Double Fudge Brownie Murder

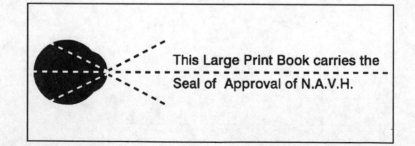

This Large Print Book carries the
Seal of Approval of N.A.V.H.

DOUBLE FUDGE BROWNIE MURDER

JOANNE FLUKE

THORNDIKE PRESS

A part of Gale, Cengage Learning

GALE
CENGAGE Learning·

Farmington Hills, Mich • San Francisco • New York • Waterville, Maine
Meriden, Conn • Mason, Ohio • Chicago

GALE
CENGAGE Learning

ALL RIGHTS RESERVED
Thorndike Press® Large Print Mystery.
The text of this Large Print edition is unabridged.
Other aspects of the book may vary from the original edition.
Set in 16 pt. Plantin.

LIBRARY OF CONGRESS CATALOGING-IN-PUBLICATION DATA

Fluke, Joanne, 1943-
   Double fudge brownie murder / by Joanne Fluke. — Large print edition.
   pages cm. — (A Hannah Swensen mystery with recipes) (Thorndike Press
   large print mystery)
   ISBN 978-1-4104-7574-9 (hardcover) — ISBN 1-4104-7574-3 (hardcover)
   1. Swensen, Hannah (Fictitious character)—Fiction. 2. Women detectives—
Fiction. 3. Bakers—Fiction. 4. Murder—Investigation—Fiction. 5. Large type
books. I. Title.
PS3556.L685D68 2015
813'.54—dc23   2015000468

Published in 2015 by arrangement with Kensington Books, an imprint
of Kensington Publishing Corp.

This book is for the newest
addition to the family,
the beautiful and charming Ellie Blue.

ACKNOWLEDGMENTS

Big hugs to the kids and the grandkids.

Thank you to my friends and neighbors: Mel & Kurt, Lyn & Bill, Lu, Gina, Adrienne, Jay, Bob, Richard, Laura Levine *(who writes the Jaine Austen series),* Dee Appleton, Dr. Bob & Sue, both Dannys, Mark B., Angelique, Anne Elizabeth, Mark & Mandy at Faux Library, Daryl and her staff at Groves Accountancy, Gene and Ron at SDSA, and everyone at Boston Private Bank. And a special thank you to Beth at Up in Stitches.

Thank you to my friends who still live in Minnesota: Lois & Neal, Bev & Jim, Lois & Jack, Val, Ruthann & Romy, Lowell, Dorothy & Sister Sue, Mary & Jim, Pat and Gary from Once Upon a Crime, and Tim Hedges.

Special thanks to my supremely patient and multitalented friend and Editor-in-Chief, John Scognamiglio.

Thanks to Meg Ruley at the Jane Rotrosen Agency for her constant support and sage advice. And thanks to Don, Rebecca, and the Christinas.

Hugs all around to all the wonderful folks at Kensington Publishing who keep Hannah baking, sleuthing, and having adventures.

Thanks to Hiro Kimura, my superb cover artist. I know I'll get a mouthful of paper, but I still want to eat that yummy-looking brownie on the cover!

Thank you to Lou Malcangi at Kensington for designing all of Hannah's delicious and stunning covers.

Thank you to my publicist, Vida Engstrand at Kensington who works tirelessly to promote the Hannah Swensen series.

Thanks to John at *Placed4Success.com* for Hannah's movie and TV spots, administering Hannah's social media, and for his voice-over on the **Blackberry Pie Murder** television commercial.

Thanks to Rudy at **Z'Kana Studios** for editing, filming, and compiling clips, for maintaining my website at **www.JoanneFluke.com,** and for administering Hannah's social media.

Thank you to Mary Avilla King at **AvoyaTravel.com** for giving me the scoop on Delores and Doc's wedding cruise to Alaska.
Now that winter's coming to Lake Eden, MN, I think Doc and Delores might want to go on a cruise to somewhere warm! Any ideas, Mary?

Big thanks to Kathy Allen for the final testing of the recipes in **Double Fudge Brownie Murder.**
Hugs to Judy Q for researching everything under the sun and helping with Hannah's e-mail at **Gr8Clues@JoanneFluke.com**

Many thanks to my friend Trudi Nash for going on book tours with me and finding all of our recipe talk just as exciting as I do. And thanks to her husband, David, for batching it while Trudi is gone.

Thanks to Holli Moncrief and her feline friend for being Moishe's inspiration.

Thank you to caterer JoAnn Hecht for making Hannah's recipes both photogenic and delicious.

Thank you to Nancy and Heiti for all sorts of wonderful recipes and plot ideas for Hannah.

Hugs to Fern, Leah, and Alicia for their work on the **Joanne Fluke Author** Facebook page and the **I Love Joanne Fluke** Facebook page. And thank you to the Double D's and the other members of Team Swensen who so willingly answer baking and other questions about Hannah online.

Thank you to Dr. Rahhal, Dr. and Cathy Line, Dr. Wallen, Dr. Koslowski, and Dr. Niemeyer for putting up with my Hannah-book-related medical and dental questions. What would Norman and Doc Knight do without you?

Huge hugs to all the Hannah fans who

10

have shared their favorite family recipes with me. (They can't guess my weight at the Winnetka Country Fair anymore!)

I'm going to suggest that we add an eighth day to the week called "Bakeday." All in favor say, *"Yum!"*

CHAPTER ONE

It was a brisk September morning and to say that Hannah Swensen was excited would be the understatement of the year. Not even the specter of her upcoming trial for vehicular homicide, which had been postponed again last week, could dampen her spirits.

"Don't worry, Moishe," Hannah told the orange and white cat who was staring at her from the top of her dresser. "I'm only going to be gone for three days and Norman should be here to pick you up any minute now. You're going to stay with Norman and Cuddles while I'm gone."

"Rrrrow!"

Hannah smiled as she slipped off her robe and dressed in her stylish, new, forest green pantsuit. Some people claimed that cats didn't understand when you spoke to them, but Moishe always reacted with an excited yowl whenever she said *Cuddles.* Norman's cat was Moishe's favorite friend. Hannah admitted that she might be anthropomorphizing, but she was convinced that Moishe loved Cuddles every bit as much as her mother loved Doc Knight.

Hannah slipped on her shoes and walked to the foot of the bed. Her suitcase was open on top of the bedspread and she checked the contents again. Claire Rodgers Knudson, the owner of Beau Monde Fashions, the upscale dress shop right next to The Cookie Jar on Main Street, had chosen what she called a mini trousseau for each of the three Swensen sisters. It was a gift from Doc Knight, their mother's groom-to-be. Of course, Delores had her own, much larger bridal trousseau, which was currently stashed in the trunk of one of Cyril Murphy's Shamrock Limousines, waiting for the wedding surprise that Doc and Delores's daughters had planned for her.

At first, all three Swensen sisters had been reluctant to accept Doc's lovely and expensive gifts. Such largesse was highly unusual in Lake Eden, Minnesota. There were a couple of rich families in town, but most people worked hard for their money and didn't have any excess to spend on luxuries. Hannah, Andrea, and Michelle fell into that latter group.

14

It had taken Doc a week, but he had convinced them to accept his generous gifts. He'd reminded them that presents for members of the wedding party were traditional, and with the exception of Doc's best man, Hannah, Andrea, and Michelle comprised the whole wedding party. He'd also stated that the lovely mini trousseaus were doubling as thank you gifts for helping him implement his wedding surprise for their mother. With that said, Doc had led them into Claire's shop and turned them over to her.

The Swensen sisters didn't shop in Claire's designer boutique very often. All three were on a budget. Hannah's bakery and coffee shop made enough money for her to live a comfortable life, but designer clothing was low on her list of priorities. Andrea, the middle Swensen sister, loved to wear designer things, but most of her commissions as a part-time real estate agent went into a college fund for her two daughters. Andrea's husband also worked. Bill was the Winnetka County sheriff, but most of his salary went toward the family's living expenses. Michelle, the youngest Swensen sister, was in college at Macalester and everything she earned from working part-time was spent on tuition, books, and living expenses.

Hannah reached out to touch the gorgeous sapphire blue dress that she would wear to her mother's wedding. Andrea and Michelle had identically styled dresses, but they were in gradiated shades of blue. Hannah's was the most vivid and the sapphire blue looked wonderful with her red hair. Michelle's dress was a lighter shade that brought out the red and gold highlights in her brown hair. Andrea's dress was the palest, an ice blue that was worthy of a winter princess. With her light blond hair worn up in a twist and secured with a rhinestone-studded comb, she looked positively regal.

Tonight, Delores would marry Doc Knight in the Little Chapel of the Orchids in Las Vegas with only Doc's best man and Delores's three daughters in attendance. The bride-to-be had no idea that Doc had planned a surprise elopement when he'd invited her to a special board member breakfast at the hospital. The breakfast had been Andrea's idea to make certain that Delores wouldn't wear her Rainbow Lady volunteer jacket and slacks.

When Delores arrived at the hospital, Doc would whisk her away in a waiting limousine that would take them to the airport. Doc had hired a second limousine to take Michelle, Andrea, and Hannah to the airport, and once they'd arrived, they would be escorted to the plane where Doc had somehow arranged for all five of them to be served a champagne breakfast.

Delores had no idea that any of this was going to happen. Hannah knew that Doc had surprised Delores several times in the past with impromptu dinner parties and gifts she hadn't expected. So far, Delores had loved his surprises. But this surprise was the biggest one of all!

Hannah readily admitted that she was a bit nervous about the whole scenario that would play out today. When her mother discovered that Doc and all three of her daughters were co-conspirators in this elopement, one of two things would happen. Either Delores would be so angry at all of them that she'd refuse to marry Doc or she'd be delighted with Doc's romantic spontaneity and grateful that they'd all helped him with her surprise.

Hannah was betting on the latter for several reasons. The most important was that Delores loved Doc totally and irrevocably. If he wanted to sweep her off her feet and elope with her, she would not hesitate. The odds in Hannah's mind tallied at ninety to ten, perhaps even steeper than that. But there was the slim chance that Hannah's mother would balk at the way that Doc had chosen to take the planning of their wedding away from her.

"That's not going to happen!" Hannah said aloud, as if by voicing that opinion, she could assure its validity. She was almost positive that Delores would go with Doc to the ends of the earth. Seeing the two of them together made Hannah long for the same kind of total consuming love. In retrospect, she knew it was the reason she hadn't accepted either Norman's or Mike's proposal. She loved both of them, but it wasn't the heart-pounding, can't-live-without-you kind of love she craved. Just once in her life she wanted to be swept off her feet by the perfect man on the perfect night with perfect love.

Did she want too much? Was there such a thing as perfect love? By refusing to settle for something less was she depriving herself of a fulfilling life?

A knock on her door pulled Hannah from her contemplative mood. She shut her suitcase, hurried from the bedroom with Moishe at her heels, and arrived at the door slightly breathless. "Hi, Norman," she said, pulling open the door.

"You didn't look through the peephole,

Hannah," Norman chided her gently as he came in.

Hannah laughed. "At eight-thirty in the morning? Besides, you said you were coming at eight-thirty and you're never late."

"Okay." Norman looked a little sheepish. "I might have overreacted, but I wish you'd remember to use the peephole. I could have been someone you didn't want to see."

"Never!" Hannah reached out to give him a hug. "You couldn't possibly be someone I didn't want to see. Not as long as you're you, Norman. I always want to see *you*!"

Norman hugged her back and Hannah knew she'd said the right thing. And he did have a point. She really ought to get into the habit of looking through the peephole before she opened the door.

"Rrrrow!"

"Hello, Big Guy." Norman bent down to pet Moishe. "Cuddles is at my house waiting for you. I hope you're ready to play all day and sleep all night."

Moishe looked up at him for a second and then he walked over to his Kitty Kastle. He jumped up to the perch and jumped down again with a toy mouse in his mouth.

"You want to take that with you?" Norman threw it down the hallway once and let Moishe retrieve it. "Okay," Norman picked

19

up the mouse. "I'm putting it in my pocket for you. I'll give it to you the minute we get to my house . . . okay?"

"Rrrrow!"

Hannah watched the interaction between cat and man with some amusement. Norman really did get along wonderfully with Moishe. Of course Mike did, too. Both of the men in her life liked her cat. And he liked both of them. Moishe hadn't helped her at all in any permanent decision making. He liked everyone . . . except Delores. And since falling in love with Doc Knight had mellowed Delores, Moishe had become much more tolerant of her.

"Do you want me to carry out your suitcase?" Norman asked her.

"Thanks, but no. Doc said the limo driver would come up to get the luggage and load it. Wheeling it out right now might upset Moishe."

"You're probably right. I just didn't want you to have to do it yourself." Norman took Moishe's harness and leash from the hook by the door and held it out. "Come on, Moishe. It's time to go and see Cuddles."

Hannah watched while Norman harnessed her pet. Moishe had always objected to getting into a cat carrier, but he loved to wear his harness. That was probably because he didn't like to be confined and preferred to roam around in the back seat of Norman's car or in the back of her cookie truck.

Norman hooked the leash to Moishe's harness and stood up. "Have a great time, Hannah. And don't let wedding fever get the best of you . . . at least not until you get back here."

"Don't worry. I won't." Hannah smiled at him. "And I won't let gambling fever get the best of me, either. I'm only taking along the money that I can afford to lose. And that's not much!"

"Do you need to borrow some from me?"

"No thanks. This way I'm not tempted. And to tell the truth, I'm really not tempted, anyway. It's just something to do while I'm there."

"I've got something else for you to do while you're there." Norman pulled an envelope out of his pocket and handed it to her. "These are for you."

Hannah opened the envelope and pulled out a sheaf of papers. "These are . . . show tickets!"

"That's right. Three tickets to Cirque Du Soleil, three tickets to the Beatles Retrospective, and three tickets to the New Irish Show Band."

"How wonderful!" Hannah threw her

arms around his neck and hugged him hard. "This is so nice of you, Norman. Michelle's been talking about Cirque Du Soleil for practically forever and Andrea just loves the Beatles. And I read about the New Irish Show Band in Sunday's paper. The dancing is supposed to be fantastic."

"That's what gave me the idea. I called the paper and found out that they had a special deal if you went through the Las Vegas visitor's bureau to order the tickets." Norman looked down at Moishe, who was trying to pull him toward the door. "I think he's anxious to go and see Cuddles."

"I know he is. When I said her name this morning, he gave me the most pitiful, yearning yowl I've ever heard."

"Just like I do when I think about you." Norman reached out to hug her again. "Have a good time, Hannah. And don't worry about a thing back here. I'll keep an eye on your place and I'll make sure that Moishe has a good time while you're gone."

Hannah had just pulled her rolling suitcase into the living room when there was another knock on her door. She gave a quick look through the peephole, thinking that perhaps Norman was back for something he'd forgotten, and gave a little gasp when she saw

22

who was standing there.

"Hannah," Mike greeted her when she opened the door. "Good for you!"

"What?"

"I'm glad you looked to see who was there before you opened the door. We'd have less crime if everyone would do that."

Hannah sent a silent thank you to Norman for reminding her and ushered Mike in. "Did you come to say goodbye?"

"That and something else." Mike pulled her into his arms and hugged her. "I got something for you to take with you. I know you've never flown before, so I brought you a good luck charm."

Hannah accepted the bag Mike handed her and opened the top a bit gingerly. She didn't really think that it was a foot from a roadkill rabbit, but you could never tell with Mike.

"Do you like it?" Mike asked, grinning widely.

"It's . . . beautiful," Hannah answered quite truthfully, staring down at the pendant inside the little jewelry box.

"It's a four-leaf clover encased in silver, and it's on a silver chain. They had silver rabbits' feet and little horseshoes, and lots of stuff like that, but I thought this would be better. So did Sharon. She said it would be perfect for you."

"Sharon?"

"She's the woman who works at the jewelry shop. The minute she said it, I knew she was right. Four-leaf clovers are harder to find than rabbits' feet or horseshoes. And Sharon personally guaranteed that there's a real four-leaf clover under that silver."

"Well, I'm not about to break it apart to find out!" Hannah slipped it on over her head and touched it gently with her fingertips. "Thanks, Mike. It's really beautiful."

"She said you'd say that. She told me she wanted one the minute she saw the display."

Hannah wasn't about to ask if Mike had gotten one for Sharon, too. She really didn't want to know. Mike was a flirt, pure and simple, and even though he wasn't Irish, he had an even bigger helping of Irish blarney than Cyril Murphy did!

"I didn't," Mike said.

"You didn't what?"

"I didn't buy one for Sharon."

Hannah frowned slightly. "I didn't ask you if you had."

"I know, but you were thinking about asking. I heard you loud and clear. This is just for you, Hannah. It's special because you're special."

Hannah didn't say anything. She just

hugged him. Mike could be really sweet when he wasn't playing his officious cop role. She was wondering if she should thank him again, she really did love the silver clover, when there was a knock at her door.

"I'll get it," Mike said, pulling the door open without looking through the peephole.

Hannah had the urge to remind him that what was good for the goose was good for the gander, but she didn't when she saw Michelle's excited face.

"Hi, Mike," Michelle said, stepping in with her suitcase. "Are you all ready, Hannah?"

"I'm ready. Did you see Andrea on your way in?"

Mike, who was still standing by the open door, pointed toward the visitor's parking lot. "Bill just dropped her off and she's wheeling her suitcase down the walkway. And your limo just pulled in. The driver's parking out by the road."

"Great!" Hannah felt a hoard of nervous butterflies take flight in her stomach. She'd never been on a plane before and she wasn't quite sure what to expect. There was something about being up in the clouds with nothing but air beneath her that was terrifying, but the thought was also exhilarating.

"I'll carry your suitcases down for you."

"But the limo driver will come to get them," Hannah said.

"That's okay. I'll do it." Mike grabbed both suitcases and started down the stairs. "Hannah?"

"Yes, Mike."

"Make sure you double lock your door."

"But the deadbolt doesn't fit right."

"It'll work if you lift up on the doorknob. Just do it, Hannah. It's important."

Hannah sighed. "All right, Mike. I'll do it."

"All cops are alike," Michelle grumbled just as soon as Mike was out of earshot. "I'll help you, Hannah. I've double locked your door before and it's a two-person job."

"Thanks, Michelle."

Hannah inserted her key and Michelle lifted up on the doorknob so that Hannah could throw the deadbolt that wasn't quite lined up correctly. It took three tries, but the bolt finally slid home.

"Mike always tells me to double lock the door," Hannah said with a sigh, dropping her keys into her purse, picking up her large carry-on by one strap, and following Michelle down the stairs. "It's a royal pain to do and I don't really have anything for anyone to steal."

"I know, but Mike's a cop and they all say

that. Lonnie told me to double lock my door when we left my place, and two of my roommates were still inside. I'll bet you five bucks that Bill reminded Andrea to double lock their door this morning."

Hannah laughed. "There's no way I'm going to take that bet, not when I'm sure you're right. People who work in law enforcement are very safety conscious."

"Oh, it's not that." Michelle turned around at the base of the stairs to smile at her older sister.

"It's not?"

"No. Lonnie explained the whole thing to me this morning and it's not a matter of safety at all. It's just that they have to file a report for every theft that occurs, and they don't want to fill out all that paperwork."

Chapter Two

"Wow!" Michelle's voice was hushed as they climbed up the ramp to the plane. "It's a private plane and I think it's a Citation X."

"Is that good?" Andrea, who was in the lead, turned around to ask.

"I think so. And I *do* know Doc must have paid a bundle to reserve it for us. I think he chartered the whole plane because there's no one else on the ramp behind us."

"Maybe the other passengers just haven't gotten here yet," Hannah suggested. "This looks like a big plane for just the five of us."

"There's also a pilot and a co-pilot," Andrea pointed out. "And maybe even a steward or stewardess. That's a total of seven or eight."

"You don't count the pilot and the co-pilot," Michelle informed them.

Hannah gave her youngest sister a surprised look. "Why not? Somebody's got to fly the plane."

"True, but they have their own cabin and they're not counted as passengers. If this is a Citation, and I think it is, it'll hold from seven to twelve passengers."

"How do you know so much about planes?" Andrea asked.

"I worked at Hubert Humphrey Terminal over part of my summer break. It's a private terminal and the planes were mostly medium-size jets like Falcons, Learjets, and Cessna Citations."

Andrea looked impressed. "That sounds exciting!"

"Not really. I worked at the Northwoods Coffee concession and all I did was make and pour coffee into to-go cups. We were right by the main gate and all the pilots came in for coffee."

Hannah was well acquainted with her youngest sister's insatiable curiosity. "So you asked them a lot of questions about their planes?"

"That's right. And that's why I'm almost positive that this one is a Citation X. If it is, we're in for a treat. It's got a top speed of six hundred miles an hour."

"That's ten miles every minute!" Hannah pointed out with a slight gasp.

"That's right. It can fly from Los Angeles to New York in four hours. That's an hour faster than conventional business jets."

"So . . ." Hannah tried to maintain a deadpan expression, but it was difficult. "I've got a question for you, Michelle. Are we going to get to Las Vegas before we even leave here?"

Michelle let out a whoop of laughter. "Maybe. Hurry up, Andrea. I want to see the inside. It's supposed to be super luxurious."

"Let's hope Mother thinks so." Hannah took a deep breath as they neared the end of the ramp. "I'm a little nervous about her reaction."

"You're not the only one," Andrea said and then she turned to Michelle. "You're not nervous about Mother's reaction?"

"It's silly to borrow trouble. Whatever's happened has already happened. It won't do us any good to worry about it now."

"But what if she's mad at all of us?" Andrea asked. "What if we have to spend the whole plane trip in uncomfortable silence?"

Hannah, who was in the lead, turned to stare at Andrea. "Mother? Mad at us and *silent*?!"

They were about to step into the plane when they heard the sound of their mother's laughter. Doc's deep baritone joined in the mirth and Hannah breathed a big sigh of

30

relief. "Mother must be okay with being whisked off to Vegas for the wedding. Let's go join them."

When they entered the plane, all three Swensen sisters stopped dead in their tracks at the sight that awaited them. The inside was like a posh cocktail lounge with seats arranged in conversational groupings around round tables. Delores and Doc sat near the rear of the spacious cabin, smiling broadly and holding crystal flutes of champagne.

"We thought you'd *never* get here!" Delores said, but she didn't sound in the least bit angry. "Doc and I were just dying to try this champagne, but we thought we should wait for you girls since you helped him plan such an exciting surprise for me."

"We're here now," Hannah said, smiling back at her mother as she walked over to takc a glass of champagne from the silver tray on the table. "Is this Perrier Jouet?" She named her mother's favorite champagne.

Doc shook his head. "No, it's Veuve Clicquot. I'm trying to convince your mother that it's her new favorite champagne."

"The only reason Mother likes the Perrier Jouet so much is because she likes the little white flowers on the bottle," Michelle informed him, reaching for a glass of champagne.

"That's simply not true!" Delores objected, but she laughed and everyone could tell that she was amused.

"Oh, yes it is." Andrea grinned as she took a glass and raised it toward their mother in a little salute. "Remember your last yard sale? I helped you set out the glassware and there were two cases of empty Perrier Jouet bottles that you wanted to sell for a dollar apiece."

"They make very lovely vases," Delores defended herself, "especially for a branch of white flowers. And this bottle," she said, gesturing toward the plain green champagne bottle with its orange label. "This bottle isn't pretty at all."

Doc laughed. "That's because it doesn't have to be pretty. The taste will convince you that it's the best champagne. Come on, Lori. Think of a toast and try it."

"To you, Doc," Delores said, clinking her glass with his. "And to us, even if we argue about the best champagne."

Glasses were raised and then lowered. And a smile appeared on Delores's face.

"You like it, don't you!" Doc responded to her smile.

"It's very good."

"Better than Perrier Jouet?"

"Well . . . yes! You're right. It's better. But it would be even better than that if it came in a prettier bottle."

"I'll write to the company tomorrow," Doc promised, smiling down at his fractious bride-to-be. "Was that a concession I heard you make, Lori?"

"Absolutely not. It might have been a compliment to your good taste, but I never make concessions."

"But I do." Doc clinked glasses with her again. "I'm marrying you, aren't I?"

"Uh-oh!" Hannah warned, even though her mother was still smiling. "Hold on a second, you two. You need to have something I brought to go with your champagne." Hannah bent down to unzip the soft-sided cooler she'd carried to the plane. She folded back the top and lifted out a platter covered with foil.

"Chocolate?" Delores asked, sounding so pathetically eager that Hannah burst into laughter.

"Yes, Mother. Your two favorite flavors, maple and fudge. I made Maple Fudge Sandwich Cookies just for you."

"You're a good daughter, Hannah," Delores said as Hannah whisked off the foil and passed the plate to her mother. Delores took one bite and a rapturous expression crossed her face. "Here, Doc. You can have a bite of my cookie."

Michelle took a cookie and sighed happily as she bit into it. "Truer love hath no other than a woman who shares one of Hannah's cookies with her beloved."

"Is that a quote?" Andrea asked.

"If it isn't, it should be," Doc answered her. "These cookies are incredible, Hannah."

"Thank you. Help yourselves, everyone. This is only the first platter. I have a second and it's still in the cooler. Since we don't have a wedding cake, I thought I'd bring these to the ceremony."

"Who needs a cake when we've got your cookies?" Delores asked, reaching for another. "And your cookies pair so beautifully with this wonderful champagne." She turned to Doc. "Do we have another bottle, dear?"

"We do. We'll have the second bottle with our breakfast."

"What do we have for breakfast?" Michelle asked him.

"We have croissants from a Minneapolis bakery, and I had Mort's Deli deliver a smoked salmon platter and three thermoses of designer coffee to the plane."

"You thought of everything!" Delores complimented him. "I'm just going to let you arrange things from now on."

Doc turned to Hannah. "You girls heard her. That constitutes a promise and I'm going to hold her to it."

"Good luck!" Hannah said, laughing along with her sisters. Delores loved to manage things, but if anyone could convince her to sit back and let someone else do it, that person was Doc.

"There are five of us," Delores pointed out, "and two bottles of champagne only go so far with five people. Did you say you had a third bottle?"

Doc smiled at her fondly. "Yes, but I'm saving it until after we say our vows. I know *I do* are only two words, but there's no way I'm taking the chance we'll get it wrong!"

MAPLE FUDGE SANDWICH COOKIES

DO NOT preheat oven quite yet — cookie dough must chill before baking.

The Cookies

2 cups white *(granulated)* sugar

1 and 1/2 cups salted butter *(3 sticks, 12 ounces, 3/4 pound),* softened to room temperature

2 large eggs, beaten *(just whip them up in a glass with a fork)*

1/2 cup maple syrup *(I used Log Cabin)*

1/2 teaspoon maple extract or flavoring *(I used McCormick Imitation Maple Flavoring)*

1 teaspoon vanilla extract

1 teaspoon salt

1 teaspoon baking soda

1 teaspoon baking powder

4 cups all-purpose flour *(pack it down in the cup when you measure it)*

1/2 cup white *(granulated)* sugar for coating the dough balls

Hannah's 1st Note: To measure maple syrup, first spray the inside of measuring cup with Pam so that the syrup won't stick to your cup.

Hannah's 2nd Note: If you can't find

maple flavoring or maple extract, don't worry about it. Your cookies will still taste like maple. It just won't be as intense a flavor.

Place the sugar in the bowl of an electric mixer. *(You can also mix up these cookies by hand, but it's easier with an electric mixer.)*

Add the softened butter and mix on LOW speed until the butter is combined. Then turn the mixer up to MEDIUM speed and beat until the mixture is light and fluffy.

Add the eggs and mix until they are well incorporated.

Add the maple syrup, the maple extract or flavoring, and the vanilla extract. Mix them in thoroughly.

Sprinkle in the salt, baking soda, and baking powder. Mix until they are combined.

Mix in the flour a half-cup at a time, beating after each addition.

Take the bowl out of the mixer and scrape down the inside with a rubber spatula. Give the bowl another stir by hand to mix everything into the dough.

Tuck a piece of plastic wrap down around the dough in your bowl. Then stick the whole bowl in the refrigerator for 1 hour.

When your dough has chilled for 1 hour, preheat the oven to 350 degrees F., rack in the middle position.

Measure out 1/2 cup white *(granulated)* sugar and place it in a shallow bowl. You'll use this to coat your dough balls.

Prepare your cookie sheets by spraying them with Pam or another nonstick cooking spray, or lining them with parchment paper.

Roll the cookie dough into walnut-sized balls with your hands. *(Lisa and I use a 2-teaspoon scooper to do this down at The Cookie Jar.)*

Roll the dough balls in the bowl of white sugar and then place them on the prepared cookie sheets, 12 cookie dough balls to a standard-size sheet.

Flatten the cookie dough balls with a metal spatula.

Bake the cookies at 350 degrees F. for 10 to 12 minutes or until they are nicely browned.

Take the cookies out of the oven. Cool them on the cookie sheets for 2 minutes, and then remove them to a rack to finish cooling. *(If you leave them on the cookie sheets for too long, they'll stick.)*

When all your cookies are baked and they are cooling on wire racks, make the Fudge Filling.

Fudge Filling

1/3 cup heavy cream *(whipping cream)*

6 ounces semi-sweet chocolate *(If you don't have semi-sweet chocolate squares, you can use a 6-ounce by weight package of semi-sweet chocolate chips.) (I used Nestle.)*

1/4 teaspoon salt

1/4 cup powdered *(confectioners)* sugar *(pack it down in the cup when you measure it — don't sift unless it's got big lumps)*

Heat the cream in a saucepan over medium heat until it begins to simmer and bubbles form around the outer edges of the cream.

Break the chocolate into pieces in a small bowl.

Hannah's 3rd Note: The advantage in using chocolate chips is that you don't have to break the chips into pieces.

Pour the heated cream over the chocolate *(or the chips)* in the bowl and sprinkle in the salt. Give it a stir with a heat-resistant spatula and then let it sit on the counter.

Wait a minute or two and then stir the mixture again to combine the cream and the chocolate. Do this until you can stir it smooth.

Let the filling sit on the counter until it cools down to room temperature.

Stir in the powdered sugar. Continue to stir until the Fudge Filling is smooth and spreadable.

When both the cookies and the chocolate filling are cool, make sandwich cookies by spreading a generous layer of filling on the bottom of one cookie and pressing the bottom of a second cookie over the top. Make sure the two flat cookie bottoms touch the filling. *(If you make a sandwich by spreading filling on the rounded tops, you won't get as much chocolate filling!)*

Let the Maple Fudge Sandwich Cookies sit on the wire racks until the Fudge Filling has "set".

Hannah's 4th Note: I'm willing to bet that you won't wait that long. Lisa and I have never managed it!

Yield: Depending on cookie size, approximately 3 to 4 dozen tasty sandwich cookies that both kids and adults will love.

Lisa's Note: When we make these down at The Cookie Jar they're gone in ten minutes flat. That's mostly because Bertie Straub from the Cut 'n Curl comes in every morning for a cookie. When she goes back to the beauty shop and tells her ladies that we baked Maple

**Fudge Sandwich Cookies, they send her
back here to buy some for them.**

CHAPTER THREE

A hot, dry breeze greeted the Swensen sisters and their mother when they emerged from the air-conditioned interior of McCarran International Airport in Las Vegas. Doc had gone ahead with the limo driver who had been waiting for them. The driver would load their luggage and meet them at the town car and limo pickup area.

"I thought Doc's best man was going to meet us at the airport," Hannah said, relishing the feel of warm sun on her shoulders.

"There's been a change of plans," Delores replied, and Hannah noticed that her mother didn't quite meet her eyes.

"He's coming, isn't he?" Andrea asked, and Hannah realized that her sister sounded nervous. What was going on, anyway?

"Yes, he's coming. It's just that he had to catch a later flight so he'll meet us at the chapel." Delores stopped for a moment and took a deep breath of the warm air. "There's a delightful scent in the air. Is it some kind of flower?"

Hannah laughed. "I think it's the absence of Deep Woods Off. You're just used to smelling insect repellent in weather like this."

"You're probably right." Delores gave a little smile as she turned to Michelle. "You've been to Vegas before, haven't you, dear?"

"Only once. We flew out here two years ago for spring break."

"Two years ago?" Delores began to frown. "But you told me you were going to stay with a friend."

"I did stay with a friend. Her family lives in Vegas. Her dad's a pit boss and her mother's a blackjack dealer."

"But you were too young to go to the casinos . . . weren't you?"

"No, Mother. The casinos have restaurants and that means anyone can go inside. You just can't gamble or drink if you're under-age, that's all. The buffets were great, especially on the Strip. We had coupon books so we never paid more than five dollars, and we ate at a different buffet every day."

"But you couldn't drink or gamble." Delores was like a dog with a bone.

43

Hannah shot her youngest sister a sympathetic look.

"I can now," Michelle replied, giving her mother a smile and neatly sidestepping the parental-set trap. "Of course, I'll probably stick to the cheap slots and poker machines. And once the gambling money is gone, I'm through."

"Very smart," Andrea said and then she pointed to a white stretch limo that was pulling up several feet from them. "There's Doc."

It took a moment or two to get into the limousine. Hannah slid all the way over on the seat and her sisters slid in next to her. Doc and Delores had the other seat and Hannah smiled as she noticed that they were holding hands.

Soon they were moving, heading into town. Hannah gazed out at waving palm trees, sparkling pools, and a riotous array of exotic plants and multicolored bougainvillea as they drove by.

"We have lilac trees and they don't grow here," Michelle said, correctly reading Hannah's envious expression. "I heard that Christmas here is sad. People come to Vegas for Christmas when they don't have anywhere else to go. Everybody else spends Christmas with family, but if you don't have any family, you have to settle for steam table turkey dinners, and artificial Christmas trees with glitzy lights, and Styrofoam snowmen."

Hannah thought about that for a minute. "That's depressing."

"I know. It makes me appreciate having a real family I can go to for Christmas with a real Christmas tree and real snow."

"That reminds me," Delores said, squeezing Doc's hand. "Where are we going to have Christmas this year? Your house or mine?"

"We'll just have to wait and see, Lori. Christmas is still three months away."

"You won't have to work on Christmas, will you?" Delores looked worried.

"Not unless there's a pandemic. My new intern's coming at the end of September."

"You'll have to spend time training him," Delores warned.

"Not really. Marlene has agreed to take care of that for me. She's met him and she thinks he's going to be perfect for our hospital. And once he's up to speed, we're going to get a third intern."

"But you only have two intern apartments."

"That's true, but there's my apartment. I don't think I'll need that now that I won't be spending so much time at the hospital."

Delores started to smile. "Really? You're going to give up your apartment?"

"I'm not exactly giving it up. I'm simply turning it over to my new chief of staff."

"Marlene Aldrich?"

"That's right. She's earned it, Lori. Marlene has accepted every challenge I've thrown her way and I'm convinced that she can run the hospital just as well as I can . . . maybe even better. I plan on taking some time off so that we can enjoy married life."

"Wonderful!" Delores looked happier than Hannah had ever seen her as she reached out to hug Doc. "Does Marlene know yet?"

"Not yet. I was waiting to discuss it with you."

"That's nice of you, but . . . why?"

"Because you've got a good head on your shoulders and you've been at the hospital long enough to have seen Marlene in action. Do you think she can handle the extra responsibility?"

"Absolutely. Marlene can handle anything that comes up. She's a very capable person and everyone at the hospital likes her. Even more important, they respect her and I can't think of anyone who would object to taking orders from her."

"That's settled then. And here we are at

the Amante del Sol."

"I've always wanted to come here," Delores said, looking out the window as their driver pulled into a circular driveway and joined a line of cars who were unloading passengers. "It's just gorgeous, Doc! I'm really going to enjoy this."

"It's only three nights, Lori."

"But . . . I thought you said we were going to be gone for ten days."

"We are. Today's Thursday. We stay tonight and Friday and Saturday nights. Then, on Sunday morning, a car picks us up to take us to the airport and we fly to Seattle."

"Seattle?" Delores looked surprised, but Hannah could tell that she was also intrigued. "Why Seattle?"

"That's where we catch the ship."

Delores gave a delighted giggle. "*What* ship?"

"The *Jewel*. It's part of the Norwegian Cruise Line. I'm taking you to Alaska to see our last frontier. I've always wanted to ride on a dog sled and touch a glacier."

Delores shivered. "But . . . I didn't bring a parka!"

"Oh, yes you did. Claire chose a whole winter cruising wardrobe for you. It'll be waiting for you when we get to our stateroom. I booked a family suite for us because, knowing Claire, I figured you'd probably need two closets."

Delores laughed. "You're probably right. Will we get to see whales and bears?"

"Definitely. Moose, too. And maybe even some timber wolves and an elk or two."

"Oh, my! I should have packed my camera!"

"You did. Or rather, Andrea did. It's in the suitcase in the trunk of this limo."

"Thank you, Andrea!" Delores turned to smile at her middle daughter.

"You're welcome, Mother," Andrea responded. "I hope I didn't forget anything."

"I'm sure you didn't, dear. And if you did, I can always replace it either here or on the boat."

"Ship," Doc corrected her. "They get testy if you call it a boat."

"Really!" Delores stared at him in confusion. "Have you been on a cruise ship before?"

"Never, but after my father died, my mother went on quite a few cruises. She said the salt air was invigorating and when she was on a ship, she felt ten years younger."

"This is sounding better and better," Delores declared. "If we just stay on that ship, will I turn into your teenage bride?"

"You *are* my teenage bride. And you're

also my beautiful young lady bride. And my lovely mature woman bride. And . . ."

"Stop!" Delores interrupted him. "I'm getting older and older and you've gone far enough. I absolutely forbid you to even think the word *geriatric.*"

Doc burst into laughter and, much to Hannah's amazement, so did Delores. As far as Hannah knew, her mother had never joked about her age before. She'd always pretended to be younger than her calendar years, but now that she was in love with Doc, she'd dropped the whole pretense. Perhaps it was because her age was clearly written on her medical records and Doc knew precisely how old she was. Or perhaps, just perhaps, it was the fact that she didn't have to pretend any longer, now that she was about to marry the man she loved.

Five minutes later, Hannah, Michelle, and Andrea were being whisked up to the eighteenth floor in an elevator that rose so quickly, it almost took their breath away. They walked down a long, beautifully carpeted hallway, following the directional signs until they arrived at the rooms the desk clerk had printed on the sleeve that held their electronic room keys.

"We're here," Andrea said, arriving at the door. "And you're right next to us, Hannah. You've got a single and Michelle and I are sharing a double."

For one brief moment, Hannah felt like offering to switch with one of them. It would be nice to have a roommate. But then she opened her door, took one look at her room, and squelched that idea. Her room was huge and it was beautiful.

"Beautiful view," she breathed as she walked down the steps from the bedroom, across the floor of the sunken living room, and out onto the balcony. Above her was an impossibly bright blue sky with lazy white clouds floating overhead like airborne white cotton candy.

Hannah turned her gaze downward. Eighteen floors below her was a huge swimming pool, its vivid blue surface sparkling in the sun. It was surrounded by beautiful tropical vegetation and flowers. A bit to one side, partially shaded by a thatched sunroof, was a large Jacuzzi. The pool area was flanked by tall palm trees, and ant-sized people in bathing suits were stretched out on lounge chairs. There didn't seem to be anyone who was actually in the water and Hannah wondered if the pool was heated. Then she laughed at herself. Of course the pool was heated. This was an expensive hotel and they did things right in Vegas. She'd seen the ads on television. The people on the lounge chairs were simply working on their tans before their vacations were over and they had to go back to colder climes.

There was a knock on her door and Hannah stepped back inside and hurried to answer it. It was the porter with her suitcase.

Several minutes later and several dollars richer, the porter had left and Hannah's suitcase was sitting on a suitcase rack by the bed. She was just unzipping it when the phone in her room rang and she reached for the extension on the bed table.

"Hello?"

"Hannah!" It was her mother's voice. "I'm so glad I caught you before you left."

"Left for where?"

"For wherever. I'm sure you girls want to explore. I just need a big favor from you."

"What is it, Mother?"

"I'm simply a wreck, dear. I'm talking to you from the bathroom, where Doc can't hear me. I need Andrea to come up here and help me while I get my hair and makeup done and dress for the wedding. And I need you and Michelle to babysit Doc. The groom isn't supposed to see the bride until we arrive at the church, you know. It's supposed to be bad luck."

"Okay," Hannah said, wondering why her

51

mother was suddenly superstitious. "I'll tell Andrea you need her, but what do you want Michelle and I to do with Doc?"

"Take him out somewhere. Or better yet, tell him you're hungry and you want to go out for something to eat before the ceremony. He'll go for that."

"Why don't I just tell him that you think it's bad luck for him to see you before the wedding?"

"Don't do that!" Delores sounded panic-stricken. "He'll think I'm being silly and tease me about it."

"All right, Mother." Hannah caved in. After all, it was her mother's wedding day. "I'll knock on Andrea and Michelle's door and get them in on it. Do you want us to come to your room and get Doc?"

"Good idea. We're in the bridal suite. It's on the top floor. Just get your sisters and come right up. I can't even unpack my suitcase with Doc here. There are just so many superstitions involved in a wedding. For all I know, that could be bad luck, too."

"You're not going to have bad luck, Mother. You're marrying Doc and that means you'll have good luck for the rest of your life."

"Don't say that! You might jinx me!"

Hannah laughed. "All right, I won't say it

again. I'll just get the girls and we'll be right up."

"I was getting a little hungry, too," Doc said, taking the last bite of his burger. "And these are really good. What do they call these again?"

"Burger Dogs," Michelle answered. "I talked to the guy in the kitchen and he said they were his idea. When his kids were small, they could never make up their minds whether they wanted him to grill hamburgers or hot dogs so he decided to combine the two."

"I think I could make these," Hannah said. And then she turned to Michelle. "And I think Lonnie could, too. We'll have to work on it when we get home. They'd be a real hit at next year's Fourth of July Picnic at Eden Lake."

Michelle nodded. "You're right and the sheriff's department always mans the barbecues. What do you think it is, Hannah? I'm thinking it's just a double hamburger patty sandwiched with chopped hot dogs in the middle."

"But they've also got a little sweet pickle relish and . . . I think there's mustard in there somewhere," Doc added.

"Mustard mixed with ketchup," Hannah

said, recognizing the taste. "And the hamburger patties have finely chopped onions in them."

"Double hamburger patties." Doc sounded thoughtful. "How do you get them to stick together long enough to grill them?"

"You press the edges together to seal them," Hannah told him. "You can do that with any stuffed hamburger patties. You just have to be careful not to put in too much stuffing."

"Is that how they do hamburgers with mushrooms and blue cheese in the middle?" Michelle asked her.

"I think so." Hannah finished the last of her Burger Dog and glanced at the menu again. "Is anyone else interested in dessert?"

Doc nodded. "I am. And we can take something up to Lori when we get back to the hotel. She's always up for dessert."

"*We* can," Hannah emphasized the word. "You can't. Mother's been thinking about all those wedding superstitions and she's convinced that it's bad luck for the bride to see the groom before the wedding. And I wasn't supposed to tell you that, so please don't mention it to her."

"I might have known it," Doc said, sighing deeply. "She's really nervous. I'm beginning to think maybe I shouldn't have planned this elopement. She might have been calmer if we'd stayed with the original plans in Lake Eden."

"No way!" Hannah was very definite. "You did the right thing, Doc. Mother's having a wonderful time. She's just a little nervous about the ceremony. And she's probably thinking about . . ." Hannah paused, not wanting to hurt Doc's feelings.

"Your dad," Doc finished the sentence for her. "Of course she is. I knew she would. It's only natural. It's one of the reasons I tried to distract her by telling her about the Alaskan cruise."

"It'll be okay." Michelle reached out to pat his shoulder. "Mother was really happy about the cruise and she'll be fine once she's actually married. This is just pre-wedding jitters and Andrea knows exactly what to do about that."

"Champagne?" Doc guessed.

"Chocolate," Hannah answered. "I left the cooler with the Maple Fudge Sandwich Cookies with Andrea. If Mother gets too nervous, we'll just calm her down with lots of delicious endorphins."

Doc was silent for a moment and then he cleared his throat. "You know that there's no real medical . . ."

"I don't want to hear it!" Hannah interrupted him. "All I know is that it works on Mother. If she's stressed, a couple bites of chocolate will snap her right out of it."

"Okay. If it works on her, that's the important thing. And I know she loves chocolate." Doc glanced down at the menu again. "They have hot fudge sundaes. Maybe I should get a hot fudge sundae to go."

"That's a good idea!" Hannah told him. "Let's take Andrea a Coney Island Sandwich. That's tuna and she loves tuna. She won't eat dessert, so Mother can have the hot fudge sundae all to herself. When we get back, Michelle can take everything up to them."

"Michelle and not you?"

"Not me. I have strict instructions to babysit you."

Doc laughed. "Instructions from your mother?"

"That's right. One of the last things she said to me before I left was that I had to keep you happy and occupied so that you didn't get cold feet and hop on the first flight back to Lake Eden."

"I wouldn't do that!"

"I'm sure you wouldn't, but Mother was still worried. And the next thing she said was that she'd just curl up and die if she couldn't marry you tonight."

BURGER DOGS

For grilling these outside, preheat your grill on medium heat.

For frying, you'll be cooking at medium heat and using a frying pan or electric grill large enough to hold 4 double hamburger patties.

1 and 1/2 pounds lean ground beef
1/2 teaspoon salt
1/2 teaspoon freshly ground pepper
Several shakes of hot sauce *(make it Slap Ya Mama if Mike is coming)*
1 Tablespoon onion, finely chopped *(I used Maui sweet onion)*
2 beef hot dogs *(I used Hebrew National)*
2 teaspoons prepared mustard *(I used Gulden's spicy brown)*
2 teaspoons ketchup *(I used Heinz)*
1 teaspoon sweet pickle relish
4 burger buns
Lettuce, sliced tomato, and sliced pickles for garnishing *(optional)*
Mayonnaise or your favorite sauce for spreading on the buns *(optional)*

In a large bowl, combine the ground beef, salt, freshly ground pepper, and hot sauce.

Add the Tablespoon of finely chopped onion and mix with your impeccably clean hands just until combined.

Tear off a sheet of wax paper *(or aluminum foil or parchment paper sprayed with Pam)* that's large enough to hold 8 hamburger patties. Put it on the counter.

Form 8 round patties about a half-inch thick. As soon as you form them, place them on the sheet of wax paper.

Cut the hot dogs into chunks and then grind them up finer by putting the chunks in a food processor and processing them with the steel blade in an on-off motion. When the hot dogs are finely ground, place the pieces in a small bowl.

Add the mustard, ketchup, and sweet pickle relish to the ground hot dogs. Mix them in until they are thoroughly combined.

Form a spoonful of the hot dog mixture into a ball. This ball should be made up of about a fourth of the mixture. *(You'll need 4 balls in all.)*

When you form the balls, place them in the centers of 4 of the hamburger patties.

Top each of those patties with another patty and seal the edges by pressing them down with your fingers.

Grill the Burger Dogs over medium-high heat, flipping them once, halfway through the cooking time.

If you like your burgers rare, it will take

about 3 minutes per side, medium will take about 4 minutes per side, and well done will take about 4 and a half minutes per side.

If you fry or cook your burgers on an electric grill, preheat your frying pan or grill to medium-high heat and follow the above cooking times.

While your burgers are cooking, prepare your buns. You can toast them on the grill if you like, or simply slather on a little mayo or a sauce of your choice.

Once your burgers have cooked to the desired degree of doneness, place them on the bottom half of the bun, garnish them with lettuce, tomato, and/or pickles if you like, slap on the top of the bun and serve to rave reviews.

Yield: 4 stuffed double-patty burgers.

CONEY ISLAND SANDWICHES

Preheat oven to 250 degrees F., rack in the middle position.

(This is not a mistake. The temperature is 250 degrees F. You need to heat these sandwiches slowly at low heat.)

1/2 pound American cheese, cut into small cubes *(I used Velveeta)*

2 five-ounce cans of water-packed tuna, well drained *(I used Chicken of the Sea white chunk tuna)*

3 large hard-boiled eggs, peeled and chopped

2 teaspoons green bell pepper, finely chopped

2 teaspoons pimento-stuffed olives, finely chopped

2 teaspoons onion, finely chopped

2 teaspoons sweet pickle relish

1/2 cup mayonnaise *(I used Best Foods which is Hellmann's if you live east of the Mississippi River)*

6 large hot dog buns *(I got the kind with sesame seeds on top — they're the same shape as hot dog buns, but wider and longer)*

Hannah's 1st Note: You can chop up

the hard-boiled eggs, green bell pepper, pimento-stuffed olives, and onion ahead of time, put it in a sealable baggie and keep it in the refrigerator so it's ready to go when it's time to mix and assemble the Coney Island Sandwiches.

Mix the cubed cheese and tuna together in a large bowl. *(I use a fork to do this because it's easier to flake the tuna with a fork.)*

Add the chopped hard-boiled eggs, green peppers, olives, and onion. Mix well.

Add the pickle relish and mix it in.

Spread the mayonnaise out on top with a rubber spatula and then use the spatula to mix it in.

Open the hot dog buns, spread the filling on the bottom halves, and close the buns again.

Wrap each bun in a piece of aluminum foil.

Place the foil-wrapped Coney Island Sandwiches, cut side up, in a baking pan.

Bake the sandwiches at 250 degrees F. for 30 minutes, or until the cheese is melted and they're warm all the way through.

Serve these sandwiches warm. Kids love them, especially because they come in their own foil-wrapped packages. Coney Island Sandwiches are also very good to take on picnics if you keep them warm in an insulated bag for the trip to the park or the beach.

Yield: 6 Coney Island Sandwiches.

CHAPTER FOUR

"Oh, Hannah! I'm so afraid I did a terrible thing!" Delores, who was sitting next to Hannah in the limo that Doc had ordered for them, reached out to touch her daughter's arm.

"You're having second thoughts about marrying Doc?"

"Oh, no! Nothing like that! It's just that I was secretive about something that I probably shouldn't have . . ."

"Mother!" Andrea reached out to grab her arm. "That's enough, Mother. We all agreed that what you did was right. And I'm sure that Hannah will agree."

"I might if I knew what it was."

"I'm afraid we kept something . . ."

"Not another word, Mother!" Michelle stepped in to silence Delores. "You did the right thing. Now let it go on and take its course."

"What course?" Hannah was feeling like

the group of blind men who were trying to figure out what an elephant looked like by grabbing various parts of it. "What are you three talking about?"

"It's nothing, Hannah. Just go with the flow," Andrea ordered.

"Yes," Michelle said. "We're almost at the Little Chapel of the Orchids and then you'll know."

Know what? Hannah's mind asked, but she bit back the question before she could ask it. They probably wouldn't tell her anyway. But her curiosity was killing her as she got out of the limo and followed her mother and sisters into the wedding chapel.

"You must be Delores," the woman at the counter said as she caught sight of the beige raw silk suit that Delores was wearing. "You look lovely, even prettier than your groom said you were. He's a very nice man, so polite. And his best man?" She stopped speaking and gave a huge sigh. "If I were twenty years younger, I'd be pulling him into a taxi to take him to my place."

"In that case, I'm glad you're not twenty years younger." Delores gave a little laugh. "We need him to make this wedding legal. I've been waiting for this for a long time, you know."

"Your groom told me. He said he fell in

love the moment he laid eyes on you. But you were already married." The woman reached under the counter and pulled out a box. "I have your bridesmaid corsages." She opened the largest white box. "And here's your wedding bouquet. Isn't it pretty?"

Andrea gave a little gasp as the woman pulled out an orchid bouquet. "It's lovely, Mother!"

"Yes, it is," Michelle said with a nod.

Hannah smiled. "It's perfect with your suit. I didn't know orchids came in all those different colors."

"It's a Rainbow Orchid bouquet," the woman told them. "Very expensive. I've only seen one before, and that was when one of our former mayors retired and married his much younger girlfriend. He was trying to impress her, but it didn't work out the way he thought it would. She said, *What are those funny-looking flowers, sweetie?* And when he told her they were orchids, she said, *Well I hope they smell good 'cause that's the only thing they've got going for them.*" She turned to Hannah, Andrea, and Michelle. "Do you girls want me to pin your corsages on for you?"

"Thanks, but we can take care of that," Hannah said, eyeing the long corsage pin nervously. There was no way she'd risk being stuck by a stranger with that fake pearl pin.

"I'll do yours, Hannah," Andrea said, and before Hannah could say yea or nay, Andrea's deft fingers had affixed the white orchid to her gown. "Michelle, you're next."

Michelle stepped up to receive her corsage and then Andrea pinned on her own corsage.

"The men are waiting for you in the garden gazebo," the woman at the counter told them. "The photographer's there and he wants to take a few pre-wedding photos." She handed the box with the wedding bouquet to Delores. "Here you go, dear. The gazebo's in the side yard off to your right."

Hannah followed her mother and sisters to the door that led to the side yard. She'd been feeling hesitant ever since she'd exited the car. She knew the uncomfortable feeling in the pit of her stomach was pure anxiety about whatever it was that Delores, Andrea, and Michelle were keeping from her. There was no doubt in Hannah's mind that it was a conspiracy and now that she thought about it, Doc was probably in on it, too. The only person who didn't know was her. It was almost like being "it" in a childhood game, shutting her eyes and counting to a hundred, and then opening them to find that all the children who'd been playing the game with her had vanished.

The gazebo garden was right next to the building and when Hannah and her sisters emerged, they found themselves surrounded by colorful flowers and lush greenery. The gazebo gleamed white in the rays of the afternoon sun and they could hear voices coming from within. One voice was Doc's. Hannah was sure of that. That meant the other two voices must belong to the photographer and to Doc's best man.

One of the unknown voices was young, still a bit high-pitched. It sounded as if it belonged to someone in his early to mid-twenties. Hannah guessed that it belonged to the photographer. Of course, some people simply had high-pitched voices and it had nothing to do with age or maturity. She realized that, but it was still a good guess.

The third voice was hauntingly familiar. It reminded Hannah of someone she couldn't quite place. She stopped to sniff the perfume of a particularly lovely rose, shut her eyes in pleasure, and listened. Yes, the third voice must belong to Doc's best man. It was definitely a mature voice, one that commanded respect. Hannah hung back a bit and let her sisters walk on toward the gazebo. The haunting quality of the third voice had all of her senses on alert. Was it someone she knew? Had her mother and sisters planned some sort of surprise from the past for her? If that were the case, who could it possibly be?

Hannah's mind went through the possibilities. It didn't take long because there weren't that many. The only date she'd had in high school was one her father had arranged for her. She'd been very excited when Cliff Schuman had asked her to be his date for the senior prom until she'd learned that her father had promised Cliff a summer job at the hardware store if he'd escort Hannah. It couldn't be Cliff anyway. The last she'd heard, he was married with three children and living in Chicago.

No one knew about the two dates she'd had as an undergraduate student in college. She hadn't told anyone, not even her friends, mostly because both dates had been first dates and there hadn't been second dates with either man. The only romance, if you could call it that, had been with Bradford Ramsey, an assistant professor in the literature department. She'd thought that Bradford was the only man in the world for her until the devastating night she'd discovered that all of his promises for a future together were lies.

The only other possibility from her past was one that caused her breathing to quicken and her heart to beat much faster than normal. What if her sisters and Doc had conspired to bring Ross Barton here? But that couldn't possibly be the case, especially when she'd spoken to Ross on the phone last night. Surely he would have mentioned it if he'd planned to fly to Las Vegas in the morning to be Doc's best man at the wedding!

As her great-grandmother Elsa used to say, *Don't shilly-shally* around. *Shilly-shally* was an irregular reduplication of *shall I.* Hannah had looked it up the first time her great-grandmother had said it. What it meant was that she shouldn't hesitate to find out if she was simply imagining things and attributing a nonexistent conspiracy to purely innocent people, and that she should march straight to the gazebo and find out the identity of Doc's best man. Hannah squared her shoulders, took a few quick steps forward so that she could catch up with her mother and sisters, and entered the gazebo only a step or two behind them.

"Hannah! You look absolutely fantastic!"

The third voice spoke and Hannah felt her mouth drop open. She clacked it shut so that she wouldn't look like the fool she felt she'd been. It *had* been a conspiracy between her sisters, Delores, and Doc! There Ross was, a bit older and somehow more handsome than he'd been the last time she'd seen him. She felt the smile spread across her face as she took in his powerful build that looked just as much at home in a suit as it did in jeans and a chambray shirt, his dark hair that always looked a bit windblown even right after he'd combed it, his brilliant blue eyes that appeared to miss nothing, and the endearing dimple in his left cheek.

"Ross!" Hannah breathed, and even though she felt more than a little irked at being left out of the secret, she couldn't help but be absolutely delighted that he was here. "They got me, Ross. I had no clue you'd be Doc's best man!"

He laughed and Hannah felt the joy of seeing him spread through her whole body.

"Come here and let me hug you. It's been way too long." Ross held out his arms and Hannah went into them. There was no way in the world she'd refuse his invitation. She'd secretly wished to hear it during college on more than one sleepless night, knowing that he was right down the hall in the apartment building on Muscrat Lane. Then there was his trip to Lake Eden when he was producing *Crisis in Cherrywood*, his independent film. He'd been distracted and stressed most of the time he'd been there, busy with the production, the amateur actors he had directed, and the murder that happened on the set. Of course she'd seen him after that, hurried visits when he had passed through Minneapolis on his way to somewhere else, but regrettably, they really hadn't had much time together. And deep in the night, when she was alone, Hannah had admitted that she wanted time with Ross to see if the sparks she'd felt so long ago could be coaxed into flames.

"You're wearing it!" Ross touched the blue sapphire ring he'd sent her from Australia and Hannah was delighted that he'd noticed. She'd worn it almost constantly since she'd received it. The color of the stone reminded her of his eyes. And then his arms were around her and it was like they'd never been apart. She was keenly aware of the clean scent of his aftershave, the heat of his cheek next to hers, his strong arms around her. Had Ross missed her every bit as much as she'd missed him?

She wanted their hug to last forever, but a voice with a really bad Southern accent intruded. "Hey, y'all!"

Hannah looked over to see a man in an

obviously fake Elvis wig staring at them. "Who's gettin' married here anyway? I thought it was them two." He pointed at Delores and Doc. "But now I think it might be you two."

Hannah felt herself blushing. Had they hugged too long? But then Ross laughed and she laughed, too. "It's them," she said, pointing to Doc and Delores. "We just haven't seen each other for a long time."

"A *very* long time," Ross said, smiling down at her. "Much too long to suit me. But we're going to have time to catch up now. I'm in the suite right next to yours and I'm here for three days."

That was exactly how long she'd be there! Hannah felt the smile spreading across her face again. She really did want to reconnect with Ross. Perhaps nothing would come of it, but it was good to have friends.

"Okay then." The Elvis impersonator turned to go. "I'm goin' inside. Y'all come in soon now."

"He's not the minister, is he?" Delores asked just as soon as the man in the Elvis wig had left.

Hannah had trouble keeping a straight face. She didn't dare look at Ross. He'd heard Delores's question, and if they made eye contact, Hannah knew she'd laugh out loud.

"No," Doc answered Delores. "He's the videographer. We're going to take a DVD back to Lake Eden with us and play it at our wedding reception."

"I don't understand." Delores glanced at Ross. "Why didn't you ask Ross to do it? He's a professional."

"Because Ross is a professional best man tonight and I don't want anything to distract him from his duties. I've been waiting for years to marry you and nothing is going to stop me."

"Oh," Delores sighed, snuggling closer to him. "That's so romantic. Let's go get married. And let's ask them to play 'Love Me Tender' for our wedding song. It'll go perfectly with our videographer's wig. And then, right after we're married, let's hurry right back to the hotel and . . ."

"Lori!" Doc warned.

Delores gave the little giggle that delighted all three of her daughters. It made their mother sound as young as a teenager.

"Don't be silly, Doc." Delores patted his arm. "I was just going to suggest that we all go out to dinner. I feel like caviar and some more of that wonderful champagne of yours."

"How about Cold Duck and anchovies?" Doc grinned down at her as he asked the question.

"That's fine with me." Delores didn't hesitate, not even for a second. "I don't care what we have as long as I'm your wife when I eat and drink it."

Hannah's legs trembled slightly as she walked down the aisle of the little chapel. *This could be your wedding,* her mind told her. *You could be the bride and Ross could be your groom.*

"You're okay with this, aren't you?" Ross asked her quietly.

"Oh, yes!" Hannah said, glad that he hadn't guessed what was on her mind. "Mother and Doc are a perfect match."

When they parted ways at the altar, Hannah walked left to take her place next to her mother and Ross walked right, to take his place next to Doc. Michelle and Andrea came next, walking down the aisle together, and they took their places next to Hannah on their mother's side.

The moment they had all finished their short journey and taken their places, Mendelssohn morphed into vintage Presley and the strains of "Love Me Tender" filled the little chapel. Hannah exchanged glances with her sisters and all three of them began to shake with suppressed laughter. Then Ross gave an audible chuckle, Doc began to laugh, and Delores giggled.

"Cut it out, everyone!" Delores hissed in an effort to silence them. "Just thank your lucky stars that Carrie isn't here or we'd have to sing it!"

That did it. Hannah, Michelle, and Andrea could no longer hold in their laughter. All three of them remembered the night that Delores and Carrie had won the karaoke contest in Anoka with their exceedingly unmusical rendition of "Bye, Bye Love".

Doc turned to the minister who was staring at them and looking confused. "It's been a long day," he explained. "And it's going to get even longer. Let's start."

The minister turned toward the photographer, who was snapping photos of the wedding party at the altar. "Pull the plug, Hank."

It took a moment, but then there was silence in the chapel and Hannah drew a breath of relief as the minister began to read the familiar wedding ceremony.

Delores's response was first. She turned, looked at her daughters and smiled, and then looked up at Doc. "I do," she said in a loud, clear voice.

Doc was next and he did the same, but he reached for her hand and brought it to his lips right after he promised to love her and cherish her.

Hannah thought of her father. She believed that if he knew, he would approve. He'd loved Delores with all his heart and she had loved him. Then Hannah glanced at Ross. He was smiling and as she watched, he blinked several times. There was no doubt that he was as happy about this wedding as she was. She reached up to brush a tear from her cheek and saw that both of her sisters were brushing away tears. It was a beautiful wedding. It was a beautiful marriage. Hannah was happy that her mother had found a love like this for the second time in her life.

"Hannah!"

Hannah blinked and came back to the present with a start as Michelle called her name. "Yes, Michelle?"

"I thought you didn't like caviar."

"I don't."

"Then why did you just eat four toast points loaded with caviar and sour cream?" Andrea asked her.

"I did that?"

"Yes," Delores looked amused as she

confirmed it. "We all watched you eat it."

Hannah was shocked. She hated caviar. Surely she'd remember it if she'd eaten the expensive delicacy she'd often referred to as *nothing but little fish eggs*! "Then I guess you'd better cut me off. I must have had too much champagne."

"That's not it," Delores told her. "You haven't even taken a sip and we've already refilled our glasses."

"Oh." Hannah glanced toward the door of the restaurant, wondering what was taking Ross so long. They were dining at one of the gourmet restaurants in their hotel and Ross had gone back to his room to make a quick phone call.

"I was like that when I fell in love with Bill," Andrea said, exchanging glances with Delores and Michelle. "Falling in love makes you very distracted."

"I'm *not* falling in love!" Hannah glared at her married sister. "And now that the subject has come up, I'm not too happy that all of you set me up. You all knew that Ross was going to be here and you didn't tell me. I don't like being left out like that."

"But we wanted it to be a surprise," Delores explained. "We all thought you'd be happy to see Ross."

"I am. It's great to see Ross again."

"Well, that's a relief." A male voice spoke directly behind her and Hannah felt her face turn as red as the bouquet of roses on their table. Ross was back. And he'd heard everything she'd said.

"You don't know how many times I almost told you I was Doc's best man," he said, sitting down next to her and taking her hands in his. "When we talked on the phone last night, I came very close to spilling the beans."

Hannah thought about that for a moment. "I knew there was something you wanted to say. I just had that feeling. I should have asked you. I was about to, but then you said you'd see me soon and I thought you were planning a trip to Lake Eden."

"I am. I'll be in Lake Eden in a week or two. I'm setting up an interview at KCOW Television. They're looking for someone to produce some original material for them."

Delores looked surprised. "I didn't know that! You didn't mention it when *we* talked on the phone."

Hannah began to frown. She hadn't known that Ross and Delores had kept in contact. Delores had never mentioned it to her.

"Ross told me last week," Andrea admitted, "but he asked me to keep it under my hat until he knew for sure about the interview. So I did."

"You could have told me," Michelle turned to Ross. "We Skyped last week and you didn't mention it."

"I know. I just didn't want to jinx the interview. I really want that job. If I get it, I'll be based in Lake Eden. I'd like to live there."

"Even after living in Hollywood?" Hannah was amazed that anyone would want to leave the entertainment capital of the world and come to sleepy little Lake Eden.

"*Especially* after living in Hollywood."

Hannah was still puzzled. "But you seemed to love it. And everything sounded so exciting when you talked about the studios and the people you met. Won't you be bored in Lake Eden?"

"Lake Eden's not boring, not with you and your family there. The fast pace out there is getting to me, Hannah, not to mention the high cost of living. A steady job with a steady income sounds like heaven to me about now."

"But . . . you have friends in California. You talk about them all the time."

Ross shrugged. "That's true, but I have friends in Lake Eden, too. There's you, your whole family, and Doc. And there are all the people I met and liked when I produced the movie in Lake Eden. I just hope I get this job, Hannah. Lake Eden is where I really want to be."

Hannah didn't say anything. She was too afraid to even breathe. It sounded as if Ross wanted to come back to Lake Eden because of her, but she didn't want to ask in case she was wrong. There would be time for a more private conversation later, after the dinner and when they were alone. But would they ever be alone?

"I'm going to have the duck," Michelle announced, shutting her menu with a snap. "How about you, Andrea?"

"Chicken Cordon Bleu. I love that and I want to find out if it's as good as Sally's."

"Red meat for me," Doc said, turning to smile at Delores. "How about you, Mrs. Knight?"

Delores laughed. "For just a second there, I thought you were talking about your mother. I'm going to have to get used to my married name. The new Mrs. Knight will have the ginger-artichoke salad, salmon en croute, and a German Chocolate Cupcake for dessert."

"They have German Chocolate Cupcakes?" Doc's face lit up in a smile. "I love German chocolate cake."

"So do I," Ross said, turning to Hannah. "You used to make a great chocolate cake when we were in college."

"Then you're bound to like German Chocolate Cupcakes," Hannah told him, "since cupcakes are little, individual cakes."

Michelle turned to the dessert page and held it up. "Look. They have a whole cupcake menu. I've never seen so many different kinds. It looks like they have a cupcake for every kind of cake."

"Except one," Hannah corrected her.

"Which one?"

"I bet you won't find angel food cupcakes on that list."

"They're alphabetical." Michelle looked at the top of the page. "You're right, Hannah. They don't list angel food cupcakes. I wonder why they don't have them."

"They don't have them because it takes a special type of pan to bake an angel food cake. I've seen cupcake-size Bundt pans, but I've never seen cupcake-size angel food cake pans."

"But couldn't you make them in regular cupcake pans?" Andrea asked her.

"I'm not sure, but I don't think it would work. Angel food cake needs that tube in the middle of the pan so the cake will bake evenly."

"I understand that. But Bundt pans have tubes in the middle. I've even got some."

"You have cupcake-size Bundt pans?" Hannah couldn't help but be amazed. Andrea baked quite a few types of whippersnapper cookies. They were her specialty. But as far as Hannah knew, Andrea had never baked a cake, not even from a mix.

"I have them, but I've never used them. You know I don't bake cakes or cupcakes."

"Then why did you buy them?" Delores, another non-baker, asked the obvious question.

"I didn't buy them. Bill's aunt gave them to us for a wedding present." Andrea turned to Hannah. "Do you want them? I'll never use them."

"Sure. Thanks, Andrea."

"Okay. I'll check to make sure they're not scratched or anything when I get back home, and then I'll bring them down to you at The Cookie Jar."

Hannah was puzzled. "How could they get scratched if you've never used them?"

"I let the girls play with the pan in the sandbox. Tracey made mud pies for Bethie that looked like cute little cakes. She even decorated the tops with dandelions. Bethie must have thought they were real cakes because she tried to eat one, and Tracey had to stop making them."

Hannah glanced at Ross. He looked every bit as amused as she was. He reached over to drape a casual arm around her shoulder, and Hannah felt a shiver of anticipation. She wanted to be alone with Ross, to find out exactly how he felt about her. Was it friendship or something more? It was all very confusing and she felt a bit unraveled as she took her first sip of champagne. Perhaps she'd better look at the menu and figure out what she wanted to order for dinner. That was a lot easier than attempting to plan out the rest of her life.

GERMAN CHOCOLATE CUPCAKES

Preheat oven to 350 degrees F., rack in the middle position.

Either spray two 12-cup muffin tins with Pam or another nonstick cooking spray, OR line the cups with cupcake papers.

Jo Fluke's Note: This is another one of Rhanna's recipes. She also gave me the Pear Crunch Pie recipe in *Devil's Food Cake Murder*.

The filling:

8 ounces cream cheese, softened to room temperature *(the brick kind, not the whipped — I used Philadelphia cream cheese)*

1 large egg, beaten *(just whip it up in a glass with a fork)*

1/3 cup white *(granulated)* sugar

1/2 teaspoon coconut extract *(optional)*

2/3 cup semi-sweet chocolate chips *(I used Ghirardelli's)*

1/2 cup chopped pecans *(measure after chopping)*

1/8 teaspoon salt

Hannah's 1st Note: There is no frosting on these cupcakes. (It would be overkill!) But some people might miss

the coconut that is found in the traditional German Chocolate Cake. If you miss the coconut flavor, add the coconut extract to the filling. If you don't, don't.

In a small bowl, beat the cream cheese, egg, and white sugar together until they are smooth and creamy. Add the coconut extract, if you decided to use it, and mix it in thoroughly.

Stir in the chocolate chips, pecans, and salt.

Set the bowl aside on the counter while you make the cupcake batter.

The Cupcake Batter:
4 ounces Bakers German Sweet Chocolate
1 cup *(2 sticks, 8 ounces, 1/2 pound)* salted butter
4 large eggs
1 and 2/3 cups white *(granulated)* sugar
1/2 teaspoon baking soda
1 cup all-purpose flour *(pack it down in the cup when you measure it)*
1 teaspoon vanilla extract

Break the squares of Bakers Sweet German Chocolate in half. *(They'll melt faster that way.)*

Cut each stick of butter into 4 pieces. *(They'll melt faster that way.)*

Place the chocolate and the butter in a microwave-safe container. Microwave it on HIGH for one minute. Wait for one minute and then stir to see if the chocolate has melted.

If the chocolate has not completely melted, microwave the butter and chocolate for an additional 30 seconds. Wait a minute and then stir. Repeat if necessary. Set the chocolate/butter mixture aside on the counter or on a cold stove burner to cool to room temperature.

Hannah's 2nd Note: You can also do this in a small saucepan over low heat on the stovetop if you wish.

In a large bowl, beat the eggs until they are light-colored and fluffy.

Add the sugar gradually and beat it in thoroughly.

Mix in the flour, baking soda, and then the vanilla extract.

Feel the container with the chocolate/ butter mixture. If the mixture is not so hot it might cook the eggs, add it gradually to the batter, beating continuously.

Take the bowl from the mixer, give it a final stir by hand, and find a scooper or a spoon to use to fill the muffin tins. *(Lisa and I use a #2 scooper down at The Cookie Jar.)*

Fill the muffin tins 3/4 full.

Drop a rounded teaspoon of the filling into the center of each cupcake.

Bake at 350 degrees F. for 30 minutes. Take the pans from the oven and let the cupcakes cool on a wire rack or a cold stovetop burner. Do not remove the cupcakes until they are completely cool. *(Rhanna says that this may take some willpower on your part because they smell SO good!)*

Rhanna's Note: These cupcakes are so good you will want to eat more than one, but they are very rich. They are great for picnics!

Yield: 20 to 24 yummy cupcakes that everyone will love.

CHAPTER FIVE

"We knocked on your door, but you didn't answer," Andrea said when Hannah met her sisters for breakfast the next morning.

"What time was that?"

"Eleven-thirty. Michelle and I couldn't sleep so we decided to go for a midnight swim."

Hannah didn't see any reason to lie about where she'd been. "I didn't answer because I wasn't there. I was still in Ross's suite."

"You were?" A broad smile spread over Michelle's face. "Good for you! I was wondering if that's where you were."

Andrea's eyes narrowed. "And just what were you doing in Ross's suite?"

"Watching his latest projects. He brought DVDs of the short films he's going to use for his interview at KCOW Television and he asked me to critique them."

"So you were critiquing Ross's films until midnight?" Michelle asked, looking disappointed.

"Not midnight. We didn't finish until after two in the morning."

"That's not very romantic!" Michelle complained. "You should have told Ross you'd critique his films today and talked him into going to the grotto pool for a midnight swim."

"That does sound lovely, but I couldn't suggest that."

"Why not?" Andrea asked, and then she started to frown. "You brought your bathing suit, didn't you? I reminded you to bring it."

"I brought it, but all the shaping panels died and went to elastic heaven. Believe me, if Ross had seen me in that swimsuit, it wouldn't have been romantic!"

"Then we'll go shopping right after breakfast," Andrea decided. "We'll get you a gorgeous, sexy, new swimsuit."

"Okay, but that's a tall order."

"Not in Las Vegas. They have everything here." Andrea pulled her phone out of her purse. "I'll check online right now and find out where we should go."

Michelle was silent for a moment, watching Andrea operate her phone and then she turned to Hannah. "Let me get this straight. You were in Ross's suite until two in the morning and all you were doing was watching his films?"

Hannah gave a little smile as she thought of a way to neatly sidestep the question. "I can't answer that, because a lady never tells."

"Not even her sisters?"

The smile on Hannah's face turned a bit mischievous. "Not even her sisters," she said.

"You really look great, Hannah. That swimsuit is a knockout on you. How about a nice tall lemonade?"

"I'd love one," Hannah said, smiling at Ross.

"Andrea?" Ross asked.

"Yes, please."

"Me, too," Michelle said even before Ross could ask her. "I'll go along and help you carry them back."

"Told you!" Andrea crowed, just as soon as Ross and Michelle were out of earshot. "Aren't you glad you bought that suit?"

"Yes. My checking account isn't, but I am."

"And aren't you glad I talked you into going for the dark teal instead of that boring black one?"

"Yes. This is much better."

91

"All right then!" Andrea looked pleased as she dipped her foot in the water. "Isn't this a real treat? There's no place in Lake Eden where we could wear our swimsuits now and dip our toes in water that wasn't almost frozen."

Hannah was about to agree with her when she thought of one place where swimsuits would be entirely appropriate. "Oh, yes there is. There's one place in Lake Eden."

"There is? Where's that?"

"Under the dome in the penthouse suite at the Albion Hotel Condos. You told me yourself that the dome was climate controlled and the pool was heated in the winter."

"You're right! I wish we could talk Mother into buying it before that corporation does. There's something about that deal that I just don't like."

"I don't know anything about any deal. You didn't mention it to me. Did someone make an offer?"

"Not someone. It's some *thing.* According to Howie, it's a corporation that calls itself Nightlife LLC. The name just sounds . . ." Andrea paused, searching for the right word. "It just sounds *off* to me, if you know what I mean."

"Nightlife LLC," Hannah repeated the

name. "I see what you mean. It sounds like the type of corporation that runs an after-hours club, or an escort service."

"I know. That's what I said to Howie, but he told me not to worry, that it wasn't like that at all. He also said I'd be very pleased when I found out who owned the corporation, but that's all he'd tell me." Andrea paused again and looked thoughtful. "Wait a minute. Do you think Nightlife LLC could be Ross and some of his movie investors? He said he wanted to move to Lake Eden. And he probably knows a lot of people with money."

"He does, but I really don't think they'd be involved in anything like Lake Eden real estate. Ross has talked about his investors. Most of them are from New York and Los Angeles and they're only interested in financing projects in the entertainment industry like plays, independent films, and concerts."

"Heads up," Andrea said as Ross and Michelle approached, each of them carrying a cardboard tray with two drinks on it.

"Here you go," Ross said, handing one lemonade to Hannah and the other to Andrea. He took his lemonade from Michelle's tray and sat down next to Hannah. "I had them put a little something extra in it."

"Liquor?" Hannah asked, wondering how a drink this early in the day would affect her.

Ross shook his head. "Raspberry syrup. That makes it a type of pink lemonade, but the common pink lemonade has grenadine or cranberry juice. I thought raspberry would be better."

Hannah took a sip. "I like this a lot better. I've had pink lemonade made with cranberry juice, but never with grenadine."

"What is grenadine anyway?" Michelle asked. "I know they put it in tequila sunrises and it's red. Is it cherry?"

Hannah shook her head. "No, it's made from pomegranates. There's an aftertaste to grenadine that I've never liked."

"But you like tequila sunrises, don't you?" Ross asked her.

Hannah shrugged. "I don't know. I've never had one."

"I can fix that," Ross told her, "But only if you promise to bake that tangerine cake you made the last time I came to Lake Eden."

"My Tangerine Dream Cake?"

"That's the one. I really like tangerines."

"I'll be glad to make it for you. I love to bake that cake."

Ross looked pleased. "It's a deal then. I'll look forward to it almost as much as I'll

94

look forward to spending more time with you."

Hannah saw Michelle exchange a look with Andrea. She wasn't sure what it meant until both of them picked up their towels and waved as they went off to take a dip in the pool. Her sisters were giving her time alone with Ross. She had to remember to thank them.

"How about meeting me at the cocktail bar an hour before we're due to have dinner with your mother and Doc? I want to find out if you like tequila sunrises."

"I'll be there," Hannah said, and then she hoped she hadn't agreed too quickly. Someone had once told her that a woman shouldn't be too eager. If she agreed too quickly, the man would get the idea that she didn't have any other prospects.

But you do have other prospects, her mind corrected her. *You've got Norman and Mike waiting at home in Lake Eden.*

"Why so quiet?" Ross asked her. "Are you having second thoughts about trying that tequila sunrise?"

"No, not at all. I love to try new things."

"Me, too. I guess we both have adventurous spirits."

Hannah almost burst into laughter. Most people thought she was too cautious and no one had ever called her adventurous before. Perhaps she was changing. And if she was, it was all because of Ross. "Perhaps that's true," she said, smiling at him over the rim of her pink lemonade glass.

Hannah was getting dressed for dinner when there was a knock on her hotel room door. "Just a minute!" she called out, slipping the top of her pantsuit over her head and slipping on her shoes before she answered the door.

"Mother!" she said, surprised to see Delores standing there. She'd expected that the knock would be from Michelle, Andrea, or Ross.

"May I come in?" Delores asked.

"Of course. There's nothing wrong, is there?"

"Not a thing. I'm supremely happy. You don't have to worry about me, dear. It's you that I'm concerned about."

Uh-oh! Hannah's mind warned her. *Something's up!* "What is it, Mother?" she asked in a voice that was much calmer than she felt.

"It's Mike and Norman. Have you heard from them since you left?"

"No, they haven't called me." Hannah felt her heart beat faster. "Is something wrong

with Moishe?"

"Oh, no dear. Everything's fine as far as I know. I just . . ." Delores stopped and looked terribly uncomfortable as she handed Hannah the bottle of champagne and the glasses she was carrying. "Pour us a glass. We're going to need it. We're going to have a mother-daughter talk."

That was enough for Hannah. She took the bottle and filled two champagne flutes. She didn't plan on having more than one sip. She wanted her wits about her, and she had a date with Ross and a tequila sunrise in less than thirty minutes. But her mother obviously had something serious on her mind.

Delores took the chair Hannah indicated and accepted a glass of champagne. She took a sip and sighed heavily. "Doc thinks I'm borrowing trouble and I shouldn't interfere, but I told him I just had to come and discuss things with you."

"What would you like to discuss?" Hannah asked, even though she really didn't want to know. There was no way she was looking forward to the forthcoming conversation.

"Well, dear . . . I think it's best to be blunt and jump right in. I'm very concerned about what you're going to tell Mike and

Norman about Ross."

"When I tell them *what* about Ross?"

"When you tell them that you were in Ross's suite last night until two in the morning."

"Those rats!" Hannah muttered under her breath, taking the one sip of champagne she'd allotted herself for this mother-daughter talk. "Andrea and Michelle must have run right up to the honeymoon suite and blabbed everything to you."

"Well . . . not exactly, dear. I called them and asked."

Hannah took a deep, calming breath. "Why did you do that?"

"Because I was concerned about you. I didn't want you to do anything rash."

"Really, Mother! I'm a grown woman over thirty. What I did or didn't do in Ross's suite is none of your business!"

"I know that, but I just wanted to ask what you planned to do about Mike and Norman."

Hannah bit back another angry retort. "I'm not planning to do *anything,* Mother. What's happening here? Are you trying to manage my love life?"

"No! I never wanted to do that! I was just concerned, that's all. And I'm glad you're having this . . . this little interlude with

Ross. But I don't want you to be swept overboard."

"Swept overboard? You're the one who's going on a cruise, not me." Delores gave a small smile, but Hannah could tell that her mother wasn't really amused. "What exactly do you mean by being swept overboard, Mother?"

Delores gave a deep sigh. "I know that you refused to accept Mike's proposal. And you didn't accept Norman's proposal, either."

"That's true."

"They both wanted to marry you, Hannah. And perhaps you were right in not agreeing to marry either one of them. That's not for me to say. But I just want you to be sure that this thing with Ross is going to be what you really want."

"What *thing*?"

"I know you, Hannah. I'm your mother. I've known you longer than anyone else on the face of the earth. I just want you to be careful that you don't make a mistake you'll regret. I probably did this mother-daughter talk all wrong, but I had to try. And now I have to go. Doc's waiting for me. But before I leave, there's one more thing I have to say. Think long and hard before you mention Ross to either Mike or Norman."

"You mean that what happens in Vegas

stays in Vegas?" Hannah repeated the line from the Las Vegas commercial that had run on KCOW Television.

"That's trite, but yes. That's exactly what I mean. I really have to go, Hannah. I'm very glad we had this talk."

Hannah walked her mother to the door, reminding herself every step that her mother only wanted the best for her.

"I love you, dear," Delores said, reaching out to hug her eldest daughter. "And I want you to be as happy as I am. I'm just worried that you're going to get caught up in all this whirlwind wedding fun and burn your bridges behind you. Ross may not be for you. You don't know yet. Please don't make any snap decisions."

"I hear you, Mother. And I won't make any decisions at all unless I'm sure. And I'm not sure yet, so you and Doc can relax."

"Thank you, dear. Dinner is at seven. Doc told me he has a surprise for us."

"I'll be there," Hannah promised before she closed the door behind her mother. She turned around, made a face at the full-length mirror that hung on an adjacent wall, and walked off to pour the rest of her champagne down the sink in the bathroom.

"I've got to talk to you about something,

Hannah. Everybody's really trying to push us together, aren't they?" Ross looked very serious as he faced her across the tiny table in the cocktail bar.

"Yes, they are and I wish they'd stop."

"So you don't want to be together?"

"It's not that!" Hannah shook her head so hard that her unruly red curls bounced. "I just don't like to be pushed. I hate it when people try to manipulate me."

"I understand perfectly." Ross reached out to take her hand. "I don't like it, either. Unless, of course, I *want* to be manipulated."

"Do you want to be manipulated?" Hannah asked and then she wished she hadn't.

"In this case, I don't really mind. I've always been crazy about you, Hannah. You knew that way back in college. Remember how we used to get together and watch vintage movies?"

Hannah smiled. "I remember."

"And do you remember who used to come up with the right movie quote most of the time?"

"You did."

"And you did. As I remember, we were tied for the championship of movie quotes when you left college." Ross stopped speaking and took a sip of his drink. "It wasn't any good after that, Hannah. I missed you too much. It just wasn't right with only Linda."

"But you loved her."

"I thought I loved her. But once you'd gone back to Lake Eden, I realized that Linda wasn't the woman I loved. It was you, Hannah."

Hannah didn't say anything. She couldn't. She just stared at him in utter disbelief.

"Don't look at me like that. It's true. I loved you way back then, Hannah, and it took me too long to realize it. By the time I did, you were gone."

"But you and Linda were engaged."

"I know. I made promises to Linda and I knew she'd never understand if I didn't keep them. I promised her that we'd get married when we graduated."

"But you didn't."

"No, but that wasn't my decision. Linda wanted to wait. She wanted to try to make it as an actress. And she did. And then she fell in love with Tom Larchmont and married him."

"How did you feel about that?"

"I was hurt . . ." Ross stopped and took a deep breath. "And I was relieved at the same time. I knew by then that it wouldn't have worked. I was grateful to Tom for coming along and asking Linda to marry him.

He kept me from the worst mistake of my life."

"But Linda loved you."

"She did, way back then. But we were kids. And when we grew up, our feelings for each other changed. We didn't know much about love and commitment back then. We were discovering things, living in the moment. You did the same, Hannah. You were living in the moment with Bradford."

Hannah took a sip of her tequila sunrise. It was good, but then she pushed it aside. "It's true. Some of it was good, and some of it was bad, but I guess all of it helped us to grow up."

There was a silence between them, but it wasn't uncomfortable. Hannah finally broke it by squeezing Ross's hands. "I'm glad we talked about all this."

"So am I. The politicians are always talking about transparency. I want everything to be transparent between us, Hannah. No secrets, no lies, just us."

"Just us," Hannah repeated. And then she leaned forward to meet him across the small table to share a kiss to seal their promise.

CHAPTER SIX

"We didn't see you at the Beatles Retrospective last night," Andrea said when Ross and Hannah met them for breakfast.

"That's because we decided not to go." Hannah picked up the jelly and put some on her toast.

"What did you do?" Andrea asked.

"We went to the pool instead," Ross answered.

"But we went to the pool afterwards and we didn't see you," Andrea said.

It was obvious that Andrea wasn't willing to stop quizzing them and Hannah felt her temper rise again. "I guess we weren't there at the same time."

"What time were you there?" Andrea asked.

"What time were *you* there?" Hannah countered. "I don't appreciate being grilled, Andrea, especially because I know you're going to tell Mother exactly what I said."

That comment made Andrea's face turn pink. "Sorry," she mumbled. "I just don't want you to . . . to . . ."

"Get hurt," Michelle finished her sentence. "We like Ross. It's not that. We practically pushed you together. But we just want to make sure you're okay."

"I understand." Ross entered the conversation again. "And I don't want Hannah to get hurt, either. But you really have to cut us some slack here. Hannah and I haven't seen each other for a while and we've got some catching up to do."

"That's right," Hannah backed him up. "If you two are monitoring our every move, it's going to get irritating in a hurry. Don't try to chaperone us. Is that clear?"

There was a moment of silence and then Andrea and Michelle nodded.

"It's clear," Andrea said.

"We're sorry if we've been too intrusive," Michelle followed up. "Maybe we're more protective than we should be."

"No kidding!" Hannah said sarcastically, and then she wished she hadn't. Her family *was* intrusive. There was no doubt about that. But they were only trying to protect her.

"Let's just forget it then," Ross suggested. "It's pretty clear that we all want the same thing. Instead of sniping at each other, let's make plans for tonight. It's our last night in Vegas and we should do something special together, at least for part of the night."

"Cirque Du Soleil," Michelle suggested, remembering the tickets that Norman had given Hannah. "I've seen it on television, but everyone says it's much more impressive if you see it in person."

"Fine with me," Ross agreed. "Shall I pick up four tickets?"

"All we need is one," Hannah told him. "Norman ordered them in advance and gave us three."

"Okay. Let me go work on that. I'm sure they'll have some at the front desk."

Hannah was thoughtful as she watched Ross walk away. Had that been a flicker of jealousy she'd seen on his face when she'd mentioned Norman's name?

"Whoa!" Michelle said, raising her eyebrows. "Ross didn't like it when you mentioned Norman."

Andrea nodded. "I caught that, too. And I agree. I think Ross was jealous."

Hannah didn't say anything, but she felt a tingle of satisfaction. If Ross felt the way she hoped he did about her, he *should* be a bit jealous or at least a bit uncomfortable when she mentioned a former boyfriend.

Former boyfriend? The rational part of Hannah's mind picked up on her phrasing. *Does that mean that Norman and Mike are out of the running and Ross is in?*

Hannah ignored the question. There was time to think about things like that later when she was back in Lake Eden. Instead, she decided to address something else that was bothering her. "Mother's worried about what I'm going to tell Mike and Norman when I get home."

"She's not the only one!" Andrea said and then she sighed. "It's like Great-Grandma Elsa used to say. *Don't put all your eggs in one basket.*"

"Mother feels the same way. And it didn't help that you told her I was in Ross's suite until after two in the morning."

Andrea looked horribly guilty. "I'm sorry, Hannah. That was my fault. It just slipped out and then there was no way to take it back. It all started when she asked about our midnight swim and why we didn't invite you to go along. I told her we were going to, but you didn't answer our knock on your door."

"That's exactly how it happened." Michelle defended her older sister. "She said you might have been sleeping, but Mother didn't buy that for a second. She said you'd always been a light sleeper and her guess was that you were still with Ross. And then she asked Andrea, point-blank, if she knew where you were."

"I couldn't lie to her." Andrea sounded sorry and guilty at the same time. "I've never been able to lie to Mother. I just wish she'd asked Michelle instead of me."

"Would you have lied about it?" Hannah turned to Michelle.

"Probably. But Mother would have caught me at it. You know what it's like to be grilled by Mother."

"Oh, yes. I know. And believe me, I can understand how the whole thing happened."

Andrea looked hopeful. "Does that mean you're not mad at us anymore?"

"I'm not mad at you. I told you I understood. I just wish Mother would mind her own business and let me take care of mine."

There was a silence and then Michelle cleared her throat. "Maybe I shouldn't ask this, but what *are* you going to tell Norman and Mike? They'll see the wedding pictures. Doc's having posters made to display at the party. They'll see that Ross was Doc's best man."

"I'll cross that bridge when I come to it," Hannah said, sounding much more confident than she felt. "There's no reason I should feel guilty about spending time with Ross. Mike's dated plenty of other women and Norman was going to marry Doctor Bev. I don't have an exclusive relationship with either one of them."

"That's true, but you haven't dated anyone else . . . have you?"

Hannah laughed. Michelle had sounded very tentative when she'd asked. "No, I haven't dated anyone else. But that's only because I haven't found anyone I want to date."

"Until now," Andrea pointed out. "Is Ross the one, Hannah?"

"I don't know. All I know is I really like to be with him. Ross and I have been friends for a long time. I lived down the hall from Ross and Linda for over three years when we were all in college. We got together at least four times a week, sometimes more."

"But you were dating Bradford Ramsey when you were in college," Michelle pointed out.

Dating isn't exactly the right word, Hannah's mind corrected, but she ignored it. "Only for a couple of months," she replied, shooting her youngest sister a warning glance. Andrea didn't need to know that both her older and younger sister had been involved with the same college professor.

"Here comes Ross," she said, giving a little wave in his direction. "I wonder if he managed to get a ticket."

"Here you are," Ross said, handing an envelope to Hannah. "The best four seats in the house. We even get to go backstage during intermission and talk to some of the performers."

Hannah opened the envelope and frowned slightly. "But . . . we already had three tickets. And you have four more in here."

"They're better tickets than the ones Norman gave you. These are premium tickets. They come with appetizers, free drinks, and that backstage visit I told you about. Not only that, we don't have to battle the crowds. With these tickets, we're entitled to enter through a special door and leave the same way."

"These must have cost a lot more than the other tickets," Hannah said.

"They did, but that's okay. You're worth it."

Ross smiled at her and Hannah felt warm all over. She also felt slightly guilty over the tickets that Norman had given her. "I wonder what I should do with the other tickets."

"You could give them away," Andrea suggested. "There's a family of three in the room next to ours and their daughter was talking about wanting to go to Cirque Du Soleil. They're sitting at that table by the door, having breakfast."

Hannah reached into her purse and handed the envelope to Michelle. "Go over there right now and see if they want them. It would be a real shame if they just go to waste. And if you see our waitress on your way over there, send her over with another menu."

Michelle was clearly surprised. "You're still hungry?"

"Not really, but I want to try a baked doughnut. I noticed that they had several kinds listed in the menu."

"A *baked* doughnut?" Ross looked puzzled. "I didn't know doughnuts could be baked. I thought they were always deep fried."

"That's exactly what I thought!" Andrea said. "It's one of the reasons I don't let Tracey have them very often. She gets a doughnut every Sunday and French fries on Wednesdays at the café when she visits me at the office after school."

When Michelle came back to their table, she was smiling broadly. "You should have seen Judy's face when I offered them the tickets." She turned to Hannah and Ross to explain. "Judy is their daughter's name. She's ten. Andrea and I talked to her mother at the pool. Judy was so excited, she bounced up and down in her chair." Michelle handed a menu to Hannah. "Here you go. I didn't see our waitress, but Judy and her parents had already ordered so they sent this menu for you."

Hannah opened the menu and found the page listing the baked doughnuts. She read down the list and was amazed at how many varieties there were. "They have chocolate, strawberry, cherry, vanilla, lemon, and something called confetti."

"Cherry," Andrea said, deciding immediately and then she turned to Michelle. "How about you?"

"Since they don't have maple, I'll take lemon."

"Ross?" Hannah turned to him.

"Confetti. It sounds interesting and I want to see what it is."

"And I'll have chocolate," Hannah decided.

"No surprise there," Michelle said.

"If I like it, I'll get another for you to take up to Mother," Hannah said, by way of explanation.

Five minutes later, no one at the table uttered a peep. They were all too busy eating doughnuts and sipping coffee. Ross was the first to finish his confection and, after he'd taken a final sip of his coffee, he gave a satisfied sigh. "These are really good."

"Mmmm," Hannah murmured by way of acknowledgment as she chewed her last bite of chocolate doughnut. "Mine was excellent. I wonder if I can get their recipe. It's not like we're in competition or anything. They're in Nevada and The Cookie Jar is hundreds of miles away in Minnesota."

"Let me try," Ross offered. "There's our waitress." He gestured toward a table across the room. "I'll ask her if she'll introduce me to the person who makes the doughnuts."

"Do you think he can get the recipe?" Michelle asked after Ross had left.

"Probably," Andrea answered, putting down her coffee cup. "He's awfully handsome."

Michelle nodded. "And he's charming, too. Ross reminds me of Lonnie. He always knows what to say to make a woman feel good about herself."

"That's Irish charm," Hannah told them. "And that's why Ross reminds you of Lonnie. Ross's mother was Irish. He told me all about his family when we were in college and he showed me a picture of his mother. She was beautiful. And his father was really good looking, too."

Ross came across the room just then, carrying an envelope in his hand.

"Looks like Ross got the recipe," Michelle commented.

He arrived at the table just in time to hear her comment. "I got *both* recipes," he told them. "One is for the baked chocolate doughnut that Hannah had. And the other one is for baked vanilla doughnuts. The pastry chef told me that the dough is the same for all of the flavors except chocolate. You just add a couple of things to the dough and glaze them differently."

"Sounds easy," Hannah commented. She took the envelope that Ross handed her and read quickly through the recipes. "There's no reason why we couldn't make these at The Cookie Jar."

"The pastry chef showed me the pans she uses," Ross told them. "And she said they're getting so popular that they come in smaller sizes for the home baking market."

"There was a kitchen supply store in the shopping center where we got your bathing suit," Andrea recalled. "Michelle and I can call there to see if they carry doughnut pans."

"If they do, we can run over there to get some," Michelle offered. "We don't have any plans for this afternoon."

Hannah glanced at Ross and found he was looking at her. As she watched, he winked and Hannah dropped her eyes quickly, hoping she wouldn't give anything away in a telltale blush. The two of them had already made plans for the afternoon, but Andrea and Michelle certainly didn't need to know about that!

"How many do you need, Hannah?" Michelle asked her.

Hannah glanced at the recipes again. "It all depends on how many doughnuts each pan holds. Lisa and I can use large pans like the ones the pastry chef uses, but I'd rather not buy those right off the bat. I need to test the doughnuts in smaller batches to see if they'll work for us. Besides, most of the chains don't carry industrial oven-sized pans in their retail stores."

Hannah thought for a moment and then she came to a decision. "I'm guessing that the home baking pans will probably hold six to eight doughnuts and be roughly the size of cupcake pans. If I'm right, get six. That's two pans for each of us and The Cookie Jar will pay you back. Every year, when Stan does my taxes, he tells me that I need to spend more money on baking equipment."

"The Cookie Jar is buying *me* two dough-nut pans?" Andrea asked, looking surprised.

"It's the least we can do," Hannah told her. "You've given us at least five great Whippersnapper Cookie recipes that our customers love."

Their waitress brought the bill and Ross grabbed it before any of them could make a move toward the black folder. "I'll get this."

"But we should pay you back," Michelle objected. "You paid for our breakfast yesterday."

"And I'll pay for your breakfast tomorrow, too," he promised. "It's only fair. I enjoy the company and I hate to eat breakfast alone."

"Me, too," Hannah said, and then she wished she hadn't just in case Ross thought she was hinting that they ought to have every breakfast together. She didn't want him to get the wrong idea. Or was it the *right* idea? She wasn't quite sure yet.

"Thank you, Ross," Andrea said as she pushed back her chair and stood up.

"Yes, thank you," Michelle echoed, also getting to her feet. "Maybe we'll see you at the pool later. I talked to Lonnie and he said it got down to forty degrees last night. I need to get some more pool time in before we go home."

Andrea nodded. "The same goes for me. Maybe we'll see you later."

Not if we see you first, Hannah thought, but of course she didn't say it. It was a cinch, however, that she wouldn't suggest going to the pool that Andrea and Michelle frequented. The look in Ross's eyes had been very romantic when they'd exchanged glances and she could hardly wait to be alone with him again.

CHOCOLATE BAKED DOUGHNUTS

Preheat oven to 350 degrees F., rack in the middle position.

2/3 cups unsweetened cocoa powder *(I used Hershey's)*

1 and 3/4 cups all-purpose flour *(pack it down in the cup when you measure it)*

3/4 cup white *(granulated)* sugar

1 teaspoon baking powder

1 teaspoon baking soda

1/2 teaspoon cream of tartar

1/2 teaspoon salt

2 large eggs

1/2 cup milk

1/3 cup sour cream

2 teaspoons vanilla extract

1/2 cup *(1 stick, 4 ounces, 1/4 pound)* salted butter, melted

1 cup *(a 6-ounce bag)* semi-sweet chocolate chips

Spray the wells in a 12-cup doughnut pan with Pam or another nonstick cooking spray. *(I used two 6-cup doughnut pans)*

In the bowl of an electric mixer, mix the cocoa powder and all-purpose flour together at low speed.

Place the sugar in the bowl and mix it in on low speed.

Add the baking powder, baking soda, cream of tartar, and salt. Mix well.

Mix in the eggs, one at a time.

Add the milk, sour cream, and vanilla extract. Mix until well combined.

With the mixer running, drizzle in the melted butter and continue to mix until the doughnut dough is smooth.

Take the bowl out of the mixer and scrape down the sides of the bowl with a rubber spatula. Give the doughnut dough another stir by hand.

Use the rubber spatula to mix in the chocolate chips by hand.

Spoon the dough into the indentations in the doughnut pan, filling them a bit over 3/4 full.

Bake the doughnuts at 350 degrees F. for 12 to 15 minutes, or until a toothpick inserted into the middle baked part of one of the doughnuts comes out clean.

Take the doughnuts out of the oven and transfer the pan to a wire rack. Cool them for 1 to 2 minutes.

Loosen the edges of the doughnuts by running a table knife around the circles. Then use potholders to pick up the pan and tip them out onto the wire rack.

Sugar/Cocoa/Cinnamon Coating:

2 Tablespoons white *(granulated)* sugar
1/2 teaspoon unsweetened cocoa powder
1/2 teaspoon cinnamon *(optional)*

Quickly fill a bag with the white sugar, cocoa powder, and cinnamon *(if you decided to use it).* You must coat your doughnuts while they are still warm so that the coating will stick.

Shake the bag to mix the ingredients and then place the warm doughnuts, one at a time, in the bag and shake them in the sugar/cocoa/cinnamon mixture. Then take them out and let them cool completely on the wire rack.

Alternatively, you can coat your doughnuts with chocolate icing, but you must let them cool completely. If you try to frost warm doughnuts, the icing will slide off. *(I know. I tried it!)*

Chocolate Icing:

1 cup semi-sweet chocolate chips *(6-ounce package)*
2 Tablespoons salted butter
2 Tablespoons cream

In a microwave-safe bowl that's large enough to hold a doughnut, combine the semi-sweet chocolate chips, salted butter, and cream.

Heat the contents on HIGH for 1 minute.

Leave the bowl in the microwave for one minute and then stir the contents with a heat-resistant rubber spatula to see if the chips are melted. If they're not, heat in 30-second increments until you can stir the icing smooth.

Quickly dip the tops of the doughnuts in the bowl of chocolate icing. Place them on a sheet of wax paper to cool.

Jo Fluke's Note: If you want to coat the entire doughnut, place it in the bowl and turn it over with a fork. Do this one at a time, transferring each coated doughnut to a cookie sheet lined with wax paper.

If you'd like to sprinkle chopped nuts on your doughnuts, do it now, before the chocolate icing has hardened. You can also put on sprinkles if you wish, or even shredded coconut.

Let the doughnuts sit until the coating has hardened. Then eat and enjoy.

These doughnuts are best eaten on the first day *(which has never been a problem in my house!)*. If there are any leftovers, put them in a covered container and eat them the next morning for breakfast.

Yield: 12 yummy baked doughnuts.

**Jo Fluke's Note: I got my baked dough-
nut pans directly from the manufac-
turer, Wilton. They're easy to find over
the holidays, but most kitchen stores
don't carry them year-round. Look
online if you can't find them by searching for "baked doughnut pans".**

ANY FLAVOR BAKED DOUGHNUTS

Preheat oven to 350 degrees F., rack in the middle position.

2 cups all-purpose flour *(pack it down in the cup when you measure it)*
3/4 cup white *(granulated)* sugar
2 teaspoons baking powder
1/2 teaspoon cream of tartar
1/2 teaspoon salt
1/2 teaspoon cinnamon
1/4 teaspoon ground nutmeg *(freshly grated is best, of course)*
2 large eggs
1/2 cup milk
1/4 cup sour cream
2 teaspoons vanilla extract
1/2 cup *(1 stick, 4 ounces, 1/4 pound)* salted butter, melted

Spray the wells in a 12-cup doughnut pan with Pam or another nonstick cooking spray. *(I used two 6-cup doughnut pans)*

In the bowl of an electric mixer, mix the all-purpose flour and the white sugar together at low speed.

Add the baking powder, cream of tartar, salt, cinnamon, and nutmeg. Mix well.

Mix in the eggs, one at a time.

Add the milk, sour cream, and vanilla

extract. Mix until well combined.

With the mixer running, drizzle in the melted butter and continue to mix until the doughnut dough is smooth.

If you are making flavored doughnuts, mix in the flavoring you want from the list below:

Orange doughnuts–1 teaspoon orange zest

Lemon doughnuts–1 teaspoon lemon zest

Coffee doughnuts–1 teaspoon instant coffee powder

Peanut butter doughnuts–1 cup *(6-oz. pkg.)* peanut butter chips

Butterscotch doughnuts–1 cup *(6-oz. pkg.)* butterscotch chips

White chocolate doughnuts–1 cup *(6-oz pkg.)* white chocolate chips

Cherry Doughnuts–1/2 cup chopped maraschino cherries, patted dry

Cranberry Doughnuts–1/2 cup chopped dried cranberries

Jo Fluke's Note: for Orange or Lemon doughnuts, you may want to use 1 teaspoon of the orange or lemon extract for 1 teaspoon of the vanilla extract.

If you are using chips to flavor your doughnuts, take the bowl out of the mixer and mix in the chips by hand. If you're using zest, just add it to your mixing bowl with the melted butter.

Spoon the dough into the indentations in

the doughnut pan, filling them a bit over 3/4 full.

Bake the doughnuts at 350 degrees F. for 12 to 15 minutes, or until a toothpick inserted into the middle baked part of one of the doughnuts comes out clean.

Take the doughnuts out of the oven and transfer the pan to a wire rack. Cool them for 1 to 2 minutes.

Loosen the edges of the doughnuts by running a table knife around the circles. Then use potholders to pick up the pan and tip them out onto the wire rack.

If you'd like a simple coating for your doughnuts, quickly fill a bag with 3 Tablespoons of white *(granulated)* sugar. You must coat your doughnuts while they are still warm so that the sugar coating will stick.

Place the warm doughnuts in the bag, one at a time, and shake them in the sugar. Then take them out and let them cool completely on the wire rack.

Alternatively, you can coat your doughnuts with Powdered Sugar Glaze, Flavored Powdered Sugar Glaze, or Chip Icing. Let the doughnuts cool completely first before you begin to make your glaze or icing. *(If you attempt to frost or glaze warm doughnuts, the icing or glaze will slide off.)*

Powdered Sugar Glaze:

2 cups powdered *(confectioners)* sugar *(pack it down in the cup when you measure it — no need to sift unless it's got big lumps)*
1/4 cup milk
1 teaspoon vanilla extract

Flavored Powdered Sugar Glaze:

2 cups powdered *(confectioners)* sugar *(pack it down in the cup when you measure it — no need to sift unless it's got big lumps)*
1/4 cup fruit juice
1 teaspoon flavor extract

(For orange use orange juice, for lemon use lemon juice, for cherry use maraschino cherry juice, for cranberry use cranberry juice. You can also add a half-teaspoon of zest to the orange and lemon if you wish.)

Combine the glaze ingredients in a saucepan large enough to hold a doughnut. Heat on MEDIUM, whisking until the glaze is smooth.

Pull the saucepan off the heat and dip a cooled doughnut into the glaze. Flip it over with a fork to glaze both sides. Extract the doughnut with the fork and set it down on a sheet of wax paper to dry.

When the glaze has "set" on your dough-nuts, you can re-dip them if you re-heat the glaze in your pan.

Any Flavor Chip Icing:
1 cup chips of your choice *(6-ounce package)*
2 Tablespoons salted butter
2 Tablespoons cream

In a microwave-safe bowl that's large enough to hold a doughnut, combine the chips, salted butter and cream.

Heat the contents on HIGH for 1 minute.

Let the bowl sit in the microwave for 1 minute and then stir to see if the chips are melted. If they're not, heat in 30-second increments until you can stir the icing smooth.

Quickly dip the tops of the cold doughnuts in the bowl of icing. Place them on a sheet of wax paper iced side up.

Jo Fluke's Note: If you want to coat the entire doughnut, place it in the bowl and turn it over with a fork. Do this one at a time, transferring each coated doughnut to a cookie sheet lined with wax paper.

If you'd like to sprinkle chopped nuts on your doughnuts, do it before the icing has hardened. You can also put on sprinkles or decorators sugar if you wish.

Let the doughnuts sit until the coating has hardened. Then eat and enjoy.

These doughnuts are best eaten on the first day *(which has never been a problem in my house!)*. If there are any leftovers, put them in a covered container and eat them the next morning for breakfast.

Yield: 12 yummy baked doughnuts.

CHAPTER SEVEN

Hannah woke up when the sky began to lighten with the promise of a new day. Even though, technically, she was still on vacation, she'd gotten into the habit of waking up early and old habits were hard to break. She smiled as she got out of bed and slipped on her bathing suit and one of the robes that the hotel had provided for its guests.

A moment later, she let herself into Ross's suite. She walked across the floor to the window, opened the drapes and the sliding door, and stepped out on the balcony. It faced east and there was a glow on the horizon. As she stood there and watched, the glow brightened and the scene below her took shape. At first, the pool was a hazy rectangle in the predawn light. The sky, reflecting on the surface of the water was a slightly lighter shade than the surrounding apron of concrete that was textured and tinted to look like brickwork.

That was when the first pale colors, muted by the gray of the sky, began to appear on the horizon. First there was a pale yellow glow that gradually lightened with a hint of coral at its base as the sun, still hidden, rose slowly in the sky. And then came the magical moment that always made Hannah's heart beat with joy at being alive. The sun, in all its stately splendor, peeked over the horizon and painted the landscape below it with brilliant color. Almost instantly, birds began to sing to herald a new day, and Hannah felt Ross's arms wrap around her waist. His lips brushed the tender skin at the back of her neck and she wondered if anything could be more perfect.

"I love to watch the sunrise," he said softly. "It's like a resurrection for me. I can forget the mistakes I made in the past because everything is fresh and new again. And if I try, I have the power to make it the best day of my life."

Hannah didn't say anything. She didn't have to. She simply turned and kissed him.

"An early morning swim?" he asked, holding her tightly. "Or is it too early?"

"It's not too early," she answered as she took his hand.

It was time to pack to go home and Hannah didn't want to go. Tears welled up in her eyes as she unzipped her empty suitcase, opened it on the bed, and began to remove her clothes from the hotel closet. She'd only folded and packed a few things when there was a knock on her hotel room door.

A smile spread across Hannah's face as she rushed to answer it. Perhaps it was Ross. Even though she'd left him less than twenty minutes ago, he might be missing her as much as she missed him.

Hannah's smile faded a bit as she opened the door and saw who was standing there. "Hello, Mother."

"Hello, dear. May I come in?"

"Of course." Hannah opened the door wider and her mother stepped into the room. Her eyes searched the space and rested on the open suitcase. "You're packing this early?"

"Yes. I'm meeting Ross and the girls for brunch later. He's going to take us to the plane."

"Good. Doc and I were planning to go along, but if Ross is taking you, we won't. He's a very capable man, Hannah."

"Yes, he is."

The silence stretched out for several moments and then Delores sighed. "I'm really

131

no good at these mother-daughter talks, you know."

Oh, I know, Hannah thought, but of course she didn't say it. Somehow, through a massive effort of will, she managed to keep her lips from twitching up in a smile.

"I just hope you know that whatever you decide is fine with me," Delores continued. "Of course I have my preferences, but it's what you want that matters."

Hannah couldn't help it. She had to ask. "You're talking about Norman and Mike?"

"Yes. Did you have a good time in Las Vegas, Hannah?"

This time Hannah did smile. "Yes, I did. It was a wonderful vacation, Mother."

"And the only thing wrong is that you want to stay here, but you have to go home?"

"That's it in a nutshell. Do you know where that phrase comes from, Mother?"

"Not now, Hannah. We're having a talk. You can tell me all about it later. I want to know if Ross is one of the reasons you had such a good time."

"Yes," Hannah said and left it at that.

"Good! I'm not sure I know how to say this."

"That's okay. Just spit it out, Mother."

"I really don't like to admit this, but Doc

and I played matchmaker. I guess you know that?"

"I know."

"And did it work?"

A happy smile spread over Hannah's face and she did a very uncharacteristic thing. She gave her mother a big hug. "Yes, Mother. It worked."

"And you're in love?"

Hannah thought about that for a minute. "I think I am."

"Do you want to be with him every minute of every day?"

"Yes."

"And can you scarcely bear the thought of being without him, even if it's only for a week?"

"Yes."

"How about Mike?"

"What about Mike?"

"Does the thought of being without Mike for a week make you unhappy?"

Hannah thought about that for a minute. "No, not really. The only time I've thought about Mike is when someone has mentioned his name."

"How about Norman? Have you thought about him?"

"I thought about Norman a little more than I thought about Mike, but I think it's because he's keeping Moishe for me."

"It's settled then. I think that you're in love with Ross."

Hannah took a deep breath. "If that's true, what do I do next?"

"You wait and see what's going to happen. And you follow your heart. Just remember this, Hannah." Delores looked very serious. "There are all kinds of love and not that many people are lucky enough to experience what I have with Doc. All I can tell you is to follow your heart and hang on tight. Don't let love slip through your fingers, dear. Love is far too precious to lose."

It was time to go. The plane was waiting and Andrea and Michelle had already boarded. Hannah turned to Ross and sighed. "I don't want to go, Cupcake."

"And I don't want you to go." He kissed her. It started as a polite, public kiss, but then his arms tightened around her and he kissed her again.

Hannah felt tears come to her eyes. He'd called her Cupcake when they were in college. And what she'd said was true. She didn't want to leave him, not even for a moment. She wanted to stay right in the circle of his arms forever.

"Hannah?"

She blinked back the tears that threatened to fall. Then she looked up at him again and answered, "Yes, Ross?"

"Do you think that maybe this could work? I mean, really, really work?"

Hannah smiled a slow smile that lit up her whole face. Ross loved her! And she loved him. It was a miracle and suddenly anything was possible. She was so happy, she was convinced that if she took Ross's hand, they could race down the runway and soar up into the skies, just the two of them.

"Hannah?" Ross looked slightly worried as he gazed down at her.

She hugged him tightly. "Yes, Ross. I think that this could really, really work."

And then she drew him down for a kiss that would seal the promise she had just made to him.

CHAPTER EIGHT

"Rrrowww!" Moishe gave an irate yowl as he jumped out of Hannah's arms and escaped to the living room carpet.

"Sorry, Moishe," she apologized. She must have been hugging him too tightly, a reaction to her anxiety about the day that was just beginning to unfold. She finished the last sip of her coffee, set the empty mug on the end table, and attempted to explain to her feline roommate. "I know you don't like hugs and I didn't mean to scare you. I guess I'm just a little nervous about what's going to happen today, that's all."

"Rrrrow."

The yowl was softer and it was accompanied by a purr as he jumped up to resume his favorite position on the back of the couch. It was obvious that he had accepted her apology by coming back into hugging range. He perched there, staring down at her and watching to see what she'd do next.

"I know," Hannah said, giving a little sigh. Even Moishe knew that this was not a typical morning. For one thing, the sun was up and it was three hours past five AM, the time that Hannah usually left for work. For another thing, she usually fed him, drank her coffee at the kitchen table, and took a quick shower just as soon as her eyes were fully open. Then she dressed for work and tossed him several kitty treats before she picked up her keys and went out the door.

"Things are different this morning," Hannah told him past the lump in her throat. "I don't have to leave for work early because my trial starts today and Howie is picking me up to take me to the Winnetka County Courthouse."

Moishe made a sound that was halfway between a growl and a purr. She'd never heard him make that particular sound before and Hannah interpreted it as an expression of sympathy with her plight.

"It's going to be okay," she reassured him. "Howie told me that the only thing happening today is jury selection. I'll be home tonight . . . probably earlier than usual."

Moishe had no reaction to that statement, either verbally or physically. He simply stared at her with a perfectly blank kitty expression. Hannah was sure he'd under-

137

stood her. At least she hoped he had.

"Howie said not to worry, so you shouldn't worry either."

"Rrrrow."

This was definitely a response to her words and Hannah took it as such. "I know. It's impossible not to worry, but I want you to think about what's going to happen when I come home tonight. I'm going to call Michelle and Andrea when court is adjourned for the day and they're going to come over with Chinese takeout. They're both helping out at The Cookie Jar today since I can't be there."

"Rrroww?"

Moishe's response was definitely a question. Hannah was sure of it. "That's right. *Chinese* takeout. And both Andrea and Michelle know that you like shrimp. When I talked to them last night they promised to bring extra. We'll all have a nice family dinner together."

As Hannah watched, Moishe's expression changed. His eyes widened in what appeared to be alarm and the fur began to bristle on his back. She was initially puzzled by his reaction and then she realized exactly what she'd said.

"You can relax, Moishe. I know I said *family dinner,* but Mother's not coming. She's still on the cruise to Alaska. I think today's the day they're going to Taku Point in a seaplane to see the glaciers and have a grilled salmon shore lunch."

"Rrrrrrow!"

Hannah laughed. She'd done it again. She'd used one of the words Moishe knew particularly well. "I know. I said *salmon*. I'll go get you some salmon treats, and then it's time for me to leave. Howie should be pulling up any minute now. He's always punctual."

She retrieved the treat canister from the kitchen and returned to the back of the couch where her feline roommate was waiting, his tail swishing back and forth like a metronome beating out a march tempo. "Here you go." She shook out several of the fish-shaped, salmon-flavored treats and placed them on the back of the couch next to him. "That ought to tide you over until I get home."

People claimed it was impossible for cats to smile, but Hannah was positive that Moishe's expression was close to glee as he stared down at his favorite treats. Then his gaze shifted back to her and he purred loudly.

"You're welcome. I'll see you tonight then. And we'll have dinner with Andrea and Michelle. And Moishe . . . one of your favorite people is coming to visit me in a week. You remember Ross when he was here with the movie, don't you?"

"Rowww."

Hannah wasn't sure if that was a yes or a no, so she didn't comment. Moishe had liked Ross the last time he'd come to Lake Eden. Ross had even carried Moishe, in his leash and his harness, out to a table at The Cookie Jar when the crew had come in for lunch. Moishe had enjoyed all the attention the film crew had given him.

Hannah gave her pet a final scratch under the chin and forced herself to walk to the door. She didn't want to leave, but she knew she had to. She unlocked it, pulled it open, stepped outside, and shut the door behind her, testing it once to make certain that it was locked. Then she stood there on the landing for a brief moment, blinking back the moisture that welled up in her eyes. She'd never been the type to break into tears at the slightest provocation, but she'd done her share of tearing up lately. If this was a by-product of being in love, she hoped she'd learn to control it soon.

"Silly!" she chided herself, descending the outside staircase and squelching the urge to glance up to see if Moishe was watching her from the living room window. She buttoned her coat and told herself that he was probably busy chowing down on his treats.

It was a chilly Minnesota morning, colder than usual for the third week in September, and Hannah shivered as she took the sidewalk that wound around the condo buildings. There was a light sprinkling of frost on the yellow and dark orange chrysanthemums in the planters that separated the buildings. Soon the gardeners would dig up the root clumps to separate them. All that would be left in the planters would be the evergreen shrubs, which would provide spots of green against the white winter snow.

The arrival of the first snowfall in Minnesota was unpredictable. It could occur at any time from the month of October on. It was not at all unusual for it to snow on Halloween, and Minnesota mothers made sure that a warm coat and warm pants could fit under their children's Halloween costumes.

Everyone who lived in the Midwest had to be prepared for a winter with sixty to seventy inches of snow. Of course some of it melted in the early months, but the banks of snow the plows left at the sides of the road could reach heights that were taller than the roofs of cars. Snow season could last for six months, starting in October and tapering off to end in April. Delores and Doc both said they remembered one year, they thought it had been in the seventies, when there had been a blizzard in May.

As she walked, Hannah thought about the long, cold winter that stretched out before her. She couldn't help but wonder if she'd be around to shovel the sidewalk at The Cookie Jar. If she was convicted of vehicular homicide and had to go to prison, would her partner, Lisa, keep their business running? Would there be enough income for Hannah to continue to make the monthly mortgage payment on her condo? And what would happen to Moishe? She'd taken care of Cuddles for Norman. Would he take care of Moishe for her? If Ross got the job and moved to Lake Eden should she ask him to take care of Moishe until she got out of prison? Or would prison mean the end of their romance? If neither man was willing to do it, would someone in her family volunteer? Questions like these had kept her from sleep for most of the preceding night.

"Don't borrow trouble!" Hannah told herself sternly. Then she looked around quickly and was relieved to find that no one else was on the sidewalk. None of her neighbors had heard her talking to herself.

Howie's car was parked right where he'd

said it would be, in the first space of the visitor's lot. Hannah hurried toward the black Lexus, an appropriate car for Lake Eden's finest lawyer. Howie gave his clients notepads with that sentiment printed on the top of every page. It was his little joke since he was also Lake Eden's *only* lawyer.

"Good morning, Hannah," Howie greeted her as she slid into the leather-covered passenger seat.

Is it a good morning, Howie? Hannah thought, but she didn't voice the question. Instead, she responded, "Good morning, Howie. Did you bring coffee for Judge Colfax?"

"We'll stop on our way to the courthouse."

"Okay. When you give him the coffee, give him this, too." Hannah handed him a small white bag.

"What is it?"

"A couple of my Double Fudge Brownies. I figured it might sweeten him up. But don't tell him they're from me. I don't want to get accused of bribery on top of everything else."

"Got it." Howie placed the bag on the backseat. "Say, Hannah . . . those brownies aren't poisoned, are they?"

"Good heavens, no!"

"Just checking. I had two of your Double

Fudge Brownies yesterday and they're great."

Hannah shivered again as Howie put the car in gear and pulled out of the parking lot. This time it wasn't from the cold. It was a shiver of guilt. She had killed someone with her cookie truck. There was no escaping that fact, even though there had been mitigating circumstances. It had happened during a summer storm with blinding rain and lightning flashing all around her. Lisa had been in the passenger seat and Hannah had been trying to make it to a grove of trees where she thought that they would be protected from the driving rain and the lightning bolts. She hadn't known that, just around the bend, there was a fallen branch that blocked the road. She'd swerved to avoid it, lost control, and hit the man by the side of the road. Even though it had been an accident, she had caused someone's death and now she had to face the consequences.

Howie glanced over at her. "Relax, Hannah. Everything will be fine. Judge Colfax isn't a bad judge. He's just incompetent."

"Is that supposed to make me feel better?" Hannah couldn't help but ask him.

"No, it's supposed to make you laugh." Howie turned to smile at her. "You're taking all this too seriously, Hannah."

"Maybe that's because I'm the one on trial and you're not."

"Yup. That could account for it. Lean back and relax. This'll all be over much sooner than you think."

Only if you're planning to ram your car into a bridge abutment, Hannah thought as Howie turned onto the access road that led to the highway.

DOUBLE FUDGE BROWNIES

Preheat oven to 350 degrees F., rack in the middle position.

Jo Fluke's Note: Last year, on a book tour for *Blackberry Pie Murder,* I asked anyone with a really good double fudge brownie recipe to please send it to me. I was overwhelmed with all the recipes Hannah fans sent. It took months to test them and I ate brownies until I didn't think I could ever face another rich, chocolate confection. (I also gained over 5 pounds in the process, but I had a wonderfully delicious time!)

This recipe is Hannah's combination of elements from all those incredible brownie recipes. If you sent a recipe to me, you'll probably recognize some element of your recipe in this one.

Thank you all for making my winter so much fun! (And also so fattening, but we won't talk about that.)

1 and 1/2 cups all-purpose flour *(pack it down in the cup when you measure it)*
3/4 cup unsweetened cocoa powder *(I used Hershey's)*
1/2 teaspoon baking soda
1/2 teaspoon salt

1 cup white *(granulated)* sugar

1 cup brown sugar *(pack it down in the cup when you measure it)*

3/4 cup salted butter *(1 and 1/2 sticks, 6 ounces)*

6 ounces semi-sweet chocolate *(I used Bakers)*

1 and 1/2 teaspoons vanilla extract

3 large eggs, beaten *(just whip them up in a glass with a fork)*

2 cups semi-sweet chocolate chips *(I used Nestle)*

Jo Fluke's Note: Be careful when you buy semi-sweet chocolate baking squares. Bakers has repackaged. A box used to contain 8 ounces in one-ounce squares wrapped in white paper. The new box contains only 4 ounces and it takes 4 little squares to make one ounce.

Line a 9-inch by 13-inch cake pan with heavy duty foil. Spray the foil with Pam or another nonstick cooking spray.

Place the flour, cocoa powder, baking soda, salt, white sugar and brown sugar together in the bowl of an electric mixer. Mix on LOW speed until they are thoroughly combined.

Place the stick and a half of salted butter

in a microwave-safe bowl. *(I used a quart Pyrex measuring cup.)*

Break the semi-sweet chocolate squares in pieces and place them on top of the butter.

Heat on HIGH in the microwave for 1 minute and then stir with a heat-resistant rubber spatula. *(If you don't have one, you really need to buy one. They're not expensive and they're dishwasher safe. You'll use it a lot!)*

Take the spatula out of the bowl and return the bowl to the microwave. Heat the butter and chocolate mixture for an additional minute.

Let the bowl sit in the microwave for 1 more minute and then take it out and stir it with the heat-resistant spatula again. If you can stir it smooth, let it sit on the counter to cool for at least 5 minutes. If you can't stir it smooth, heat it in increments of 30 seconds, letting it sit in the microwave for 1 minute after each increment, until you can stir it smooth.

Hannah's 1st Note: You can also do this on the stovetop over LOW heat, but make sure to stir it constantly so it won't scorch.

Stir the vanilla into the melted butter and chocolate mixture. Let it continue to cool on the counter.

Add the eggs to your mixer bowl and beat everything together at MEDIUM speed until everything is incorporated.

Turn the mixer down to LOW speed and slowly pour the chocolate, butter, and vanilla extract mixture into the mixer bowl. Mix this until it's combined, but do not over-beat.

Roughly chop the chocolate chips into smaller pieces. *(I used my food processor with the steel blade.)*

Take the bowl out of the mixer and fold in the chocolate chips by hand. *(You can use the same heat-resistant spatula that you used earlier.)*

Scoop the mixture into your prepared pan. The mixture will be very thick. Use the same rubber spatula to scrape the bowl and get every wonderful bit of yummy batter into the cake pan.

Smooth the batter out and then press it down evenly with the back of a metal spatula. Make sure the batter gets into the corners of the pan.

Bake your Double Fudge Brownies in your preheated oven at 350 degrees F. for exactly 23 minutes. DO NOT OVERBAKE! If you do, you'll end up with dry brownies that taste like chocolate cake instead of chocolate fudge!

When you take your brownies out of the oven, set them on a cold stove burner or a wire rack to cool.

Hannah's 2nd Note: My cake pan always has one square, the size of a brownie, missing when I make the frosting. I'm not going to admit to anything here. I think the brownie thief must have come into my kitchen to take one brownie when I wasn't looking.

Make the Milk Chocolate Fudge Frosting.

Milk Chocolate Fudge Frosting:

2 Tablespoons *(1 ounce)* salted butter

2 cups milk chocolate chips *(I used Nestle Milk Chocolate Chips, the 11.5-ounce package)*

1 can *(14 ounces)* sweetened condensed milk *(NOT evaporated milk — I used Eagle Brand)*

Place the butter in the bottom of a microwave-safe bowl. *(I used a quart Pyrex measuring cup)*

Place the milk chocolate chips on top of the butter.

Pour in the 14-ounce can of sweetened, condensed milk.

Heat on HIGH for 1 minute. Then remove from the microwave and stir with a heat resistant rubber spatula.

Return the bowl to the microwave and heat for another minute.

Let the bowl sit in the microwave for 1 minute and then take it out *(careful — it may be hot to the touch!)* and set it on the counter. Attempt to stir it smooth with the heat-resistant spatula.

If you can stir the mixture smooth, you're done. If you can't stir it smooth, return the bowl to the microwave and heat on HIGH in 30-second increments followed by 1 minute standing time, until you can stir it smooth.

To frost your Double Fudge Brownies, simply pour the frosting over the top of your brownies, using the heat-resistant rubber spatula to smooth the frosting into the corners.

Give the microwave-safe bowl to your favorite person to scrape clean. *(If you're alone when you're baking these brownies, feel free to enjoy the frosting that's clinging to the sides of the bowl all by yourself.)*

Let the frosted brownies cool to room temperature until the frosting is "set". Then cover with a sheet of foil and store them in a cool place.

CHAPTER NINE

Howie used his gate card to enter the garage and he parked in the area that was set aside for lawyers. The sign read COUNSELORS ONLY and Hannah wondered why they still used the British term for lawyers. Did that make American lawyers feel superior? And how about Gil Surma, the counselor at Jordan High. Could he park there if he had to come to the courthouse for any . . . ?

"Hannah? Let's go."

Hannah's thought process stopped in mid-sentence as she realized that Howie had turned off the ignition, gotten out of the car, and walked around to open her door. "Sorry," she apologized, getting out of the car. "Why are we parking here instead of on the street?"

"Because it's secure parking. Reporters aren't allowed inside. And this door leads directly to the elevators."

Hannah noticed Howie's use of the plural.

"There's more than one elevator?"

"Yes, and the people around here are all up in arms about it. They say it's a waste of taxpayer money, but we have to comply with the new state mandate. The second elevator is for handicapped judges and it was put in less than a year ago. It leads up to a specially equipped courtroom on the second floor and similarly equipped chambers on the third floor."

"How does it work?" Hannah asked.

"It's simple. The judge enters the elevator and locks his wheelchair down. The elevator goes up to the second and third floors. If he chooses the second floor, the rear door of the elevator opens and deposits him directly behind the judge's bench. If he chooses to go to the third floor, the elevator takes him directly to his specially equipped chambers and he can wheel out directly to his desk."

"That sounds very convenient."

"It is, but this is an old courthouse. The whole thing had to be retrofitted and it cost a fortune."

"I can imagine it did, but I'm sure the judges in wheelchairs are delighted with it. How many handicapped judges are assigned here?"

"A grand total of zero. There's only one in the entire county judicial system and he's at the Ramsey County Courthouse in St. Paul. That's what the taxpayers are so upset about. Every single courthouse in the county system had to comply with the mandate, whether they had any handicapped judges or not."

"Government," Hannah said, and left it at that as Howie used his gate card again to open the interior door built into the garage wall. It led to a narrow hallway completely devoid of any decoration and painted an industrial green that Hannah recognized from school lunchrooms and bathrooms.

"Is this how they bring the prisoners in?" she asked, and then she immediately wished she hadn't. She didn't want to think about being a prisoner and having to reappear in court in this fashion.

"Yup." Howie slipped his card in the slot by the elevator and the doors opened.

"But I didn't come in this way when I came from jail for my bail hearing. They just parked on the street and brought me up the steps and in the front door."

"That's because you had preferential treatment. Bill knew you weren't a flight risk."

And Bill also knew that Andrea would never forgive him if he brought me in this way, Hannah thought, but she didn't say it. "I see," she said instead, stepping into the small elevator.

When the elevator doors opened again, Hannah found herself stepping out into a small waiting room. Benches with metal loops sticking up every few feet were along one wall. Hannah had watched enough television cop shows to know why the loops were there. If inmates were handcuffed, one wrist would be released and the empty handcuff would be locked around the loop.

"Let's sit at the table until they call us," Howie said, leading the way to a table flanked by two wooden chairs, one on either side. He pointed to the chairs. "Any preference?"

"It doesn't matter as long as one of them isn't hooked up to two-twenty."

Howie stared at her for an instant and then he burst into laughter. "Good. I'm glad you've got your sense of humor back. It'll make things a lot easier."

Hannah had just taken a seat when an official-looking man rushed in. He nodded to Hannah and then turned to Howie. "Good morning, Counselor," he said, handing Howie a note. "Judge Colfax told me to give you this note the minute you came in."

"Thanks, Dave." Howie took the note, unfolded it quickly, and read it. Then he turned to Hannah. "Mr. Johansen is Judge Colfax's clerk. Actually, Dave is Judge Flemming's clerk, but he's helping Judge Colfax while he's here."

"Nice to meet you, Mr. Johansen," Hannah said, doing her best to smile.

"It's Dave. I'm glad to meet you too, Miss Swensen."

"It's Hannah."

Dave gave a little chuckle. "Most of the people I meet here aren't this polite. It really *is* nice to meet you." He turned to Howie. "Aren't you going to tell her what's in the note?"

"Yup. Just as soon as you two are through being polite." Howie glanced down at the note again. "Judge Colfax has some pressing business he has to take care of. When that's concluded, he wants to see us in his chambers." Howie turned to Dave. "Any idea how long that'll take?"

"No, but I'll ask. All he did was tell me to bring you to the anteroom next to his chambers. He'll call you in when he's ready."

"He didn't tell you why he needed to see us?" Howie asked.

"No. He wasn't . . . ." Dave paused and Hannah could tell he was choosing his words carefully. "Let's just say that Judge Colfax wasn't very talkative this morning."

156

Howie handed the white bag with the coffee and Hannah's Double Fudge Brownies to the clerk. "Will you take this in to the judge, Dave?"

"A giant latte?" the clerk guessed.

"You got it. And a couple of brownies."

"That ought to put him in a better mood." Dave began to smile. "I'll run this up to him right now. It'll only take a couple of minutes. And then I'll come back for you."

Hannah and Howie exchanged glances once the door had shut behind the clerk. There was no need for words. Hannah knew they were thinking the same thing. Judge Colfax was in a bad mood and that wasn't a good sign. All they could do was hope that his favorite coffee and her brownies for breakfast would sweeten him up.

Dave was true to his word. It took less than two minutes for him to return. "Judge Colfax thanks you for the coffee and brownies, especially since he didn't have time for breakfast. He said to tell you that he'll only be tied up for a few more minutes and then he'll call you in."

Hannah and Howie followed the clerk down the hall and rode up to the third floor in the elevator. Dave showed them to the anteroom and they took seats inside. The clerk had just left when Howie's phone rang.

"Uh-oh!" Howie said, after glancing down at the display. "I've got to take this, Hannah. I'll be right outside the door. Just poke your head out and alert me when Judge Colfax calls us in."

Hannah nodded, wishing that she could stand out in the hall with Howie. It would be more comfortable than sitting in the anteroom, waiting. The wooden chairs in the anteroom were terribly uncomfortable.

There was a clock on the wall and Hannah watched the seconds tick by. There was no sound from the judge's chambers next door and Hannah wondered if Judge Colfax had left and forgotten that he'd summoned them. She wished she were somewhere else, anywhere other than sitting in a hard wooden chair designed by a sadist in this small room smelling of old furniture, stale sweat, and dread.

Hannah shut her eyes to block out the sight of the clock, which was moving in what had to be slow motion. She hadn't gotten much sleep last night and she was bone tired. If she hadn't been so uncomfortable, she might have dozed off. At least then the time might have passed faster.

The only sound was the tick of the clock and it was mesmerizing. Hannah let her head loll forward and her eyes closed against the bright fluorescent lights. Then they snapped open again when she heard the sound of a crash, followed by a heavy thud.

Hannah jumped to her feet. Had the sounds she'd heard come from the judge's chambers? Or had she fallen asleep and dreamed the whole thing?

She could feel her heart beat hard as she tiptoed to the interior door that led to the judge's chambers. She didn't hear anything else alarming so she put her ear to the surface of the door. If she heard pages rustling as Judge Colfax read a brief or the sound of his voice talking on the phone, she'd know he was all right. The temporary judge she'd drawn for her trial was elderly and had come out of retirement to fill in for Judge Flemming, the regular judge. It was entirely possible that Judge Colfax had slipped and fallen. If that had happened, perhaps he was unable to get up. He could be in dire need of help.

Hannah hesitated one more moment and then she decided that she had to do something. The defendant in a trial couldn't just burst into the judge's chambers. That was not only impolite, it might even be grounds for further charges against her. Her hand trembled slightly as she knocked on the door and waited for a response. The interruption might make Judge Colfax angry, but she would explain that she had heard a crash and a thud and just wanted to check to make sure he was all right. Surely he couldn't object to that!

There was no answer, no sound at all from within the chambers. Hannah took a deep breath and knocked a second time. What if Judge Colfax couldn't answer her knock, or even call out for her to come in? What if he'd fallen, hit his head on something, and he was on the floor unconscious? She had to do something and she had to do it now.

Hannah knew she'd be risking the judge's wrath by entering his chambers without his permission, but there was no time to waste. Carefully, silently, she pushed the door open a crack and peered in.

At first glance, the room appeared empty. No one was moving and there were no sounds. But then she saw something that made her push the door open all the way and rush inside. A wooden gavel lay on the floor near the far corner of Judge Colfax's desk. It was only inches from a pool of something dark red in color and looked a lot like blood!

Hannah stepped over the gavel, avoided the dark red pool, and raced around the side of the desk. And there she found Judge Colfax. He was crumpled in a heap on the floor, a half-eaten Double Fudge Brownie on the floor near his hand, and his desk chair upended beside him. As she stared at his head she realized that there was no longer any doubt about the origin of the dark red pool on the floor. The contents were, most certainly, Judge Colfax's blood.

The scene was horrific and Hannah averted her eyes. If only she'd rushed in the second she'd heard the sounds! But another glance at Judge Colfax's head told her that it wouldn't have made a particle of difference. She was no doctor but she was almost certain that there was no way Judge Colfax could have recovered from the massive damage done by the gavel to the side of his skull.

Get help! Hannah's shocked mind told her and her shaking legs carried her across the floor to the door that led to the hallway. She opened it, stepped out, and motioned frantically to Howie who was pacing near the water cooler, his cell phone to his ear.

Hannah watched as Howie ended his call, dropped his phone in his jacket pocket, and approached her. "Judge Colfax called us in?" he asked her.

Hannah opened her mouth to answer, but she couldn't seem to find her voice. She shook her head from side to side, cleared

161

her throat, and somehow managed to choke out the words she needed to say. "Get help! Judge Colfax is dead. He's been murdered!"

Chapter Ten

"How much time would you say elapsed between the time you heard the crash and the thud, and the time you entered Judge Colfax's chambers?"

Hannah blinked and stared up at Mike's face. She was still in shock and she had no idea how much time had passed. "I don't know."

"Give me your best estimate."

"Not very long. Maybe . . . two minutes? Or three at the most?"

"Okay." Mike paged back through his notes. "Do you have any idea why Judge Colfax wanted to see you before the trial started?"

"No."

"Does Mr. Levine have any idea?"

"I don't know. Howie got a phone call and went out to the hall to take it right after the clerk left us in the anteroom."

"And he was still on the phone when you

left the judge's chambers?"

"Yes."

"Was it still in response to the original call that came when both of you were in the anteroom?"

Hannah frowned slightly. What difference could that make? But this was an official interview and she had to answer. "I don't know. When I went out into the hall, I didn't hear anything Howie said. He was standing down by the water cooler. I just saw him end the call."

"You mean you heard him end the call?"

"No, I *saw* him end the call. At least I *think* he ended the call. He dropped the phone back into his pocket so that's what I assumed."

"And then you told him that Judge Colfax was dead?"

"Yes. And I waited in the hall while he went to get help. I . . . I didn't want to go back inside the judge's chambers and be alone with . . ." Hannah's voice trailed off and she shuddered visibly.

Mike reached out to give her a comforting pat on the shoulder. "It's okay, Hannah. I understand."

"And I didn't want to go back in the anteroom, either. The connecting door was open. And I didn't want to see . . . you know."

"Of course you didn't."

Was Mike being condescending? Hannah searched his expression, but she still wasn't sure.

"I mean . . . I've seen lots of dead bodies before, but this was . . ." she stopped and swallowed hard. "This was particularly brutal."

"Do you think that whoever killed him really hated him?"

"It looked that way. And it was personal. The killer had to get right up next to Judge Colfax to hit him with the gavel. It's not like he was shot from the doorway. And the gavel belonged to Judge Colfax's father. He was a judge, too."

"How do you know that?"

"Howie mentioned it when I was in court for the bail hearing."

"Do you think there's any significance to the fact that his father's gavel was used as the murder weapon?"

Hannah thought about that for a moment. "I don't know. It's possible there could be a connection. I guess we'll have to catch his killer to find out."

Mike began to frown. "*We'll* have to catch the killer?"

Hannah sighed. It seemed she was on the outs with Mike and the sheriff's department again. There were times when Mike welcomed her help in solving a murder case, but at other times he resented it. She'd thought about his inconsistency a lot and she still wasn't sure what caused it. Of course, she didn't know exactly what caused the wind to blow, either.

"Let me rephrase that," Hannah said, deciding it was time to tiptoe around Mike's moods or whatever they were. "What I meant to say was, I guess you and your detectives in the sheriff's department will have to solve the case before we can know for sure."

Mike's frown eased a bit and Hannah was glad. She wanted this interview to end so she could check with Howie and find out what would happen to her court case now that Judge Colfax was no longer in charge.

"You're the prime suspect, you know," Mike said, lowering his voice so that no one else could hear even though they were completely alone in the anteroom.

"*What?* Why would *I* want to kill Judge Colfax?"

"To delay the trial until Judge Flemming comes back. You were worried about Judge Colfax's competency. You said that the last time we all got together for dinner at your place."

"Well . . . yes. I admit I felt that way and I probably mentioned it. But things changed."

"What things?"

Hannah thought fast. She knew why things had changed. Now that she was involved with Ross, she didn't want anything like a trial hanging over her head. She'd hoped that the trial would be over by the time Ross came to Lake Eden for his job interview at KCOW Television. And of course she'd hoped that she would be acquitted.

"What things changed, Hannah?" Mike expected an answer and she wasn't about to tell him about Ross. She would tell both Mike and Norman, but this was neither the time nor the place. "The stress of waiting was getting to me," she answered quite truthfully. "I just wanted everything to be over as soon as possible."

Mike didn't say anything. He just nodded and scribbled for several minutes in his notebook. That made her wonder what she'd said that was so interesting, but at last he looked up. "I have what I need for now, Hannah. You can . . . oh, wait a second." He drew a folded note out of his pocket. "This is from Norman. He caught me on the way in. He wanted to wait for you, but I told him that you already had a ride."

"But I don't. I rode here with Howie." Hannah stuck the note in her pocket. It could be personal and she'd read it later.

"I know. I saw his car in the garage when I pulled in. Howie's waiting for you in the hall."

"But I thought Lonnie was going to be interviewing Howie."

"Lonnie did, and the interview's over. Howie's waiting for you outside by the water cooler."

Hannah was puzzled. Mike had been in the anteroom with her the whole time and she knew he hadn't made any phone calls. "How do you know that?"

"I told Lonnie to text me when he was through with Howie. See?"

Mike held out his phone and Hannah looked at the screen.

Done. He's waiting for her in the hall by the water cooler.

"Okay," Hannah said, getting up from the tortuous wooden chair. She remembered that Mike's phone had made a little dinging sound during the interview and he'd glanced down at the display. That must have been when Lonnie's text message had come in.

As she walked toward the door, she wondered if she should update her cell phone to one that could send and receive text messages. Her mother and her sisters had been trying to persuade her to get a new phone for the past two years. Even though she'd insisted that all she needed was a phone that would make and receive calls with none of the fancy extras, perhaps they were right. They'd been right about buying a computer to store her recipes and using the Internet to search for ingredients that Florence didn't carry at the Red Owl. She'd resisted when they had suggested it, but now she loved being able to print out a clean copy of a recipe and search the Internet for hard-to-find ingredients. That had come in very handy. They could be right about updating her cell phone, too.

"Hannah?" Mike stopped her as she was about to open the door.

"Yes?"

"If I have any more questions, I'll drop by your condo later. I still have to interview Judge Colfax's clerk. And do me a favor, okay?"

Hannah wasn't about to agree until she knew what Mike's favor was. She'd learned her lesson when she'd promised to do a favor for Andrea without knowing what it was. "What is it?"

"See if you can figure out how to shut off your *slaydar* before you discover another dead body."

"I'll try," Hannah promised, heading for the hallway. Mike accused her of having *slaydar.* He said it was like radar except that instead of using it to locate speeders, she used it to locate murder victims. If she had *slaydar,* then Mike had *foodar* and he used it to locate a meal. She had no doubt that he would knock on her door just as she and her sisters were sitting down to eat their Chinese takeout.

"That'll be Mike," Hannah said, spooning a bit of Kung Pao shrimp over the small helping of rice on her plate. "Will you girls let him in while I get another plate?"

She took another plate from the cupboard, along with a place setting complete with chopsticks. Then she headed back out to the living room and stopped in the doorway as she saw Norman sitting at the table.

"Hi, Hannah," Norman said, smiling at her. "I brought Cuddles. She's already in the bedroom, playing with Moishe. Why did you buy so much food? I told you I was bringing Chinese."

"You did?"

"Yes. In my note. Mike promised to give it to you."

"He did."

"Then you knew?"

Hannah was mortified. "Not exactly. I . . . I really hate to admit this, but . . . I was so upset when I left the courthouse that I forgot it was in my pocket. I'm sorry, Norman."

"That's okay. It's entirely understandable. Now we have only one problem."

"What's that?"

"I brought takeout and you've already got takeout. We have to think of five other people to invite."

The doorbell rang as if right on cue. Hannah laughed. "We don't have a problem, Norman. That'll be Mike."

"You invited Mike?"

"No, but he said he'd drop by if he had any more questions for me."

Norman chuckled. "And you figured it would be right when you were sitting down to eat."

"We all figured that," Michelle spoke up. "That's his pattern. Mike always drops by when we're eating. I think it's the only time he gets a hot meal."

"I'll go let him in," Andrea offered.

"And I'll get another place setting." Michelle got up from her chair. "Chopsticks or a fork?"

"Both. That way he can have his choice." Hannah sat down next to Norman and took a small helping of chicken chow mein. She loved to take a bite or two of everything to sample it. She had just sprinkled on a few crispy noodles when Mike came up to greet her.

"Sit down and join us, Mike," Michelle offered, placing the plate, napkin, and utensils on the other side of Norman's chair.

"Are you sure? It seems I always drop by at mealtime."

Norman turned to Mike. "We've got plenty of food tonight. Andrea and Michelle brought takeout and I brought takeout. We need someone to help us eat it. Dig in, Mike."

"Thanks. I was busy doing interviews and I didn't have time for lunch. This looks really good."

"It is," Andrea told him. "It's from the Lan Se Palace."

"Lan Se means *blue* in Mandarin Chinese," Hannah told her. "That's why they hung those blue mirrors on the outside of the building."

"I remember when it used to be the Watering Hole," Andrea said. "It was a rundown wreck inside. Now it looks really nice."

Hannah began to frown. "Wait a second. When did you go inside? You were still in high school when the Watering Hole shut down."

"Oh. Yes, yes I was. I was . . . um . . . out with Bill one night and it was . . . raining. And his car got stuck in the mud. He didn't want to leave me in the car alone at night, so we walked to the Watering Hole to see if some of the guys there could help us push his car out."

"Right," Mike said, giving her a knowing grin. "I heard about that night from Bill."

Andrea looked shocked. "You did?!"

"I like those blue mirrors," Michelle said, quite obviously trying to change the subject. "How about you, Norman?"

Before Norman could answer, the doorbell rang again. "Will you get that, Andrea?" Hannah asked, trying to save her sister from further embarrassment.

"Check the peephole," Mike warned as Andrea got ready to open the door.

"Right." Andrea peeked out and when she turned to face them, her eyebrows were raised in a question. "It's Howie Levine. Any idea what he wants?"

"No," Hannah answered, "but let him in and he'll tell us."

Andrea opened the door, Howie stepped in, and he began to frown as he saw the full plates at the table. "I'm sorry," he apologized. "I didn't know you were just sitting down to eat."

"Join us," Hannah told him, getting up from her chair. "I'll get another plate."

Howie looked a bit uncertain. "That's nice of you, Hannah, but are you sure I'm not interrupting?"

"Not at all. We've got way too much food."

"And it's from the Lan Se Palace," Andrea told him. "Do you know that Lan Se means *blue* in Chinese?"

"As a matter of fact, I do. I looked it up for them when they were trying to think of a Chinese name for their restaurant."

"They're Chinese and they couldn't think of a Chinese name?" Andrea was clearly surprised.

"Adam Wang is third generation American. And his wife is second generation. As far as I know, they've never been to China and I know for a fact that they don't speak Mandarin." Howie gave a little smile. "You've never seen the chef, have you?"

Andrea looked thoughtful. "I don't think so. I've never been back to the kitchen."

"Well, his name is Carlos Fernandez. He used to work at a Chinese restaurant in the Cities. It was the Wangs' favorite restaurant and when it closed, they jumped at the chance to hire Carlos as their head chef."

Hannah looked down at her plate. She wasn't sure why Howie had come and it made her so nervous, she didn't feel like eating. She decided to take the bull by the horns and ask the important question. "Why did you come to see me, Howie?"

"Later, Hannah. Let's enjoy the meal."

"I can't, not unless I know if the reason you came is good news or bad news."

"It's good news."

Hannah glanced at the plate that had looked so unappetizing a few moments before and did an abrupt turnaround. The Kung Pao shrimp now looked mouthwateringly delicious and so did the chow mein. "Thanks, Howie." She smiled, picking up a succulent shrimp with her chopsticks.

CHAPTER ELEVEN

"Dessert and coffee?" Hannah asked after everyone had eaten. When her question was followed by a chorus of assents, she smiled.

"What's for dessert?" Mike asked her. "Fortune cookies?"

Hannah gestured toward the white bag on the table. "The fortune cookies and almond cookies are right there, but we also have Salted Cashew and Milk Chocolate Whippersnappers. Andrea baked them this morning."

"Those whippersnappers sound a lot better than takeout fortune cookies and almond cookies," Mike said, giving Andrea a smile. "I've never met one of your whippersnapper cookies I didn't like."

Howie gave a little laugh. "Neither has anyone else. If you're late getting to The Cookie Jar in the morning, they're already gone."

Hannah glanced at Andrea who was smiling widely. It wasn't often that Hannah's middle sister was praised for her abilities in the kitchen, but Andrea was learning how to take a basic recipe and embellish it in ways that were tasty and creative. Perhaps her forte was cookie baking. Hannah knew it certainly wasn't sandwich making! Andrea had never had a flop with whippersnappers the way she had with peanut butter and mint jelly sandwiches on raisin bread.

"Are you cold, Hannah?" Howie asked.

Hannah shook her head. "No . . . just thinking about something."

"Judge Colfax's death?" Mike asked, his eyes narrowing slightly.

"No, it was something totally unrelated," Hannah told him, realizing that she'd shuddered at the thought of Andrea's favorite sandwich.

"Have you heard anything from your mother and Doc?" Howie asked, reaching for another whippersnapper cookie.

"I have," Michelle pulled out her phone. "She e-mailed this morning from Juneau. She says, Unseasonably warm here. Announcer on the Duck Boat wearing shorts. She said it was only the third time this year."

"She must have sent it to all three of us." Andrea turned to Hannah. "Did you get it?"

"Probably. I haven't turned on the computer today."

"You need a smartphone," Howie advised her. "Then you can stay in touch with your messages. I couldn't do my job without it."

Norman reached out to touch her arm. "Now I know what to get you for an early Christmas present. I'll take you out to the mall tomorrow and we'll get you a new phone with all the bells and whistles."

They were ganging up on her! That realization made Hannah feel like rebelling stubbornly and insisting that she didn't need a new phone. But she *did* need a new phone.

"How about it, Hannah?" Mike urged her. "Are you ready to update and join all the rest of us?"

Hannah gave a little sigh. "Maybe," she admitted, swallowing her pride. "It would have come in handy today when Howie and I were waiting for Judge Colfax to call us into his chambers. I could have called to let everyone know what was happening."

"But you didn't know everything that was happening," Howie said.

"What do you mean?"

"I'll tell you, but you have to promise not to cheer too loudly."

Hannah turned to Mike. "You caught the killer?!"

Mike shook his head. "Not yet."

"Then you don't know what Howie's talking about?"

Mike shook his head again, and Hannah turned to Howie. "Okay. You'd better tell us before we all die of the same malady that killed the cat."

As if on cue, Moishe ran into the living room followed closely by Cuddles. They circled the table once before Hannah could reach out to steady the coffee carafe.

"Feet up!" Norman warned as the cats raced around the table.

"But they're gone now," Howie pointed out as the cats left the table area and ran into the kitchen. "I can see them from here. They're drinking water in the kitchen."

"We got a break, but they'll be back any sec . . ." Norman stopped speaking and reached for the container of sweet and sour soup. "Somebody get the chicken chow mein."

Everyone except Howie knew the drill and acted almost instantaneously. Michelle grabbed the black mushrooms with oyster sauce and the orange beef, Mike stabilized the kung pao shrimp and the shredded pork with hot garlic sauce, Andrea picked up her plate of cookies and the chicken chow mein, and Hannah held on to the coffee carafe with one hand and the beef with black bean sauce with the other.

The lapping of tongues ceased and there was a second's silence followed by the sound of running feet.

"Here they come!" Norman told Howie. "They're after the shrimp with lobster sauce."

The words were no sooner out of Norman's mouth when the cats were racing around the table again. They circled once and then there was a crash as Moishe ran into the table leg.

"Did he hurt himself?" Howie asked, looking horrified at what he believed to be an accident.

Hannah laughed. "Not a bit. He does it on purpose and he hits the table with his hindquarters. Watch! Here they come again."

They all watched the cats speed through the living room and jump up on the couch. They ran across the back, paws flying, and then jumped down to circle the table again. Just as Hannah had predicted, Moishe ran into the table leg again.

"You're right!" Howie said, sounding a bit puzzled. "Why does he do that?"

"They got a piece of Lonnie's steak one night at Norman's house," Hannah explained. "Lonnie didn't grab his plate in time, and intermittent reinforcement makes an action very difficult to extinguish."

"In other words they keep hoping it'll happen again?"

"That's right. They know they get a piece of shrimp in the kitchen after dinner. And that means they know there's at least two pieces left. Cats aren't known for their patience."

"Everybody can relax now," Norman informed them, watching as Moishe and Cuddles jumped up to sit on the back of the couch. "Cuddles doesn't have that crazed look in her eyes any longer."

Hannah poured more coffee for all of them and then she turned to Howie. "What were you going to tell us before the feline marathon began?"

"That you don't have to go back to court."

"I don't?"

"No. I got a call at my office and all charges against you have been dismissed."

"Judge Flemming came back?" Hannah guessed.

"No. Judge Colfax dismissed the charges against you this morning. His clerk found the signed papers in his out-box."

Hannah was astonished. Could it all truly be over? "Judge Colfax dismissed the charges before he even met with us?"

"Apparently he did. The clerk read me the pertinent parts. Judge Colfax determined that there were extenuating circumstances and in this case, you were exempted from following the statutes. He also chastised the prosecutor's office for wasting the taxpayers' money by filing the charges in the first place."

Hannah zeroed in on the last piece of information Howie had given her. "Then Judge Colfax's nephew is in trouble?"

"Dave seemed to think so. He's worked for Judge Flemming for years and he's privy to all the scuttlebutt at the courthouse. He said that Chad Norton was already in hot water with his boss for bringing this case against you in the first place. The fact that he caused Judge Colfax to publicly criticize the district attorney's office is going to make Chad's situation even worse."

Hannah watched as Michelle picked up the carafe of coffee, saw that it was empty, and carried it into the kitchen. She heard the water running and knew that her thoughtful youngest sister was making another pot of coffee. She wished she'd thought to ask Michelle to bring in her stenographer's notebook so that she could write down Chad Norton's name on the suspect list she'd started in what she called her Murder Book. If he'd known that Judge Colfax intended to dismiss her case, he could have had a motive to kill his uncle to keep him from signing the papers.

"Norton's in the race for district attorney and he's running against his boss," Howie told Norman. "I talked to Rod Metcalf. He said the *Lake Eden Journal* just got the declared candidate list and Chad Norton's name is on it."

Norman gave a humorless laugh. "If Norton knows what's good for him, he'll pull out immediately and try to save his job. There's no way he can win after people find out about Judge Colfax's decision."

"I really don't think he could have won, anyway," Andrea said. "Too many people supported Hannah. And every single one of them thought the case against her was ridiculous."

Howie nodded. "You're right. It *was* ridiculous. Everyone thought so. If Judge Flemming had been here, it would never have gotten this far."

Michelle came back from the kitchen and handed Hannah her stenographer's notebook. "Here's your Murder Book. I thought you'd probably want to add Chad Norton to the suspect list."

"Who's on your list?" Mike asked Hannah.

"Nobody yet. I'm going to write in Chad Norton right now."

"Better put yourself down, too. You had a motive."

Hannah just stared at him for a second or two. "That's absurd!" she finally said. "I don't have a motive. Judge Colfax dismissed my case."

"But did you know that before you went into his chambers?"

Hannah counted to ten. Unfortunately, it wasn't long enough and the fire was still in her eyes as she turned to face him. "No, I *didn't* know that before I went into his chambers."

"So when you entered his chambers, you still had a motive to kill him."

"Yes."

"So, Miss Meddlesome, put yourself on your suspect list."

"*What* did you call me?"

"Miss Meddlesome. That's my new name for you, Hannah. It fits you perfectly since you're always meddling in my official cases. Don't you usually add anyone with a motive to your suspect list?"

Hannah took a deep breath and somehow managed to hang on to her temper. "Yes, I

184

usually do."

"Then it's just like I said. You'd better add yourself."

Hannah gave him a long-suffering look. "Think about it, Mike. I can't investigate myself!"

"Maybe not, but I can. You're still on *my* list."

The tension around the table was palpable and the silence was long and unbroken. Hannah realized that everyone was waiting for her to say something. Somehow she had to turn the uncomfortable moment around so that it could become a nice family dinner again.

"Well," she said, swallowing her ire. "If I'm on your list, I do hope I'm at the very top."

Norman chuckled and the tension was broken. Then Mike laughed and reached out to pat her hand. It was all Hannah could do not to pull back, but she didn't. The dregs of discomfort were still in the room and there was no need for any more tension tonight. Her whole day had been filled with anxiety. She wished that she could be magically transported to California to be with Ross, but since that was impossible, she needed to put aside her urge to tell Mike that if he couldn't be polite to her, he was no longer welcome in her condo.

She tried. She really did. She told herself that Mike hadn't been picking on her specifically, that suspecting people, even people like her, was his job and that was what made him such a good detective. That didn't work so she gave up on Mike and switched her focus to Norman.

Norman hadn't said a word to support her. He'd just sat there letting Mike go right on giving her a hard time. Norman insisted that he loved her. Shouldn't a man who loved a woman come to her defense?

This wasn't the first time that similar situations had occurred. She'd been simmering about it for a while. It had been a slow build and it had almost reached the boiling point tonight. Both Mike and Norman said that they loved her, but neither one was willing to defend her against everyone and everything.

Hannah tried to shake off the lonely feeling that was growing inside her, but she couldn't help wondering what Ross would have done if he'd been there.

"What is it, Hannah?" Michelle leaned close to whisper in her ear.

"Everything," Hannah said quietly. "Ever since I got back, everything seems static. Nothing's changed. Nothing's grown. This

186

may sound crazy, but I think I'm overdue for a change in my life."

SALTED CASHEW AND MILK CHOCOLATE WHIPPERSNAPPER COOKIES

DO NOT preheat your oven quite yet — this cookie dough needs to chill before baking.

1 box chocolate cake mix, the size you can bake in a 9-inch by 13-inch cake pan *(I used Betty Crocker Super Moist Chocolate Fudge, net wt. 15.25 oz.)*

1 large egg

2 cups Cool Whip, thawed *(measure this — a tub of Cool Whip contains a little over 3 cups and that's way too much!)*

1 cup milk chocolate chips *(Andrea used a 6-ounce package of Nestle milk chocolate chips)*

1/2 cup salted cashews, finely chopped *(measure AFTER chopping)*

1/2 cup powdered *(confectioner's)* sugar in a separate small, shallow bowl for rolling dough balls. *(You don't have to sift it unless it's got big lumps.)*

18 to 24 maraschino cherries without stems, drained and cut in half

Place approximately HALF of the cake mix in a large bowl.

Whisk the egg in a medium-size bowl.

Stir the 2 cups of thawed Cool Whip into the egg mixture.

Add the egg and Cool Whip mixture to the cake mix in the large bowl. Stir only until everything is combined. You don't want to stir all the air out of the Cool Whip.

Sprinkle the milk chocolate chips on top.

Sprinkle the 1/2 cup of chopped cashews on top of the milk chocolate chips. Gently stir until they're combined. Again, don't over-stir!

Sprinkle in the rest of the cake mix and fold it in with a rubber spatula, stirring only until everything is combined. The object here is to keep as much air in the cookie dough as possible. Air is what will make your cookies soft and have that melt-in-your-mouth quality.

Hannah's 1st Note: This dough is very sticky. It's much easier to work with if you chill it before you try to form the cookies. Just cover the bowl and stick it in the refrigerator for an hour.

When your cookie dough has chilled for one hour, preheat your oven to 350 degrees F., rack in the middle position. DO NOT take your chilled cookie dough out of the refrigerator until after your oven has pre-heated to the proper temperature.

While your oven is preheating, prepare your cookie sheets by spraying them with Pam or another nonstick baking spray, or lining them with parchment paper.

When your oven is ready, take your dough out of the refrigerator. Using a teaspoon from your silverware drawer, drop the dough by rounded teaspoonful into the bowl of powdered sugar. Roll the dough around with your fingers to form powdered sugar coated cookie dough balls.

Place the dough balls on your prepared cookie sheets, no more than 12 cookies on a standard-size sheet.

Press a half cherry, rounded side up, on top of each cookie.

Hannah's 2nd Note: Work with only one cookie dough ball at a time. If you drop more than one in the bowl of powdered sugar, they'll stick together.

Andrea's Note: Make only as many cookie balls as you can bake at one time and then return the dough to the refrigerator. I have double ovens so I prepare 2 sheets of Whippersnapper Cookies, one for each oven.

Bake the Salted Cashew and Milk Chocolate Whippersnapper Cookies at 350 degrees F., for 10 minutes. Let them cool on the cookie sheets for 2 minutes or so, and then move them to a wire rack to cool completely. *(This is a lot easier if you line your cookie sheets with parchment paper — then you don't need to lift the cookies one by one. All you have to do is grab one end of the parchment paper and pull it, cookies and all, onto the wire rack.)*

Once the cookies are completely cool, store them between sheets of waxed paper in a cool, dry place. *(Your refrigerator is cool, but it's definitely not dry!)*

Yield: 3 to 4 dozen soft, chewy cookies, depending on cookie size.

CHAPTER TWELVE

Something was tickling her nose. Hannah opened her eyes to find Moishe only inches from her face, so close that his whiskers were brushing against the bridge of her nose.

"What time is it?" she asked sleepily before she realized how ridiculous her question was. Even if Moishe could speak, he didn't know how to tell time.

Or did he? she thought as his rough tongue shot out to lick her cheek. It was clear that he wanted her to get up. He was probably hungry. What time was it anyway?

With great effort, Hannah sat up in bed. Sunlight was streaming through her bedroom window. That was odd. It was always dark when she got up to get ready to go to work. She turned her head to glance at her alarm clock. It was ten to seven, hours later than she habitually got up on a work day. Had her alarm failed to go off?

Hannah reached out to feel for the button on the back of the clock, the one she pulled out to activate the alarm. It was pushed all the way in. Had she forgotten to set the alarm last night? Or had Michelle tiptoed into her room in the wee hours of the morning and deliberately pushed the button so that her alarm wouldn't go off?

Moishe was purring so loudly he sounded like a car with a nonfunctioning muffler. It was definitely time to feed him. She usually fed him right after she poured her first cup of coffee and . . .

Hannah's mind stopped in mid-thought. She smelled coffee. She was sure of it. And there was another wonderful scent in the air. It smelled like apples. And cinnamon. And nutmeg. And something else, a darker, richer scent. Cardamom?

That did it. Cardamom was Hannah's favorite spice and she swung her legs over the side of the bed and felt for her slippers. The light had dawned and it was obvious that Michelle had gotten up early, baked something that smelled incredibly yummy, and gone off to work at The Cookie Jar. What a wonderful baby sister she had!

"Come on, Moishe! Let's go see what Michelle baked!" Hannah slipped her feet into her favorite sheepskin-lined moccasins and headed for the kitchen. She was wide awake, her mouth was watering, and she could hardly wait to see whatever it was that Michelle had left for her.

"It's some kind of breakfast bread," she told Moishe, zeroing in on the loaf of bread that sat on the counter. "I know you'd rather have shrimp, but it smells incredibly good to me."

"Rowwww!"

Hannah turned to glance at Moishe who was standing in front of his empty food bowl. "Okay," she told him. "Just let me pour my coffee and then I'll get your kitty crunchies."

As she passed by the breakfast bread, it beckoned to her, but her furry roommate came first. Her stomach growled almost as loud as Moishe's purring as she filled his bowl and got him fresh water.

"My turn," she said, taking her first sip of coffee, the best of the day, incredibly good and rich. She took another sip and then headed straight for the counter to cut a piece of Michelle's breakfast surprise.

The bread was dark and moist, and reminiscent of apple pie. She always put cardamom in her apple pies, even though it had gotten very expensive over the years. She didn't need much, only a half teaspoon to mix with the cinnamon and nutmeg. And her Mom's Apple Pie, the recipe that had come from her great-grandmother Elsa, was very popular at The Cookie Jar.

A moment later, Hannah was seated at her kitchen table and she took a bite of bread. It was every bit as good as it smelled, perhaps better. She had to get the recipe from Michelle. Her customers would absolutely love it.

A note was propped up on the table and Hannah read it.

Good morning, Hannah. Lisa picked me up and we're at The Cookie Jar. Stay home as long as you like. We've got everything covered.

Ross called. He's coming in earlier than he expected. They moved up his interview to this Thursday. He wanted to know if that was okay with you so please call him back after noon, your time, today.

The bread on the table is Applesauce Bread. I got the recipe from one of the girls in my acting class. She said it was her grandmother's recipe. I hope you like it. It's good just the way it is, room temperature with butter, or toasted and buttered.

See you when you get to The Cookie Jar. Lisa wants you to fill her in on what happened yesterday so she can start telling the story.

The note was signed with an *M* for Michelle and there was a postscript on the bottom.

P.S. — I fed Moishe.

Hannah turned to look at her cat who was staring up at her with a perfectly innocent expression. "You've been busted," she told him. "Michelle said she'd already fed you."

Moishe's expression didn't change one bit. He still looked as innocent as a newborn kitten. Hannah sighed and shook her head. He'd duped her and there was nothing she could do about it now. His food bowl was empty again. If Michelle did this again, she'd make sure to read the note *before* she put Moishe's breakfast in his bowl.

Hannah and Michelle had baked Applesauce Bread and the kitchen at The Cookie Jar smelled wonderful. After they'd finished cleaning up their baking dishes, Hannah had poured coffee for both of them, and they were sitting at the stainless steel work island in the center of the kitchen, enjoying a well-deserved break.

"Lisa's about to start telling the story," Michelle said, noticing that the chatter coming from the coffee shop had abruptly ceased. "You're jam-packed with customers out there. I went in to check while you were putting the Applesauce Bread in the oven and it's standing room only."

"I'm not surprised. They love Lisa's stories. Some of our customers come back two or three times to hear them all over again."

"Lisa ought to join the Lake Eden Players," Michelle said, naming the amateur theater group that had taken over the old shoe repair shop and turned it into a small theater.

"If she did, she'd draw a huge crowd. And then they'd have to move to bigger quarters. Lisa's a natural actor."

"Do you all know about Judge Colfax's death?" Lisa's voice carried clearly to them from the coffee shop. There was a chorus of yesses and Lisa went on. "And do you all know that our Hannah was the first on the scene?"

"Hannah has slaydar. She's always first on the scene!" a deep voice commented and several customers laughed.

It was Cyril Murphy. Hannah recognized his slight Irish brogue.

"You're right," Lisa said. "Let's start when Hannah got up yesterday morning. It wasn't an ordinary day for her and I think some of you know why."

"She had to go to court," a woman answered.

Hannah recognized the voice, but she couldn't quite place it. It belonged to either Bertie Straub or her accountant's wife, Lolly Kramer.

"That's right, Bertie," Lisa said. "Hannah was nervous because Howie was picking her up at her condo to take her to the county courthouse."

"I'll testify to that," Howie Levine said. "I know because she didn't laugh at my first two jokes."

Hannah turned to Michelle. "Could you go out right after Lisa finishes her story and drag Howie back here? I need to talk to him."

"Are you going to ask him about Judge Colfax's background?"

"That's right." Hannah was impressed. Michelle had learned a lot by helping her investigate. "I want to hear what Howie knows about Judge Colfax's family and any cases he tried that may have played a part in his murder."

"Good idea. I did a little research this

198

morning on the Internet."

Hannah was surprised. Michelle must have been up all night if she'd done computer research. "Before you left my place?"

"No, in Lisa's car on the way here. I used my smartphone."

"I see," Hannah said, and she did. It was yet another reason to buy and learn to use a smartphone. *If* she could get Tracey to teach her how to use it. And *if* she didn't have to publicly admit that she'd been foolish to dig in her heels and stubbornly refuse to even consider updating her old phone.

"I ordered some groceries from Florence's website while I was at it. I'll cook dinner the night Ross comes to town if you'll make the dessert."

"Deal," Hannah said, visions of desserts dancing through her head. "Did you order the groceries on your smartphone?"

"Yes. All we have to do is pick them up at the Red Owl on the way home." Michelle turned to glance at the clock on the wall. "You should call Ross right after Lisa finishes her story. It's noon already."

"Thanks. I'll call right now."

"But don't you want to hear Lisa's story?"

"Not really. I was there and I know what happened. I've already told everything to Mike and to Lisa. Twice is enough."

"Okay. I'll slip into the coffee shop so I can hear Lisa better."

Hannah smiled. "That was a very nice way of putting it."

"Putting what?"

"The fact that you're going into the coffee shop to give me privacy for the call."

"Oh. Yes. Well . . . that's okay, isn't it?"

"It's fine. I was complimenting you on your sensitivity."

"Mother should be that sensitive!" Michelle said, getting up from her stool. "I just about died every time I talked to a boyfriend on the phone in the hall. I knew she was listening to every word I said."

"Yes, but not the way you think."

"She wasn't listening at the door?"

"No. We had an extension in the kitchen, remember?" Hannah waited until Michelle had nodded and then she continued. "She listened in there."

"Did you catch her at it?"

"If you mean did I walk in the kitchen and see her, the answer is no. But I know she did it. One time I was talking to a friend and I heard the dishwasher go on the rinse cycle. There was no way I could have heard it from the hallway unless the phone in the kitchen was off the hook."

"Did you ever accuse her of eavesdropping?"

"No. I just told all my friends what she was doing and they were careful not to say anything that they didn't want repeated on the Lake Eden Gossip Hotline."

"Smart," Michelle said, picking up a full jar of cookies to take into the cookie shop. "I always wondered how she knew I was going to the movies with a boy instead of studying with one of my girlfriends."

Hannah waited until Michelle had left and then she checked the timer. The Applesauce Bread had only a minute or two left to bake. She waited until the timer rang and then took the loaves out of the oven and transferred them to the baker's rack. By the time she finished calling Ross, the bread would be cool enough to take out of the pans. She would test the warm bread on her customers, a kind of unexpected treat.

Hannah took a deep breath of the wonderfully aromatic air as she picked up the remote phone and stepped out the back door to make her call. There was no doubt in her mind that her customers would love Michelle's Applesauce Bread, and she suspected they'd have to bake several more batches to handle all the orders they were bound to receive.

APPLESAUCE BREAD

Preheat oven to 350 degrees F., rack in the middle position.

3/4 cup salted butter *(1 and 1/2 sticks, 6 ounces)* softened to room temperature

1 package *(8 ounces)* softened cream cheese *(the brick kind, not the whipped kind)*

2 cups white *(granulated)* sugar

2 large eggs, beaten *(just whip them up in a glass with a fork)*

1 teaspoon vanilla extract

1/2 teaspoon baking powder

1/2 teaspoon baking soda

1/2 teaspoon salt

1 teaspoon ground cinnamon

1/2 teaspoon ground nutmeg *(freshly grated is best)*

1/4 teaspoon ground cardamom *(optional)*

1 and 1/2 cups applesauce *(I used Mott)*

3 cups all-purpose flour *(don't sift — pack it down in the cup when you measure it)*

1 cup chopped nuts *(I use pecans or walnuts)*

Hannah's 1st Note: You can mix this up by hand, but it's a lot easier with an electric mixer.

Beat the softened butter, softened cream

cheese, and sugar together until they're light and fluffy.

Add the beaten eggs and the vanilla extract. Mix them in thoroughly.

Sprinkle in the baking powder, baking soda, salt, ground cinnamon, ground nutmeg, and ground cardamom *(if you decided to use it)*. Mix until they are well combined.

Measure out the applesauce and add it to your mixing bowl. Beat until it is well combined.

Add the flour in one cup increments, mixing after each addition.

Shut off the mixer and remove the bowl. Scrape down the sides with a rubber spatula and give it a final stir.

Use the rubber spatula to mix in the chopped nuts by hand.

Spray the inside of a loaf pan with Pam or another nonstick cooking spray. *(My pan was 8 inches long, 4 inches wide, and 3 inches tall.)* Alternatively, you can spray 3 small loaf pans with nonstick cooking spray and use those. *(My small loaf pans are 5 inches long, 3 1/4 inches wide, and 2 inches tall.)*

Give your dough a final stir by hand, and use a large spoon to fill your prepared loaf pan(s). Smooth the top with a rubber spatula.

Bake your bread at 350 degrees F., for 60 to 70 minutes, or until a cake tester, a long toothpick, or a thin wooden skewer inserted into the middle of the bread comes out clean. *(My bread took the full 70 minutes.)*

If you used the 3 small loaf pans, bake them at 350 degrees F. for 25 to 35 minutes or until a long toothpick or a thin wooden skewer inserted in the middle of the loaf comes out clean.

Hannah's 2nd Note: If the top of your loaf is browning too fast, tent a piece of foil over the top of the pan and finish baking with the foil in place.

Cool your Applesauce Bread in the pan on a wire rack until the bottom of the pan is warm but not hot to the touch. Then loosen the bread by running a knife around the inside of the pan.

Tip the bread out of the pan and place it right side up on the wire rack.

Hannah's 3rd Note: This bread is yummy if you toast and butter it. It's also wonderful to use for pork or ham sandwiches.

Yield: 1 large loaf or 3 small loaves of incredibly tasty bread.

Hannah's 4th Note: If you want to make these as muffins, preheat your oven to 375 degrees F. with the rack in

the center position. Spoon the batter into greased muffin tins. Alternatively, you can spray the inside of the muffin cups with Pam or another nonstick cooking spray, or line them with cupcake papers. Bake the muffins at 375 degrees F. for 25 minutes or until the muffins are golden on top. (Mini muffins should bake for 15 to 20 minutes or until slightly golden on top.)

CHAPTER THIRTEEN

She could hardly wait to hear his voice! Hannah was so busy thinking about Ross, she didn't notice that the crisp September day had turned colder. A light wind was blowing and it was definitely sweater weather, but she didn't feel the drop in temperature. She closed the back door behind her, walked over to lean against the side of her cookie truck, and took a deep breath of the chilled air. Then she dialed the number, her heart pounding in excitement.

Ross answered on the third ring. "Hannah!" he greeted her before she'd even identified herself.

"Yes. How did you know it was me?"

"I have caller ID."

"Michelle said you might be coming to Lake Eden early."

"That's right. They moved up the date of my interview."

"That's great!" Hannah said, feeling like the sun had suddenly emerged from the gray clouds overhead to turn the colorless day into a spectacle of beauty. "What time do you think you'll be through with the interview?"

"I doubt it'll run more than an hour, or two at the most. I should be through by four."

"Then dinner at six will work?"

"It'll work." Ross's voice was warm. "Where shall we go?"

"My place. Michelle's cooking dinner and I'm making dessert."

"Your tangerine cake?"

"My thoughts exactly. I had Florence special order some tangerines and they should be in today. Do you want me to pick you up at the airport?"

"No. I'm renting a car. I can hardly wait to see you again, Cupcake. I know it's only been two days, but I miss you."

"And I miss you."

"I reserved a room at the Blue Moon Motel."

"But you could have stayed with me."

"I knew you'd offer, but I didn't think that was a good idea."

"You mean . . ." Hannah felt tears come to her eyes and she paused to wipe them away. "Do you mean you don't want to stay with me?"

"Of course not! I want to stay with you! I want to spend every minute I'm in Lake Eden with you. But you have a reputation to protect. There's no way I'd want to jeopardize your status in town."

"Maybe I could drive out to see you at the Blue Moon?"

Ross laughed. It was a low sexy laugh that made Hannah catch her breath. "We'll work out the details when I see you. Only fifty-six hours to go."

He was counting the hours! Hannah's smile was beatific. She'd never felt like this about anyone before and it thrilled her to the core.

"I'm counting the hours, too," she admitted. "Do you want me to greet you at the door with a tequila sunrise? I called Sally at the Lake Eden Inn and she told me how to make it."

"You liked it that much when we had them in Vegas?"

"I loved it! It was delicious, but the night that followed it was even better." The moment the words were out of her mouth, Hannah regretted them. Was she being too forward?

"I'm glad," Ross said.

Hannah drew a deep breath and let it out in relief. She hadn't been too forward. There was genuine caring in Ross's voice. She could hear it and she felt warm all over from the top of her head to the tips of her toes. "So would you like me to greet you at the door with that tequila sunrise?"

"I'd rather have a kiss from you."

"I feel exactly the same way," Hannah said, giving a little shiver of anticipation. She was about to tell him what they were having for dinner when she heard a voice calling her from the kitchen. "I have to go, Ross. I'm meeting with Howie in the kitchen."

"But you told me last night that Judge Colfax dismissed your court case before he was murdered."

"He did."

"Then why are you meeting with your lawyer?"

"Howie's worked with Judge Colfax in the past. I need to ask him some questions about the judge's personal life and any high profile cases he might have tried."

"That means you're investigating again?" Ross waited until she confirmed it and then he laughed. "That was a really dumb question on my part. Of course you're investigating. You found the judge's body. Is Mike all bent out of shape about the fact you're working on it?"

"He's not happy. As a matter of fact, he's investigating *me.*"

"*You?* Why?"

"Because I was the one to discover the body. And at that time, I didn't know that Judge Colfax had dismissed my case. That means I had a motive to kill him."

"But you didn't. I can't believe Mike thinks that! He should know that you'd never do something like that!"

Ross was clearly outraged with Mike's attitude and Hannah hurried to explain. "I don't think Mike really *believes* I did it. He suspects everyone with a motive until he proves them innocent. That's just the way he is."

"Well, that's asinine! Think about it, Cupcake. If Mike's your friend, he should trust you."

Hannah didn't say anything even though it was exactly the way she'd felt. She just waited to see what Ross would say next.

"I think he's just trying to pull your chain. He's probably jealous."

"Of you?"

"Maybe. Does he know that we met in Vegas?"

"No. Mother and Doc and the girls know

because they were there, but I didn't tell anyone else."

"Why not?"

"Because I wanted to keep it to myself and just enjoy the secret. It's too new and too wonderful to share with everyone right away."

"I agree. But I still think Mike's jealous. He probably resents the fact that you're so good at cracking his cases."

Hannah felt a flush of pride. "Do you really think so?"

"I do. Solving murder cases is one of the things you do so well." Ross paused for a moment and then he said, "Maybe there's some way I can help you on this one when I get there."

"Maybe," Hannah said, her spirits lifting so high, they threatened to float away. Ross wanted to help her investigate. He wanted to be a part of her life. And she wanted to be a part of his.

They said their goodbyes and Hannah ended the call. She was glowing with good feelings as she opened the door and stepped back into the kitchen.

"Hi, Howie," she said when she saw him sitting at the work island, a cup of coffee in his hand and half a slice of Applesauce Bread sitting on a napkin in front of him. "I hope I didn't keep you waiting too long."

"Not at all. It's a nice break for me. I've got to file bankruptcy papers for a client later and that's a royal pain. Can I talk you out of another slice of that Applesauce Bread? It's really good."

"I'll wrap one for you to take home. I think your wife would like it."

"I think *both* of us would like it. Kitty will probably want the recipe."

"She can have it. I share my recipes."

Howie gestured toward the door to the coffee shop. "Lisa's really something, isn't she? She had us all sitting on the edge of our seats. You lead an exciting life, Hannah."

"That's true." Her thoughts turned to Ross and their secret romance. "But as far as finding murder victims goes, there are times that I wish my life were a little less exciting."

"I know what you mean. Yesterday was a hard day. I didn't like Judge Colfax that much, but I do feel sorry for him, especially because he did us a real favor before he died."

"Me, too. That's why I wanted to talk to you. He didn't deserve to die like that and I want to help bring his killer to justice."

"I figured that. Before we start delving

into Judge Colfax's background, can I have that second slice of Applesauce Bread? I was going to let this one cool to see if it was good that way too, but I can't wait."

"It's good cold," Hannah said, heading for the counter to cut another slice for Howie. "Michelle baked a loaf and I had it that way for breakfast. And she says it's good toasted with butter on it."

"It would be great for sandwiches. Just think about it, Hannah. A little mayo, a slice of Swiss cheese, some deli-cut smoked turkey slathered with cream cheese . . ." Howie stopped and swallowed. "That would be really good."

"It sounds good," Hannah agreed, setting a plate with two more slices in front of him. "Can we get started now?"

"We can. What do you want to know?"

"Tell me about Judge Colfax's family." She reached into her apron pocket for her Murder Book and her pen.

"Sorry, Hannah. I really don't know that much about him. He's married and has children. And he was with a law firm around here somewhere. He told me once that he'd tried a lot of cases in our courthouse."

"Tell me about his children."

"He has one son."

"How old is he?"

Howie shrugged. "I don't know. Since Judge Colfax had to be over seventy, his son's probably married with kids of his own."

Hannah jotted that down, but she knew she needed more information. "How can I find out more about him?"

"Try the Internet. He was a public figure and there's bound to be something there. And maybe you could . . ." Howie stopped speaking for a moment and then he nodded. "Yes. That'll work."

"What will work?"

"You can go out to the courthouse with me to file those bankruptcy papers. We're bound to run into Dave Johansen and you can ask him about Judge Colfax."

"But he doesn't really know me. Do you think he'll tell me anything personal about the judge?"

"He will if you take him some cookies with chocolate. Dave's crazy about chocolate."

"Then I'll take him some Double F Double M Crunch Cookies. It's a new recipe I baked."

"That should work. Okay. I will."

Hannah was puzzled. "You will what?"

"I'll test one for you. I know I ate all that Applesauce Bread, but I have enough room left to test a cookie."

Hannah laughed and went to the baker's rack to get a cookie for Howie. He loved her baking and that was gratifying. She brought him a cookie on a paper napkin and she watched as he took his first bite.

"Perfect!" Howie said. "I like these, Hannah. They're crunchy and they have a lot of chocolate. What's in them?"

"M&Ms and crushed Frosted Flakes."

"So the hard candy coating on the M&Ms makes them crunchy?"

"Either that or the crushed Frosted Flakes. I'm not really sure if it's the candy coating or the cereal. Maybe it's both."

"I'll analyze it for you as long as I don't spoil my supper tonight. Kitty's making lasagna and she'll be disappointed if I don't have at least two helpings. I probably shouldn't have had that Triple Threat Breakfast at the café this morning, but I think I could handle one more of those cookies for you . . ." he paused and grinned, "as long as it's in the interests of research, of course."

"Of course," Hannah said, retracing her steps to the baker's rack to fetch another cookie. She'd known Howie for years and as far as she could tell, he'd never been overweight. She wished she knew his secret of eating three eggs, three slices of bacon, three sausage links, and two biscuits smothered in gravy, followed less than three hours later by three slices of Applesauce Bread and two cookies, and not even counting the two helpings of lasagna he'd told her he was going to have at supper tonight, without ever gaining an ounce!

"These are great!" Dave Johansen said, reaching into Hannah's distinctive bakery bag for another cookie. "Howie said you were a great baker, but I've never tasted anything like these before."

"Thanks," Hannah said, wondering how soon she could ask him what he knew about Judge Colfax.

Dave picked up the extra-large cappuccino that they'd stopped to purchase at Howie's favorite coffee place and took a big swallow. "Okay. Go ahead and ask me your questions. Howie said you were investigating Judge Colfax's murder."

Hannah pulled out the list of questions she'd written on the ride to the courthouse. Her first set of questions concerned Chad Norton and a possible motive for killing his uncle. "When did you find the papers Judge Colfax signed dismissing the charges against me?"

Dave reared back in his chair. "Hold on

there! Are you investigating *me*?"

"No." She'd been expecting that reaction. "I just need to know the time line on those documents."

"Okay then." Dave seemed satisfied with her answer. "I found them right after the crime scene people left and I went in to straighten up the judge's chambers. I noticed that there was something in his out-box and that's when I found the papers. The minute I realized what they were, I called Howie from Judge Colfax's office phone and told him about it. And then I hightailed down to file the papers so they'd get recorded."

Hannah gave him a smile. "Thank you, Dave. That's what I thought, but I had to ask. Do you think anyone else knew that Judge Colfax had signed those documents?"

"Not unless he told someone he was going to do it. Or unless the killer came into his office to talk to him, saw the signed papers in his out-box, and went into a killing rage."

Hannah swallowed hard. She'd seen the crime scene with her own eyes and she could believe that whoever had bludgeoned Judge Colfax to death had been in a killing rage. "Do you know anyone who might fit that pattern?"

"Every lawyer who steps into the court-room is capable of flying into a rage if the case he's worked on for months is summarily dismissed just minutes before the trial is scheduled to begin."

"I can understand how they might fly into a rage at a last-minute dismissal. But you said a *killing* rage. Is there anyone in particular that you were thinking of?"

Dave looked slightly embarrassed. "I should have known you'd pick up on that. And yes. There *is* one lawyer who's legendary for having a hair-trigger temper and blowing his stack, even in the courtroom."

"Chad Norton?" Hannah guessed.

"So they say. He's never had an outburst like that in front of me, but the story around here is that Chad exploded in front of another judge when he lost what he thought was an open and shut case. That judge threw him in jail for contempt, and in order to be released, Chad had to apologize to the judge, pay a hefty fine, and complete an anger management course."

"From what I hear about his personality, something like that must have stuck in Chad's craw."

"I'm sure it did. And it would have put an end to his career plans if it had been made public, but it wasn't."

"Why not?"

"I'm not sure, but the matter was kept under wraps. The whole thing was like it never happened. Nobody except Chad and the judge know about it."

"Except for whoever told you."

"That's true. Word gets around in these hallowed halls, but we know the rules. We talk to each other, but never to any outsiders."

"You're talking to me."

"Yes, but you're investigating Judge Colfax's murder. And Howie told me that you can be trusted. I want to give you any information I have that'll help you catch the killer."

Hannah's eyes narrowed. "I was under the impression that you didn't like Judge Colfax. Was I wrong?"

"You're not wrong. Judge Colfax was a royal pain in the you-know-where, but he was murdered while I was on duty. That makes me partly responsible. If I'd been in his chambers at the time, it never would have happened."

Guilt, Hannah's mind told her. *Dave feels guilty because he wasn't there to protect Judge Colfax.*

"You probably couldn't have stopped it even if you'd been there," Hannah said, in

219

an effort to make him feel better. "It looked to me as if the killer went berserk with anger. Getting back to Chad Norton . . . has he ever gotten violent again?"

"Not that I've heard of. And I would have heard. People tell me things."

"So as far as you know, he's never had an outburst in court since he took that anger management course?"

Dave shook his head. "If he has, I haven't heard about it."

"Tell me what you know about Judge Colfax's personal life. Does he have a family?"

"One son by his first wife. They're divorced. Bitterly from what I hear. The son is trying to make his living as a musician. His name is Seth, but he took his mother's family name when they divorced."

"You said the son was *trying* to make his living as a musician. Isn't he doing well?"

"I don't think so. One of the clerks heard him once and she said he wasn't very good. He sings with a band called Liquid Steel."

Hannah wrote that in her book. "What else can you tell me about him?"

"He's a mama's boy. Judge Colfax told me Seth doesn't work at a regular job and that Sheila is supporting him."

"She works?"

"No, Sheila doesn't work. She doesn't

have to. Her father died and left her enough money to set her up for life, but she still cashes her monthly alimony check from Judge Colfax. I know because he told me the alimony check was a day late and she'd already called him about it three times. He asked me to hand it to her personally so that he would know exactly when she got it."

"Did you happen to notice what her last name was?"

"Sure did. It's the same as my wife's grandmother's last name. Dortweiler."

Hannah jotted Sheila Dortweiler in her book. "What was Mrs. Dortweiler doing when you handed her the check?"

"She was sitting in her living room drinking coffee and eating a peanut butter and banana sandwich."

"Do you remember where Mrs. Dortweiler lives?"

"I do. She's got a big place on the lake in Annandale. It's less than an hour from here. I'll give you the address. Judge Colfax told me that after I'd hand delivered his check, I could take the rest of the day off. I thought that was really nice of him until my paycheck came and I found out that what it amounted to was taking the rest of the day off without pay."

Hannah held her pen poised over a blank line. Was telling someone to take the day off and not paying them a motive for murder?

"And don't start writing my name in that book of yours," Dave said. "I didn't do it and I've got an alibi. I was talking to my wife on the phone when the judge was killed and it'll be on my phone records. Have the cops check, if you like. The phone company won't give the records to you, but they always cooperate when the request comes from someone in law enforcement."

"That's not necessary," Hannah said, even though she was already wondering if the deputies in charge would do that with all their persons of interest and if Michelle would ask Lonnie to make a copy for her. "What's Judge Colfax's current wife's name?"

"Nora. She's really nice. I've met her and I like her."

Hannah noticed the omission. Dave had met Nora and he liked her. He'd also met Sheila if he'd delivered Judge Colfax's check to her house, but Dave hadn't said he liked her.

"Did Judge Colfax and his current wife have any children?"

"No."

"Then he had only the one son?"

"Actually . . . no. He has a daughter by a woman named Margaret George. He was reminiscing about her one afternoon. I guess she was a really nice gal and he was going to marry her, but he met Nora and that was that."

"Do you know anything about Judge Colfax's high profile cases?"

"Not really. He just filled in around here. All the high-profile cases were delayed until the regular judges got back."

Hannah glanced down at her notes. Dave Johansen had given her a wealth of information and it was a good place to start her investigation. She had only one question left to ask. "Do you know anyone in addition to Chad Norton who had a motive to kill Judge Colfax?"

Dave thought for a moment and then he shook his head. "No, not unless someone he convicted wanted revenge. He didn't have any cases like that here, but if I were you, I'd check his case records. Even murderers get out on parole eventually. And there's always the families of the victims. Someone like that might have thought their loved one's killer or rapist got off too easy."

"That's a good idea," Hannah said, even though she'd already thought of it. "Thanks, Dave. You've been a big help."

"You're welcome. He wasn't a bad guy, you know. He just got crotchety in the last year or so. Maybe he was in pain. That'll make some people cantankerous."

Hannah said her goodbyes and went out to the lobby to meet Howie. He wasn't there yet and she sat down in a chair to write another note in her Murder Book. *Check with Nora C. about Judge Colfax's health.*

DOUBLE F DOUBLE M CRUNCH COOKIES

Preheat oven to 350 degrees F., rack in the middle position.

1 cup white *(granulated)* sugar

1 cup brown sugar *(pack it down in the cup when you measure it)*

1 cup salted butter *(2 sticks, 8 ounces, 1/2 pound)* softened to room temperature

1 teaspoon baking soda

1 teaspoon salt

2 teaspoons vanilla extract

2 large eggs, beaten *(just whip them up in a glass with a fork)*

2 cups Frosted Flakes

2 and 1/2 cups flour *(pack it down in the cup when you measure it)*

1 cup M&M's candy *(regular, not the kind with nuts in the middle)*

Hannah's 1st Note: I use an electric mixer to mix up these cookies at The Cookie Jar. If you don't have an electric mixer, you can do it in a large mixing bowl with a wooden spoon.

Place the white sugar and brown sugar in the bowl of an electric mixer. Mix them up together.

Add the softened butter and beat until the mixture is light and fluffy.

Sprinkle in the baking soda and salt. Mix them in thoroughly.

Add the vanilla extract and the beaten eggs. Beat until everything is thoroughly incorporated.

Measure out the 2 cups of Frosted Flakes and place them in a closeable plastic food storage bag. Crush them with your hands or roll a rolling pin over the bag to crush them.

Add the crushed Frosted Flakes to your bowl and mix them in.

Hannah's 2nd Note: 2 cups of Frosted Flakes will equal approximately 1 cup when crushed.

Add the flour in half-cup increments, mixing after each addition.

Scrape down the sides of the mixing bowl with a rubber spatula and take the mixing bowl out of the mixer. Give it a final stir by hand.

Gently, using a folding motion with the rubber spatula, mix in the M&M's candy.

Let the dough sit on the counter for a minute or two to rest. *(It doesn't really need to rest, but you probably do.)*

Prepare your cookie sheets by spraying them with Pam or another nonstick cooking spray, or by lining them with parchment paper.

Form the dough into walnut-sized balls with your impeccably clean hands and place them on the prepared cookie sheets, 12 to a standard-size sheet.

Press the dough balls down just a bit so they won't roll off on the way to the oven. *(Don't laugh. This happened to Lisa when she made these cookies at home. Her two dogs, Dillon and Sammy, chased the cookie dough balls and gobbled them up before she could stop them! She called Doctor Hagaman because there was chocolate in the cookies and chocolate isn't good for dogs, but he said not to worry when she told him that they only got two dough balls apiece.)*

Bake your Double F Double M Crunch Cookies at 350 degrees F. for 10 to 12 minutes. Cool on the cookie sheet for 2 minutes, then remove the cookies to a wire rack until they're completely cool. *(If you used parchment paper, you can leave them on the paper. Just pull it over on the wire rack. The cookies will be easy to peel off when they are cool.)*

Yield: approximately 6 to 8 dozen, depending on cookie size.

Hannah's 3rd Note: If your first pan

of cookies spread out too much in the oven, chill the dough in the refrigerator for one hour before baking the rest of your cookies.

Delores's Note: I love these cookies! They're so sweet and chocolaty. Hannah told me that the M&M candy name came from Forrest Mars Sr., of the Mars candy company, when he struck a deal in 1941 with Bruce Murrie, son of famed Hershey president William Murrie, to develop a hard shelled candy with chocolate at the center. The two M's stand for Mars and Murrie. Hannah should really go on *Jeopardy!* She knows a lot of little facts like this. If she won, she could replace her old cookie truck with something that runs better.

CHAPTER FOURTEEN

When she walked in the back door of The Cookie Jar, Hannah found Norman waiting for her at the stainless steel work island. There was a cup of coffee in his hand and a welcoming smile on his face.

"We didn't get a chance to talk very much last night," Norman said, patting the stool next to him. "Sit down, Hannah, and tell me all about Vegas and the wedding."

"Vegas was good. Michelle and Andrea took me to buy a new bathing suit and all three of us enjoyed the pools. We really loved the show tickets you gave us, too."

"That's great. How was the wedding?"

"It was fun. You'll see the video at the party. The wedding chapel was small, but it was nice, except for the videographer in the Elvis wig."

"Oh, no!" Norman laughed. "Was your mother really upset about that?"

"Not really. She was having too much fun

to be upset. She said the wig was so awful, she was going to ask them to play 'Love Me Tender' at the ceremony."

"She didn't!"

"Oh, yes she did. It was a great wedding, Norman. Mother and Doc looked very happy."

"They deserve to be happy. Did you meet anyone interesting?"

He knew! Hannah felt an instant of panic and her heart jumped up to her throat. Somehow Norman knew about Ross! What should she do? What should she say? Somehow she had to handle this without hurting Norman's feelings.

The truth, Hannah's mind instructed. *Tell him the truth.*

Hannah knew her instinct was right and fair. There was no way she could lie to Norman. But caution prevailed. The whole truth could wait until they were in private . . . if she told him at all. Perhaps she'd change her mind about Ross when she saw him again.

Fat chance! her mind mocked her. *You're in love with Ross and you know it. It's a lot different from the way you feel about Norman. Norman's a friend, a wonderful friend, and there's no denying that you do love him. But, as you've thought so many times in the past, you don't love him enough to marry him.*

Was she thinking clearly? Or was she deluding herself? She had to consider the fact that her mother's wedding was very romantic. Just seeing Delores and Doc together had made her long for someone she could love the way that they loved each other. There was also the romantic atmosphere of Las Vegas to consider. She had been on vacation and alone in a hotel room. Ross had been in a suite only a few steps down the hall. It was possible that what she was feeling for Ross was a vacation fantasy that had no part in the reality of everyday life. She should wait to tell Norman until she was sure that her feelings for Ross were real.

Nice job of rationalization, her mind said sarcastically. *Are you going to tell him, or not?*

Not, Hannah's inner voice answered. *I won't tell him everything until I find out if it's real.*

Hedging your bets?

Hannah made a conscious decision to stifle her sarcastic mind. She would refuse to listen and go with her heart.

"I didn't meet anyone that interesting," she responded, hoping her answer hadn't taken too long, "with the exception of Doc's best man. That was a complete surprise."

"Who was it?"

Norman didn't know, and Hannah drew a deep breath of relief. "Ross Barton," she answered. "You remember him, don't you?"

"Sure I do. What happened to the friend from medical school that Doc was going to ask?"

"He was doing something for Doctors Without Borders and couldn't get back to the States in time."

Norman looked thoughtful. "Was Ross working on a project in Vegas?"

"I'm not sure, but he did have a meeting with someone while he was there. He told us he wasn't happy in Hollywood and he was looking for something else."

"Then he was probably flying to Vegas anyway for that meeting. What's he looking for anyway?"

"I don't know. He didn't go into specifics with us. But I do know he's coming to Lake Eden for an interview at KCOW Television."

"Good. He's a nice guy, and I'd like to see him again. How long is he staying?"

"I don't know that either," Hannah answered quite truthfully since Ross hadn't told her . . . yet. And then she said something off the top of her head that she wished she could call back the instant the words left her mouth. "Michelle's making dinner on Thursday night and we invited Ross. Would you like to join us?"

"Sure. I haven't seen Ross since he shot that movie here in Lake Eden. And if there's food involved, Mike will probably show up, too. It'll be like old home week."

Not exactly, Hannah thought, but she didn't say it. What on earth had gotten into her, extending the invitation to Norman?!

"What time is dinner?" Norman asked her. "And do you want me to bring Cuddles?"

"Come at six o'clock and yes, please bring Cuddles. That'll make Moishe very happy."

"Now I have an invitation for you," Norman said, smiling at her. "Will you come to dinner with me at the Lake Eden Inn tonight? I already invited Michelle and Lonnie, and I'm going to invite Andrea and Bill. I thought it would be fun to celebrate the fact that your court case was dismissed."

"How nice!" Hannah was genuinely touched at Norman's thoughtfulness. "Are you going to invite Mike?"

"I'd better. After all . . ."

"There's food involved!" Norman and Hannah said together. And then they shared a laugh.

Hannah was just slipping the last pan of

cookies in the oven when Michelle came into the kitchen from the coffee shop. "Did Norman invite you to dinner at the Inn?"

"Yes. And I invited him to dinner Thursday night."

"Then Ross isn't coming?"

"Ross *is* coming. He thought he'd finish his interview by four at the latest and then he's coming to my place."

"So Norman is coming and Ross is coming."

"Yes. And Mike will probably show up. He usually does . . ."

"When food is involved," Michelle finished Hannah's sentence with a laugh. But then she quickly sobered and a worried expression crossed her face.

"What's the matter?" Hannah asked her.

"I was just thinking about dinner with Norman, and Mike, and Ross. Won't it get ugly with all three of them there at the same time?"

Hannah thought about that for a moment and then she shook her head. "I don't think so. Norman likes Ross and so does Mike. Norman even said that it would be like old home week."

Michelle didn't say anything. She just stared hard at Hannah.

"What?" Hannah asked her, puzzled by

that reaction.

Michelle gave a little sigh. "Sometimes Hannah, you're a babe in the woods, especially when it comes to men. You really don't know what you're doing, do you?"

"What do you mean?"

"You're clueless. I can tell. You're getting the three rivals together in one place at the same time. That means what you're doing is comparison shopping!"

Hannah blinked. And then she blinked again. Finally she said, "Maybe you're right, but I never *meant* to do that! Really I didn't."

"I believe you. I said it before, you're clueless."

"Can't you at least say guileless? It sounds much better."

"Okay, you're guileless. I think I knew more about men in high school than you do now."

Hannah was silent for a long moment. Perhaps she had made a big mistake. Unfortunately, she didn't know how to correct it. "What do you think I should do, Michelle?"

"There's nothing you can do to reverse things. My advice would be to sit back and let it all play out between Norman, Mike, and Ross."

"But you said it might get ugly!"

"It might. That depends on how you act and how Ross acts. I think Ross will be fine. I'm sure he's been in situations like this before."

Hannah caught her sister's inference. "But you're not so sure about me."

"That's right. I think we need a distraction. So far it's just you and me and the three guys. I'll invite Lonnie. That'll help. And I'll give Andrea a call at the office and ask her to come over here to discuss it."

"I'll do it," Hannah said. "I have to talk to her anyway. I want Tracey to run out to the mall with me when she gets out of school."

"Going comparison shopping?"

Michelle eyes were twinkling and Hannah knew she was kidding. "I think I've done enough of that, at least for today! I'm going out there to pick up a new phone."

"You're emerging from the Dark Ages?"

"I guess you could say that. It shouldn't take long. Tracey's an expert when it comes to the new phones. She'll steer me in the right direction."

"I have no doubt of that. Tracey's a genius when it comes to anything electronic. When you talk to Andrea, ask her to think of another couple we can invite. The more people we have, the more the distraction. And the more the distraction, the less the tension."

After Michelle went back to the coffee shop, Hannah got herself a big glass of water. She felt like she'd been hit between the eyes with a sledgehammer. She'd really had no concept of the problems she'd created by inviting Norman. Now they'd have only forty-eight hours to plan and prepare a dinner party and that meant more work for both of them.

"I think we've got it, Hannah," Andrea said. They were sitting at the work island and all three sisters had just sampled Hannah's latest batch of cookies and pronounced them excellent. "Read the list of guests and we'll see if we have enough."

"You and Bill, Michelle and Lonnie, Lisa and Herb, Norman, Mike, and Ross. Counting me, that's ten."

"I think we need a couple of single women," Michelle suggested. "They'll be a distraction for Mike and Norman. With other women there, they won't be concentrating so much on you."

"Agreed," Andrea said. "It's really too bad Mother and Doc aren't here. Mother could distract anyone."

"Is that a compliment?" Hannah asked her.

"I don't know. Mother does tend to dominate the conversation, but in this case, we need someone who can do that."

"I've got an idea," Hannah said. "How about Tracey and Bethie? I think they'd be just as distracting as two single women."

Andrea groaned. "I *know* they'd be distracting, especially in Bethie's case. Grandma McCann just taught her the 'Itsy Bitsy Spider' song and she wants everyone to sing it with her. And Tracey can take you away from the group by helping you with the new phone she helps you buy."

"Then Tracey and Bethie are in." Michelle sounded very certain. "Kids are a great distraction. And we'll ask Norman to bring Cuddles."

"He's bringing her," Hannah said. "I already asked him to."

"That means *Feet Up.* It's a perfect distraction. Let's make sure we drop little pieces of pork chop to bait them."

"Let's ask Grandma McCann, too," Andrea suggested. "That way she can take the girls home at bedtime, and Bill and I can stay until Mike and Norman leave."

"Good idea," Michelle gestured for Hannah to write it down.

Hannah flipped the page in her notebook and added her nieces and Grandma Mc-

Cann. "We've got thirteen."

Andrea frowned. "I'm not that superstitious, but thirteen is an unlucky number."

"In some cultures it's a lucky number," Hannah told her.

"But we don't live in those cultures. I think we ought to have at least one more. How many people can you fit around your table, Hannah?"

"I have fourteen chairs and a highchair for Bethie. Fifteen would be crowded, but it's possible, especially since Tracey is small."

"It *is* fourteen counting Cuddles," Michelle pointed out. "Moishe and Cuddles are distractions, too."

"And they don't have to sit at the table," Hannah said with a laugh.

"You're right, Michelle," Andrea agreed. "I think we've got the ideal crowd to take Hannah off the hot seat." She turned to Hannah. "I can bring some applesauce to go with the pork. Grandma McCann makes it from scratch."

"Applesauce would be great with pork," Hannah told her, looking down at her notebook and flipping the page to the menu they'd come up with earlier. "We've got your applesauce with Michelle's Lick Your Chops Pork." She turned to her youngest sister. "Your pork dish has potatoes, doesn't it?"

"Yes. It has potatoes and gravy, with onions, bell peppers, and mushrooms on the side. It's yummy and goopy, if you know what I mean, so we'll need some kind of bread to soak up the gravy."

"How about a quick bread?" Hannah suggested.

Andrea looked puzzled. "What's a quick bread?"

"A bread without yeast," Hannah explained. "Savory muffins are a quick bread and so are biscuits. Actually, so is banana bread, but I wouldn't serve it with pork chops. How about cranberry biscuits? Cranberries go well with pork."

"Do you have a recipe for those?" Andrea asked.

"No, but I can wing it. I'll try them out later this afternoon to see if they work."

"I'll be at the office until five," Andrea informed her. "You can always call me and I can taste them for you. I could even take a couple home to Bill to get his opinion."

Hannah smiled. She knew exactly what Bill's opinion would be. He loved biscuits in any way, shape, or form and he was also fond of cranberries. "Good idea," she told Andrea. "I'll call you when they're ready."

■ ■ ■ ■

Hannah was just sitting down with her mid-afternoon cup of coffee when Lisa came into the kitchen carrying an empty display jar. "Thanks for the invitation, Hannah. Herb and I would love to come to dinner at your place."

"Good," Hannah said, motioning toward an empty stool. "Did Michelle cue you in about my goof with Norman?"

"Yes, between delivering cookies and refilling coffee cups, I got the whole story in eleven parts and we'll be glad to help you out." She glanced at the empty package of sweetened dried cranberries on the counter. "Are you making Boggles? Or cranberry muffins?"

"No, but you're close. I'm not making cookies and I'm not making muffins. I'm baking Cranberry Biscuits."

"Are they an experiment?" Lisa guessed.

"Yes. If they turn out all right, we'll serve them for dinner Thursday night."

Just then the timer rang. Lisa followed Hannah to the oven and watched as she opened the door. "They smell good," she said. "Hold on for a second and I'll get the empty baker's rack."

241

Hannah waited until Lisa wheeled the rack into position and then she took out the first two pans of biscuits. She slid them onto the rack and was just turning around to grab another set of pans when Lisa spoke again.

"They look good, too. I think you've got a winner, Hannah."

"We'll have to taste them before we know for sure," Hannah said as she took out another two pans. As she placed them on the racks, she decided that Lisa was right. The biscuits were a beautiful golden color and they smelled so good her mouth began to water.

"I don't know if I can wait until they cool," Lisa said, her eyes fixed on the top rack as Hannah removed two more pans.

"Wait for what?"

Both Hannah and Lisa turned to see Michelle standing in the doorway.

"Wait for these cranberry biscuits of Hannah's to cool," Lisa explained.

"You'll have to wait a few minutes at least," Michelle informed her. "Everyone is clamoring for you to tell the Judge Colfax story again. Bertie Straub is back for the fourth time today."

Lisa turned back to Hannah. "Promise to save one of those cranberry biscuits for me?"

"I promise, but I don't think that'll be a problem. I just baked eight pans."

Lisa hurried back into the coffee shop and Michelle went to the full baker's rack to fill the empty display jar Lisa had brought in with Peanut Butter and Jam Cookies. "Mike came in a couple of minutes ago. He said he wanted to listen to Lisa's story. Do you want me to send him back here when Lisa finishes so that you can invite him to dinner in person?"

Hannah almost groaned. She really didn't want to see Mike. She'd already done the wrong thing with Norman and that made her leery of doing the wrong thing with Mike, too. She wanted to ask Michelle to invite him, but since she'd invited Norman, she supposed it was only right to invite Mike herself and not rely on a third person to do it. When she did, she'd be very careful what she said.

"Okay," Hannah gave a little nod. "Tell Mike I'd like to see him. I'll be right here, reading over the notes I made at the courthouse this morning."

After Michelle left, Hannah got out her notes. Dave had given her the names of five suspects. One was Chad Norton. She'd already written his name on her list, but she made a notation next to it. *Temper,* she

243

wrote. *Court ordered anger management course.*

The next suspect she'd added was Sheila Dortweiler. She noted the fact that Sheila had inherited from her father and that she was supporting her musician son. Hannah would definitely go to visit Sheila in Annandale.

Seth Dortweiler was the third suspect on Hannah's list. She'd talk to Michelle about going to see Seth when he was performing with Liquid Steel.

And then there was Nora Colfax, Judge Colfax's widow. Hannah added her name to the suspect list because family members of the victim were always suspect until proven innocent.

That left only two other suspects and Hannah wrote in Margaret George and her daughter. As she wrote them down, she frowned slightly. She'd met a woman with the last name of George, but she couldn't remember where. She had a feeling it was right here in Lake Eden, but she wasn't sure. It was a pity that Delores couldn't answer her cell phone while she was on the ship. She knew everyone in Lake Eden and if there was a woman named Margaret George, in town, Hannah's mother would know of her.

The enticing aroma of the Cranberry Biscuits pulled Hannah off her stool. She followed the scent like a hunting dog and touched a biscuit on the top rack. It was still a bit on the hot side of warm, but she didn't care. She simply had to taste one to see if she'd succeeded.

Hannah didn't bother with a napkin. She juggled the hot biscuit from hand to hand as she walked back to the workstation. She broke it open, dropped the two halves quickly, and went after the butter. She got a stick out of the walk-in cooler and placed it on a plate. Of course, she'd prefer softened butter, but the biscuits were still so hot, they'd melt the butter in no time at all.

A moment later, part of the biscuit was buttered. She'd been right. The butter melted almost immediately. Hannah picked up her creation and bit into it, chewing rapidly so that she wouldn't burn the inside of her mouth. The cranberries were tender and the taste was good. As a matter of fact, it was much more than good. Her Cranberry Biscuits were incredibly delicious and that meant she'd succeeded!

CRANBERRY BISCUITS

Preheat oven to 425 degrees F., rack in the middle position.

3 cups all-purpose flour *(pack it down in the cup when you measure it)*

2 teaspoons cream of tartar *(this is important)*

1 teaspoon baking powder

1 teaspoon baking soda

1 teaspoon salt

1/2 cup salted butter *(1 stick, 4 ounces, 1/4 pound)*

8-ounce package cream cheese, softened *(I used Philadelphia in the silver box)*

2 large eggs, beaten *(just whip them up in a glass with a fork)*

1 cup sour cream *(8 ounces)*

1/2 cup milk *(see Hannah's 1st Note)*

1/2 cup sweetened dried cranberries *(I used Craisins)*

Hannah's 1st Note: Sometimes you may need to add more or less milk so that all the ingredients combine in a wet/dry mixture that's about the consistency of cottage cheese. I've made these biscuits several times and I've never

had to use less or more than a half-cup of milk. I don't think you'll have to adjust it either, but you can if you need to.

FIRST STEP
Prepare your baking sheets by spraying them with Pam or covering them with parchment paper. If your baking sheets are small, you may need to prepare 2 sheets since this recipe makes 12 very large biscuits.

SECOND STEP
Use a medium-size mixing bowl to combine the flour, cream of tartar, baking powder, baking soda, and salt. Stir them all up together. Cut in the salted butter just as you would for piecrust dough.

Hannah's 2nd Note: If you have a food processor, you can use it for the first step. Cut 1/2 cup COLD salted butter into 8 chunks. Layer them with the dry ingredients in the bowl of the food processor. Process with the steel blade in an on-and-off motion until the mixture has the texture of cornmeal. Transfer the mixture to a medium-sized mixing bowl and proceed to the next step.

THIRD STEP
Stir in the softened cream cheese. Add the beaten eggs and the sour cream in that order. Mix everything all up together.

Add the milk and stir until everything is thoroughly combined.

Sprinkle in the sweetened dried cranberries and mix them in thoroughly.

FOURTH STEP
Use a soup spoon to drop the biscuits by rounded spoonfuls onto the baking sheet(s) you've prepared. Leave at least and inch and a half clearance between each biscuit.

Once the biscuits are on the baking sheet(s), wet your fingertips and shape them into nice-looking rounds. (I leave mine slightly irregular so everyone will know that they haven't come out of a paper tube in the refrigerated section of the Red Owl.)

FIFTH STEP
Bake the biscuits at 425 degrees F. for 12 to 14 minutes, or until they're golden brown on top.

Cool the biscuits for at least 5 minutes on

the cookie sheet, and then remove them with a metal spatula. Serve them in a towel-lined basket so that they stay warm.

Yield: Makes 12 large biscuits that every-one will love, especially if you use them to accompany ham, pork, or turkey!

Hannah's 3rd Note: If there are any leftover biscuits, store them in a plastic bag at room temperature. They're won-derful for breakfast the next day. All I do is split them, toast them, and slather them with butter.

Lisa's Note: I'm going to try these for turkey sandwiches the day after Thanks-giving. I think Herb will love them!

CHAPTER FIFTEEN

"Hi, Hannah," Mike said, coming in the swinging door from the coffee shop. "How are you?"

"I'm fine," Hannah said.

"How was Vegas?" Mike asked. "I was going to ask you right away, but I had a lot on my mind when I saw you at the courthouse yesterday."

Interrogated me would be a better description than saw me, Hannah's mind said. *And of course you couldn't ask me when you came to the condo, because you were too busy continuing to interrogate me!*

"Vegas was good." Hannah answered, leaving it at that. She knew that Mike was going to pump her for information right after he'd finished with the niceties. That was his pattern. She also knew because he was wearing the perfectly innocent expression that she'd seen on Moishe's face as he waited for exactly the right instant to pounce on a mouse. "The wedding was great."

"That's what Norman told me. He said that Ross was Doc's best man. And he told me that Ross is coming to Lake Eden for an interview at KCOW Television."

"That's right."

"Is he moving back to Lake Eden?"

There was no hint of jealousy in Mike's voice and Hannah realized that Norman hadn't acted very jealous either. Perhaps neither one of the men she'd dated would be upset if Ross got the job and returned to Lake Eden. Hannah wasn't sure if she should be relieved, or upset so she tabled that thought to think about later. "I don't know if that'll happen or not, but we have an invitation for you. Michelle and I are throwing a little dinner party for Ross on Thursday night. Can you come?"

"Sure. It'll be good to see Ross again. What time?"

"Six o'clock. We'll probably eat around six-thirty."

"Okay. What are you baking, Hannah? Whatever it is, it sure smells good."

That was a hint if she'd ever heard one! Hannah's lips twitched in amusement. Mike was never subtle. "I have some Secret Spice Cookies that should be cool enough to eat.

251

Would you like to try one?"

"That'd be great! I had a couple of Lovely Lemon Bar Cookies in the coffee shop, but I missed lunch and it wasn't quite enough."

Hannah plucked three cookies off the top shelf of the baker's rack and carried them to Mike. "Here you go. This is a new recipe from Lisa's Aunt Nancy. Let me know what you think."

Mike took a bite and chewed. "Nice spice," he said, taking another large bite. "These cookies are really good. They're unusual, too. I can taste cinnamon and nutmeg and maybe cloves, but there's some spice in there I can't identify."

"I know," Hannah said, getting up to fetch another couple of cookies as Mike wolfed down the second one. She carried them to the work island, set them down, and said, "It's ketchup."

"What?!"

"There's ketchup in these cookies."

"You mean like what you put on hamburgers?"

"The very same thing. Lisa's Aunt Nancy fools people with these cookies all the time. Nobody can guess the secret spice."

Mike took another cookie and chewed thoughtfully. "I can almost taste it, but not quite. And I never would have guessed it.

I'll buy two dozen before I leave and take them out to the sheriff's department. Wait until Lonnie and Rick taste these! They'll never believe what's in them. Are you going to serve them for dessert Thursday night? I bet Ross won't be able to guess it either."

"Probably not. Aunt Nancy says nobody ever has. But I'm serving Tangerine Dream Cake on Thursday."

"That's a great cake! I'll be there unless I'm arresting Judge Colfax's killer. And that reminds me. How's your investigation coming?"

Hannah shrugged and tried to look casual. She was glad she'd asked Mike to dinner before he'd started to grill her about what she'd learned. If she'd waited, she might not have felt like asking him. "It's going okay, I guess. I haven't gotten very far yet."

"You got far enough to interview Dave Johansen at the courthouse this morning."

Mike knew, and that meant he was keeping tabs on her. Hannah didn't like it, but there was nothing she could do about it. "Yes, I went out to talk to him," she admitted. "When I met Dave yesterday, Howie mentioned that Dave had worked there for years, and I thought talking to him would be a good place to start. I'm assuming that you interviewed him, too?"

"That guy knows everything about every-body involved with the courthouse."

"That's exactly what Howie said about him." It was a good opening and Hannah wanted to find out what Dave had told Mike. "Did Dave tell you about Judge Colfax's first wife?"

"Yeah. He said that it was a bitter divorce so I'll go to talk to her. The son is another person I want to contact. Kids from broken homes can have big grudges against the absent parent. I've seen that more times than I can count. His name is Seth, right?"

"That's what Dave said."

"Did he mention anyone else?"

"He talked about Chad Norton first. He told me that Chad has a hair-trigger temper, and one of the judges found him in contempt of court and ordered Chad to complete an anger management course. I added his name to my suspect list."

"He's on my list, too. Actually, he's my prime suspect right now, but that could change. I'm calling him in this afternoon to see if he's got an alibi."

"Will you let me know?"

"Why?"

"Because I thought we were sharing information."

"We are. Just don't forget that you're a

civilian. Law enforcement is privy to certain information that civilians aren't.""

Same old, same old, Hannah thought, but she didn't say it. She just sat there and waited to hear what else Mike would say.

"I know it's not fair, but those are the rules. As a sworn law enforcement officer, I can't break the rules."

Hannah knew she should remain silent, but she simply couldn't. "You've broken those rules before."

"I know, but I won't do it again. It's not the sort of thing an ethical cop should do." Mike glanced down at his notebook. "Let's get back to business. Is there anyone else on your suspect list?"

Hannah dropped her gaze so that Mike couldn't see how angry she was. He expected her to share her information with him, but he wasn't willing to return the favor. Was he holding out on her? There was only one way to find out.

"Any other suspects on your list?" Mike asked her again.

"I gave you my suspects," she said, quite truthfully. She *had* given him her suspects. Perhaps not *all* of her suspects, but information sharing was a two-way street. "It's time for you to reciprocate, Mike. Are there any other suspects on your list?"

Mike looked down at his list. "Nope. That's it for now."

He was lying! Either that, or Dave hadn't told him about Margaret George and her daughter. Whatever the case, Hannah wasn't about to share Dave's information with Mike, at least not until she had the chance to ask Delores about Margaret George.

There was an uncomfortable silence and then the swinging door opened and Tracey came running in. "Hi, Aunt Hannah. Mom said I could go to the mall with you to get your new phone. I did a little research online and I found some new ones that are super and have lots of apps."

"You're going out to the phone store?" Mike asked her.

"Yes. I decided it was time to upgrade when I tried my old phone and it wouldn't turn on."

Mike's eyes narrowed suspiciously. "Did you forget to charge it again?"

"I don't remember, but it doesn't really matter. It's an old flip phone and it's time to replace it."

"It sure is!" Tracey said, plunking down on a stool next to Hannah. "That phone is a real dinosaur."

"What kind of dinosaur?" Mike asked her.

Tracey thought for a moment and then

she smiled. "A Brachiosaurus."

"Why did you compare it to a Brachiosaurus?" Hannah asked her. Tracey always had a reason and she wanted to hear it.

"Because the Brachiosaurus could weigh up to forty-five metric tons and your old cell phone is heavy. It's big, too, and a Brachiosaurus could grow as long as eighty-five feet."

Mike whistled. "That's long!"

"Yes, it is. It's more than three-quarters the length of the football field at Jordan High!"

"That's right," Hannah said. "I'd hate to have something that big coming after me."

"The Brachiosaurus is an herbivore," Tracey informed her. "They only eat plants, but they eat a lot. They could eat through almost nine hundred pounds of plants a day."

"Were they the biggest dinosaur?" Mike asked her.

"No. That's the T-Rex." Tracey turned back to Hannah. "Another reason I chose the Brachiosaurus is because some of them lived right here in the United States. Not only that, but the first fossils were found by a farmer and we have a lot of farmers around here."

"Those are all good reasons," Hannah told

her. "Just hearing them convinced me that I should buy a new phone. If I keep my Brachiosaurus cell phone, we won't have any plants left in my whole condo complex."

Tracey giggled and Hannah was gratified. She loved to hear both of her nieces laugh.

"I'll take you both out to the mall with me," Mike offered. "I have to pick up a new phone, too. I had a little accident with my phone this morning."

"Thanks, Uncle Mike," Tracey accepted his offer before Hannah could say a word. "What happened to your phone?"

"I . . . uh . . . I dropped it in the toilet."

"You don't have to be embarrassed about that," Tracey told him. "My dad's done it three times already. Mom told him not to take his phone with him in the bathroom anymore, but Dad says he has to check his e-mail first thing in the morning."

"That's exactly what I was doing," Mike said.

"Toilets and cell phones don't play well together," Tracey said, looking wise. "This boy in my class, Calvin Janowski, did the same thing and his mother took his cell phone away for a whole month! Do you have yours with you?"

"It's in a bag in the cruiser."

"Oh, good! We're going in the cruiser?"

Mike nodded and Tracey looked delighted. "Can I sit in back and pretend to be a dangerous criminal?"

"If you want to."

"Thanks, Uncle Mike. It'll be fun."

"But it's just pretend, right?" Hannah asked. "You don't really want to be a dangerous criminal, do you?"

"Of course not!" Tracey was clearly shocked. "I just want to practice my acting skills since Uncle Ross is coming to town. You're coming to dinner, aren't you, Uncle Mike? Our whole family is going to be there."

"I know. Your Aunt Hannah told me. I'll be there."

"Maybe you can help me teach Aunt Hannah how to use her phone, especially if you get the same kind. I'll download the instruction manual on Mom's computer at work. They've got a faster printer than we do." Tracey turned to Hannah. "You'd better make sure you have your credit card, Aunt Hannah. New cell phones are expensive."

"I'll go check right now," Hannah said and went off to get her purse. It was hanging by the back door and even though she was out of sight, she could still hear Tracey and Mike's conversation.

"Mom said Aunt Lisa and Uncle Herb are

259

coming, too," Tracey told him. "And Uncle Norman is bringing Cuddles so she can see Moishe. Maybe they'll play chase and bang into the table leg again."

Hannah smiled. She *knew* they'd play chase, especially if she baited them with bits of her pork chop.

"I can hardly wait to pick out Aunt Hannah's phone," Tracey said, sounding excited at the prospect. "She needs lots of help with technology. And I'm glad we're all going shopping together."

"Me, too," Mike said. "I'm just thinking that maybe I should upgrade my phone, too. It's almost two years old."

"That's ancient," Tracey told him. "Are you due for an upgrade from your provider?"

"Not yet, but I'll just buy it out-of-pocket."

"You might not have to. Check with the clerk at the phone store. Sometimes you can get a new phone or some kind of a discount if you switch providers."

"That's a good idea. I'll do that."

"And take your old phone in anyway to have it dried out. That way you can give it to Helping Hands to sell in their thrift store, and take a deduction on your income tax. That's what my mom did with her old cell phone. I'm going to try to convince Aunt Hannah to do the same thing with hers."

"Maybe you'd better hold off until you talk to someone at Helping Hands," Mike cautioned.

"Why should I do that?"

"Because they might not take dinosaurs."

"That's a good one, Uncle Mike!" Tracey gave a little giggle and then she broke into delighted laugher.

Mike joined in and Hannah smiled at the sound of their mirth.

When their laughter trailed off, Tracey spoke again. "Thanks for inviting us to go with you, Uncle Mike. It's kind of warm this afternoon and it would be hot inside the cookie truck. Aunt Hannah's air-conditioning doesn't work right."

"I know. Her climate-control system is practically nonexistent. Your Aunt Hannah's truck has four-sixty air-conditioning."

"What's that?"

"Four windows rolled down at sixty miles an hour. It's the only way you can cool off in her cookie truck."

Buying a new phone didn't take long and Hannah was glad to get back to The Cookie Jar. When she walked in the back door, she found Lisa and Michelle waiting for her in the kitchen.

"Did you get it?" Michelle asked.

"Yes. It's beautiful, but I have to wait until tomorrow night to learn how to use it."

"Why?"

"Because that's when Tracey promised to teach me."

"You don't have to wait," Lisa said, looking extremely confident. "You can always get the instructions online. That's what I did when I got my new phone."

"Good for you, but that won't work for me."

"Why not?"

"Because I don't even know how to turn it on. I'll just have to wait until Tracey teaches me."

Michelle and Lisa exchanged glances, and Hannah knew what they were thinking. "I know you think I'm clueless. You're right. I am. Maybe I could figure it out, but I'm going to wait for Tracey. She's very proud of the fact that she gets to teach her dinosaur aunt how to use her new cell phone."

"I'll bet she is!" Lisa said, smiling at the thought. "We teach her things all the time. Just the other day, she asked me how our oven worked, so I showed her."

"I taught her something, too," Michelle told them. "Tracey came in yesterday, after school, and she said she knew I'd taken a dance class in college and she wanted me to teach her to dance."

"That's exactly why I want to wait," Hannah told them. "Adults teach her things all the time, but this time it'll be different. Tracey can be the teacher and attempt to teach a clueless adult like me how to use my new cell phone."

SECRET SPICE COOKIES

Preheat oven to 350 degrees F., rack in the middle position.

2 cups all-purpose flour *(pack it down in the cup when you measure it)*
2 teaspoons baking soda
2 teaspoons ground ginger
1 teaspoon ground cinnamon
1/2 teaspoon ground allspice
1/2 teaspoon salt
1 cup white *(granulated)* sugar
1/3 cup tomato ketchup *(I used Heinz)*
1/4 cup salted butter *(1/2 stick, 2 ounces, 4 Tablespoons)*
1/4 cup vegetable oil
1/4 cup molasses
1 large egg, beaten *(just whip it up in a glass with a fork)*
2 teaspoons vanilla extract
1/4 cup white *(granulated)* sugar for coating the dough balls prior to baking

Either spray your cookie sheets with Pam or another nonstick cooking spray or line them with parchment paper.

Place the flour in the bowl of an electric mixer *(or in a mixing bowl if you want to stir the cookie dough by hand, but it'll take some muscle).*

Sprinkle in the baking soda and turn the mixer to low speed to combine them.

Add the ginger, cinnamon, allspice, and salt. Mix them in at low speed.

Mix in the granulated sugar at low speed.

In a microwave-safe bowl, combine the ketchup, butter, oil, and molasses. Heat the mixture on HIGH for 30 seconds or until the butter has melted.

Let the bowl sit in the microwave for another 30 seconds and then stir to combine the ingredients.

With the mixer running, add the ketchup, butter, oil, and molasses mixture. Beat until thoroughly combined.

Add the egg and mix it in at medium speed. Then mix in the vanilla extract and beat until all ingredients are thoroughly combined.

Take the bowl from the mixer, scrape down the sides with a rubber spatula, and give the bowl a final stir by hand.

Place the 1/4 cup sugar in a small, shallow bowl.

Using a small scooper *(Lisa and I used a 2-teaspoon size at The Cookie Jar),* form dough balls from the cookie dough. If the dough isn't firm enough to do this, cover it with plastic wrap and refrigerate it for one hour. *(Don't forget to turn off your oven if you do this!)*

Roll the dough balls, one at a time, in the bowl of sugar to coat them. Then place them on a prepared cookie sheet, no more than 12 cookie dough balls to a standard-size sheet.

Hannah's Note: Lisa is going to try rolling some dough balls in powdered sugar the next time we bake these. She thinks it'll have a different visual effect, but we may miss the crunch of granulated sugar.

Bake the Secret Spice Cookies at 350 degrees F. for 10 to 12 minutes or until the cookies are golden brown around the edges.

Take the cookies out of the oven and let the cookie sheet sit on a cold stovetop burner or a wire rack for 2 minutes. Then pull the parchment paper off the cookie sheet and onto a wire rack to allow the cookies to cool completely.

Yield: approximately 3 dozen tasty cookies, depending on cookie size, spiced with a secret ingredient that no one who didn't watch you make them will be able to identify.

CHAPTER SIXTEEN

"It always smells so good in here!" Michelle took a deep breath as they walked past the huge stone fireplace in the lobby of the Lake Eden Inn.

"That's because Sally is a great cook," Hannah told her, heading for the stand that was positioned just inside the dining room door.

"I think I smell chicken Kiev. Maybe I'll have that tonight. I love Sally's chicken Kiev."

"I agree it's wonderful, but wait until we hear the specials. Sally's specials are always . . . special."

Their favorite waitress was working at the reservation stand and Hannah greeted her with a smile. "Hi, Dot. Is Norman here yet?"

"He's here and so are Lonnie and Mike. Andrea just called. They're running late, but they're leaving the house right now and coming straight out here. They said to start and not wait for them. Just follow me and I'll take you to Norman's table."

"Thanks, Dot," Hannah said, choosing to walk beside her instead of following. "How's the baby?"

"Not a baby anymore. Just ask him. If you do, he'll tell you that he's a big boy. My mother told him that *big boys* don't wear diapers and she's got him in training pants. And then she said that *big boys* had to learn to use the potty and he did!"

"That's amazing. He's still really young, isn't he?"

"Twenty months and he's already potty trained . . . most of the time. He still has an occasional mistake, but he's really pretty good. My mother is incredible with things like that. I wouldn't be surprised if she taught him to read next year." Dot stopped as she reached Norman's table. "Here you go, ladies. I'll be back."

"She walks in beauty like the night," Lonnie said as Michelle approached.

"I just love guys who quote poetry to me," Michelle said, giving him a little kiss on the top of the head before she sat down.

"How about an appetizer while we wait for Andrea and Bill?" Norman suggested.

"Good idea!" Mike said. "I skipped lunch and I'm starved."

Hannah was amused, but she didn't say anything about the fact that Mike had eaten two cookies in the coffee shop and even more cookies with her in the kitchen. It seemed that Mike's appetite rivaled Howie's.

"Hi, everyone," Sally said, arriving at their table in time to hear Norman's suggestion. "How about my baked Brie for your appetizer? It's brushed with butter and has French herbs on the top. I serve it with little knots of fresh bread that you can dip in the cheese that runs out when you cut a slice."

"I'm for that," Hannah said quickly and then she looked at everyone else around the table. "Does anyone else want Sally's baked Brie?"

"I do," Michelle said. "I'm in a cheese mood."

"I feel like meat," Mike said, turning to Sally for advice.

"How about our flatbread covered with pulled pork, cheddar, and baked apples? Or flatbread that's topped with mozzarella, feta cheese, caramelized onions, and chopped fresh tomatoes with a hint of fresh basil? Both of them are really good. I had pulled pork flatbread today for lunch."

"Let's try both," Norman suggested. "And I'd like to order some wine. "What do you have in a white?"

"I'd recommend the Stone Cellar Chardonnay, the Matua Sauvignon Blanc, or the Rodney Strong Sauvignon Blanc. They're all excellent wines."

"Hannah?" Norman turned to her. "What's your preference?"

"I'll let Sally choose. I know I'll be fine with whatever she thinks will go best with her baked Brie."

"Sally?" Norman looked up at her.

"I'll bring the Matua. I think Hannah will like that. Do you want wine, Michelle? I know you're over twenty-one."

Michelle hesitated for a moment and then she nodded. "Just half a glass. I really enjoy white wine with Brie."

"How about you boys? Would you like a red?"

"I wish!" Mike said, sounding wistful. "Unfortunately, I have to write some reports when I get back tonight."

"How about you, Lonnie?"

Lonnie glanced at Mike, who nodded. "Go ahead. You're off duty and I won't need you anymore today."

"Thanks," Lonnie told him and then he turned to Sally. "I won't drink any more than one glass. It's a waste to open a whole bottle for just me."

"It won't be just you," Hannah told him. "Bill will have some when he gets here. He likes red wine. And I know that Andrea will share our bottle of white."

"She'll like it, I'm sure," Michelle said, deliberately avoiding Hannah's eyes. Both of them knew that Andrea adored the wine that Hannah privately called Chateau Screwtop. Andrea fancied herself a wine snob and the last time she'd tasted it, she'd described Hannah's wine as "a delicate but impish white with a hint of citrus." Both Hannah and Michelle knew that Andrea would be horribly embarrassed if she ever found out that Hannah bought it by the jug at CostMart for well under ten dollars. Hannah kept the jug hidden behind a large pickle jar on the bottom shelf of her refrigerator and never let Andrea pour her own wine.

"So what else did you do in Vegas for fun?" Norman asked Hannah when Sally had left.

Hannah avoided glancing in Michelle's direction. "We discovered a couple of new recipes."

"For what?" Mike asked.

"German Chocolate Cupcakes," Michelle answered him. "They were delicious."

"I'd like to taste those," Lonnie said. "My

mother made German Chocolate Cake. It was one of her specialties."

Hannah thought this was a bit strange, considering Bridget Murphy's background. Bridget O'Sheehan had come to Lake Eden as a high school exchange student from Ireland and Cyril's parents had hosted her. Cyril had shepherded the pretty Irish girl through the six months she'd spent at Jordan High. When Bridget went back to Ireland, Cyril had stayed in touch and when he'd taken over his father's business, he'd called Bridget and asked her if she'd like to come back to Lake Eden and run his front office. Bridget had accepted his offer and the rest was history.

"I'm surprised Bridget didn't make an Irish dessert her specialty," Hannah told Lonnie.

"I asked her about that once. She said she grew up eating Irish desserts and she wanted to make something completely different."

Dot came up with the wine before Hannah could ask any more questions about Irish desserts. She handed a full, two-serving wine carafe to Norman, along with an empty tumbler. "Here you go, Norman. Do you want me to pour?"

"I can do it, Dot. Go ahead and open the wine for everyone else."

Everyone at the table knew the identity of the liquid in Norman's carafe. It was ginger ale. Norman didn't drink, but only Hannah knew why he never touched alcohol. He'd told her one day in strict confidence and she'd never told anyone else. It all had to do with a night, several years before he'd moved to Lake Eden, when he was working as a dentist in Seattle. He'd gotten drunk, done some things he knew would embarrass his mother, and ended up in jail. Norman hadn't touched a drop of alcohol since.

"Here come Bill and Andrea," Hannah said, spotting her sister and brother-in-law coming in the door to the dining room.

"Hey," Bill said when they got to the table. "How's my crackerjack detective team?"

"Good," Mike said, and Lonnie nodded.

"Hannah, Michelle . . . I've been so busy, I haven't seen either one of you since you got back from Vegas, but Andrea tells me you had a great time."

"We did," Michelle said.

"It was fun," Hannah responded, glancing at Andrea who gave a little shake of her head. Hannah knew what the shake meant. Andrea hadn't told Bill anything personal about Hannah's relationship with Ross.

"Norman?" Bill went on. "Thanks for the

invite. It's always good to see you again, unless I have to sit in your dental chair. Then it's a real pain."

"Not true," Norman looked perfectly serious, but Hannah noticed that his eyes were sparkling with humor. "Don't you know? I'm the *painless* dentist."

There was laughter around the table, and Bill and Andrea joined in.

Then Andrea said, "I hope we didn't keep you waiting too long. Bethie wanted to watch *Snow White* and it took me awhile to find it. We have over a hundred children's movies. Our den is practically a kid theater!"

When they were seated Norman said, "We ordered some appetizers and some wine." He gestured toward the bottles Dot was opening. "Red wine, Bill?"

"That would be good. I'm through for the day."

"And white for you, Andrea?"

Andrea nodded. "What is it?"

"Matua Sauvignon Blanc," Dot answered her. "I haven't tasted it yet, but Sally says it's very good."

Andrea smiled. "If Sally says so, it's got to be good. She really knows her wines. Of course, nothing can compare to the wine that Hannah lays in for me. It's the best I've ever tasted."

"Thanks," Hannah said, and her mind went into high gear to search for another topic to discuss. Her gaze focused on Andrea's lovely red and gold scarf and she knew she had the perfect conversation changer. "That's a beautiful scarf, Andrea. And that reminds me . . . did you leave a scarf at my place the last time you were there?"

"I don't think so. What does it look like?"

"It's silk and it's over . . ." She turned to Michelle. "How long would you say that scarf was?"

"It's just a guess, but I'm sure it's around three feet. I didn't measure it."

"I have some long scarves. Bill gave me one for Christmas. What color is it?"

Hannah did her best to remember. "It has gorgeous blue flowers on a green background."

"It's not a geometric design," Michelle added. "The flowers are large and almost abstract. And each one is a different size and a slightly different shade of blue."

"That sounds beautiful, but it's not mine. I've never had a scarf like that. Where did you find it?"

"Moishe found it. He had it on the floor in the living room when Michelle and I got back after work."

"It could be Mother's," Andrea suggested. "She always wears a scarf with her suits. Do you want me to text her?"

"Not really. If it's hers, I can't get it to her until she comes home anyway. In the meantime, we'll just ask everyone who's been at my place if it's theirs."

"I don't suppose you know where Moishe found it," Mike said, and Hannah figured his detective mind wasn't idle.

"No," she answered him. "I'm sure it wasn't in the living room. I would have found it long before this. It's a mystery."

Mike smiled. "Well, you like mysteries. I'm sure you can solve a little one like that. All you have to do is make out a list of women who've been in your condo. And then you have to call each one and ask her if she's missing a scarf. That's what I'd do."

Hannah wanted to tell him that she wasn't an idiot and she'd already done that, but she didn't say it. This was Norman's party and she wasn't about to spoil it. "Thanks, Mike," she said sweetly and hoped her thanks hadn't come out too sarcastically.

"You're welcome, Hannah."

Hannah searched Mike's face and decided that he hadn't heard any sarcasm in her tone. If he had, he would have returned their exchange with a nasty comment.

"This isn't the first time we've found something like that," Michelle said. "Moishe was playing with some kind of sash the other day. It looked like it was from a robe or a dressing gown."

"And I don't have anything in that color," Hannah added, and then she turned to Mike. "And we don't know where he got that, either."

"Maybe you've got a kleptomaniac cat," Norman suggested, and everyone laughed.

"I know waitresses aren't supposed to comment on people's private conversations, but there are kleptomaniac cats." Dot said, arriving with an ice bucket for the white wine.

"You're kidding!" Michelle turned to Dot in surprise.

"No, I'm not. When I get off work late, sometimes I can't fall asleep right away. That's when I get up, go to the living room for a cup of tea, and turn on one of those late night news programs."

"That's exactly what I do," Mike said. "It gets my mind off whatever case I'm working. And it's so boring, it gets me sleepy."

Dot gave him a smile. "That's right. So I was sitting there sipping my tea and letting some anchorman jabber away when I heard something about a kleptomaniac cat."

"So you listened," Michelle guessed.

"Yeah. And the story didn't come on for fifteen minutes. I was almost ready to turn off the TV and give up when he showed this picture of a tabby cat with a necklace in her mouth."

"Photoshopped?" Norman asked.

"I don't think so. I don't remember exactly where she lived, but this lady said her cat went out prowling during the day and came home with other people's things. She said the cat, I think she said her cat's name was Tippy, had started coming home with her loot. She wanted to tell people about it and say that if they were missing any jewelry or clothing, they should come over to her garage on Saturday and claim their stolen items."

"Do you think that could possibly be true?" Hannah asked.

Mike shrugged. "Maybe. I've heard of crows and ravens flying off with sparkling things and putting them in their nests. I guess cats could do the same thing."

"Well, I just thought I'd mention the possibility." Dot refilled any wineglasses that needed it and placed the white wine in the bucket of ice she'd brought. "I'm going to go check on your appetizers. They should be coming out in the next couple of minutes."

"Thanks, Dot," Hannah told her. "And thanks for telling us about that cat. I don't think that's the case with Moishe, but it's really interesting."

"Why can't it be the case with Moishe?" Mike asked her after Dot had left them.

"Because he can't get out."

"Do you have any loose screens?" Mike asked her.

"I could have loose screens, but they wouldn't do him any good. I never leave any windows open when I leave the condo in the morning."

"Is there any other way you can think of that Moishe could be using to get out?"

Hannah shook her head. "No. I always check the windows to make sure they're closed and locked. And right after I step out on the landing, I check the door to make sure it's locked."

"And there's no other entrance or exit to your apartment?"

"No." Hannah frowned slightly. Mike was acting as the interrogator again and she didn't like it. "You've been there enough times to know that all I have is the one staircase."

"How about a dryer vent? That would

have access to the outside."

"That's true," Hannah conceded. "But I close my dryer door after I use it and it's still hooked up to the vent. I know because I used it last night and it was working just fine."

"An attic?"

"I have an attic. It serves the whole building. But the only way to get up there is to go through a little trap door in the ceiling of my bedroom walk-in closet."

"Have you checked that trap door lately?"

Hannah thought about that for a moment. "Actually . . . no. I'll check it as soon as I get home."

"If that's not it, call me," Mike said, looking amused. "I've got a new surveillance system that a security company asked me to test for them. I'll come over and install it at your place and we'll make sure that Moishe isn't getting out."

"Thanks, Mike," Hannah said, and this time she was totally genuine in her gratitude. If Moishe was getting out during the day, she wanted to know about it so she could cut off his escape route and keep him safely at home.

CHAPTER SEVENTEEN

She was getting dressed for church in a phone booth. It wasn't an ordinary phone booth like the ones they had outside city hall in Lake Eden. This phone booth had stained glass on three sides, very like the church windows in Reverend Bob's church. And now that she looked, she noticed that there were pews in front of the fourth side of the phone booth, the one with clear glass.

The pews were beginning to fill up with people. As she watched, Hannah realized she had to hurry to get ready or church would start without her. She turned to Ross, who was in the phone booth with her, and handed him his tuxedo jacket. Now Ross was ready, but she wasn't. Where was her wedding gown? She couldn't get married like this!

There was laughter from the front pew. Bertie Straub. Hannah recognized her laugh. Rod Metcalf sat beside her and he was taking photos. They would be in tomorrow's paper and she couldn't find her wedding gown. She searched the phone booth, but it wasn't there. Had she left it at home in her closet?

And now the phone was ringing, one ring, two rings. She had no choice. She was forced to answer it.

She reached out and her fingers touched the phone on her bed table. *Her bed table.* It was a dream, but the phone was still ringing.

"Hello," she managed to say, sitting up in bed and shaking her head to clear it.

"Hannah? Did I wake you?"

It was Mike. Was he real, or was he part of her dream?

She wasn't in the phone booth any longer and she was wearing the sleep shirt she usually wore when she went to bed. "What time is it?" she managed to ask.

"Eight o'clock. I called The Cookie Jar, but Michelle said you weren't in yet."

Hannah glanced at her alarm clock. Mike was right. It was eight o'clock. Michelle must have turned off her alarm so that she could sleep late again.

"I *did* wake you, didn't I?" Mike sounded apologetic, a rarity for him.

Hannah hurried to reassure him. "Yes, but

I'm glad you did. I have to get up and get started. I have a ton of things to do today."

"Don't we all!" Mike gave an audible sigh. "Did you get a chance to check that trap door in your closet?"

For a moment, Hannah was at a loss. What was he talking about? Then she remembered why he'd asked about the trap door. "I checked it when I got home last night. It was closed."

"And there's no way Moishe could have opened it to get up there, and closed it when he came down?"

Hannah laughed. "He's smart, but he's not *that* smart."

"Right. I was just exploring all the possibilities. I brought that surveillance system with me to work this morning. If you want me to, I can run out there and install it right now. It should only take ten or fifteen minutes."

"That'd be great!"

"Then I'll leave here in five and you'll see me in twenty. Does that work for you?"

"Perfectly," Hannah said. "Thanks, Mike."

Five minutes later, she had gulped her first cup of coffee and was stepping into the shower. Ten minutes later, she was dressed and back in the kitchen, wondering what she could fix for breakfast. That was when

283

she saw the note Michelle had left propped up between the salt and pepper shakers on the kitchen table.

Baked Fruited Oatmeal in the oven. Lisa picked me up again this morning and we've got it covered. Take your time coming in.

Hannah glanced over at her double ovens. The bottom one was set on WARM and the light was on. She could see a casserole dish inside and it was obviously filled with baked oatmeal. What in the world was baked oatmeal? She'd never heard of it before. It would be good. She knew that. Everything Michelle made was good.

A second or two later, she opened the oven door with a spoon in hand. As she did, a wonderful scent drifted out to entice her and she dipped in her spoon to taste the breakfast dish that Michelle had created. Once she'd blown on her spoon several times to cool it, she tasted the baked oatmeal. "Cinnamon," she said aloud. "And vanilla, and brown sugar. And . . . apricots!" The complexity of flavors was wonderful. Michelle's Baked Fruited Oatmeal was utterly delicious.

She wanted a whole bowlful immediately,

but Hannah forced herself to put the lid back in place and have another cup of coffee instead. She'd wait for Mike and once he'd installed the surveillance system, they could enjoy Michelle's breakfast dish together.

"I like your baked oatmeal," Hannah said, the instant her youngest sister came into the kitchen of The Cookie Jar. "Mike liked it, too. He came over to install the surveillance system and said he hadn't had time for breakfast, so I gave him a bowlful. He told me he doesn't usually like oatmeal, but your oatmeal is the exception."

"Mike doesn't seem like the oatmeal type. Are you sure he wasn't just being polite?"

"I don't think so. He had three helpings."

Michelle laughed. "Then he must have liked it. I'll give you the recipe if you want it."

"I want it. How are the cookies holding out?"

"We're okay so far, but we'll probably blow through what we have left when the noon rush comes in."

"Then I'd better start baking."

"Good idea. I'll help you."

"But don't you have to go out there?" Hannah gestured toward the swinging door that led to the coffee shop.

"Not really. Aunt Nancy's out there and she said she'd stay and help Lisa. She wants to meet you later."

"I want to meet her, too. I'd like to thank her for all the recipes she's given us. We use a lot of them here."

Michelle smiled. "She noticed that right away. She asked Lisa if the spice cookies she was serving were made with her Secret Spice Cookie recipe."

"Was she pleased when Lisa told her that they were?"

"*Pleased* isn't the word. She was practically ecstatic, especially when she realized that people were trying to guess what the secret spice was."

"That's a great recipe and so are all the others she gave us. Is she all moved in?"

"She's in, but she hasn't unpacked everything yet. Right now she's looking for someone who can build floor-to-ceiling bookcases for her kitchen."

Hannah was surprised. Most people had cookbooks in their kitchens, but they didn't need a floor-to-ceiling bookcase to hold them. "She's going to put a floor-to-ceiling bookcase in the kitchen?"

"That's what she said, except think bigger. She's going to cover one whole wall with floor-to-ceiling bookcases."

"Why isn't she putting her books in her living room?"

"She is. She's having bookcases built for the living room, too. And her bedroom."

"How many books does she have?"

"I asked her that and she said she had enough books to make two brawny movers weep."

Hannah laughed. "I think I'm going to really like Aunt Nancy. So she's going to put her overflow books from the bedroom and the living room into her kitchen?"

Michelle shook her head. "Oh, no. The kitchen bookcases are for her cookbooks. And she's buying three file cabinets for her loose recipes."

"Good heavens!"

"I know. We've got to go over and look at her place when everything's unpacked. She might have even more recipes than you do."

Two hours later, Hannah stood back and surveyed her work. The baker's rack was full of cookies and she needed a break. She'd go out into the coffee shop to tell Lisa the cookies were ready and meet Aunt Nancy. If there were some tactful way to ask, she would find out how long Lisa's aunt would be staying to help and if it was long enough, she'd ask Michelle to go with her to see Sheila Dortweiler, Judge Colfax's ex-wife.

Just as Hannah was about to go into the coffee shop, Lisa came through the swinging door. "Oh, good!" she said eyeing the full baker's rack. "We're about to run out of cookies. Would you like to go up front and meet my Aunt Nancy?"

"I'd love to," Hannah said. "Do you have any idea how long she'll be here?"

"In Lake Eden? Or here at The Cookie Jar?"

"Here at The Cookie Jar. If she'll stay to help you in the coffee shop, I'll borrow Michelle and go to see Judge Colfax's ex-wife."

"She'll be happy to stay until closing. As a matter of fact, she asked if she could. She wants to meet Herb and he wants to meet her, so he's dropping by when he gets off work. After that, we planned to stop to see Dad and Marge, but I'll call and ask them to meet us here. We can have coffee and cookies."

"Then it's okay if I take Michelle with me?"

"It's fine. You two go ahead. Aunt Nancy really enjoys meeting new people and she caught on to the coffee shop routine right away. She's always been very sociable and she's helped us a lot this afternoon. If it's okay with you, we might stick around after I close and bake a batch of cookies. She's got a new recipe she wants to show me."

"That's fine with me," Hannah said quickly.

"Oh, good! This is turning into a great day!" Lisa sounded happy and energized, an amazing feat for someone who'd already worked a nine-hour day and still had three hours to go. For the first time in her life, Hannah wished she were ten years younger. She'd been working for less than six hours and she was already craving mindless television and her comfortable living room couch.

"I'm going to invite Dad and Marge if they want to come over to our house for dinner tonight. I made a big pot of spaghetti sauce this morning and I've got Dad's favorite garlic cheese bread all ready to stick in the oven. All I have to do is stop at the Red Owl to pick up salad fixings and Neapolitan ice cream for dessert."

"Take some leftover cookies home with you," Hannah told her. "You can have them with the ice cream."

"Great idea! Aunt Nancy already said she'd come and we'll have a family party."

"Sounds like fun," Hannah said, even

more impressed with Lisa's enthusiasm for what sounded like a lot more work for her.

"Oh, I know it'll be fun! I'll drag out the old photograph albums and if Dad is having a good day, he can tell us family stories."

For one brief moment, Hannah felt sad for Jack Herman. Lisa's father had been diagnosed with Alzheimer's disease and he had good days and not-so-good days. On good days he was almost his old self, a very bright and sociable man.

"Dad loves to tell the story about Uncle Buster and the fish," Lisa went on. "That fish gets bigger every time he tells it!"

Hannah laughed. "That's what usually happens with fish stories. The fish grow in drama, weight, and length. My dad had one he used to tell and Mother always said that the fish started out the size of a minnow and ended up the size of a whale."

"Men are all the same when it comes to fish stories. Come up front with me and I'll introduce you to Aunt Nancy. Then you and Michelle can leave. Grab a few cookies for the ex-Mrs. Colfax. It can't hurt and it might make her put on the coffee and start talking to you."

Hannah smiled and shook her head. "I'll do it, but from what I've heard about Sheila Dortweiler, I'd need a whole display jar full of cookies to sweeten her up."

BAKED FRUITED OATMEAL

Preheat oven to 350 degrees F., rack in the middle position.

Michelle's 1st Note: I got this recipe from Grandma Knudson. She told me it was another recipe from her granddaughter-in-law, Janelle.

2 large eggs

1/2 cup brown sugar *(pack it down in the cup when you measure it)*

1 and 1/2 teaspoons baking powder

1 teaspoon salt

2 teaspoons vanilla

1 teaspoon cinnamon

1/2 cup salted butter, melted *(1 stick, 4 ounces, 1/4 pound)*

1 cup whole milk

3 cups dry oatmeal *(either the original or the Quick 1-Minute) (I used Quaker Quick 1-Minute)*

1 cup raisins or dried fruit *(your choice)*

Grandma Knudson's 1st Note: Janelle says everyone in her family likes dried blueberries in their Baked Oatmeal.

Lightly grease a 2-quart baking dish. Alternatively, you can spray it with Pam or another nonstick baking spray.

Crack the 2 eggs into the baking dish and whisk them up.

Add the brown sugar, baking powder, salt, vanilla, and cinnamon. Mix until everything is well combined.

Stir in the melted butter.

Add the whole milk and stir it in.

Sprinkle in the oatmeal and the dried fruit. Stir until everything is well combined.

Bake, uncovered, at 350 degrees F. for 25 to 30 minutes or until the baked oatmeal is "set" in the center. *(This means that if you hold the baking dish with potholders and shake it gently, the center does not look as if it's still liquid. If it does, bake it until the center is firm.)*

If you're not going to serve this oatmeal immediately, turn off the oven, put a cover on the dish, and leave it in the oven until everyone arrives for breakfast or brunch.

To serve, spoon the oatmeal into cereal bowls and accompany it with a pitcher of warm milk or cream. Alternatively, you can serve it with a dollop of vanilla yogurt and fresh fruit.

Michelle's 2nd Note: My roommates at college like this with raspberries or strawberries. When Lonnie comes to visit, he likes his oatmeal made without fruit and he slices a banana to put on

top of his bowl.

Grandma Knudson's 2nd Note: I make this on Saturday night, cover it with plastic wrap, and stick it in the refrigerator. Then, when I get up early on Sunday morning, I take off the plastic wrap and set it out on the counter for 30 minutes or so to warm up. Then I bake it so that Claire and Bob have a hearty breakfast before Sunday School and morning church services.

CHAPTER EIGHTEEN

"This is pretty," Michelle said as they drove down a well-maintained private road that wound through a grove of pine trees. "I can hardly wait to see the house."

"We may not get to see the house," Hannah told her. "Look over there toward the left."

"What do you mean, we may not . . . oh!" Michelle spotted the set of ornate, wrought-iron gates that blocked the winding road ahead.

Hannah hit the brakes and they stopped at the side of the road. "We need a game plan before we get to those gates. There's probably a buzzer I can press to connect with someone at the house. Whoever answers is going to ask us why we're here. What do you think I should say?"

"We have a cookie delivery for Mrs. Dortweiler from The Cookie Jar bakery in Lake Eden? That's not exactly a lie."

"No, it's not and that might work to get us through the gates, but once we drive up to the house, someone on her staff may come out to the truck to pick up the cookies. And then we may not get inside to see Mrs. Dortweiler personally."

"You're right. But how do we get inside the house?"

Hannah thought for a long moment. "I could say that Judge Colfax ordered the cookies for her because he tasted them and liked them. That much is true. Howie's taken him cookies from my bakery on several occasions. And then I could say that Judge Colfax told me that he wanted to apologize for being late with her last alimony check."

"But won't they still come out to get the cookies without letting us in?"

"Probably. I'd have to add something like, "Judge Colfax gave me a message for Mrs. Dortweiler.""

"They might ask you to write out the message so that they can give it to her."

"I've got an answer for that. I'll say that Judge Colfax asked me to deliver it personally and not divulge it to anyone else."

Michelle was silent for a moment. "That should get you in. But how about the personal message? What are you going to tell her?"

"I'm going to say I lied."

"What?" Michelle looked completely confounded.

"I'm going to tell her I lied. And then I'm going to tell her why. And after that, I think she'll cooperate and answer any questions I have."

"This I've got to see! Go ahead, Hannah. Try it."

Five minutes later, Hannah and Michelle were sitting in surprisingly comfortable chairs with gold velvet upholstery and spindly legs in the south wing of Sheila Dortweiler's massive home. The home was what Hannah would have called a mansion and the room was what her mother, a Regency romance fan and writer, would have referred to as a "withdrawing chamber."

They heard the sound of someone walking toward them in the hallway outside and Michelle sat up a little straighter. "Here she comes."

Sheila Dortweiler entered the room with the force of a whirlwind. She was a thin woman, beautifully dressed in an obviously expensive suit with obviously expensive jewelry adorning her ears, throat, and fingers, and obviously colored coal-black hair worn in an elaborate style. She was wearing an obviously annoyed expression on her face, which had obviously seen some extensive cosmetic surgery. "Who are you and what are you doing here?"

"I'm Hannah Swensen, Mrs. Dortweiler, and this is my sister, Michelle. I own a cookie shop and bakery in Lake Eden, Minnesota, called The Cookie Jar. I brought two dozen Banana Frosted Peanut Butter cookies for you. Your husband ordered them."

"My ex-husband."

"Yes. I believe the order was by way of apology for a late alimony check."

"Well . . . that's a first!" Mrs. Dortweiler's expression may have softened a bit at Hannah's explanation, but if it had, it wasn't discernible. "You *do* know my ex-husband is dead, don't you?"

"I do. I found his body."

Mrs. Dortweiler reared back slightly in surprise. "Really! They told *me* he died at the courthouse."

"That's true. I was waiting for my case to be called when the clerk told me that Judge Colfax wanted to see me in his chambers. I was waiting in his anteroom when I heard a crash and went in to investigate."

"Investigate?" Mrs. Dortweiler's eyes narrowed. "*Hannah Swensen!* I knew I'd heard that name before! You're the nosy one that solves murders!"

Hannah knew that it was time to take charge of the conversation before they were shown out of Mrs. Dortweiler's house and her life. "That's right," she said, meeting the older woman's eyes. "I don't appreciate your terminology, but your facts are correct. I do solve murder cases and I'm going to solve your ex-husband's murder case. He dismissed the case against me despite the fact that it was brought by his current wife's nephew, and I owe him one."

This time Mrs. Dortweiler's expression *did* soften. It wasn't much, but Hannah noticed it. "I read about your court case, too. It was about as bogus as it gets. Nora is an idiot and so is her whole family, including that nephew of hers. So why are you here, Miss Swensen? You don't think I killed my ex-husband, do you?"

"Not you. You were having too much fun punishing him for leaving you. Why would you give that up?"

Mrs. Dortweiler let out a short bark of laughter. "How perceptive of you! And you're right. I *was* punishing Geoffrey. But if you know that I didn't kill him, why are you here?"

"I need answers. And I need those answers from someone who has no vested interest in killing Judge Colfax, or in keeping him alive. You fit the category and that's why I'm here."

"So you need a disinterested party!" Mrs. Dortweiler crossed to a chair and sat down. "But are you sure I'm really disinterested? How about the alimony? I didn't want that to stop, did I?"

"I don't think that you cared about the alimony, one way or the other. You didn't need the money, but it was amusing to put the bite on your ex-husband every month. You wanted to be a thorn in his side."

"Very true. But perhaps I tired of the game and decided to take revenge for past wrongs. Geoffrey was a bit of a . . . player, you know. Perhaps I was jealous because I wasn't the most important person in his life."

"That's not it," Hannah said, shaking her head.

"Why not? I knew that he was having an affair while we were married."

"If you'd been that jealous and upset, you would have killed him instead of filing for divorce."

As Hannah watched, a slow smile played over Mrs. Dortweiler's lips. "You're good at

300

this, Miss Swensen. And I'm beginning to enjoy it. Are your cookies as delicious as your questions?"

"Try one and see." Hannah opened the box and smiled as Mrs. Dortweiler chose a cookie and began to eat it.

"Excellent!" she pronounced, once she'd finished the cookie. "I'll ring for tea."

"How about changing that to coffee, Mrs. Dortweiler?" Hannah suggested. "Coffee is a better complement for peanut butter and bananas."

"I agree. And call me Sheila." She turned to Michelle. "And you're Michelle. Do you ever talk, Michelle?"

"Only when she lets me."

Sheila laughed. "Humor runs in your family, I see. Just let me order the coffee and then I'll give you the dirt on Geoffrey and all the people in his life. I just love to dish dirt about Geoffrey. This is going to be the best afternoon I've had in years!"

BANANA FROSTED PEANUT BUTTER COOKIES

Preheat oven to 350 degrees F., rack in the middle position.

1 cup melted butter *(2 sticks, 8 ounces, 1/2 pound)*

2 cups brown sugar *(firmly packed)*

1/2 cup white *(granulated)* sugar

1 teaspoon vanilla extract

1 teaspoon baking powder

1 and 1/2 teaspoons baking soda

1/2 teaspoon salt

1 cup peanut butter *(I used Skippy Creamy Peanut Butter)*

2 beaten eggs *(just whip them up in a glass with a fork)*

1/2 cup chopped salted peanuts *(measure AFTER chopping)*

3 cups flour *(don't sift — pack it down when you measure it)*

Microwave the butter in a microwave-safe mixing bowl for approximately 90 seconds on HIGH to melt it. Mix in the brown sugar, white sugar, vanilla, baking powder, baking soda, and salt. Stir until they're thoroughly blended.

Measure out the peanut butter. *(I spray the inside of my measuring cup with Pam so it won't stick.)* Add it to the bowl and mix it in. Pour in the beaten eggs and stir it all up. Add the chopped salted peanuts and mix until they're incorporated.

Add the flour in one-cup increments, mixing after each increment. Mix until all the ingredients are thoroughly blended.

Prepare your cookie sheets by spraying them with Pam or another nonstick cooking spray or lining them with parchment paper.

Form the dough into walnut-sized balls with your impeccably clean hands and arrange them on the cookie sheet, 12 to a standard-size sheet. *(If the dough is too sticky to form into balls, chill it for an hour or so, and then try again, but don't forget to turn off your oven if you chill the dough.)*

Flatten the dough balls a bit with a metal spatula or with your palm.

Bake at 350 degrees F. for 10 to 12 minutes, or until the tops are just beginning to turn golden. Cool on the cookie sheet for 2 minutes, then remove to a wire rack to finish cooling.

When your cookies are cool, make the Banana Frosting.

Banana Frosting

1 ounce *(2 Tablespoons)* salted butter, melted

1/2 cup baby food mashed bananas *(I used Gerber)*

1/2 teaspoon banana extract *(if you can't find it, use vanilla extract)*

3 to 3 and 1/2 cups confections *(powdered)* sugar *(no need to sift unless it's got big lumps)*

Stir the melted butter into the mashed bananas. Mix until it is smooth.

Add the banana extract. Mix it in thoroughly.

Add the confectioner's sugar in half-cup increments stirring the mixture smooth after each addition. Add more confectioners sugar, if needed, to bring it to spreading consistency.

Spread the frosting on top of the peanut butter cookies, one by one, stopping just short of the edges. Replace them on the wire rack as you do so.

Let the frosting "set" for 30 minutes, then enjoy!

You can store these cookies at room temperature, layered in a box and separated by wax paper.

Yield: approximately 5 dozen cookies, depending on cookie size.

Hannah's Note: We sprinkle the top of the

frosting with chopped salted peanuts or a piece of dried banana before it hardens at the Cookie Jar.

Jo Fluke's Note: If you have leftover frosting, make graham cracker sandwiches for the kids.

CHAPTER NINETEEN

"Me or you?" Michelle asked Hannah, who was following her up the stairs.

"You," Hannah said. "I'll take your grocery bag."

"Okay." Michelle handed her the bag with tomorrow night's dinner ingredients and Hannah watched her brace herself on the second floor landing outside the door. "It's quiet inside your living room. Maybe Moishe is sleeping."

Hannah shook her head. "He's not sleeping. And if he was sleeping before we got here, he opened his eyes the second he heard us coming. Norman was here, waiting for me to come home one day, and he said that Moishe went on the alert the moment he heard my cookie truck pull into the garage."

"How can you tell when Moishe goes on the alert?"

"His ears perk up and his tail starts swishing back and forth. Norman knew I was coming home because Moishe started purring, jumped down from Norman's lap, and headed straight for the door."

"Impressive," Michelle said, taking up a stance with her feet apart in the center of the landing. She leaned forward to use her key and then she turned around to look at Hannah. "Ready?"

"I'm ready. And I'm willing to bet that Moishe is, too."

Michelle leaned forward to unlock the door. She pushed it open and a flying bundle of orange and white fur went airborne and hurtled into her waiting arms.

Michelle made a sound midway between a gasp and a grunt with the emphasis on the grunt. Hannah had heard that sound only once before. It was at a family picnic when her father and uncles had decided to throw their father's medicine ball to each other. It had looked similar to a bowling ball, but it was covered with leather. And instead of weighing twelve or thirteen pounds, her grandfather's medicine ball weighed in at almost thirty pounds. The merriment had stopped after only a few throws and that night Delores had rubbed her husband's back with liniment.

"Either Moishe's gaining weight or I'm

growing weaker," Michelle said, carrying him into Hannah's living room and placing him on the back of the couch.

"It might be both," Hannah commented, smiling to show her sister that she was teasing. Michelle had always been strong and athletic. "Let's go change, relax for a couple of minutes, and then we'll bake my cake. Ross asked me to bake it. He told me he loves tangerines."

Hannah fed Moishe and then she went off to her bedroom to change into what Andrea called her "at-home ensemble," which consisted of a pair of grey sweatpants and an old college sweatshirt. When she came back into the living room, she found Michelle sitting on the couch in a similar outfit with Moishe in her lap and two glasses of white wine sitting in front of her on the coffee table.

"You're only twenty-one," Hannah told her. "Are you turning into a two-fisted drinker already? And why on earth did you put ice cubes in my jug wine?"

Michelle laughed. "It's not your jug wine. It's lemon soda. I bought it at the Red Owl because Florence convinced me that we'd like it. And the reason I added ice is because it's not chilled. I put it in a wineglass because it looked prettier that way."

"Is it any good?"

"I don't know. I was letting it chill down a little. Try it and see what you think."

Hannah took a cautious sip. "Yes."

"What does *yes* mean?"

"It's not bad at all. It might even be good." Hannah took another sip. "Actually, I like it. It's lemonade with fizz."

"Thanks for being my taste tester," Michelle said with a smile. "Now that I know it's not awful, I'll try it, too."

"So I was your guinea pig?"

"You could say that." Michelle took a sip. "You're right, Hannah. It *is* good. I'll pick up another six-pack tomorrow."

They sat in companionable silence for several minutes with the exception of Moishe, who was purring loudly every time Michelle scratched him behind the ears.

Then Hannah took her last sip of lemon soda and stood up. "I'd better start baking. If I sit here much longer, I'll nod off."

Michelle got up and picked up her glass. "Didn't you sleep long enough?"

"I did, thanks to you. That was really nice of you, letting me sleep. I never get the chance to do that when you're not here."

"It's one of the reasons I like to stay with you. When I stay at Mother's, I don't feel helpful. When I stay with you, I do. And sometimes I even get to help you with an investigation. I really like that."

"You do?"

"I really do. It's such a change from my classwork."

"I should hope so! Unless, of course, those lectures you go to are deadly boring."

Michelle laughed and so did Hannah. They were still laughing when Hannah placed the recipe she'd printed out at The Cookie Jar on her kitchen counter and they went off to gather the ingredients. Hannah was just picking the seeds from the last tangerine when she heard soft footfalls that meant Moishe had entered the kitchen.

"Don't tell me you're hungry again!" she said, expecting a yowl in response. But there was no yowl from Moishe. Instead, he made a muffled cry.

"What's the matter?" Hannah responded immediately, whirling around to discover that Moishe was holding a blue and white mitten in his mouth. "Moishe! Where did you get that mitten?" She made a grab for the mitten and managed to extricate it without any damage to either her fingers or the mitten.

Michelle turned to look at the mitten that Hannah was holding. "Is it yours, Hannah?"

"No, and I don't recognize it. How about you?"

Michelle shook her head. "It's not mine. I've never had a pair of blue and white mittens."

"It's pretty," Hannah said, examining the mitten. "I like the little snowflake design."

"I like it, too. And I think this mitten's homemade. See that thumb? It reminds me of the mittens that Grandma Ingrid used to knit for me."

"That's because the thumbs were always a little crooked and placed in the wrong spot. Grandma Ingrid hated to knit thumbs. I watched her finish a pair of mittens once, and I asked her why she had little needles around the hole on the side. She said that it was the thumbhole and she hated to knit thumbs because she could never get them right."

"Well, this mitten has to belong to somebody we know."

"That's right," Hannah said. "And that someone has another one just like it."

Michelle rolled her eyes. "Very funny."

"I thought so," Hannah said with a smile and then she quickly sobered. "It's not mitten weather yet so this mitten must have been left here last year."

"*If* it was left here."

"Yes, if it was *left* here." Hannah said, glancing at Moishe who was sitting in front of the refrigerator looking as pure as the driven snow.

Hannah and Michelle stared at the mitten for long moments and then Hannah gave an exasperated sigh.

"What?" Michelle asked.

"I totally forgot. We've got a perfect way to tell if Moishe got out and brought this mitten home."

"The surveillance system," Michelle said, catching on immediately. "You told me that Mike installed it this morning."

Hannah placed the mitten on the counter. Then she thought better of it and stuck it in a drawer. Moishe could jump up on the counter, but he'd never opened a kitchen drawer. "Let's get that cake into the oven and then we can watch the surveillance tape while it's baking. Maybe we can catch our cat burglar red-pawed and it'll show us how he gets out."

"There's nothing on the tape," Michelle said, sighing deeply. "All we did was watch Moishe jump up on the couch and down from the couch a bunch of times, and walk back and forth between the kitchen and the hallway."

"That's true, but we did learn a lot."

"Like what?"

"We learned that Moishe didn't go out the door to the landing, but he still had something that didn't belong to us."

"Okay," Michelle conceded, "but we don't know if he got that mitten today. For all we know, he could have stolen it three days ago, hidden it under a bed, and just now got it out to play with it."

"You're right. The only thing we know for sure is that Moishe had it in his mouth when he walked past the camera on his way to the kitchen. And the camera was trained on the outside door. Let's reposition the surveillance system so it shows the length of the hallway. Mike showed me how to do it."

"What good will that do?"

"It'll narrow things down. Maybe Moishe does have a stash of hidden bounty somewhere. If he does, and if we find it, we might discover something we'll recognize. Then, if we can identify the owner, at least we'll know where Moishe's been."

"But we won't know how he got there," Michelle pointed out. "I can't believe we're spending all this time tracking a cat!" Hannah raised her eyebrows. "Don't sell him short, Michelle. My felonious feline is a cagey one."

Michelle laughed. "He certainly is! Maybe we'd better look around for a hidden treasure map."

"Or a tunnel like the ones the pirates used to move stolen goods between their ships and the coastal towns. It's pretty obvious that Moishe knows how to dig. I have to sweep up kitty litter every morning."

"Then a tunnel is a definite possibility." Michelle looked very serious. "I wonder where his tunnel could be. Do you think we should tear up the living room carpet to take a look?"

Hannah glanced down at her faded green carpeting. She'd hated the color when she'd moved in and she hated it even more now. She gave a little sigh, but she shook her head. "This carpeting's so old, it might be an improvement, but let's not do anything that rash until we give up on Mike's surveillance system. New carpeting is expensive. Come on, Michelle. Let's reposition that camera and hope for the best."

Fifteen minutes later, the job was done. Hannah started to walk back into the living room when she noticed that Michelle was standing motionless, staring up at the camera that was positioned over the doorway to her bedroom. "What is it?" Hannah asked her.

"It's that camera. It's going to catch me every time I go in and out of my bedroom."

"What's wrong with that?"

"It's a *camera*!"

"Okay, it's a camera. What's wrong with a camera?"

"It's a camera and I'm an actress. Every time an actress sees a camera, she gets the urge to perform. I don't think you're going to appreciate hearing the first three numbers from *Jesus Christ Superstar* when I get up to go to the bathroom at three in the morning."

"That's better than Hamlet's soliloquy, but I see what you mean. Can't you perform any quieter scenes? Like the body in the pool at the beginning of *Sunset Boulevard*?"

"But the body in the pool doesn't have any lines until they go back in time to when he was alive."

"I know. That's the whole point."

Michelle laughed. "I'll work on it. Or better yet, I just won't look up at the camera in the middle of the night." She was quiet for a moment and then she glanced at her watch. "Are you tired, Hannah?"

"Not really. Why?"

"Because Seth Dortweiler is performing at the Eight Ball Bar in Grey Eagle tonight. His set starts at nine."

"And you want me to interview him to-night?"

"Why not? Unless you'd rather wait until tomorrow night when Ross gets here."

Hannah shook her head. She certainly didn't want to work on a murder case the first night that Ross was in town. "I'd rather go tonight. And then, tomorrow morning, we can try to catch the judge's widow at home."

TANGERINE DREAM CAKE

Preheat oven to 350 degrees F., rack in the middle position.

Hannah's 1st Note: I think it's possible to make this cake by hand, but it will take a strong arm to do it. Lisa and I use an electric stand mixer. Some people may still have a food grinder in their kitchen cabinet. If you do, get it out and use it. If you don't, use a food processor and the steel blade to process the tangerines after you juice them, the raisins, and the pecans.

3 ripe tangerines *(choose the ones with perfect skin — you'll be using that, too!)*

1 cup golden raisins *(Regular raisins will also work, but I think that the golden raisins work best in this recipe.)*

2/3 cup pecans

2 cups all-purpose flour *(Don't pack it down. Just scoop it out and level off the top of your measuring cup with a table knife.)*

1 teaspoon salt

1 teaspoon baking soda

1/2 teaspoon nutmeg *(freshly grated is best)*

1 and 1/3 cups white *(granulated)* sugar

1/2 cup *(1 stick, 4 ounces, 1/4 pound)* salted butter, softened to room temperature

1 teaspoon vanilla extract

3/4 cup whole milk

2 large eggs

1/4 cup whole milk *(This brings the milk total up to one cup.)*

Grease and lightly flour a 9-inch by 13-inch cake pan. *(Alternatively, you can spray the pan with baking spray, the kind with flour in it.)*

Wash the outside of your tangerines, then cut them in half and juice them. Save one-third cup of the juice. You'll be using it in the Tangerine Dream Cake topping. If there is more than *1/3* cup of tangerine juice, pour the excess into a little container and save it to add to your cake batter.

Pick out the seeds and throw them away, then cut the pulp and rind into quarters.

If you have a food grinder, grind the tangerine pulp and rind with the raisins and the pecans. If you don't have a grinder, simply put the tangerine pulp and rind into the bowl of your food processor with the steel blade in place. Add the raisins and the pecans. Process them with an on and off motion until they're chopped as finely as they'd be if you'd used a food grinder. *(They should look as finely ground as hamburger.)*

Set the ground tangerine, raisin, and pecan mixture aside in a bowl on the counter.

Leave your steel blade in the food processor and don't wash the bowl. You'll be using it to finely chop a quarter-cup of pecans for the topping once your Tangerine Dream Cake has baked.

If you had any excess tangerine juice *(anything over the 1/3 cup you're saving for the cake topping)* add it to the tangerine, raisin, and pecan mixture. Stir it in and return the bowl to the counter.

Measure out one cup of flour and put it in the bowl of your electric mixer. Add the salt, baking soda, nutmeg, and white sugar. Mix them together at LOW speed.

Add the second cup of flour. Mix that in at LOW speed.

Add the softened butter, the vanilla extract, and the *3/4* cup whole milk. Beat at LOW speed until the flour is well moistened. Then turn the mixer up to MEDIUM HIGH speed.

Beat for 2 minutes. Then shut off the mixer and scrape down the sides of the bowl.

Turn the mixer on LOW and add the eggs, one at a time, beating all the while. Then beat in the 1/4 cup whole milk. Once the eggs and the milk are incorporated, turn the mixer up to MEDIUM HIGH.

Beat for 2 minutes. Then shut off the mixer and scrape down the sides of the bowl again.

Remove the bowl from the mixer. You're going to finish the Tangerine Dream Cake by hand.

Gradually add the ground tangerine, raisin, and pecan mixture to the mixing bowl, folding it in gently as you go. The object is to keep as much air in the cake batter as you can.

Pour the cake batter into the pan you prepared earlier. Smooth out the top with a rubber spatula.

Bake your Tangerine Dream Cake at 350 degrees F. for 40 to 50 minutes, or until a thin wooden skewer or a cake tester that you poke into the center of the cake comes out clean. *(I started testing my cake at 40 minutes, but there was still sticky batter clinging to the tester. The last time I baked this cake, it took the full 50 minutes.)*

When your cake is done, take it out of the oven and place it on a wire rack or a cold burner on the stovetop.

Tangerine Dream Cake Topping:

1/3 cup tangerine juice *(from the tangerines you juiced earlier)*

1/2 cup white *(granulated)* sugar

1/4 cup finely chopped pecans

Hannah's 2nd Note: You must make the topping and put it on your cake while the cake is still piping hot from the oven.

Drizzle the 1/3 cup of tangerine juice over the top of your hot cake.

Sprinkle the sugar over the top of the tangerine juice on your cake.

Finely chop more pecans. Measure out 1/4 cup and sprinkle them on top of the sugar on your cake.

Let your cake cool to room temperature. Then cover it and refrigerate it. This will keep it nice and moist.

You can serve your Tangerine Dream Cake at room temperature or chilled. It freezes well if you wrap it in foil and put it in a freezer bag.

If you'd like to dress it up a bit, cut pieces, put them on pretty dessert plates, and decorate each piece with a dollop of sweetened whipped cream.

CHAPTER TWENTY

"I feel stupid in this outfit," Hannah said, glancing down at her oldest, tightest pair of jeans and the shocking pink tank top that was at least two sizes too small for her. Michelle had bought it in Las Vegas and it was the epitome of glitz, with sparkling gold lettering proclaiming that the wearer was a SHOWGIRL IN TRAINING.

"You look perfect for the Eight Ball. You'll see I'm right just as soon as we go in."

"You looked that up online, too?"

"No, I've been there before."

"With Lonnie?"

"No! Lonnie wouldn't be caught dead in a place like the Eight Ball. The first time I went there, it was a girls' night out in high school and we thought it was far enough away from Lake Eden so that no one would recognize us."

"And it wasn't?"

Michelle shook her head. "I got busted."

"Did Mother read you the riot act?"

"I would have preferred that, but she gave me the silent treatment when I came in the door. There she was in her robe and slippers. She held out her hand for the car keys and after I handed them over, she motioned for me to go into my room."

"And you worried about it for the rest of the night because you didn't know what else she was going to do?"

"That's right." Michelle gave Hannah an assessing look. "How do *you* know about that?"

"I had one memorable experience with Mother's silent treatment and that was enough to keep me home for a solid month!"

"What did you do?"

Hannah shrugged. "Not much, but I *did* lie to her about where I was going. I had a friend named Marilyn. She was a bookworm, just like me, and every once in a while, we'd study together for a big test. Mother approved of Marilyn, but there was a group of three girls that she wanted me to avoid. As it turned out, she was right. All three got into big trouble in their senior year. But this was in our junior year and one of the girls begged me to come over and help them with their term papers in history. It was the night before they were due and I'd handed mine in that morning, so I said I'd help them."

"That was nice of you."

"Too nice, as it turned out. What they wanted wasn't a critical review, or help in wording a section. They wanted me to actually write the term papers for them."

"So you refused?"

"Yes. I told them I'd help them, but I couldn't write their papers for them, that our teacher would recognize my style and we'd all get into trouble. They didn't like that and they left me sitting there at the library."

"So you went home?"

"Not right away. I'd told Mother that I was going to study with Marilyn so I had to stay there for a couple of hours. *Then* I went home."

"How did Mother find out that you weren't studying with Marilyn?"

"Marilyn called to talk to me an hour after I'd left home."

"Busted!"

"Oh, yes. Mother didn't say a word. She just handed me one of those little pink notes she always used to log in phone calls."

"The ones with the blank line at the top and words under it that said, *Called while you were out,* and another blank for the time of the call and the telephone number?"

"Yes. She'd written *Marilyn* on the top line, and that was all. I tried to explain, but she just pointed to my room, so I went. And just like you, I worried all night about how she was going to punish me."

"What did she do?"

"Absolutely nothing. In the morning, things were the same as they'd been on any other morning. And that was worse than any punishment she could have given me. I kept waiting for the other shoe to drop, but it never did."

"She's a smart mother," Michelle said. "That's exactly what she did to me."

"Perhaps *diabolical* would be a better description than *smart,*" Hannah said, and both of them laughed as she pulled into the parking lot for the Eight Ball Bar.

"Park over there, under that tree," Michelle pointed out a spot in the back of the lot. "We don't want anyone to see your cookie truck and identify us if things go bad."

"Bad? How could things go bad?" Hannah asked as she parked in the spot that Michelle had indicated.

"Maybe Seth won't want to be interviewed and he'll sic one of the bouncers on us.

Then we won't want him to know who we are or where we came from, but your cookie truck will give us away."

"This place has more than one bouncer?" Hannah asked, picking up on the fact that Michelle had mentioned *bouncers.*

"Four or five, at least. Things get a little rowdy on music nights."

"And tonight is their music night?"

"Their music nights are Monday through Saturday. They're closed on Sundays. Come on, Hannah. Let's go."

What have you gotten yourself into this time? Hannah's mind chided her as she got out of the truck, locked it securely, and followed Michelle across the parking lot. *You don't belong in a place like this!*

"Neither does Michelle!" Hannah said aloud.

Michelle turned back to her. "What did you say?"

"Nothing. Just talking to myself. Is there a cover charge?"

Michelle laughed. "In a place like this . . . hardly! There's a two-drink minimum, that's it. Get something in a can or bottle. It's safer. The last time I was here, they had a C minus rating from the health board tacked to the door. That's one violation short of closing them down."

"Thanks for telling me," Hannah said as they neared the door and she saw the health board sign for herself. "I was thinking of ordering a hamburger."

"Not here. I'm hungry, too. When we finish here, we can stop in at the Corner Tavern. They've got great hamburgers and it's on our way home." Michelle arrived at the door and pulled it open.

Hannah followed her into the dim and crowded interior of the building. "Do you come here often?" she asked Michelle.

"Only when Crystal's working."

"Who's Crystal?"

"One of the girls who lives in our house. She bartends here some weekends and a couple of us make the commute with her."

"That's an hour's commute!"

"I know, but the tips are really good. That's how I know the Corner Tavern is open late. We always call ahead for burgers and eat them on the way back to the house."

Hannah remembered what Michelle had said about Lonnie. "So Lonnie doesn't mind when you come here without him?"

"I'm not sure if he minds, or not. It's no big secret, but I'm not sure if he even knows we drive down with Crystal and come out here." Michelle stopped speaking and frowned slightly. "Lonnie and I aren't married and we aren't engaged to be married. I love Lonnie and I think he loves me, but we don't have a firm commitment. I don't know everything he does when he's not with me, and he doesn't know everything I do when I'm not with him. Our situation is a little like the situation you had with Norman and with Mike."

Hannah noticed Michelle's use of the past tense when she referred to Hannah's situations with Norman and with Mike. Michelle was sure that her big sister was ready to make a commitment to Ross. *But are you sure?* Hannah's mind asked her. *I'll know soon,* Hannah answered the question, and this time she was very careful not to voice her answer aloud.

"Hi, there," a cocktail waitress came bustling up to them.

"Hi, Laney."

The waitress gave Michelle a closer look. "You're a friend of Crystal's . . . right?"

"That's right. I'm Michelle."

"Crystal's not working tonight."

"I know. She's at home cramming for a test, but she'll be in this weekend."

"Good. She makes a great Appletini. All the girls love them. A table for two?"

"Could you make it a table for three? And just as close to the stage as we can get?"

Michelle asked, handing Laney a folded bill. "Somebody may be joining us later."

"Sure thing. Just follow me."

With the agility of a mountain goat, Laney wove a narrow path between the too many tables in the too small a space, until she stopped at a tiny cocktail table with three chairs that was placed directly in front of center stage. "This okay with you?"

"Perfect," Michelle told her. "Bring us two Bartles and Jaymes, any flavor, and two small bottles of water. And Laney? Can you do us a favor and open them right here at the table?"

"Sure thing. I would have done that anyway for any friend of Crystal's, especially the way Jimmy is eyeing your friend."

Hannah turned to look at the older man behind the bar and discovered that he was staring at her. At first she thought his left eye was twitching, but then she realized that he was winking at her and she turned away quickly. "What would he do?" she asked Laney.

"Put a couple shots of vodka in the bottles," Laney answered her. "And then, when he saw you were having trouble walking straight, he would follow you out to the parking lot."

Hannah gave a relieved sigh. "I'm glad we

didn't sit at the bar!"

"You should be," Laney gave a little laugh. "Jimmy's been on a tear ever since his wife up and left him. Even the waitresses have to watch it around him."

When Laney left to get their drinks, Hannah glanced at the Eight Ball Bar patrons. The age range was wide, from the mid-twenties to the early sixties. The older women seemed cut from the same mold, dressing in clothing designed for younger, more toned bodies and sporting hair colors that probably weren't real. They wore too much makeup, drank too many alcoholic fruit drinks, and laughed too loudly at each other's jokes. There were a few couples, but not many.

And there was a definite segregation of the sexes. There were tables of women and tables of men, but very few mixed tables. The women were quite obviously vying for the attention of the men, but the men appeared oblivious to their attempts at flirtation.

Hannah turned to Michelle. "What's going on here? Those women over there, the one in the red top for instance, is flirting with the man in the black shirt at the next table. She's really loud and I'm sure he notices her, but he just keeps on talking to his buddies and doesn't acknowledge her at all."

"Of course not. It's not last call."

"What?"

"He's waiting until it's closer to closing time. If he notices her now, he'll have to buy her drinks all night. If he waits, he can get away with one or two rounds."

"He's that cheap?"

"Yes, but so are most of the guys who come here. Crystal told us about it and I've seen it for myself. When they flick the lights for the last round, the men scurry around like rats, trying to pick someone up."

"And the women let them?"

"Some do, some don't. If we stayed, you'd see it for yourself, but I hope we won't have to stay that long. The band's due to start any minute now, and if we play our cards right, we can talk to Seth and get out of here in an hour tops."

"I hope so," Hannah said, trying not to sound as upset as she felt. She was sorry she'd asked about the dating ritual. It was sad to see these desperate women try to attract such callous men. Didn't they realize that there was more to life than spending their nights like this?

It was a welcome distraction when the band arrived. There were four men, all dressed in show clothes. Their pants were skin-tight and black in color, and they wore gold satin cowboy shirts decorated with rhinestones. They had similar haircuts that emphasized their bleached-blond spiky hair, and they all wore pasted-on smiles. Hannah tried to decide which one was Seth Dortweiler, but since she'd never seen a photo of him, and since all of the band members looked alike, this was no more than guesswork.

"I'll find out which one is Seth," Michelle said, and Hannah wondered if her baby sister had been taking mind-reading classes at Macalester.

"Good idea," Hannah replied. "I'll pay for the drinks when they come."

"Don't tip Jimmy if he brings them," Michelle warned, getting up from her chair. "He may think you're paying him in advance for something a little more than delivering our drinks."

Hannah sent up a silent prayer that Laney would be the one to deliver their drinks. And her prayers were answered almost immediately when Laney arrived at their table with a tray holding four bottles.

"I just saw Michelle up there," she pointed to the raised stage, "talking to the boys in the band. I didn't know she was a fan."

"Neither did I," Hannah said quite truthfully.

"There she goes through the kitchen door," Laney announced, standing on tiptoe to follow Michelle's progress through the overcrowded room. "She's probably going out to the trailer to see Seth."

"You're probably right."

"She's a theater major, isn't she?"

"Yes."

"I figured that. So is Crystal and she said everybody in their house is some kind of drama person. If Michelle gets in to see Seth, she's in for the surprise of her life!"

"She is?" Hannah felt a seed of worry begin to grow rapidly. It rivaled time-lapse photography with the speed it took for the worry to bloom into full-blown fear. "What's the surprise, Laney?" she asked.

"Seth looks like a Dee-Dee," Laney told her, "but he's not like that at all."

"What's a Dee-Dee?"

"A Degenerate Doper. That's what he looks like onstage. But he isn't. It's part of his act."

Hannah was slightly relieved, but not entirely. "You seem to know Seth pretty well."

"I should. His mother used to live on our

333

block before she inherited that mansion of hers."

The seed of worry had bloomed and died, and Hannah was grateful to Laney for the information. "So the degenerate doper persona is all an act?"

"You bet it's an act!" Laney accepted the tip Hannah handed her and smiled her thanks. "Seth graduates from law school this year. The guys in the band go to law school, too."

"With that hair?" Hannah glanced at the men, who were almost through setting up their equipment.

"They wear hairpieces. You ought to see them when they come out in their regular clothes. They could walk right in here and sit at a table, and no one would know who they were. By the way . . ." Laney leaned closer and lowered her voice, "I hope you brought earplugs. They're pretty awful, but they put on a good show and the women love them. They're especially crazy about Seth. He sings, if you can call it that."

Hannah wasn't sure she completely understood. "Do they do this for the thrill of it?"

"No, they do it for money. It's helping to put all five of them through law school."

"Did Seth's father know he was going to law school?" Hannah asked.

"I don't know for sure. All I know is that Seth's mother doesn't know. He told me he wants to shock her by inviting her to his graduation."

"That's a little odd, isn't it?"

"Maybe, but he's probably got his reasons. I never asked. I just promised never to tell her. Actually . . . I shouldn't have mentioned it to you." Laney looked very uncomfortable. "I guess that's because you're easy to talk to. You won't tell his mother, will you?"

"Absolutely not. I only met her once and I don't plan on seeing her again."

Laney laughed. "I can appreciate that! Sheila is a piece of work. I'm surprised the judge lasted with her as long as he did. That was really awful what happened to him, wasn't it!"

"It was awful," Hannah agreed.

"I heard he was married again and that it was going fine. He deserved a little happiness after Sheila. Do you know that she kept right on cashing those alimony checks of his even after she inherited all that money from her family? She didn't need his money. And she knew he was married again and didn't have a big retirement. What a witch!"

CHAPTER TWENTY-ONE

Hannah had taken only one sip of her wine cooler when Michelle came rushing back to the table. "Let's go!"

"Go where?"

"Through the kitchen to the band trailer. Seth's got ten minutes before he has to go on and he can see us right now."

A moment or two later, Hannah was following her sister through the kitchen, a crowded little room with more unwashed dishes and cockroach traps than food. They emerged through the back door and crossed the asphalt parking lot to a dented camping trailer.

"Seth?" Michelle knocked on the door. "It's Michelle and Hannah."

There was a muffled sound from the interior which Michelle must have taken for permission to enter because she climbed up the step and opened the door.

"Come on, Hannah," she said, stepping

through the doorway and into the interior.

Hannah followed her, stepping into a brightly lighted room with a couch, a mirror that ran the length of one wall with a counter beneath it, and three chairs positioned in front of the reflective surface.

"This is my sister, Hannah," Michelle introduced her. "And Hannah? This is Seth Dortweiler. I told Seth that you were investigating his father's murder."

"Hello, Hannah." Seth rose from his chair in front of the mirror and reached out for her hand. "Good to meet you."

"Thanks. You, too," Hannah said, trying not to stare at Seth's skintight, red satin jumpsuit that left very little to the imagination.

"I go to William Mitchell and there was an article about you in the *St. Paul Pioneer Press.* Michelle told me you're investigating my dad's murder and I want to help you any way I can, but I have only a few minutes before I go on. We can also meet during our break if you have more questions for me."

Hannah noticed that Seth's voice was shaking slightly and that could be due to one of three reasons. Either he suffered from a bit of stage fright, he was still terribly upset about his father's death, or he was nervous about being questioned because he was guilty.

"When is the last time you saw your father?" Hannah began in an attempt to narrow it down.

"Last week. We met for lunch at The Corner Café. That's only five minutes from the courthouse and Dad was hearing a trial there."

"Did you talk about the trial?"

"No, we talked about law school. He was . . ." Seth stopped speaking and swallowed hard. "He was really happy that I was almost through. It was . . . our secret."

"Did he know about the band?"

Seth smiled for the first time since they'd entered the trailer. "Yeah. He got a real kick out of it. He said he bartended at a real dive when he was going to law school."

"He went to William Mitchell, didn't he?" Michelle asked.

Seth nodded. "He helped me get in. Alumni pull and all that. My grades weren't really good enough, but they took me anyway because of his recommendation."

"And you're due to graduate this year?"

Seth nodded again. "He was really pleased that I was going to law school."

Hannah picked up on the obvious omission. "Isn't your mother pleased?"

"Sheila?" Seth gave a little laugh. "Nothing pleases Sheila."

"I noticed you called her *Sheila* and not *Mother.*"

"That's her choice. Other kids had mothers. I had Sheila." Seth took a deep breath and let it out in a sigh. "It's not fair, you know!" He stopped and swallowed again. "I . . . I wish Dad had lived to see me graduate. He was so proud of me for getting this far. And he would have loved to come to my graduation. I'm going to invite Sheila, too, but I'm almost sure she won't come."

"Why not?" Michelle asked.

"Because the one thing she doesn't want is for me to follow in Dad's footsteps. She hated him. When I first heard that Dad had been murdered, I wondered if she'd done it, but she didn't."

"You're convinced of that?" Michelle asked him.

"Yeah . . . now, I am. I checked up on her."

"How did you do that?" Hannah asked, trying to keep the shock out of her voice. It was a terrible state of affairs when a son had to check to make sure that his mother hadn't murdered his father.

"This cop called me at ten forty-five that morning to tell me. They called the law school because they found the number in Dad's private phone book. I asked when it had happened and this cop named Mike something-or-other told me that Dad's clerk had seen him at nine, so it was after that."

"That's right," Hannah said, not mentioning the fact that she'd gone into Judge Colfax's chambers to find his body.

"I knew that Sheila had a standing appointment at the spa at ten every Monday morning. And I know that it takes forty-five minutes to drive from our house to the courthouse. Since the spa is an hour from our house in the opposite direction, it would have taken Sheila an hour and forty-five to get from the courthouse after she killed Dad to the spa. That means if Sheila kept her ten o'clock appointment at the spa, she couldn't have killed Dad."

"And you found that she'd kept the appointment?" Hannah asked.

"Yes. The woman at the receptionist's desk checked the sign-in sheet and she said that Sheila had arrived fifteen minutes early."

"Did you tell that to the authorities when they questioned you?"

Seth shook his head. "They haven't come around to question me yet. They asked me a couple of things on the phone, but so far that's it."

"You'd better go," Hannah said after glancing at her watch. "You're supposed to be on at nine and it's already five after."

"That's okay. The band's warming them up for me. Can't you hear them?"

Hannah listened. She'd been dimly aware of something loud and unmelodious happening in the distance, but she hadn't guessed that it was Seth's band.

"Pretty awful, huh?" Seth asked, reading the expression on her face.

"Well . . . let's just say that it's not my thing," Hannah replied.

"It's not mine either, but it pays well." He turned to give a final glance in the mirror, and then he opened a small box on the counter. "Uh-oh. I'm going to have one heck of a headache when I get back here after the show!"

"Were you looking for aspirin?" Hannah asked him. "I've got some in my purse."

"Actually, no. I was looking for earplugs. I usually wear them when I perform."

"I have those, too," Hannah said, taking out a package of earplugs and handing them to him.

"These are great earplugs," Seth commented. "They block out a lot."

"But you're the singer!" Michelle said, and Hannah noticed that she looked confused. "How can you sing in the right key if you can't hear the band?"

"Oh, I can still hear them, just not as loudly. And it doesn't really matter if I'm on or off key. They come to see us, not to hear us. And since none of us are real musicians, that's a really good thing!"

The message light was blinking on Hannah's phone when they got back from the Eight Ball Bar. Hannah grabbed the phone to retrieve the message while Michelle went off to her room to change to her pajamas and robe.

Hi, Hannah. It's Lisa. If you get home before eleven, please call me back. I've got good news for you, *the disembodied voice said.*

Hannah glanced at her watch. It was ten-thirty. She punched in Lisa's number and sat down on the living room couch. Three seconds later, she had a purring cat on her lap and Lisa answered the phone.

"Where were you?" Lisa asked after Hannah had identified herself.

"At the Eight Ball Bar in Grey Eagle."

"You went to the Eight Ball Bar for *fun*?" Lisa sounded shocked.

Hannah laughed. "No, to conduct an interview with Judge Colfax's son."

"A judge's son hangs out in that place?"

"No, he was singing with a band that was playing there."

"But . . ." Lisa stopped speaking and sighed. "Never mind. I don't think I should ask any more questions."

"That's good because it just gets curiouser and curiouser," Hannah told her, borrowing heavily from Lewis Carroll. "What's the good news, Lisa?"

"You and Michelle don't have to come in at all tomorrow. Dad and Marge are coming in to help out, and so is Aunt Nancy. I'm going to have all the help I need. Aunt Nancy's coming early to bake with me. She's got a couple of new recipes she wants to try. Relax, Hannah. You and Michelle take the day off to get ready for your dinner party. We can handle it at The Cookie Jar," Lisa gave a little laugh, "unless, of course, you find another dead body. I could use a new story to tell."

"I'm not planning on finding any more . . ." Hannah stopped speaking as she thought of something Lisa could use for a story. "Could you use a story about a cat burglar?"

"Sure. That sounds exciting. Our customers love new stories."

"That's because you tell them so well,"

Hannah complimented her.

"Thank you. Tell me about this cat burglar you mentioned, and I'll use it for tomorrow's story."

By the time Hannah had finished telling Lisa about Moishe and the objects that came from unidentified owners, Michelle had changed to her nightclothes and was in the kitchen, frying something that smelled delicious.

"What are you doing?" Hannah asked her, arriving in the kitchen doorway.

"Browning the pork chops for tomorrow. I'm going to make the whole meal in the slow cooker, but the pork chops taste better if they're browned."

"I'll help you," Hannah offered.

"It's a one-person job, but you can pull out a chair and talk to me while I'm working. And if you're not too tired, would you please pour us both something cold to drink before you sit down?"

"Sure thing." Hannah headed to the refrigerator and was about to open the door when she saw an object on the floor. "Uh-oh," she said, bending down to pick it up.

"What is it?" Michelle asked, turning around to see what was in Hannah's hand.

"A hat. It's one of those knitted ski caps. And this one has white snowflakes just like the mitten we found earlier."

"The cat burglar strikes again?"

"It certainly seems like it. Moishe must have gotten the mitten and the ski cap from the same place."

"When I'm done here, let's check the tape," Michelle suggested.

"Good idea. He didn't have it hidden in the kitchen. I would have found it when we baked the Tangerine Dream Cake. Maybe we'll get lucky and see him carrying it in from wherever he goes to sneak out."

While Michelle watched her pork chops brown, Hannah filled two tall glasses with ice. She added an ounce of white jug wine and a generous splash of lemon soda. She filled the rest of the glasses with club soda, and added two frozen strawberries.

"What are you making?" Michelle asked, watching Hannah with interest.

"I don't know. I'm just experimenting to see what I can make with this awful white wine. That wine cooler we had at the Eight Ball Bar gave me the idea."

"Hand it over. I'll be *your* guinea pig this time."

"I didn't put much wine in it," Hannah warned her, handing one of the glasses to Michelle.

"That's all to the good. It means that if I

like it, I can have another."

Hannah waited while Michelle tasted her concoction. "Well? What do you think?"

"I think I'll have another when I'm through with this one. It's refreshing and it's absolutely perfect for someone who's standing over a hot stove." Michelle flipped the pork chops so that she could brown the other side, and went to the refrigerator to get the bell peppers and onions she'd bought at the Red Owl. "If you want to, you can help me clean the peppers and cut them in strips. I need to peel and chop the onions, too. Just as soon as I brown the other side of these pork chops, I'll take them out and use the same pan to brown the pepper strips and the onions."

The two sisters worked in tandem, peeling, chopping, and putting the vegetables they'd prepared in a bowl. When the last pepper was julienned and the last onion was peeled and chopped, Michelle checked the pork chops, took them out of the frying pan to rest on a platter, and began to sauté the raw vegetables.

"I love colored bell peppers," she said, smiling at the colorful array of green, red, orange, and yellow. "I could have used all green, but this is much more fun."

"The color is a function of maturity,"

Hannah told her. "Green bell peppers have been on the vine for the shortest amount of time before they're harvested. Red bell peppers reach full maturity before they're harvested."

"And yellow and orange are somewhere between the shortest and the longest vine ripening?" Michelle asked.

"Yes, generally speaking. Of course, there are differences in the plants. Some have been cultivated to produce a certain color. For instance, orange bell peppers could be a slightly different strain, but all bell peppers come from the same seeds."

"I think they taste different, but maybe that's in my imagination."

"No, it's not. They're actually nutritionally different. The green ones have more chlorophyll and they're not as sweet. Yellow peppers have more lutein and zeaxanthin carotenoids, orange have more alpha, beta, and gamma carotene, and red bell peppers have more lycopene and astaxanthin."

"I think I could have lived my whole life without knowing that," Michelle said.

"You're probably right. I have no idea why I remembered it. The important thing is that color in bell peppers depends on how long they're allowed to ripen and the red ones are the sweetest and the ripest."

"The whole color thing is interesting. What do they turn into after they turn red?"

"Mush."

"What?"

"They turn into mush. And then they fall off the vine and onto the ground."

Michelle cracked up and so did Hannah. It seemed to take forever for them to stop laughing. Perhaps their hilarity was due to the fact they'd worked all day and conducted two interviews. And now that they were back at the condo, they could relax and have a good time. Hannah wasn't sure exactly why her comment was so funny and she didn't try to analyze it. It simply felt good to laugh.

"Do we have room for three crockpots in the bottom of the refrigerator?" Michelle asked when they'd finally stopped laughing. "Just the crocks with their covers."

"I think so. It's a really big refrigerator. I didn't measure when I bought it and it barely fit into the space when it was delivered. They had to cut a hole in the ceiling to vent it."

"I can't believe you didn't measure."

"I know. It was stupid of me, but I'd never bought a refrigerator before, and I just assumed that anything I bought would fit into the space."

Hannah opened the refrigerator and did a little housekeeping, throwing out a severely wrinkled apple, three senior potatoes that had surpassed their life span, a bag of carrots that had reached and exceeded its golden years, and a package of blue cheese that wasn't bleu cheese. When she was through, she turned to Michelle. "Yes, there's room for three crocks now."

Michelle got out three of Hannah's crockpots and sprayed the crocks with Pam. "Will you help me peel the potatoes?"

"Sure." Hannah chose a paring knife and handed one to Michelle. With both of them working, the potatoes were peeled in record time. "Do you put them in whole?" she asked.

"No. They have to be cut in half lengthwise. That way they cook a little faster and they'll get done when everything else is done."

"That makes sense. What else do you have to do before we can fill the crocks?"

"Open the soup cans. That's it. I need two cans of condensed cream of mushroom, one can of condensed tomato, and one can of condensed celery for each crock. We have to mix them together, along with the package of pork gravy. I could have just used three cans of condensed golden mushroom soup and one can of condensed celery soup, but Florence didn't have the golden mushroom soup in stock."

Once the soup cans were open and mixed together, Hannah watched Michelle assemble the first crock. "I think I've got it. You do the second crock and I'll do the third."

"Okay. That'll save time," Michelle agreed. "Just ask if you have any questions. Lisa says this is a very forgiving recipe. Even if you don't assemble it exactly right, it still turns out to be delicious."

"I wonder if you could do it with chicken breasts," Hannah said as she assembled the ingredients in her crock.

"I don't know why not. If you have any doubts, ask Aunt Nancy. It was her recipe in the first place."

"I'll ask and then I'm going to try it. I think I'll add some Hungarian paprika. That should be really tasty. And maybe I'll use a can of condensed cream of chicken soup for one of the cans of condensed mushroom soup."

"That's the nice thing about this recipe," Michelle said, putting the lid on one of the crocks and carrying it to the refrigerator. "You know it works and you can start playing around by switching ingredients. I do that with muffins all the time."

"And I do it with cookies to come up with new varieties for my customers." Hannah put the lid on her crock and put it on the bottom shelf of the refrigerator, right next to Michelle's.

"Will you hold the door open?" Michelle asked, picking up the last crock and carrying it to the open refrigerator. When that was safely stowed away, she went to the kitchen sink to wash her hands.

"We have eighteen pork chops," Hannah said.

"And they're double thick," Michelle pointed out. "I think that should be enough to feed everyone, even Mike."

LICK YOUR CHOPS PORK (ONE-DISH PORK CHOPS)

Hannah's 1st Note: Here's another recipe from Lisa's Aunt Nancy. It's so easy it's almost sinful. If you serve it to your family, you should run your fingers through your hair so it looks like you didn't have time to brush it, dab a little flour on your face, and rumple your apron a bit before you carry it out of the kitchen. That way your family will think you spent hours in the kitchen cooking just for them.

You'll need a large frying pan, a 6-quart or larger slow cooker *(crockpot),* OR a 9-inch by 13-inch cake pan.

6 center-cut pork chops, 3/4 inch to 1 inch thick

2 Tablespoons vegetable oil

1 Tablespoon salted butter

2 cans of **condensed** cream of mushroom soup *(I used Campbell's, 10 3/4 ounce cans — see Hannah's 2nd Note below)*

1 can of **condensed** tomato soup *(I used Campbell's, 10 3/4 ounce can — see Hannah's 2nd Note below)*

1 can of **condensed** cream of celery soup *(I used Campbell's, 10 3/4 ounce can — see*

Hannah's 2nd Note below)

1 package DRY pork gravy mix *(I used Schilling, the kind that you heat with one cup of water.)*

2 medium-size onions, chopped

2 medium-size green peppers *(or one red and one green, OR a small package of frozen tri-color pepper strips)*

3 or 4 medium-size potatoes, peeled and cut in half lengthwise

1 additional package of pork gravy mix *(for later)*

Salt *(for later when you adjust the seasonings)*

Pepper *(for later when you adjust the seasonings — freshly ground is best, of course)*

Hot Sauce *(make sure it's Slap Ya Mama hot sauce if you invite Mike Kingston!)*

Hannah's 2nd Note: It's becoming more difficult to find condensed soups in the stores. Make sure you look for the word *condensed* and read the directions, just to make sure. It should say to mix one can of water or milk with the can of soup before heating as soup. If it doesn't say that, you don't have condensed soup. If you buy Campbell's

soups, the condensed versions are generally in red and white cans with the words "Great for Cooking" on the label, but that could change before this recipe is published!

In a large skillet on MEDIUM HIGH heat, sauté the pork chops with the vegetable oil and butter until they're browned on both sides. Remove the pork chops to a plate and pull the frying pan from the heat. DON'T WASH IT! Use a spatula to loosen any tidbits of pork on the bottom of the skillet, but leave them there.

Lisa's Note: I always spray the inside of my crockpot with Pam when I make this recipe. Herb does the dishes when I do the cooking and it makes it easier for him to wash my crockpot.

Mix the 4 cans of condensed soup and the dry pork gravy mix together in a large bowl on the counter.

Place 1/4 of the soup mixture in the bottom of the crockpot.

Place a layer of pork chops on top of the soup. Turn them over with a fork so that the tops of the pork chops are coated and then cover them with another layer of pork chops. Slather the top layer of pork chops with another 1/4 of the soup. *(You have*

354

now used half of the soup.)

Turn the crockpot on LOW heat and cover it to begin cooking.

Place the chopped onions and peppers in the skillet you used for the pork chops and fry them over medium heat until the onions are translucent. Stir constantly, scraping the bottom of the pan to lift and mix in any tidbits of browned pork that have stuck to the pan.

Remove the onions and peppers from the pan with a slotted spoon and place them on top of the pork chops in the crockpot.

Slide the potato halves around the pork chops and slather on the rest of the soup in your bowl.

Replace the crockpot lid and cook until the pork chops and potatoes are fork tender, approximately 4 hours. *(Mine took the full 4 hours.)*

Taste the gravy that has formed and adjust the seasonings if necessary. If the gravy is not thick enough, sprinkle in the 2nd package of pork gravy mix, stir it in, put on the lid, and let it cook in the crockpot for an additional 15 minutes.

Serve with a small green salad if you wish, and you will have a complete meal with salad, meat, vegetable garnish, potatoes and gravy! You can also add a side dish of chilled applesauce or cranberry sauce.

Jo Fluke's Note: You can also make this meal in a 9-inch by 13-inch cake pan in the oven. Assemble it the same as you would in a crockpot, cover it with 2 layers of heavy-duty foil to seal in all that goodness, and bake it in a 350 F. degree oven for 3 hours or until the potatoes and pork chops are fork tender.

CHAPTER TWENTY-TWO

Straw-ber-ry fi-elds for-ev-er. She was running effortlessly through an endless expanse of strawberry fields, her diaphanous white gown streaming out behind her and her bare feet stroking the sun-warmed earth in perfect time to the Beatles song.

It was a sun-dappled summer afternoon with flitting butterflies decorating the fragrant, strawberry-scented air. The sunshine was warm on her shoulders, caressing her bare arms as she ran. Her feet kissed the ripe berries and they sent up waves of delightfully aromatic perfume as she crushed them beneath her toes.

Her toes . . . strawberries . . . Moishe!

Hannah sat up in bed, startling the cat who was licking her feet with his rough tongue. "Cut that out, Moishe! I was having the most wonderful dream and . . ." Hannah stopped speaking and rubbed her eyes to wake up.

Sunlight was streaming through her bedroom window. Or was that a part of her dream? It must be because she could still smell the strawberries, even though the lovely summer afternoon and the strawberry fields had disappeared.

There was only one way to tell if she was still dreaming and Hannah reached down for her slippers. She pulled them on and sighed as she stood up. She was awake. There was her alarm clock and it was ten after eight. And there was Moishe, staring up at her from his perch on her pillow. "Why do you always take *my* pillow? I bought you your own pillow and it's exactly like mine. Tonight I'm going to take your pillow and see how you like it."

The scent of strawberries was still in the air. If it was not a dream, the residual effect was lasting a long time. Hannah slipped on her robe and padded down the hallway toward the kitchen. With each step she took, the strawberry scent intensified.

"Good morning, Sleepyhead." Michelle greeted her the way Hannah had greeted her when Michelle was in grade school. "Sit down and I'll pour a cup of coffee for you." She indicated a pan of muffins sitting on a wire rack on the counter. "These muffins should be cool enough to eat in about ten minutes."

"They smell great!" Hannah said, a bit surprised that she could vocalize before her first sip of morning coffee.

"I hope they're as good as they smell. I just threw them together when I got up. I've never made strawberry muffins before."

Hannah watched as her sister filled a mug with coffee and carried it to the kitchen table. "Thanks," she managed to say.

"You're welcome. You don't have to talk before you've had your first cup. I know how difficult that is."

Hannah gave a nod and picked up the mug. She brought it to her lips and sipped the wonderfully restorative morning brew. "Good," she said, lifting the mug for another sip.

"What time would you like to see the judge's widow?" Michelle asked after Hannah had finished her first cup of coffee and had refilled the mug.

"How about ten? We have a good chance of catching her at home then. And she should be up and awake."

"You're not going to call first?"

"No. I almost always get more information when I surprise suspects."

"Then Mrs. Colfax is a suspect?"

"Yes, until I clear her. Family members

are always suspect until their alibis are checked out. Emotions run high in families." Hannah glanced over at her sister's strawberry muffins. "Do you think those muffins are cool yet?"

"Probably. I'll get one for you, but be careful when you take off the cupcake paper. It could still be hot in the center."

Hannah watched as Michelle plucked a muffin out of the pan and brought it over to her. There was softened butter and a knife on the kitchen table. Hannah felt the cobwebs in her mind begin to dissipate as she peeled off the fluted paper cup and took her first bite without benefit of butter.

"Mmmph," she said in a sound that was partly a sigh and partly a sound of pleasure. "These are great, Michelle!" She glanced over at the wire racks on the counter. "You made two dozen?"

"Yes. I thought that if I made a double batch, we could take some to Mrs. Colfax. Most people bring things when they pay condolence calls."

Hannah smiled. Michelle was turning into a good investigator if she'd figured out the reason that Hannah would give for seeking out the judge's widow. "That's just perfect. Thanks for baking them, Michelle."

"My pleasure. I love to bake in the morning. There's something magical about the sweet scents that fill the kitchen when you're sitting at the table, drinking coffee and waiting for whatever you baked to come out of the oven."

"Exactly right," Hannah said, agreeing with her sister wholeheartedly. "Judge Colfax's clerk gave me Nora Colfax's home address and it's less than a half hour from here. Let's get on the road by nine-fifteen, just to be on the safe side."

"That sounds like a plan," Michelle said, and then she chuckled softly.

Hannah was puzzled by the chuckle. As far as she knew, she hadn't said anything humorous. "Why are you laughing?"

"I was thinking that leaving early was a good idea, because it's harvest season and we might run into a Minnesota traffic jam."

"Two cars behind a tractor?"

"Right." Michelle refilled their coffee cups and grabbed a muffin for herself. She peeled off the paper and bit into it. "I think these worked well. I'll add them to the recipe file on my laptop."

"Make a copy for me," Hannah said, pushing her chair back and getting to her feet. "I'm awake now and I'm going to take a quick shower and get dressed."

"Okay. But don't you want another muffin?"

"Yes, when I get back. You've heard of the carrot on a stick in front of the donkey, haven't you?"

"Incentive," Michelle said. "That should work for both of us. I'll shower and dress, too. Our muffins will be right here waiting for us when we're ready."

At thirteen minutes before ten, Hannah pulled up in front of a modest house on the fifteen hundred block of Elmwood Street. The house was covered in pale blue stucco with white shutters on the sides of the windows and a white metal awning over the front door to protect the caller from the elements. There were still some late-blooming chrysanthemums in the window boxes and snowball bushes stood sentinel on the sides of the red brick walkway that led up to the front steps.

"Nice little house," Michelle said. "It's quite a contrast to the ex-Mrs. Colfax's mansion."

"The house and the flowers are well-kept," Hannah noted. "Those snowball bushes have been trimmed recently. If you let them go, they'll take over your whole yard."

"Snowballs are hydrangeas, aren't they?"

"Some are, some aren't. There are a lot of different types of hydrangeas. These look like the Japanese variety to me, and the soil must have a lot of aluminum because the blooms have a blue tint. The color depends on the acidity. It's late summer so these are already turning a bit green. I don't think they're the other type of snowball bush. Those are viburnum bushes, and I actually like them better because they have huge white blooms. But I'm no expert."

"You sound like an expert to me."

"But I'm not. It's just that I had to research hydrangeas and viburnums when Norman and I designed our dream house for that newspaper contest we won. Part of the planning included the landscaping around the house."

The two sisters walked up to the front door and Hannah rang the bell.

A moment or two later, the door opened to reveal a pleasantly plump woman dressed in a navy blue suit, white blouse, and dress shoes. Her hair was carefully styled and it was a beautiful shade of gray. Hannah judged her to be at least ten years younger than Judge Colfax.

"Mrs. Colfax?" Hannah asked her.

"Yes."

"I'm Hannah Swensen and this is my

sister Michelle. I knew your husband and we're both terribly sorry for your loss."

"Hannah Swensen. Oh, my! Do come in, my dears. My husband's clerk called me and said you might drop by."

"That's kind of you, Mrs. Colfax," Hannah said, beckoning to Michelle and then following the older woman to a small kitchen in the rear of the house.

"Sit down and have a cup of coffee with me."

"Are you sure you have time?" Hannah asked her. It was obvious that the judge's widow was dressed to go out.

"I have plenty of time. My appointment isn't until noon." She poured three cups of coffee and carried them to the table. "Cream or sugar?"

Hannah shook her head. "Just black for us."

"These are for you, Mrs. Colfax." Michelle handed her the box of muffins. "I baked strawberry muffins this morning."

"You girls are so talented!" Mrs. Colfax lifted the lid and peeked inside. "Oh, my! They smell just marvelous." She turned to Hannah. "My husband called me right before . . ." she stopped and cleared her throat. "He'd just eaten one of the brownies your lawyer brought for him. He said you'd probably baked them because you owned a bakery. Was he right?"

"Yes. They were my Double Fudge Brownies."

"Well, he really enjoyed them and he said he had to call to tell me how wonderful they were. Thank you, my dear, for giving him that pleasure. He was a wonderful man!"

Hannah felt tears come to her eyes. It was clear that Mrs. Colfax had loved her husband. "I'm so sorry," she repeated the sentiment.

"Seth called this morning and told me you'd been to see him last night. He told me not to worry, that you were a nice person and you were determined to catch my husband's . . ." Mrs. Colfax stopped speaking and cleared her throat again. "Geoffrey's killer."

"That's true, Mrs. Colfax."

"Nora. Please call me Nora, both of you." She turned and smiled at Michelle and then she turned back to Hannah. It wasn't much of a smile, but it was there nonetheless. "My heart goes out to you, Hannah. It must have been terrible, being the one to find Geoffrey like that."

Hannah nodded. It *had* been terrible, but she wasn't about to describe the scene to Judge Colfax's widow. "Do you know anyone who might have wanted to hurt your husband?"

"Oh, my yes! I'm sure quite a few people did. There are all the criminals he put behind bars, his ex-wife, Sheila, who despised him, and his former mistress. I'm not really sure how she felt about Geoffrey. He left her for me, you know. I loved Geoffrey very much, but there are those who felt quite the opposite."

"How about his son? Did Seth resent the fact that his father left the family?"

"I imagine he did at first. Seth was eleven and that's a difficult time in a young boy's life. And I'm sure Sheila filled his head with all sorts of nonsense about Geoffrey. He didn't leave Sheila for me, you know. I didn't even know Geoffrey then. He left Sheila because he could no longer stand living with her. He was wracked with guilt about leaving Seth behind. He tried his best to win custody of Seth, but the judge was old-fashioned and thought that children should stay with their mothers. The best Geoffrey could get was joint custody and Sheila didn't live up to her bargain with that."

"But Seth developed a good relationship with your husband as he grew older?"

"Oh, my yes! In the past three years

they've been practically inseparable. When Geoffrey worked as an interim judge, they had lunch together at least once a week. Seth just loves my meatloaf and he came to the house for Sunday dinner every week, and he always brought me little gifts like flowers and candy. He is a very thoughtful person and Geoffrey was so proud of him. He graduates from law school in June, you know."

"He told us. That's wonderful, Nora."

"Geoffrey certainly thought so. He said that his son had come into his own at last."

The moisture was building again in Nora's eyes and Hannah hurried with her next question. If Nora could concentrate on giving information that could assist in the murder investigation, it might help her deal with her grief.

"Have a muffin, Nora." Michelle pushed the box closer. "I'd really like to know what you think of them."

"Why . . . thank you. I think I will. Just sitting here smelling them is wonderful, but it isn't quite enough." Nora reached for a muffin, peeled off the paper, and tasted it. "Oh, my! These are delicious, Michelle! I wish I could bake like this. Would you girls like to have one with your coffee? Heaven knows, I don't need all of them!"

"Thanks, but we already had two apiece for breakfast," Hannah told her.

Nora smiled. "Well, I know that I'll enjoy them. My sister's coming in to help with all the arrangements and she loves strawberries. She's bound to love these muffins, too."

Hannah glanced down at her list of questions. She already knew that Judge Colfax had called his wife only minutes before he was killed. Nora had mentioned that. And Mike would be sure to pull the record of calls made from the judge's chambers. She was almost positive that Nora was telling the truth, but it couldn't hurt to check. There were times when intuition was the mother of disaster and Hannah wasn't about to assume anything when it came to investigating a murder.

The most difficult question was next and Hannah knew she had to phrase it carefully. If Nora took offense at the inference, she might refuse to answer any more questions. "I imagine your nephew was very upset," Hannah said, hoping that she sounded sympathetic.

"Chad?" Nora looked shocked. "I doubt he cares, one way or the other. Geoffrey didn't like Chad and I'm sure that Chad felt the same way, especially after the tongue-lashing Geoffrey gave him for pursuing the case against you in spite of his advice."

Hannah was surprised at this news. "Judge Colfax tried to talk Chad out of prosecuting me?"

"Several times. Geoffrey met with him privately and he told Chad that the charges were ridiculous, that no judge worth his salt would consent to even hear the case. But Chad wouldn't listen. He was always stubborn, even as a child."

"Do you think Chad was angry with Judge Colfax for dismissing my case?" Hannah asked her.

"I *know* he was angry. That's practically a given. Chad has quite the temper, and everyone in the judicial system knew it. Geoffrey told me that one of his female colleagues ordered Chad to attend a course in anger management before she'd allow him in her courtroom again."

"Judge Colfax's clerk told me about that."

Nora took another sip of her coffee. "Dave knows everything about everyone at the courthouse. I'm glad you talked to him. He's a very good source of information." Nora turned to Michelle, who'd just finished her coffee. "Would you like more coffee, my dear?"

"Yes please, and I'll get it," Michelle said,

rising from her chair to pour a second cup for all of them.

"I know where you're going with this, Hannah," Nora continued when Michelle had replaced the carafe in the coffeemaker and returned to her chair. "It does sound conceivable to an outsider, but I've known Chad since he was a baby and I don't think he could ever become angry enough to get physically involved in an altercation. He lets his mouth run away with him, but he's a physical coward at heart. He might have been terribly angry with Geoffrey, but to . . . to strike him like that?" Nora shook her head. "No, Hannah. Chad just doesn't have it in him."

Hannah nodded, but she wasn't convinced. Although she respected Nora's opinion, she wasn't about to cross Chad's name off her suspect list. She still planned to find out about the phone calls Judge Colfax had made in the days before his murder. If he had called Chad, she would be even more suspicious.

The last and final inquiry Hannah had on her list required great tact, and tact was a skill that Hannah did not possess naturally. Again, she knew that she had to be very careful about the way she phrased her question. "We've already talked about your husband's son," she said. "Did Judge Colfax have any other children?"

Nora sighed and shook her head. "No. Geoffrey and I never had children. I was over fifty when we married, and . . . well . . . it just didn't happen."

She doesn't know about the judge's daughter! Hannah's mind reminded her. *Dave told you, but he didn't tell her. What does that mean?* Hannah tabled that thought for future consideration and stood up. "Thank you so much for your hospitality, Nora. I'm very sorry we had to meet under such sad circumstances."

Michelle smiled at Nora as she stood up. "Please call us if there's anything we can do for you. And thank you very much for the coffee."

Hannah waited until they were in the cookie truck, driving away, before she glanced at Michelle. "Well? What did you think?"

"She's a nice lady who's hanging on by the skin of her teeth. And she doesn't know about Judge Colfax's daughter."

"Right."

"Dave told you, but he didn't tell her. And Judge Colfax didn't tell her, either."

"Right again." Hannah turned onto the highway and merged with the traffic. "I wonder what that means."

"You'll find out. Whatever it is, it may have something to do with Judge Colfax's murder. It's possible that your court case doesn't have any bearing on his murder. And the same goes for his other court cases. Judge Colfax could have been killed for a completely different reason."

Hannah gave a little groan. "You're right. I could have been interviewing the wrong people all this time. And if that's the case, the fact that Judge Colfax was a lawyer and a judge could be the biggest red herring I've ever encountered!"

STRAWBERRY MUFFINS

Preheat oven to 375 degrees F., rack in the middle position

The Batter:

3/4 cup salted butter *(1 and 1/2 sticks, 6 ounces)*

1 cup white *(granulated)* sugar

2 beaten eggs *(just whip them up in a glass with a fork)*

2 teaspoons baking powder

1/2 teaspoon salt

1/2 teaspoon cinnamon

1 cup fresh or frozen sliced strawberries *(no need to thaw if they're frozen)*

2 cups plus one Tablespoon flour *(pack it down in the cup when you measure it)*

1/2 cup whole milk

1/2 cup strawberry jam

Crumb Topping:

1/2 cup sugar

1/3 cup flour

1/4 cup salted butter *(1/2 stick)*

Grease the <u>bottoms only</u> of a 12-cup muffin pan *(or line the cups with double cupcake papers — that's what I do at The Cookie Jar).* Melt the butter. Mix in the sugar. Add the beaten eggs, baking powder, salt, and cinnamon. Mix it all up thoroughly.

Put the one Tablespoon of flour in a baggie with your cup of fresh or frozen sliced strawberries. Shake it gently to coat the strawberries and leave them in the bag for now.

Add half of the remaining two cups of flour to your bowl and mix it in with half of the milk. Then add the rest of the flour and the milk, and mix thoroughly.

Here comes the fun part: Add the half cup of strawberry jam to your bowl and mix it in. *(Your dough will turn a beautiful shade of pinkish red.)* When your dough is thoroughly mixed, fold in the flour-coated fresh or frozen sliced strawberries.

Fill the muffin cups three-quarters full and set them aside. If you have dough left over, grease the bottom of a small tea-bread loaf pan and fill it with your remaining dough.

Crumb Topping:

Mix the sugar and the flour in a small bowl. Add the butter and cut it in until it's crumbly. *(You can also do this in a food processor with chilled butter and the steel blade.)*

Fill the remaining space in the muffin

cups with the crumb topping. Then bake the muffins in a 375 degrees F. oven for 25 to 30 minutes. *(The tea-bread should bake about 10 minutes longer than the muffins.)*

When your muffins are baked, set the muffin pan on a wire rack to cool for at least 30 minutes. *(The muffins need to cool in the pan for easy removal.)* Then just tip them out of the cups and enjoy.

These are wonderful when they're slightly warm, but the strawberry flavor will intensify if you store them in a covered container overnight.

Hannah's Note: Grandma Ingrid's muffin pans were large enough to hold all the dough from this recipe. My muffin tins are smaller and I always make a loaf of Strawberry tea-bread with the leftover dough for my nieces. If I make it for Tracey and Bethie, I leave off the crumb topping. They love to eat it sliced, toasted, and buttered for breakfast. Andrea told me that her girls love strawberries so much, they even put strawberry jam on top of the butter!

CHAPTER TWENTY-THREE

"Here she is. My cell phone technology teacher," Hannah said to Michelle as she slid over in the booth so that Tracey could sit beside her. Hannah and Michelle had arrived at Hal and Rose's Café twenty minutes ago and they had been sipping coffee while they'd waited for Tracey to join them.

"Hi, Aunt Michelle." Tracey hugged Michelle and then she slid in beside Hannah. "This is *so* exciting! I've never gone out to lunch in the middle of a school day before! Mom had to write me a note and everything!" She leaned in a little and lowered her voice. "You should have seen all the other kids. They were jealous of me. Calvin Janowski even asked me if I'd bring him back one of Rose's pickles!"

"So you've got a thing going with Calvin?" Michelle asked her.

Tracey giggled merrily. "Oh, Aunt Michelle! You must be teasing me. Calvin's so immature!"

Hannah covered her laugh with a cough. There were times when Tracey sounded like her grandmother. "You're a little young for that, aren't you, Tracey?"

"Unfortunately, yes. But I'll get there. At least that's what Mom and Grandma Mc-Cann tell me. Could we please order now, Aunt Hannah?" Tracey glanced at her watch. "I have only thirty-three minutes left before I have to walk back to school. I don't want to be late for noon recess today. The girls are taking on the boys in kickball. And the ball isn't the only thing we're going to kick!"

"Tracey!" This time Hannah didn't cover her laugh. "I'd better not ask you what you mean by that."

"You can ask me. I'm just repeating what Grandma McCann said when I told her about the kickball contest. And when I asked her what she meant, she said that the girls would kick the score up so high, the boys couldn't possibly win. Isn't that funny?"

"That's funny," Michelle said, exchanging smiles with Hannah.

"I know that's not what Grandma Mc-Cann meant at all, but she recovers well, and I pretended to believe that."

"Oh, Tracey!" Hannah said, bursting into even more laughter. "You're cracking us up today. Do you know what you'd like for lunch?"

"Hamburger, fries, and a chocolate shake. I've been dreaming about that all morning. I almost lost my place in Bluebird Reading because I was so busy trying to decide between a strawberry and a chocolate shake. I'm just glad that Cheryl reads with her finger. All I had to do was look at her and I found my place again. It's a good thing I did because Miss Gladke called on me next. And she gets very upset with us when we lose our places."

"Cheryl reads with her *finger*?" Michelle asked, picking up on that part of Tracey's explanation.

"Yes." Tracey opened the menu and traced her finger along the line of print that described Rose's roast turkey sandwich on whole wheat bread. "Like this."

"I see," Michelle said. "And you don't read with your finger?"

"Not anymore. Mom said I used to in preschool, but now I just use my eyes. And I don't read with my lips, either. Calvin still does, but he's trying to stop. And I'm getting really good at keeping my place unless I'm too distracted by thoughts of hamburgers, fries, and chocolate milkshakes, of course."

"That's good, Tracey," Hannah said, motioning to Rose that they were ready to give her their order. "You're going to teach me how to text today, aren't you?"

"Yes. I think you're ready for that lesson. And if you're not, we'll just table it until tomorrow after school. And after I teach you to text, I'll take a look at Aunt Michelle's cell and see if there are any new apps that I can explain to her."

Hannah saw Michelle turn away and pretend to cough into her napkin and she looked grateful for the interruption when Rose arrived to take their order.

"Okay, Tracey," Hannah said, after Rose had gone off to prepare their lunch. "What do I do first?"

"You get out your cell phone."

"Right." Hannah retrieved it from her purse and handed it over to her young teacher. "There's a text I have to send. It's important and I'd like to learn how to do it while we're waiting for Rose to fix our lunch."

Twenty-five minutes later, Hannah had sent her text message and all three of them had finished Rose's delicious hamburgers, fries, and shakes.

"That was really good, Aunt Hannah!" Tracey said. "Thank you for buying me lunch." She turned to Michelle. "And thank you for asking Rose for an extra pickle for Calvin."

"I'll give you a ride back to school," Hannah offered. "Then you won't have to hurry. And I hope you girls do kick the boys' whatevers in kickball."

Tracey laughed and climbed into the back of Hannah's cookie truck. It was only a couple of blocks to the school, and Hannah pulled right up in front. "Do you see that pink box in the back, Tracey?"

"I see it, Aunt Hannah."

"Grab that and take it in with you. There are three dozen assorted day-old cookies inside. You can enjoy them with your classmates after the kickball game."

"Thanks, Aunt Hannah! I'll be over after school to enter your contacts."

"My what?"

"Your contacts. They're the phone numbers you call on a regular basis. How many of those numbers do you have?"

"I'm not sure." Hannah thought about it for a moment. "I call your mother, Michelle, Grandma Delores, Doc, Ross, Norman, Mike, and Lisa. I think that's it."

"But that's only eight!"

Hannah shrugged. "I know. I really don't use my cell phone that often."

"You will now that you have a smartphone. I'll put my number in your contacts. You can call me if you have trouble with your phone."

"Okay."

"And I'll need to put in your land line at the condo."

"Why?"

"So that it'll be listed under HOME. That way, if you ever lose your cell, the person who finds it can call your answer machine and leave a message."

"Okay," Hannah said. "That makes sense."

"Just remember, all you have to do is type the first couple of letters of somebody's name and their number will come up on your display. Then just hit CALL or TEXT and your phone will take care of the rest automagically."

"Automagically?"

"That's what I call it when my smartphone does something I like and I don't know how it does it." Tracey grabbed the cookie box and came around the truck to hug both Michelle and Hannah before she ran off toward the entrance. Hannah waited until her niece was safely inside and then she started the truck again.

381

"So who did you text?" Michelle asked after they'd pulled away. "I didn't want to ask you in front of Tracey in case it was personal."

"I sent a text to Mother to see if she knows Margaret George. That name is really familiar and I think I met her when I catered one of Mother's launch parties."

"Did she get back to you?"

"Not yet. Tracey used a special ring tone for text messages when they come in. It's a series of chimes that sound like Big Ben. It's totally different from the ring tone she used for phone calls."

"What do you have for phone calls?"

"It sounds like a ringing phone."

"That figures," Michelle said with a smile.

Hannah gave her a sharp look. "You think it should be something else?"

"No, it's perfect for you. Let's stop by The Cookie Jar and taste Lisa's new cookies. And then we'd better get back to your condo to get ready for the dinner party tonight."

"Uh-oh!" Hannah said as something dreadful occurred to her. "I didn't plug in the crockpots. Did you?"

"I've got all three on timers. By the time we get back, they should be bubbling away."

"What if they aren't?"

"Then we throw everything in a pan and bake it in the oven. It takes less time in the oven than it does in slow cookers. Don't worry, Hannah. Dinner will be ready on time. And we'll all have a wonderful evening."

Hannah thought of being in Ross's arms again and she began to smile. It was a slow smile that started with the corners of her lips and grew to encompass her whole face. "Yes," she breathed. "I *know* that I'll have a wonderful evening."

"Don't dress the salad now!" Michelle looked horrified as Hannah poured salad dressing into the bottom of the bowl.

"I'm not going to dress it," Hannah told her, sprinkling thinly sliced red onions on top of the dressing and then adding fresh spinach leaves.

"But . . ." Michelle stopped speaking, unsure of herself. "I've never seen you do that before."

"That's because I haven't done it before. It's a trick I learned from Sally out at the Lake Eden Inn. When she caters a large party and one course is a salad, she puts the dressing in the bottom of the bowl, adds something like onions that won't soak up the dressing or wilt, and then adds the greens on top of that. She finishes it off with tomatoes, but she doesn't slice them. And then she fills little Baggies with all the extras, like croutons, bacon bits, and shredded cheese, puts those on top, and then covers the whole thing with plastic wrap and puts it in her walk-in cooler. Then all her waitresses have to do is slice the tomatoes, add the baggies with the extras, and toss the salad when it's time to serve it."

"That makes a lot of sense."

"I know. I figured I'd try it tonight." Hannah added Baggies with bacon bits, freshly grated parmesan, and croutons, and put it on top of the lettuce. Then she covered it all with plastic wrap and stuck it in the bottom of the refrigerator.

The doorbell rang and Michelle glanced at the clock. "That'll be Andrea and Tracey . . . unless Ross bombed on his interview and came straight over here."

Hannah shook her head. "Ross didn't bomb on his interview," she said, heading to the door to open it. "He wants the job so he can move here." She opened the door and smiled when she saw Andrea and Tracey. "Hi, you two. Come on in."

"Can we please go in the kitchen, Aunt Hannah?" Tracey asked in tandem with her first step into the condo. "You said you had something special to show me."

"And I do. I'll show you right now if your mother and Aunt Michelle will set the table."

"Fine with me," Michelle said. "I'm through in the kitchen and it's all yours."

Andrea handed Michelle the bulky package she was carrying. "I'll help you, Michelle. Put this somewhere safe, will you, please? It's a floral centerpiece for the table. Grandma McCann is bringing the applesauce."

Hannah walked to the kitchen with Tracey at her heels. The first thing Tracey did was open the drawer with aprons, take out one, and hold it out to Hannah. "Is this one okay for me to wear, Aunt Hannah?"

"Of course. That's the one I bought for you, Tracey."

"What are we baking?" Tracey asked, slipping into the child-size, cobbler apron and going to the sink to wash her hands.

"We're not baking anything. We're making Pop in Your Mouth Chocolate Candy."

"No baking?" Tracey looked a bit disappointed.

"No baking," Hannah repeated, "but we're going to heat some chocolate in the microwave after we make the candy balls and we'll dip them in the chocolate."

385

"Oh, good. I love to use the microwave. Grandma McCann taught me how."

"That's good," Hannah said, and she meant it. Andrea was almost a total non-cook and non-baker. The only exceptions were her Jell-O molds and her whippersnapper cookies.

"Oreos?" Tracey asked, spotting the familiar package on the counter. "Are they in the Pop in Your Mouth Chocolate Candy, Aunt Hannah?"

"They are and I'll want you to crush them for me. Do you know how to use a rolling pin?"

"Sure. Grandma McCann lets me crush the graham crackers she uses for pie crusts."

"Good." Hannah handed her niece a rolling pin and a freezer-weight closable plastic bag. "Put one row of Oreos in here and then crush them with the rolling pin."

"As small as I crush graham cracker crumbs?"

"Yes. That small."

"Okay, Aunt Hannah, but wouldn't it be easier with the food processor?"

"It would be. But you're not allowed to use the food processor alone at home . . . are you?"

"No. Both Mom and Grandma McCann say the blade is too sharp. But if you set it up for me, I know how to pulse it."

"All right then," Hannah walked over to the counter and pulled the food processor into position. She attached the steel blade, plugged it into the outlet, and motioned to Tracey. "Are you allowed to put in the graham crackers for Grandma McCann?"

"Yes, as long as I drop them in one at a time, and don't get anywhere near the blade. Grandma McCann watches me like a hawk."

"Then so will I."

Hannah watched as Tracey opened the package and dropped the Oreos into the bowl of the food processor. "I think that's enough," she said when the bowl was about a third full. "The Oreos are stickier than graham crackers and I don't want to put in too many."

"Exactly right." Hannah put on the top and stepped aside to let Tracey stand in front of the machine. "Go ahead, Tracey. Pulse it."

Tracey pulsed the cookies until she was satisfied and then she turned to Hannah. "Do you have a plastic spatula, Aunt Hannah? I'm not allowed to reach inside with my fingers, but I can stir things up a little with a spatula."

Hannah reached into the container of

plastic utensils that sat on the counter and removed the type of spatula that Tracey wanted. "Here you go, honey. Check it to make sure there aren't any big chunks."

Tracey removed the top of the food processor and checked. "It looks fine to me. Do you want to check, Aunt Hannah?"

"No. You checked and that's good enough for me. I'll take out the blade and you can dump the crumbs in a bowl. And then we'll do another batch."

It didn't take long for Tracey to convert all of the sandwich cookies to sticky crumbs. When they were in the mixing bowl, Tracey turned to her aunt. "What's next, Aunt Hannah?"

Hannah went to the refrigerator and got a package of brick cream cheese. She opened it, put the cream cheese in a microwave-safe container, softened it in the microwave, and added it to the mixing bowl with the crumbs. "Stir it all up with a wooden spoon, Tracey. Make sure it's well mixed."

Tracey stirred the mixture until it was a homogenous mass. "I'm done," she reported.

"Now we have to cover it with plastic wrap and put it in the refrigerator for at least three hours."

"But will it be ready when the company

comes?"

"No. You'll take it home with you when you leave tonight. But I staged this recipe for you so you'll be able to have candy for everyone to taste."

"Oh, good!" Tracey sounded relieved as she carried her bowl to the refrigerator. She slipped it on a shelf and turned to Hannah. "Where do I find the stages?"

"The first stage is in that blue bowl on the second shelf. "It's been chilling for you. Bring it over to the counter and I'll show you what to do."

In very little time, Hannah had showed her niece how to roll balls with the chilled mixture, place them in a single layer in a wax paper-lined cake pan, and stick toothpicks in each of the balls."

"I'm done," Tracey said, sticking in the last toothpick. "What now?"

"Now put the balls in the refrigerator and take them home with you when you leave tonight. You can put them in your refrigerator at home and have Grandma McCann help you finish them when you come home from school tomorrow."

"Okay. But what do we do here? You said I'd have candy to give to the dinner guests."

"You will. I rolled balls from my first stage this morning, so the second stage is ready to be dipped. Do you like things dipped in chocolate?"

"You're teasing, Aunt Hannah. You know I do! And so does Bethie. Do I get to dip yours now?"

"You do. There's a box of balls with toothpicks in place on the top shelf of the refrigerator. We'll melt the chocolate and then we'll get them out."

"Okay." Tracey watched with interest while Hannah put a cup of chocolate chips in a Pyrex measuring cup and melted them in the microwave. She stirred the chips smooth and then she carried the measuring cup to the counter.

"Shall I get out your box of balls?" Tracey asked.

"Just as soon as you put wax paper in another box." Hannah indicated the empty box she'd placed on the counter. "The wax paper is in the third drawer down under the silverware."

Once the box was ready, Hannah and Tracey dipped the balls in the melted chocolate and placed them on the wax paper. "Put the box in the refrigerator, Tracey."

Tracey carried the box to the refrigerator and placed it on a shelf. When she came back to the counter, she looked very proud of herself. "I did it. It was easy, but you told me exactly what to do. You'll give me a copy of the recipe, won't you?"

"Of course. You saw how many balls we made and I know our guests won't eat them all. What are you going to do with the leftovers?"

Tracey thought about that for a moment. "I think I'll give them to Daddy to take in to work tomorrow . . . as long as Mom doesn't eat them in the middle of the night. She loves chocolate almost as much at Grandma Delores does!"

POP IN YOUR MOUTH CHOCOLATE CANDY

Do Not Preheat Oven — This Is a No Bake Recipe!

1 package Oreo Cookies *(14.3 ounces by weight — about 36 sandwich cookies)*

8 ounces brick-style cream cheese *(not whipped — I used Philadelphia Cream Cheese)*

1 cup *(6-ounce by weight package)* semi-sweet chocolate chips *(I used Nestle)*

Hannah's 1st Note: This recipe is from Rhonda, who earmarked it for Tracey.

Crush the Oreo cookies with the steel blade in a food processor or by placing them in a ziplock freezer bag and crushing them with a rolling pin.

Unwrap the cream cheese and soften it by placing it in a microwave-safe bowl and heating it on HIGH for 1 minute.

Add the crushed Oreo cookies to the bowl and mix them up thoroughly.

Cover the bowl with plastic wrap and place it in the refrigerator for at least one hour so that the mixture will firm up. *(Longer than one hour is fine, too.)*

Using impeccably clean hands, roll pop-in-your-mouth size balls from the cookie and cream cheese mixture.

Stick a toothpick into each ball and place the completed balls on a cookie sheet lined with wax paper. *(The toothpicks will make it easier for you to dip the balls in melted chocolate chips once they've firmed up in the refrigerator again.)*

Place the cookie sheet with the Pop in Your Mouth Chocolate Candy in the refrigerator for another 1 to 2 hours. *(Overnight is even better.)*

Once your balls have chilled again and you're ready to dip them in chocolate, place one cup of chocolate chips in a microwave safe bowl. *(I used a 2-cup Pyrex measuring cup.)*

Heat the chocolate chips on HIGH for 1 minute. Let them sit in the microwave for an additional minute and then stir to see if the chocolate chips are melted. If they're not, continue to heat in 20-second increments until they are.

Take the cookie sheet with the balls out of the refrigerator and set it on the counter. Using the toothpicks as handles, dip the balls, one by one, in the melted chocolate and then return them to the cookie sheet. Work quickly so that the balls do not soften.

If you want to decorate the balls with sprinkles, sprinkle them on while the chocolate coating is still wet.

Return the cookie sheet with the Pop in Your Mouth Chocolate Candy to the refrigerator for at least 2 hours before serving.

When you're ready to serve, remove the candy from the refrigerator, arrange the balls on a pretty plate or platter, and remove the toothpicks.

Hannah's 2nd Note: If you plan to serve these at a party, use pretty toothpicks when you make the balls and leave them in place so that your guests will have a way to pick them up off the platter without getting chocolate on their fingers.

Yield: Approximately 100 Pop in Your Mouth Chocolate Candies depending on the size of the balls.

CHAPTER TWENTY-FOUR

Hannah knew it wasn't physically possible, but she was willing to testify that she felt her heart jump up to her throat when the knock came at her door. "I'll get it," she gasped, and raced to the door to answer it.

"Hannah!" Ross stood on her landing, smiling and holding out his arms.

She wasn't aware of moving, but she must have stepped forward because before Hannah could draw another breath, she was standing on the landing with Ross, his arms clasped tightly around her. "You're here," she said breathlessly.

Her sarcastic mind countered, *What an idiotic thing to say! Of course he's here. You're standing on the landing with him.*

Hannah didn't give it another thought. She simply raised her face to his and kissed him.

Bells rang, birds chirped, strains of beautiful music floated through the air, and Hannah felt warm all over. Her mind told her how ridiculous her thoughts were, but she ignored it and ceased to think of anything except how wonderful it was to be in Ross's arms again. The kiss seemed to last forever, or at least until a female voice interrupted.

"Hey, Hannah!" Michelle roused her older sister from the fantasy that was no longer a fantasy. "Are you going to stand there kissing all afternoon? Or are you going to invite Ross in?"

Hannah blushed. She'd forgotten that she had people waiting inside. "Come in, Ross. Michelle's here, but you already know that. And so are Andrea and Tracey. I guess I got a little . . . distracted."

"Me, too." Ross chuckled and slipped his arm around her shoulders. And then he said quietly, so no one else could hear, "I've been dreaming about this moment ever since I left you at the airport in Las Vegas."

"Uncle Ross!" Tracey raced up to him. "You're here!"

"Rrrrrow!" Moishe yowled, following her.

"I'm so glad you're back!" Tracey said, hugging Ross. "We had so much fun the last time you were here."

"We did," Ross said, picking her up to give her a hug. "You've got to be at least a foot taller than the last time I saw you."

"Almost, but not quite. Grandma Mc-Cann says I'm growing like a weed. Is that a good thing?"

"Sure. Weeds are plants and some of them are really pretty. Have you ever seen a milkweed pod? They're beautiful."

Tracey thought about that for a moment while Ross reached down to pet Moishe, who was rubbing up against his legs.

"I don't think I've ever seen a milkweed pod," Tracey told him.

"Maybe we can go looking for some this weekend. I'm pretty sure your Aunt Hannah knows of some good places to look."

"I do," Hannah said quickly. "I've seen some by Eden Lake. Cattails, too."

"Rrroww!" Moishe let out a yowl, and everyone laughed.

"Not real ones, Moishe," Tracey told him. "We're talking about the plant variety."

The dinner was going very well and Hannah could hardly wait until everyone left. She chided herself internally for her impatience to be alone with Ross, and concentrated on being a good hostess. Thank goodness no one seemed upset that Ross was in Lake Eden! Mike and Norman appeared to be very happy to see him, and Hannah hoped that their acceptance would continue if they guessed that she was in love with him.

As it turned out, they hadn't needed any distractions. The green-eyed monster had not put in an appearance and everyone was getting along famously. Perhaps she was being a bit unrealistic, but it gave Hannah hope that she could remain friends with Mike and Norman even if her relationship with Ross intensified in the way she hoped it would.

"I'll help you put on the coffee, Hannah," Andrea said once they'd finished the salad, which had worked well, and eaten their main course of pork chops, peppers, and potatoes.

"Thanks," Hannah said quickly. Either Andrea had gotten a bit of dust in her left eye and was trying to blink it out, or she was attempting to send her a signal.

"What is it?" Hannah asked, when they were alone in the kitchen and the conversation had resumed at the table.

"Here," Andrea said, pulling a sheaf of papers from the shoulder bag purse she'd carried into the kitchen and handing them to Hannah. "The top one is Mike's report on Chad Norton."

"How did you get these?"

"I ran them through the scanner this

morning while Bill was in the shower." Andrea looked very proud of herself. "He always brings paperwork home with him when the detectives are working on a big case. I saved the files to my computer and I printed them out after Bill left."

"Very smart and very sneaky," Hannah complimented her.

"Thanks. I was going to give them to you earlier, but then you got busy baking with Tracey, and then Ross came, and there wasn't any time I could get you alone. I figured you could go over them with Michelle after everyone's left."

"That's exactly what I'll do." Hannah placed the papers on the top shelf of her cupboard. "Does Bill think Chad did it?"

"Not anymore. Mike cleared him. It's all in the report. Chad was on the phone to his boss when Judge Colfax was killed."

Hannah used a word she would never have used if Tracey had been in the kitchen. "I was almost hoping he was guilty."

"Bill felt the same way," Andrea said. "And so did everyone else at the station. They all think that Chad is an arrogant . . ." she stopped and grinned, "another word that starts with an *a*. I'm sure you know what I mean."

Hannah laughed. "Of course I do. You

meant arrogant *attorney.* Or perhaps, arrogant *assistant* DA."

"Right," Andrea said with a laugh, just as Tracey came into the kitchen, followed by Ross.

"Norman says to tell you that Cuddles has that look in her eyes again," Ross reported. "What does that mean?"

"I told him that it meant *feet up,* Aunt Hannah, but Uncle Ross didn't get it," Tracey tried to explain. "You'd better tell him."

"I'll do better than that," Hannah promised. "I'll show him." She motioned to the platter of cake she'd just sliced and the tray of coffee cups. "Will you carry the tray with the cups, Ross? I'll bring the coffee, Tracey can carry the cream and sugar, and Andrea can take the cake."

"I always did take the cake," Andrea quipped, following them to the table.

They actually managed to eat a little cake and take several sips of coffee before Hannah heard kitty footfalls coming down the hallway. "Feet up!" she warned, steadying her coffee cup and picking up the carafe. Those who knew the drill lifted or steadied anything on the table that might fall as Moishe raced into the room, followed closely by Cuddles, who was chasing him.

Ross raised his feet like everyone else as the cats raced around the table. "So that's what *feet up* means! But why do you steady the . . ." He stopped speaking as Moishe slammed into the table leg and their coffee sloshed in the cups. "Oh! *Now* I get it."

"Hannah's cat got my steak that way one night at Norman's house," Lonnie explained. "Moishe crashed into the table leg, and my steak fell on the floor. Before we could pick it up, he grabbed it and ran up to Norman's bedroom with it. By the time we got up there, both cats were under the bed eating it."

"So now he does it on purpose," Ross said, catching on immediately. "It's almost impossible to wipe out the effects of intermittent reinforcement. Moishe and Cuddles will probably do this every time you have food on the table."

"He's right," Hannah said, exchanging glances with her sisters. There was no need to say that they'd helped the intermittent reinforcement along by dropping some of the little bits of pork they'd secreted in their napkins. "If they keep on doing this, we may have to eat behind closed doors."

"Or take them to my house every time we eat here," Norman said. "And bring them here, every time we eat at my house."

"Or you could simply come to our house," Lisa suggested, "except then we'd have to deal with our dogs because Dillon and Sammy beg at the table."

Hannah turned to her partner in surprise. "I thought you weren't going to give them scraps from the table."

"I wasn't. And I haven't." Lisa turned to Herb. "He does it all the time, but they know better than to beg from me."

"How about at breakfast?" Herb asked Lisa, and Hannah noticed that Lisa's face turned slightly pink. "You know as well as I do that breakfast is a free-for-all at our house."

"Not all the time! And it's only when we have bacon." Lisa turned to Hannah. "It's those sad puppy dog eyes. I just have to give Dillon some of my bacon. And in the interest of fairness, I simply have to give Sammy the same amount."

"Let me get this straight," Hannah said. "You feed them bits of bacon at breakfast, but you don't feed them anything at lunch or dinner?"

Lisa nodded. "That's right."

"And somehow you expect them to know that they can beg from you if there's bacon on the table but they can't beg from you if you don't serve bacon?"

"Exactly right. That's the way I trained them."

Hannah began to grin. "So . . . you're telling me that you never serve bacon at lunch or dinner?"

"Well . . . there are exceptions. Sometimes we have BLTs for lunch, but they smell entirely different than just plain bacon. A dog's sense of smell is very acute, you know."

Hannah turned to Herb. "Does this actually work?"

"Not at all, but Lisa keeps trying."

Everyone at the table laughed, including Lisa. "Herb's right. It's not really working, but you know me. I refuse to give up. One of these days one of them will get it . . . maybe. And in the meantime, they get lots of bacon."

"Maybe you should try to pair it with a signal," Tracey suggested. "You know, like ringing a bell when it's bacon for breakfast, but not ringing it when it's bacon for lunch. After a while, they might not expect anything when the bell doesn't ring."

Just as Tracey finished speaking, a bell rang. It sounded like a clock way off in the distance, but Hannah didn't have any clocks with chimes.

"Did you do that for effect?" she asked Tracey.

"No, you did. You're getting a text message, Aunt Hannah."

"Oh!" Hannah exclaimed, and then she laughed at herself. "It'll stay there until I retrieve it, won't it?"

"Yes," Tracey assured her. "It'll stay there until you read it and then it'll go into the old text mode unless you erase it."

"Right. That's what you taught me at lunch."

"Yes. And you taught me how to make Pop in Your Mouth Chocolate Candy. Do you think they're ready yet, Aunt Hannah?"

Hannah glanced at the clock. "I'm sure they are. Why don't you go get them right now, Tracey?" She looked around the table. "You all want to try one, don't you?"

"You have to ask when it's *chocolate*?" Grandma McCann questioned with a laugh.

"Chockit!" Bethie said, clapping her hands. "I want *chockit*!"

"She knows how to say that," Bill commented. "Andrea says it's the first word she learned."

Andrea shook her head. "Actually, it's not. Her first word was for you, Bill. She called you Da-da, just like Tracey did. It's pretty obvious that Daddies count more than

Mommies in our family."

"Now you know that's not true," Bill said with a laugh, but Hannah noticed that he looked very proud. She hoped that Andrea would never admit that both Tracey and Bethie had said *Ma-ma* first.

After more coffee refills and several Pop in Your Mouth Chocolate Candy pieces that everyone pronounced incredibly delicious, Norman got up. "I'd better check on the cats."

"Because they're quiet . . . too quiet?" Hannah asked him.

"That's right. It generally means that they're into something when they do that at my house. The last time it was the cat food. One of them knocked the bag down from the counter and they were in the kitchen gorging themselves."

"That's why I have a padlock on my broom closet and I keep the cat food in there," Hannah said. "Moishe hasn't figured out how to pick that lock yet."

Mike smiled. "Give him time, Hannah. And if he can't get to his dry food, he'll learn how to use a can opener and steal your tuna and salmon."

"Or your salad shrimp," Lisa said. "I bet he could open your freezer if he really put his mind to it."

"Look at this!" Norman came back holding a small teddy bear.

"Where did you find that?" Hannah asked him.

"The cats had it under your bed and they were chewing on it. I think I got it just in time. They punctured it a few times with their teeth and they were probably getting ready to pull out the stuffing." Norman stopped and frowned slightly. "It's not a cat toy, is it?"

Hannah took the teddy bear from Norman and examined it. "No, and it's not mine, either." She turned to look at Michelle. "Is it yours?"

"No, it's not mine." Michelle turned to Andrea. "Is it yours?"

Andrea shook her head. "It's not mine and it's not one of Bethie's toys. It has beads for the eyes and we don't let her play with anything she could pull off and choke on."

"It doesn't squeak, does it?" Lisa asked.

"I don't think so." Hannah squeezed it several times, but the teddy bear didn't make a sound. "No squeak," she reported.

"Then it's not a dog toy. They usually have squeakers inside."

"Could I see it, Hannah?" Grandma McCann asked.

Hannah handed the teddy bear to

Grandma McCann, and Ross, who was sitting next to Bethie's high chair, watched as she examined it. "Maybe that loop at the top of its head is a hanger," he said. "You could slip it over a nail, or . . . wait a second! It's made of red and green plaid. Do you think it could be a Christmas tree ornament?"

"I think that's exactly what it is," Andrea told him. "I've seen bears like that at the mall. I was thinking of doing a bear Christmas tree, but I decided to wait until the girls were older and they could help me pick out the ornaments."

"I'm older," Tracey pointed out.

"I know you are. Let's wait until Bethie is old enough to appreciate it and then we'll do it."

"Okay," Tracey said, smiling at her mother. "It'll be more fun if Bethie can go shopping with us, too."

"Looks like the cat burglar struck again," Mike said. "I think we'd better put a tail on Moishe."

"He's got a tail, Uncle Mike!" Tracey said, and then she giggled.

Mike laughed and so did everyone else with the exception of the cats who had come into the room and were looking at them curiously.

"Aha!" Mike said. "Here's my prime suspect, right over there in the orange and white coat. Lonnie? I want you to interrogate the suspect for me."

"Sure thing, boss." Lonnie patted his lap and Moishe jumped up. "Please state your name for the record."

"Rrrrrow!" Moishe said.

"Could you spell that for the record?"

"Rrrrrow."

"Thank you. All right, Mr. Cat. If you're honest with me, it'll go easier on you. Where were you on the night of . . ." Lonnie turned to Bill. "What's the right date, Sheriff Bill?"

Bill was laughing so hard, he couldn't answer and so was everyone else around the table.

"All right then," Lonnie continued. "We'll concentrate on the previous three nights, Mr. Cat. That would be Wednesday, Tuesday, and Monday."

Moishe stared up at Lonnie blankly. His expression was so comical, it sent everyone off in gales of laughter again.

"Stop!" Hannah said at last. "I'm going to have sore ribs tomorrow from laughing so hard."

Lonnie lifted Moishe and lowered him to the rug. "Thank you for your cooperation, Mr. Cat. You may now leave in the company of Miss Cat . . . or is that Miss Chief?"

"Mischief!" Tracey almost collapsed as she caught on to what Lonnie was saying. "That's funny, Uncle Lonnie!"

"I missed you all so much," Ross said, smiling at Hannah. "I never laughed like this in California. It's really good to be back."

"So how did the interview go?" Mike asked him.

"Yes," Norman jumped into the conversation. "Did you get the job, Ross?"

Hannah held her breath and crossed her fingers the way she had as a child when she wanted something she didn't think she could live without. She not only crossed her middle fingers with her pointer fingers, she also crossed her ring fingers with her pinkies. And then, for good measure, she crossed her thumbs together in her lap. She would have willingly crossed her toes, if she'd been able to figure out how to do it.

"The interview went well," Ross told them. "I have the job on a week's trial basis."

"They're pretty cheap out at KCOW," Lonnie said. "One of my sisters worked there until she found something better. Did they try to get you to work that trial week without pay?"

"No, it's half-pay. But that's okay for a

week. They'll let me know by next Friday at the latest. Then, if I've got the job, I'll go up to full pay, benefits, and bonuses for every project I film for them."

Mike whistled. "Not bad. You must have driven a hard bargain."

"I did. I told them that, in the interest of full disclosure, I also had an upcoming interview at WCCO Television in Minneapolis."

"Do you?" Bill asked.

"Actually . . . yes. What I didn't tell them was that all WCCO was interested in was using the film I shot here in Lake Eden to kick off their Minnesota at the Movies month."

"Smart," Norman said, smiling at Ross. "KCOW might have tried to work you at half-pay for more than one week if you hadn't told them that."

Hannah listened to the ensuing conversation, but she was concentrating much more on her inner thoughts. *KCOW offered Ross a job! It's a temporary job, only for a week, but they're bound to be impressed with him. Say they hire him full-time and pay him a full salary. What, exactly, does that mean for me? Will Ross ask me to marry him? And if he does, what will I say?*

"Earth to Hannah," Norman said, stilling

her inquisitive mind and bringing her back to the conversation with a jolt.

"Yes, Norman?" Hannah smiled. "Sorry about that. I was thinking about . . ." she thought fast and came up with something, ". . . baking a new cookie."

"What kind of cookie?" Tracey asked her.

"A tea cookie."

"A refrigerated one?" Lisa asked and Hannah noticed that she looked interested.

"Actually . . . no. I was thinking about baking a cookie with tea in it. Mother's Regency Romance Readers Group would love it."

Ross gave her a look that said *Maybe you can fool them, but you can't fool me. That wasn't what you were thinking about at all.*

Hannah could feel herself beginning to blush and she quickly dropped her eyes, but not before she saw his amused smile.

Grandma McCann glanced at her watch. "It's getting late and it's a school night. I'd better take my little lambs home."

"Widdow Wamm," Bethie said and then she laughed.

"That's right," Tracey told her. "You're Grandma McCann's little lamb."

"Widdow Wamm," Bethie repeated again. It obviously delighted her because she said it over and over as Grandma McCann got

her into her coat. Bill collapsed the foldable high chair, Andrea made sure that Tracey's jacket was zipped up, and they all went down the stairs together to help Grandma McCann get them safely into the car.

CHAPTER TWENTY-FIVE

"Alone at last," Ross said when everyone had left. "How long do we have before Michelle and Lonnie come back from their walk around the complex?"

"I don't know," Hannah said. "I guess it depends on how cold it is out there."

"Fair enough. You said you had the makings for tequila sunrises. Would you like me to make one for you?"

"That would be nice. Will you have one with me?"

"Sure. I could use something to relax me after the flight and the interview. Come to the kitchen with me and show me where everything is. We'll make our drinks together."

Hannah felt her spirits rising as she walked to the kitchen with Ross's arm warm around her shoulders. It was great to be together again.

"I've been thinking about the motel," Ross

said and he sounded very serious. "I don't think you should drive out there, Hannah."

"Why?" Hannah asked, wondering if he knew that she'd been having second thoughts about that. She'd offered to drive out because she'd wanted to be alone with him, but now she wasn't sure it was the right thing to do.

"Don't take this wrong, Hannah." Ross gave her a little hug. "I want you to come out there with me, but someone's bound to see you. We can wait, can't we?"

"Yes, we can wait." Hannah turned to kiss him. "Thank you, Ross. That's exactly what I was thinking." *Wait for what?* her mind asked. *Wait for the cows to come home? Ask him what he means. You know you want to know.*

But Hannah squelched the urge to ask. Ross would tell her what he'd meant when the time was right. In the meantime, she was happy just to be with him doing things like eating dinner, enjoying company, and talking. More serious things would come later. She was sure of it. And if Ross could wait, so could she.

Hannah didn't think about the text message until she was in bed for the night. She was tired and she wanted to go to sleep, but perhaps her mother had responded to her question about Margaret George.

"I'll be right back," Hannah told the cat she knew would claim her pillow the instant she was out of the room, and went to get her phone. She flicked on the light in the living room, glanced at the display on the screen, and pressed the button Tracey had taught her to press to retrieve text messages.

There it was! She must have done it right! Hannah was so excited about her success, she almost forgot to read the text message. When she did, a wide smile spread across her face.

Hello, dear. You were right. Margaret George is in my Regency group. She'd rather be called Peggy than Margaret and she lives in Elk River. Carrie has her street address. Go see her. I know she'll remember you. She was wild about your Regency Ginger Crisps. Love, Mother.

"Thank you, Mother," Hannah said aloud, and made a promise to herself that she'd text her mother in the morning when she wasn't so tired and was capable of remembering the instructions that Tracey had given her. She plugged in her phone to charge it and went back to her bedroom.

415

Just as she'd expected, Moishe had commandeered her pillow.

"Fine. I'll use yours." She grabbed his pillow and crawled into bed for a much-needed rest.

Morning came much too early. Hannah groaned when her alarm went off and she resisted the urge to press the snooze button with every fiber of her being. She let the electronic beeping go on as she dangled her feet over the side of the bed and forced herself to sit up. She wanted nothing so much as to crawl back into the nest of blankets still warm from her body, and cuddle up for another five minutes that could turn into ten with another press of her snooze button, or fifteen, or twenty.

"Up!" she commanded her body and reached under the bed for her slippers. Her nose began to function and she smelled the invigorating scent of freshly brewed coffee.

"Michelle," she said with a gratefulness that bordered on the pathetic. There was another scent in the air as well, something with the delightful aroma of cinnamon and raisins and brown sugar. Coffee cake? Rolls? Whatever it was, she wanted some!

She told herself that she had to shower and dress before she could taste whatever it was that Michelle had made for breakfast. With that inducement firmly in place, she made short work of it.

Ten minutes later, she was walking down the hallway with Moishe at her heels, and she was eager to taste the reason for her haste. "Good morning, Michelle," she greeted her youngest sister as she hurried into the kitchen. "What smells so delicious?"

"Cinnamon Raisin Scones." Michelle turned around to look at her. "You're dressed!"

"That's your fault."

"What?"

"I told myself that I couldn't come out to see what you were baking until after I'd showered and dressed. So I did. Really fast."

"Turn around," Michelle said, and then she laughed.

"Why are you laughing?"

"You have your sweater on backward."

"I do?" Hannah rolled her sweater up to her armpits, slipped her arms out of the sleeves, and turned the sweater around on her neck. Once her arms were back in the sleeves, she rolled the sweater back down and went to pour herself a cup of coffee. "I thought it was a little tight around the neck."

"See what happens when you dress without your first cup of coffee? It's a good thing I was here. You would have gone to work with your sweater all wonky."

"You're probably right." Hannah took her first scalding sip of coffee and smiled. "Ross is probably getting ready for his first day of work right now."

"He's ready. He called twenty minutes ago to see if we were up. I hope you don't mind, but I invited him over for scones and coffee. I was just coming to wake you up when I heard you in the shower."

"Ross is coming here?"

"That's right. That's okay, isn't it?"

"That's not okay, that's great. I'll get to see him before work. I look all right, don't I?"

"You do, now that your sweater's on right. Do you want to go and put on some makeup?"

"Not really, unless . . ." Hannah began to frown. "Do I need makeup?"

"No. You look fine without it. And it's breakfast, not a gala evening out."

"Good," Hannah said, finishing her coffee and going back for more. "I'm almost awake and once I have my second cup of coffee, I should be able to text Mother."

"So it was Mother who texted you?"

"Yes. She told me how to reach Margaret

George. She's in Mother's Regency group, except she doesn't go by Margaret. She prefers to be called Peggy."

"Okay. If she's a member of the Regency group, she'll probably like scones. We can take her some if you want to. This recipe made twelve large or eighteen medium scones."

"That's the same yield as my Easy Cheesy Biscuit recipe."

Michelle laughed. "Where do you think I got the basic recipe? It's yours with modifications."

"Good for you! There are a limited number of basic recipes. All the others come from modifications of the ingredients that influence the taste, the shape, and the texture. It's a little like a melody. There are a limited number of musical tones that the human ear can hear. The melody depends on how you arrange them. And that whole subject is a little too involved for a discussion before breakfast. Aren't those scones of yours almost ready to come out of the oven?"

"Are you hoping I get this job, Hannah?" Ross asked when Michelle went back to her room to get ready to leave.

"Yes," Hannah answered him quickly.

"And do you want me to move here to Lake Eden?"

"Oh, yes!" Again, the answer came quickly and from her heart.

"The dinner was fun last night and I don't think that either Mike or Norman was too upset at the prospect of me coming back here permanently. Am I wrong?"

"You're not wrong." She hesitated and then blurted out exactly what was on her mind. "They might have been more upset if they'd known about Las Vegas."

"They don't know that I met you in Vegas?"

"Oh, they know that!" Hannah stopped and tried to think of a way to explain. "It's just that they don't know that we became . . . involved when we met in Las Vegas."

"You didn't mention that I love you?"

Hannah shook her head. "Not yet."

"Some people might think you were being evasive just in case things didn't work out between us."

"I know. I thought about that, but that's not it at all. I just want to break it to them gently so that we can all remain friends. Do you think that's possible? Or am I deluding myself?"

"I don't know. I guess we'll just have to

wait and see."

"One step forward at a time?"

"Yes. The first step is this job at KCOW Television. Let's see how that turns out. If I get it, we'll take the next step. And if I don't get it, we'll figure out where to go from there. Is that all right with you?"

"Yes." Hannah smiled as he stood up and pulled her into his arms for a kiss. "That's absolutely fine with me, Ross."

It was ten in the morning when Hannah pulled up in front of Peggy George's home. It was a condo complex with one-story units that had red brick exteriors and dark green doors that matched the trim around the windows. Judging from the outside, Peggy's unit appeared to have three bedrooms. Hannah figured that one bedroom was for Peggy, one for her daughter, and one for Peggy's office where she wrote her Regency romances.

"Nice place," Michelle said as Hannah parked in the space set aside for visitors.

Hannah agreed with her sister's assessment as they got out of the cookie truck and walked down a winding brick path to Peggy's unit. Late-blooming flowers lined the paths and the lawns were still green and manicured. Adult trees provided shade for the units and Hannah spotted a children's playground with slides, a jungle gym, and swings, along with a paved bike path and a tennis court.

"I hope we're not too early," Hannah said, glancing at her watch before she prepared to ring the doorbell.

"It's ten-fifteen," Michelle said. "She should be up, unless she spent all night writing."

"There's only one way to find out." Hannah pressed the button that rang the doorbell. And then they waited. And waited. And waited for some response from inside.

"Do you think she's gone?" Michelle asked.

"Maybe. I'll ring the doorbell again and if she doesn't answer, we'll go somewhere for coffee and try again later."

The second attempt garnered no more response than the first. Hannah turned from the door and was about to step away when she heard a voice.

"Hello! Are you looking for me?"

A woman came rushing along the path toward them, her brown, curly hair bouncing as she ran. She was wearing an aqua blue jogging suit and sneakers.

"It's her," Hannah said to Michelle, and

then she turned to greet the woman. "Hi, Peggy."

"Hannah!" Peggy looked pleased to see her at first and then a doubtful expression flickered across her face. "You found his body."

"Yes."

"It must have been horrid for you. Are you all right?"

Hannah nodded, a bit taken aback. It was not the reception she'd expected.

"It was in the papers," Peggy said, answering Hannah's unspoken question. "I called Delores to ask her about it, but she wasn't home."

"She eloped with Doc," Hannah explained. "Right now they're on a cruise to Alaska for their honeymoon."

"How lovely!" A smile spread across Peggy's face. "I took my daughter Sara on an Alaskan cruise last year when she got her master's in biology. She fell in love with the seals on the ice floes. We took hundreds of pictures from our balcony on the ship, especially when we went through Sawyer Bay. We actually got to hear a glacier calving."

"What's that?" Michelle asked her.

"Calving is when a piece of ice breaks off a glacier and falls down into the water. It makes the loudest sound you'll ever hear. It was phenomenal!" Peggy stopped speaking and turned to smile at Michelle. "I'm sorry, but I don't even know your name."

"Michelle Swensen," Michelle responded before Hannah had time to introduce her. "I'm Hannah's youngest sister. If you came to Mother's last launch party, I was there serving canapés."

"Of course. I thought you looked familiar." Peggy unlocked the door and pushed it open. "Come in, girls." She turned to Hannah. "I assume you want to ask me about my connection with Geoffrey. Your mother mentioned that you investigate things like this."

They made polite conversation about Delores and Doc's wedding and Peggy's cruise to Alaska until Peggy had made coffee and they were all sitting in comfortable chairs in the small living room, sipping coffee and eating Michelle's scones.

"All right," Peggy said to Hannah after she'd complimented Michelle on her scones. "I knew you'd be coming so feel free to ask me your questions."

"How did you know?" Hannah asked her.

"Dave called and said he'd told you about me because you were trying to catch the person who'd murdered Geoffrey. Poor

Geoffrey. And my heart goes out to Nora. She couldn't have children and Geoffrey was her whole life. You probably know that he chose not to tell Nora about Sara."

"Yes. Why was that?"

"Geoffrey was afraid it would break Nora's heart. She'd tried so hard to get pregnant. And she wanted so badly to give him a daughter. He was afraid it would be devastating for her to learn that he had a daughter by his former mistress."

"Did you think he was right?"

"I'm not sure. It could have gone either way, I guess, but I didn't know Nora's mental state at all. I've never met her and I wasn't in any position to judge, so I did as Geoffrey wanted. He spent time with Sara and he was good to her. That was all that really mattered to me."

"You didn't resent the fact that he left you and married Nora?" Michelle asked the question that was hovering on the tip of Hannah's tongue.

"Oh, I did. At first. But I didn't really want to marry Geoffrey. It wasn't him. I just didn't want to marry at all. I didn't find out that I was pregnant with Sara until after Geoffrey left."

Hannah asked the first question on the list she'd prepared. "Where were you when

Judge Colfax was killed?"

"Right here," Peggy reached out to pat the couch next to her chair. "And I do mean right *here*. I had a deadline to meet and I'd spent all night proofing the manuscript. When I finished, I sent off the file to my editor in New York and I was just too tired to get ready for bed. I grabbed a blanket from the closet and fell asleep on the couch."

"Did anyone see you here on the couch?"

"Just Sara, but she left early and that won't do you any good. Dave said that Geoffrey was killed between nine and nine-thirty and Sara left at seven. She's an assistant professor at the community college."

"Is there anyone else who might know that you were here when Geoffrey was killed? Perhaps someone knocked on the door and you had to get up to answer it? Or you made or received a phone call?"

"Not that I can think of. The phone didn't ring and . . ." Peggy stopped speaking and began to smile. "Of course there's a way to tell I was here. I forgot all about the guard at the gate. Didn't he stop you to ask who you were visiting and log in your license plate number?"

"Yes, he did."

"Well, they do that with the residents, too.

They have a checklist and they log you out if you leave. If I'd been logged out, the guard would have told you to come back later, that I wasn't home."

"Perfect," Hannah said, jotting it down. And then she asked the question she'd been dreading to ask. "How about your daughter, Sara? Where was she at the time of Judge Colfax's death?"

"*Sara?*" Peggy looked as shocked as a person could possibly look. "You think that Sara killed Geoffrey?! Why she couldn't even go to work on Tuesday because she was crying so hard!"

"Of course I don't think Sara killed him," Hannah said hastily. "It sounds as if they had a very good relationship and I'm so sorry to bring it up, but I simply want to cross her name off my suspect list."

"Then you don't really think . . . ?"

"Absolutely not!" Hannah interrupted the question. "All I want to do is clear Sara's name the way I've cleared yours."

"Oh. That's fine then." Peggy drew a deep, shuddering breath. "I'm sorry I overreacted."

"That's quite all right. Let's try to think of a way we can prove that Sara was nowhere near the Winnetka County Courthouse on Monday."

"Why that's easy!" Peggy exclaimed. "Sara teaches a lab in biology from nine to ten on Monday mornings. All you have to do is check with the college to make sure she was in the lab."

"I'll do that," Hannah promised. "Now I have one final question and I want you to think very hard about it and call me if anything occurs to you after we leave. Will you please do that?"

"Of course. What is it?"

"I want you to think about your life with Geoffrey and all the people you met or heard about. Is there anyone you can think of who might have wanted Geoffrey to die?"

"His ex-wife Sheila?"

"Not Sheila. I've already cleared her."

Peggy was silent for long moments and Hannah could tell that she was giving the question some serious thought. Several minutes passed and then Peggy looked up. "No one. I can't think of anyone at all. But please leave me your number and if I think of someone, I promise I'll call you and tell you."

CINNAMON RAISIN SCONES

Preheat oven to 425 degrees F., rack in the middle position.

3 cups all-purpose flour *(pack it down in the cup when you measure it)*

1/3 cup brown sugar *(pack it down in the cup when you measure it)*

2 teaspoons cream of tartar *(important)*

1 teaspoon baking powder

1 teaspoon baking soda

1 and 1/2 teaspoons cinnamon

1/2 teaspoon salt

1/2 cup salted butter *(1 stick, 4 ounces, 1/4 pound)*

2 large eggs, beaten *(just whip them up in a glass with a fork)*

1 cup vanilla yogurt *(8 ounces by weight)*

1 cup raisins *(I used golden raisins)*

1/2 cup whole milk

Use a medium-size mixing bowl to combine the flour, brown sugar, cream of tartar, baking powder, baking soda, cinnamon, and salt. Stir them all up together. Cut in the salted butter just as you would for piecrust dough.

Hannah's Note: If you have a food processor, you can use it for the first

step. Cut the half-cup COLD salted butter into 8 chunks. Layer them with the dry ingredients in the bowl of the food processor. Process with the steel blade in an on and off motion until the mixture has the texture of coarse corn-meal. Transfer the mixture to a medium-sized mixing bowl.

Stir in the beaten eggs and the vanilla yogurt. Then add the raisins and mix everything up together.

Add the milk and stir until everything is combined.

Drop the scones by soup spoonfuls onto two cookie sheets sprayed with Pam or another nonstick baking spray. Alternatively, you can line your baking sheets with parchment paper. Divide your dough so that there are 9 scones for each cookie sheet.

If you have two ovens, you will bake one sheet in the upper oven and one in the lower oven. If you have only one oven, it will probably have 4 racks inside. Bake your scones on the two middle racks, switching their positions halfway through the baking time.

Once the scones are on the cookie sheets, wet your impeccably clean fingers and shape them into more perfect rounds. Then flatten them with your moistened palms. They will rise during baking, but once you flatten them, they won't be too round on top.

Bake the scones at 425 degrees F. for 10 to 12 minutes, or until they're golden brown on top. *(Mine took the full 12 minutes.)*

Cool the scones for at least five minutes on the cookie sheet, and then remove them to a wire rack with a metal spatula. *(If you used parchment paper, all you have to do is position the cookie sheet next to the wire rack and pull the paper over to the rack.)*

When the scones are cool, you can cut them in half lengthwise and toast them for breakfast.

Yield: Makes 18 delicious scones.

CHAPTER TWENTY-SIX

It had been a productive morning and Hannah congratulated herself as she baked a batch of Orange Dreamsicle Bar Cookies for her customers. Lisa was in the coffee shop telling the newest installment of the cat burglar story and Aunt Nancy and Marge were helping to take care of the customers. Michelle was in the kitchen with Hannah, sitting on a stool at the work station, involved in research on her laptop computer.

"How's it coming, Michelle?" Hannah asked her as she slipped the pans of bar cookies into the oven.

"Not so hot. I think we struck out on Judge Colfax's court cases. I've looked at all the ones that received press coverage and there's nothing that could provide a motive for murder. Initially, there were five cases that might have qualified, but the criminals he sentenced are still behind bars."

"No rapists that got off or any three-strike offenders?"

Michelle shook her head. "He didn't try any rape cases. The three-strike rule was only in effect for a few of his cases and none of those are candidates."

"Did you get time to check with the community college?"

"Yes. Sara George was there for her lab and she didn't leave the campus until four that afternoon. Assistant professors have to check in and out with the department secretaries."

"I hate to admit it, but I'm stymied. I'm fresh out of suspects, Michelle."

"No, you're not. There's still the unknown suspect for the unknown reason."

"So what am I supposed to do with him? Arrest him for an unknown reason?"

Michelle laughed. "It's good to see you still have your sense of humor. If you want my advice, you'll come up with a new recipe and bake. That always gets you thinking. Let's go down to Florence's and walk up and down the aisles. Maybe we'll get an idea for an ingredient that no one else has ever used in a cookie before."

Hannah seized the opportunity. "That sounds like more fun than sitting here tearing out my hair. Just let me ask Aunt Nancy if she'll take these bar cookies out of the oven when the timer rings, and we'll go."

Twenty minutes later, Hannah and Michelle were in the condiment aisle of the Lake Eden Red Owl Grocery Store, walking past an array of jars and bottles.

"I just walked past a jar of raspberry mustard," Michelle said.

"Interesting, but no. Let's keep looking."

"How about raspberry vinegar?"

"Been there, done that. Whoa! What's this?" Hannah stopped in front of a row of jams and jellies.

"What's what?" Michelle asked her.

"This jelly." Hannah pointed to a jar on the shelf. "It's called Hot Pepper Jelly."

"Made with red jalapeños." Michelle read the label aloud. "But you're not thinking of . . ."

"Oh, yes I am!" Hannah interrupted her. "I thought I had the jump on Mike when Dave didn't give him Peggy George's name or tell him about her daughter, but it turned out that going to interview her was just another blind alley."

"But I liked her," Michelle protested.

"So did I. That's not what I meant, Michelle. It's just that I thought I had the advantage over Mike, and I didn't."

"It's a contest with you two. Whatever made you think that you might marry him?"

"I don't remember," Hannah said with a laugh. "It was probably because he's so . . . so . . ."

"He certainly is!" Michelle said. And then both of them laughed.

"What's so funny?" Florence asked, coming around the end of the aisle.

"Hot Pepper Jelly," Hannah said, holding up the jar.

"Oh, that. They sent two cases by mistake. I've got to remember to send them back, unless . . . You don't want any, do you?"

"I think we do," Hannah said, deciding on the spot.

"But only at a greatly reduced price," Michelle added.

Florence nodded. "I can do that. It'll save me the time and the trouble of returning it. And it'll save me the shipping cost, too. How about a dollar a jar?"

"Sold!" Michelle said, grabbing jars and putting them in their shopping cart. "We'll take all the red you've got and we'll take the green, too."

"There's green?" Hannah turned to her sister in surprise.

"Right here. Mild Pepper Jelly. It's made from green jalapeños. Red and green.

435

They're Christmas colors. Just think about what you can do with this jelly for the holidays!"

Florence stared at Michelle as if she were from another planet. "If you girls bake any red and green cookies for Christmas, I'm not eating any," she announced.

Hannah had just finished sprinkling the Orange Dreamsicle Bar Cookies with powdered sugar when there was a knock on the kitchen door. She glanced at the clock. It was too early to be Ross. "Will you get it?" she asked Michelle.

A moment later, Michelle led Norman into the kitchen and got him settled with a cup of coffee at the stainless steel work station.

"Hi, Hannah." Norman said.

"Hello, Norman. Would you like to try one of my Orange Dreamsicle Bar Cookies? They're new."

"I'd love to. Thanks Hannah. I just stopped by to see if you'd recovered from last night."

"From last night?"

"Yes, from the dinner party. You and Michelle must have worked very hard to get ready for a party that big."

"Don't worry about us. We've recovered."

"How's Ross?"

"He was fine this morning. He stopped by for one of Michelle's scones on his way to work."

"I hope he gets that job, Hannah. He's a really nice guy and everybody here gets along with him. I think he'd be a nice addition to our group."

Not if you knew how I felt about him, Hannah's mind said. *Then you'd want him to stay away.* But she didn't say that. Instead, she said, "I guess we'll just have to wait and see what happens."

"These are really good, Hannah," Norman said when he'd tasted the bar cookies she brought him. "And the name is perfect. They do taste like Orange Dreamsicles."

"Thanks," Hannah said, hoping he wouldn't notice how distracted she was.

"How are you coming along with the investigation?"

"I'm not," Hannah replied with a sigh. "I've cleared every suspect on my list except the unknown suspect with the unknown motive. There's got to be a reason Judge Colfax was killed. I don't believe it was random. Someone had a very personal reason for wanting him dead."

"Maybe we're missing something," Norman said, and Hannah noticed that he'd used the plural. Norman always wanted to help when she investigated murder cases.

"Maybe." Hannah said, but she was doubtful. She'd gone over everything with Michelle and she'd reviewed her own notes countless times. "If we're missing something, I don't know what it is."

"Of course you don't," Norman said with a grin. "If you did, you wouldn't be missing anything."

Hannah groaned and then she reached out to give him a hug. That comment was pure Norman and she adored his sense of humor. She wanted to be with Ross. That hadn't changed. She'd told her mother that she didn't love Norman the way she loved Ross, but was that because she'd taken Norman for granted and assumed that he would always be around for her? Could she ever be completely happy if she lost Norman as a result of loving Ross?

ORANGE DREAMSICLE BAR COOKIES

Preheat oven to 350 degrees F., rack in the middle position.

Orange Cookie Crust:

2 cups all-purpose flour *(pack it down in the cup when you measure it)*

1 cup cold salted butter *(2 sticks, 8 ounces, 1/2 pound)*

1/4 teaspoon orange zest

1/2 cup powdered *(confectioners)* sugar *(no need to sift, unless it's got big lumps)*

Orange Filling:

4 beaten eggs *(just whip them up in a glass with a fork)*

2 cups white *(granulated)* sugar

1/4 cup orange juice *(I used Minute Maid)*

1/4 teaspoon orange zest

1/4 cup orange liqueur *(I used Triple Sec)*

1/2 teaspoon orange extract *(optional)*

1/2 teaspoon salt

1 teaspoon baking powder

3/4 cup all-purpose flour *(pack it down when you measure it)*

Extra powdered *(confectioners)* sugar to sprinkle on top

Hannah's 1st Note: Orange zest is the finely grated peel from an orange. Use just the colored part. The white is bitter. One orange will yield approximately 1/2 teaspoon of orange zest and that's enough for this recipe.

To make the Crust:
Place the 2 cups of flour in the bowl of a food processor.

Cut each stick of butter into eight pieces. Place them on top of the flour.

Sprinkle the 1/4 teaspoon of orange zest on top of the butter.

Sprinkle the powdered sugar on top of the orange zest.

Process with the steel blade in an on-and-off motion until the resulting mixture looks like coarse cornmeal.

Prepare a 9-inch by 13-inch rectangular cake pan by spraying it with Pam or another nonstick cooking spray. Alternatively, for even easier removal, line the cake pan with heavy-duty foil and spray that with Pam. *(Then all you have to do is lift them out of the pan, peel off the foil, and cut them up into pieces.)*

Spread the crust mixture out in the prepared pan and pat it down with your impeccably clean hands. Then use a metal spatula to even it out and make it smooth on top.

Get ready to put your crust in the oven. You will prepare the Orange Filling while your crust is baking.

Bake the crust at 350 degrees F. for 15 to 20 minutes, or until it's golden around the edges. When it's baked, you will be removing the pan from the oven and pouring on the filling you'll make, so **don't turn off the oven until both the crust and the filling are baked!**

Hannah's 2nd Note: If your butter is a bit too soft when you make the crust, you may end up with a mass that balls up and clings to the food processor bowl. That's okay. Just scoop it up and spread it out in the bottom of your prepared pan.

Hannah's 3rd Note: Don't wash your food processor quite yet. You'll need it to make the orange filling. (The same applies to your bowl and fork if you made the crust by hand.)

To make the Orange Filling:
Combine the eggs with the white sugar. *(You can use your food processor and the steel blade to do this, or you can do it by hand in a bowl.)*

Add the orange juice, orange zest, orange

441

liqueur, orange extract *(if you decided to use it),* salt, and baking powder. Mix thoroughly.

Add the flour and mix until everything is incorporated. *(This mixture will be runny — it's supposed to be.)*

When your crust is baked, remove the pan from the oven and set it on a cold stovetop burner or a wire rack. **Remember, don't shut off the oven! Just leave it on at 350 degrees F.**

Pour the orange filling you just made on top of the crust you just baked. Let it sit on the cold stove burner for a full 5 minutes. *(This helps the filling stick to the crust.)*

When the 5 minutes are up, use potholders to pick up the pan and return it to the oven. Bake your Orange Dreamsicle Bar Cookies for an additional 30 minutes.

Remove the pan from the oven and cool your bar cookies in the pan on a cold stovetop burner or a wire rack. When the pan has cooled to room temperature, sprinkle some of your extra powdered sugar on top.

Cover your pan with foil and refrigerate it until you're ready to serve. Then take it out of the refrigerator, sprinkle the top with more powdered sugar, and cut your Orange Dreamsicle Bars into brownie-sized pieces.

Place them on a pretty platter, and serve them with plenty of hot, strong coffee or tall glasses of milk. Yum!

Hannah's 4th Note: If you would prefer not to use alcohol in these bar cookies, simply substitute another 1/4 cup of orange juice for the orange liqueur. That's what Lisa and I do at The Cookie Jar. This recipe works both ways and I can honestly tell you that I've never met anyone who doesn't like Orange Dreamsicle Bar Cookies!

CHAPTER TWENTY-SEVEN

"I'm so glad we're baking!" Hannah said to Michelle as they gathered the ingredients for a sugar cookie dough. "I didn't realize how depressed and frustrated I was about Judge Colfax's murder case. All I could think about was how I was getting nowhere fast."

"It's not just the murder case," Michelle told her, bringing several pounds of salted butter to the work station.

"What do you mean?" Hannah set the sugar and flour canisters on the stainless steel surface.

"I came back in from the coffee shop when you were hugging Norman. Are you having second thoughts about Ross?"

"No! I just don't want to lose Norman's friendship, that's all. You know how I feel about him. We're . . ." Hannah stopped in mid-sentence and sighed. "I'm not sure how to describe it."

"Completely compatible? Soul mates? Joined at the hip? Cut from the same cloth?"

"Yes. All of the above. I can't bear the thought of losing him."

"How about Ross?" Michelle ducked back into the walk-in cooler to get the eggs and brought them to the work table. "Can you bear the thought of losing Ross?"

"No!"

"Then you've got a problem that has nothing to do with Judge Colfax's murder case."

"I know. Let's bake. I'm getting stressed again just talking about it."

"Sounds to me like you're in a real emotional jam," Michelle told her. "And that's what we should call these cookies."

"Emotional jam?"

"No, Hot Jam Cookies. That way the name won't give them away. They could be hot from the oven, not hot from hot peppers."

"But the name doesn't work. We're not using jam. We're making these cookies with jelly."

"Picky, picky," Michelle said with a grin. "Jelly? Jam? What's the difference?"

"Jelly is made from clear fruit juice. And jam is made from pureed fruit. They look entirely different."

"Okay, let's call them Hot Jelly Cookies. But that doesn't sound as good as Hot Jam Cookies."

Hannah thought about that for a moment. "You're right," she admitted. "Hot Jam Cookie it is. Let's taste the jelly and see just how spicy it is. That way we'll know how much to use."

"You first."

Hannah laughed. "Okay. I'll taste the green and you can taste the red."

"Oh, sure! I might have known it. You're giving me the hotter one." Michelle smiled to show she was teasing. "Let's taste and then let's switch. We should know what both jellies taste like."

"Deal."

The two sisters tasted their respective jellies. "What did you think of yours?" Michelle asked.

"The green's really tasty and it has a little kick, but not all that much," Hannah answered. "I like it. How about the red?"

"It's hot, but not too hot. I like it, too."

"Take a sip of coffee to clear your palate and then let's switch," Hannah said. "I want to make sure they're both good enough to use in the cookies."

"Good idea," Michelle replied, handing her a clean spoon.

446

Both sisters sipped coffee for several moments. Then they switched jars, and tasted again.

"I think they're both perfect," Michelle said. "All you have to do is tell your customers which is which and they can choose how much heat they'd like."

"I agree. Let's mix up the cookie dough and try them. I want to see what effect baking has on the jellies."

They worked in companionable silence until Hannah heard the faint strains of the "Wedding March." At first she thought she was imagining things, but then she realized it was coming from Michelle's purse. "Your purse is playing the 'Wedding March.' "

"My *phone* is playing music," Michelle corrected her. "It's a text from Mother. That's her text ring tone."

"Don't even think about asking Tracey to set that up for me!" Hannah warned her.

"I wouldn't dream of it. You've got enough problems of your own when it comes to the subject of weddings." Michelle wiped her hands and went off to get her purse. She glanced at the screen and said, "It's a long one. Mother must be feeling chatty. I'll read it to you."

"Great." Hannah covered the cookie dough with plastic wrap and put it in the coldest spot in the walk-in cooler to chill. Then she came back, poured fresh coffee for both of them and sat down to hear the message.

"I've never had so much fun in my life!" Michelle said.

"Making cookie dough?" Hannah asked her.

"No. I'm reading Mother's message to you."

"Oh. Go ahead."

"I've never had so much fun in my life!"

Michelle repeated. **"Doc and I went to the Empress Hotel for high tea! It's in Victoria, British Columbia, and that's a port of call on the trip back from Alaska. It was just wonderful and Doc doesn't even like tea! They brought out a round silver serving platter with five tiers. It was filled with delicious tiny sandwiches on bread with no crusts, crumpets, scones with clotted cream, biscuits — that's what the English call cookies, you know — and petite bites of cakes and desserts with creams and fruit. The smallest, top tier had four absolutely amazing chocolate truffles. That's not exactly a tradition for high tea, but neither Doc nor I minded once we'd tasted them. They were from a chocolate shop just down the street and I'm bringing you**

girls some. Don't tell Hannah, but I'm worried about . . . Uh-oh!"

Hannah frowned. "Mother's worried about uh-oh?"

"The uh-oh! was mine. I wasn't supposed to read you any of the next part."

"You can't leave me hanging like that. You started it. Now finish reading it."

"You're not going to like it."

"So what? I want to know what Mother doesn't want me to know."

Michelle covered her face with her hands. "That was really convoluted," she said in a voice that was muffled by her fingers.

"You know what I mean. Now read it."

Michelle sighed deeply and looked down at her phone again. "All right. If you insist."

"I insist."

"Don't tell Hannah, but I'm worried about her reaction to Ross. I know she knew him in college, but I've never seen her so starry-eyed before, not even when she was dating that horrid English professor who duped her into thinking he was an available suitor when he was nothing but a cad and a bounder."

Hannah laughed. She couldn't help it. "An available suitor? A cad and a bounder? I think high tea in British Columbia affected

Mother more than she realizes."

"And how!" Michelle laughed right along with Hannah. "Do you want me to finish reading Mother's text or shall we just forget about it?"

"Let's hear the rest."

"Okay." Michelle picked up her phone again. **"Let us hope that Ross does get the job at KCOW. Then Hannah will have time to judge whether her affections for him are real or simply a reaction to her boring, single life."**

Hannah didn't say anything at first. She just thought about what her mother had written. Then she shrugged. "I don't think my single life is boring, but Mother's got a point. Las Vegas was a romantic fantasy. A man from my past that I'd always wanted to date showed up unexpectedly and swept me off my feet in an exciting interlude away from my ordinary life."

"Was that *all* it was?" Michelle asked, and Hannah thought she sounded a bit disappointed.

"I don't think that's the case at all, but I can see why Mother might think so."

"She's interfering in your life again, isn't she?"

"Yes, but only because she loves me and wants the best for me."

Michelle looked thoughtful. "I guess that mitigates it a little, but I know that I wouldn't like it."

"Of course not. I don't like it either. I understand it, though."

"You're a bigger woman than I am!"

"Oh, I know that," Hannah said with a perfectly deadpan expression. "I haven't been a size three since I was two years old!"

Hannah had just taken the Hot Jam Cookies from the oven when there was a knock on the back door. "That'll be Mike."

"How do you know?"

"I made Hot Jam Cookies for him. That means there's food involved. Need I say more?"

"Probably not," Michelle said and went to open the back door. "Hi, Mike."

"Hi, Michelle. Is Hannah here? I need to talk to her."

"Of course," Hannah called out. "Come in, Mike. I'll pour a cup of coffee for you."

"Something sure smells good," Mike said, taking his usual place on a stool at the stainless steel work island.

"Hot Jam Cookies," Hannah told him. "If you wait three or four minutes, you can taste them for me."

"I've got time. I need to talk to you

anyway. Are you busy right now?"

"Not at the moment." Hannah poured a glass of juice for herself and sat down across from Mike.

"So," Mike said, "I understand you went to see Mrs. Colfax."

Hannah tried to read his expression. He didn't really look that angry. "Yes, I did," she admitted. "Michelle and I went to pay a condolence call. Michelle baked Strawberry Muffins and we took some to Nora."

"And Seth Colfax. I checked in on him this morning and he said he'd talked to you and Michelle at the Eight Ball Bar. Really, Hannah!"

"What are you so upset about? The fact that I'm meddling? Or the fact that Michelle and I went to the Eight Ball Bar?"

Mike stared at her for a long minute. "I'm not sure which one's the worst."

It was time to take the bull by the horns, but it might help to sweeten that hunk of beef up first. Hannah got up. "Hold that thought. I'll be right back." Hannah headed straight for the baker's rack where she picked up two cookies for Mike.

"Try these," she said, carrying them back to him. "The green is mild pepper jelly. The red is hot pepper jelly."

"Pepper jellies?" Mike said, biting into the

green one. "Wow! That's really good."

"That's the mild one. Let me know what you think when you get to the hot one."

Mike picked up the other cookie and took a bite. "Oh, yeah! *Really* good!"

"Do you think the red jelly is too hot for ordinary people?"

"No. I know about twenty guys that'd love it. Can I have a couple more, Hannah?"

Hannah got more cookies and then she handed him something else, a piece of information he might not have. It was time to trade it for something he had that she didn't have. "I went to see Margaret George. And Michelle checked out her daughter, Sara."

"Who are Margaret and Sara George?"

"Judge Colfax's mistress and the daughter he fathered by her. Michelle and I interviewed the mother this morning."

"How did you find them?"

Hannah hesitated. She didn't want to get Dave Johansen in trouble. "I don't exactly remember. Does it matter?"

Mike thought about that as he ate another cookie. "Not really, as long as you cleared them. And you didn't go to see Chad Norton?"

"Uh . . ." Hannah thought fast. "No, I didn't."

"Then how did you clear him?"

Hannah hemmed and hawed for a moment and then she noticed that Mike was laughing. "What?"

"I know how you cleared him. I just wanted to put you on the hot seat for a minute. I know you cleared him. You saw the phone records."

"How do you know *that*?"

"Because I made *sure* you saw those phone records. I gave them to Bill and told him to put them in his briefcase to take home."

"But . . ." Hannah stopped speaking as the full implication of what Mike had just told her sunk in. "You *knew* Andrea would find them and copy them for me?"

"Sure, I knew. She always does."

"But if you knew what was going to happen, why didn't you just give them to me in the first place?"

"I couldn't. I told you before, cops have rules. I couldn't deliberately break them, but I figured out a way around them."

"And you're not hiding anything from me?"

Mike shook his head. "No, I'm not. I'm stuck on this one. And there's a lot of pressure on me to solve it fast. You're not hiding any leads from me, are you?"

"No. I don't have any other leads."

"So we're both stuck."

Hannah sighed and nodded. "We're both stuck, Mike."

"Okay. If you think of anything, will you call me? Or text me? Tracey told me she taught you how to text."

"I will. Can I count on the same consideration from you?"

"You can. You're good at this, Hannah. You're better than anyone else in my department. I don't really want to admit this, but you might even be better than me."

"Never," Hannah said. "You're the best. Don't you remember all the advice and the books you gave me? What I learned, I learned from you."

"I wish you'd learn one more thing from me, Hannah."

"What's that?"

"I wish you'd learn how much I love you," Mike said. And then he turned and walked out the door.

HOT JAM COOKIES

Preheat oven to 350 degrees F., rack in the middle position.

2 cups white *(granulated)* sugar

1 and 1/2 cups salted butter, softened to room temperature *(3 sticks, 12 ounces, 3/4 pound)*

1/4 cup pepper jelly *(I used Reese Mild Pepper Jelly made with green jalapeno peppers, but if you want more heat, you can use Reese Hot Pepper Jelly made with red jalapeno peppers)*

2 large eggs, beaten *(just whip them up in a glass with a fork)*

1/2 teaspoon baking soda

1 teaspoon salt

4 cups flour *(pack it down in the cup when you measure it)*

1/3 cup white *(granulated)* sugar for later

1/2 cup pepper jelly *(use whatever kind you used in the cookie dough)*

Hannah's 1st Note: I used an electric stand mixer to mix these up. You can also do it by hand in a large bowl with a wooden spoon if you don't have a mixer.

Hannah's 2nd Note: When Lisa and I make these cookies down at The Cookie

Jar, we use mild pepper jelly for half the cookies and seedless hot pepper jelly for the other half. It's become almost like a test of manhood with the men in Lake Eden. If one of our male customers orders two Hot Jam Cookies, everyone cheers. If he orders one mild and one hot, everyone claps politely. If he orders two mild, everyone just shrugs.

Place the white sugar in the mixer bowl.

Add the softened butter and beat until it's light and fluffy.

Melt the jam in the microwave or in a saucepan over low heat. Once it's the consistency of syrup, take it off the heat *(or out of the microwave)* and let it cool on the counter for 5 minutes.

Mix the melted jam in with the butter and sugar. Beat until it's thoroughly incorporated.

Add the eggs and beat until everything is well mixed.

Sprinkle in the baking soda and salt. Mix well.

Add the flour in half-cup increments, beating after each addition.

Scrape down the sides of the mixing bowl with a rubber spatula and then take the bowl from the mixer. Give it a final stir by hand and stick it in the refrigerator to chill slightly while you prepare your cookie sheets.

Prepare your cookie sheets by spraying them with Pam or another nonstick cooking spray, or lining them with parchment paper.

Place the 1/3 cup of white sugar in a shallow bowl for coating the cookie dough balls.

Take the cookie dough out of the refrigerator and roll it into one-inch diameter balls with your impeccably clean hands.

Hannah's 3rd Note: If the cookie dough is too sticky to roll into balls, cover it with plastic wrap and stick it back in the refrigerator for more chilling, but if you do this, don't forget to turn off your oven. You can preheat it again when the dough has chilled enough to roll.

One by one, place the cookie dough balls in the bowl of sugar and roll them around until they're coated.

Place the sugar-coated cookie dough balls on your prepared cookie sheet, 12 balls to a standard-size sheet.

Flatten the dough balls slightly with a greased spatula or your impeccably clean hand.

Use your thumb to make an indentation in the center of each cookie. Be careful not to poke all the way through the cookie. Then the jelly you're going to drop in the indentation will leak out from the bottom of the cookie. *(Lisa and I use a tool for this at The Cookie Jar, but when Lisa bakes these cookies at home, she uses the small end of a wine bottle cork to poke the holes.)*

Use a small spoon to fill the indentation with the pepper jelly you've chosen, but be careful not to overfill.

Bake the Hot Jam Cookies at 350 degrees F. for 10 to 12 minutes.

Let the cookies cool on the cookie sheet on a cold stovetop burner or a wire rack for 2 minutes. Then use a metal spatula to transfer them to a wire rack to finish cooling. *(If you used parchment paper, there's no need to take the cookies off the paper. Just pull the paper onto the wire rack and wait until the cookies are cool to remove them.)*

Yield: 8 to 10 dozen, depending on cookie size.

Hannah's 4th Note: If you'd like to make a half-batch of these cookies, simply reduce each ingredient by half EXCEPT for the baking soda. Leave that measurement at 1/2 teaspoon.

CHAPTER TWENTY-EIGHT

Hannah and Michelle were just mixing up the last batch of cookie dough when Ross came through the swinging door that separated the coffee shop from the kitchen.

"Hi, Ross," Hannah greeted him. "We're almost through here."

"Great. Why don't you let me take you two to dinner at the Lake Eden Inn? I haven't seen Sally and Dick yet."

"Thanks for the invitation," Michelle said quickly, "but I can't. I promised Lonnie that I'd go over to his parents' for dinner."

This was the first that Hannah had heard of it and she wondered if Michelle was refusing because she wanted to give them more time alone together. Whatever the reason, Hannah wasn't about to quibble about it.

"Hannah?" Ross turned to her.

"Thank you, Ross. I'd love to have dinner with you. Just let me stick this cookie dough in the cooler, and I'll be ready to go."

"I'll take your truck, Hannah," Michelle offered. "I'll feed Moishe for you. Lonnie's picking me up at the condo anyway and then you two can go straight out to dinner."

Hannah glanced down at her second-best pants and top. "I was going to change clothes."

"You look great just the way you are," Ross told her. "Let's go."

"I never argue with a man who has food on his mind," Hannah said, smiling at Ross. "Especially when I'm hungry, too."

They arrived at the Lake Eden Inn just as it opened for dinner. Dot was at the reception desk and she ushered them to one of the elevated, curtained booths.

"I'll be right back with your water and rolls," she said, rushing off toward the kitchen.

"I love these booths," Ross said, reaching across the table to take Hannah's hand. "I feel like king of the world up here."

"We're the first ones here," Hannah said, looking down at all the empty and perfectly set tables. "I don't think I've ever been the first diner here before. It's like preferred seating in an empty banquet room."

Dot came back to their table much faster

than they'd expected. She set down a basket of rolls and two glasses filled with water, lemon slices, and ice. "Sally's making you a drink," she said, and then glanced at their clasped hands. She looked from Hannah to Ross and then back again, and promptly left, pulling the curtains shut behind her.

"I guess Dot thinks we need privacy," Hannah said with a laugh.

"She's right. We haven't had much of that. This gives us a chance to talk in private."

"What would you like to talk about?" Hannah asked, and then she wondered if that was too forward. Perhaps Ross was only making idle conversation.

"I'd like to talk about us, but we'll get to that later when we're really alone. Right now I want to know how your interview with Peggy George went."

"It went just fine. She was very co-operative, and Michelle and I found out that she has an alibi for the time of Judge Colfax's murder."

"You sound disappointed."

"Not really. She's a very nice woman."

"How about the daughter?"

"Same thing. She's an assistant professor of biology at the community college. She was teaching a lab session when her father was killed. I'm fresh out of suspects, and I don't know where to go next. It's the first time this has happened to me."

"How about Mike? Do you know how he's doing?"

"Yes. Mike dropped by this afternoon and told me he has the same problem. Not only that, but the department is getting a lot of pressure to hurry and make an arrest."

"Pressure? From whom?"

"I don't know. I didn't ask him. Do you think that's important?"

"It could be. Why don't you call Andrea and see if she can find out who's applying that pressure? Call Michelle, too. Lonnie's working with Mike, isn't he?"

"Yes. That's a good idea, but I won't call. I'll send Andrea and Michelle a group text message. Tracey showed me how to do that and they're both techno geeks. They'll respond faster to a text than a phone call."

"Atta girl!" Ross said, watching her send the message. "I'm glad to see that you're catching on to all this. And that reminds me . . . did you get the text I sent you this afternoon?"

"No. My phone was in my purse and I guess I didn't hear Big Ben chime."

"You can read it now," Ross told her.

Hannah checked her phone and found Ross's text immediately. When his message

463

came up on the screen, she began to smile.

I'm taking a break and I just want to say
how much I love you, Hannah.

Instead of looking up, she sent another
text message, this one to Ross.

I love you, too.

Ross's phone beeped almost immediately
and he looked down at the screen. There
was a smile on his face as he looked up at
her again. "Do you realize that we'd never
have to talk? We could just text each other
all the time, even when we were together."

"But where's the fun in that?" Hannah
asked, reaching out to touch his arm. "Some
things are better said and done in person,
aren't they?"

"They are," Ross agreed, capturing her
hand and bringing it to his lips for a kiss.

A moment later, Sally came by with two
champagne cocktails. "I made these for
you." She turned to Ross. "It's really good
to see you again. Are you here in Lake Eden
for long?"

"I hope so. I applied for a job at KCOW
Television. If I get it, I'll be moving here."

"That's good to hear. I can name quite a

few people who've missed you." She turned to look at Hannah.

Hannah blushed slightly. "Can you join us for a minute, Sally?"

"Just for a minute. I've got a new sous-chef in the kitchen and I want to keep an eye on him." Sally slid into the booth next to Hannah. "Are you working on Judge Colfax's murder case?"

"Yes. It's a tough one."

"I wish I had something for you. I do keep my ear to the ground out here. And sometimes I even use your invisible waitress trick."

Ross turned to look at her inquiringly, and Hannah explained. "If people are talking about something important, they don't seem to notice the waitress when she refills their coffee cups or brings things to the table. They just go right on talking."

"Unfortunately, I haven't heard a thing about Judge Colfax," Sally continued, "except for the lunch reservation, of course."

"What lunch reservation?" Ross asked her.

"The one he made for the day he was murdered. It was a little strange. He placed the call himself instead of having his clerk do it. And he reserved a table for two, but he didn't mention who the other party would be."

Hannah felt her interest rise. "And he usually tells you?"

"Yes. It's almost always his son. Seth loves to have lunch here. He's crazy about my bleu cheese–stuffed burgers. I even asked the judge if Seth was joining him, but he said no, he was lunching with someone else."

"And he didn't say who it was," Hannah repeated, just to make sure.

"No, but I think it was someone important because he asked if they could park by the back door. When he comes with Seth, they always park in the lot."

"Could it have been someone with mobility issues?" Ross asked.

"It could have been, but I think he would have mentioned that up front. He might have even asked if someone could help them with a wheelchair or a walker."

"But he didn't say anything like that?" Hannah reached for the steno pad she carried in her purse and jotted it down when Sally shook her head.

"He did ask for a private booth, though. And he said he was coming earlier than usual, at eleven instead of when I open at eleven-thirty. I got the feeling he didn't want to be seen, or maybe whoever he was taking to lunch didn't want to be seen. It was a little curious, that's all."

Hannah nodded. "And of course he never showed up because he was dead by then."

"That's right. It was this booth, the one you're sitting in. I saved it through the whole lunch hour for him."

When Sally left to check on her sous-chef, Hannah turned to Ross. "I wonder why Dave didn't tell me about Judge Colfax's lunch plans."

"Maybe he didn't know about them. If you have his home number, why don't you call him and ask?"

Before Hannah could reach for her phone, Dot arrived again. Hannah waited until they'd given her their order and then she placed the call. It only took a few moments and she had her answer. Dave hadn't known about Judge Colfax's lunch plans because the judge, usually meticulous about letting Dave know precisely where he'd be, hadn't written the luncheon on his calendar.

"My curiosity is prickling," Ross told her when she'd related what Dave had told her. "How about yours?"

"It's doing a little more than prickling. It's nudging me hard. There's something very strange about these lunch plans."

"Because they don't fit Judge Colfax's pattern?"

"Exactly right. It feels like another piece of the puzzle, a big one. I just have to figure out where it fits."

"No, *we* have to figure out where it fits," Ross corrected her. "I'm helping you on this one, remember?"

"I remember. And I'm very glad," Hannah said, closing the little gap Dot had left in the curtains and reaching for his hand.

Hannah had just taken her last bite of Sally's excellent Beef Wellington when a text message came in. She retrieved it, read it, and then looked up at Ross. "It's Andrea. She said the phone call urging Bill to hurry and make an arrest came from Senator Eric Worthington's office. Whoever called said that the senator and Judge Colfax became friends when the senator clerked at Worthington Law and Judge Colfax was a junior partner. Bill thinks that the senator is eager for justice for his old mentor."

"Did you say Senator *Eric* Worthington?" Ross asked.

Hannah checked the text message again. "Yes. That's what Andrea wrote. Why?"

"I knew Mr. Worthington had gone into politics, but I didn't realize that he'd become a state senator. I should have guessed he'd follow in his father's footsteps."

"His father?"

"Yes, Governor Clayton Worthington. My family lived across the street from the Worthingtons when I was growing up. Their youngest son, Clay, was my best friend all the way through high school. Clay's father, that's Senator Eric Worthington, used to take us to Twins games and Vikings games. Clay's older brother, Ray, was the high school quarterback when Clay and I were in junior high, and he earned an athletic scholarship and quarterbacked for the Cougars in college."

"The Brigham Young, Houston, or Washington State Cougars?"

"Washington State." Ross looked a bit surprised that she knew.

"I follow college football," Hannah told him. "The pros are more practiced athletes, but college football is more fun." She paused and took a sip of her champagne cocktail. "Tell me more about the Worthington family."

"Everyone was an athlete except Clay. His grandfather, the governor, played competitive tennis. He was always after Clay to take up a sport. And Clay's father was a third-round draft pick for the Vikings when he finished his junior year in college, but he decided to finish his degree and go to law school instead of going pro. I think he always regretted it, because he really enjoyed the Vikings games and knew a lot about football strategy."

"Was Clay's mother an athlete, too?"

"Yes. She was a long-distance runner. She competed in college and ran marathons all over the country after she married the senator. Clay and I watched the whole Boston Marathon so we could see her reach the finish line. As far as I know, she still runs marathons."

"What does Clay's older brother do now?"

"Ray ended up coaching college football. The last I heard, he was with the Gators."

"Gainesville, Florida?" Hannah was surprised. "He's a long way from Minnesota. Where did your friend Clay end up?"

"He stayed in Minnesota and lives in Mankato. He's an economics professor at the state university there. He married his college girlfriend and they've got two daughters. I get a Christmas card from them every year. And Clay's sister lives in Duluth. She went to college up there and liked it so much, she stayed."

"Is she an athlete, too?"

"A swimmer. She almost made it to the

Olympics her first year in college."

"So Clay's older brother is the only one who moved away from Minnesota?"

"That's right. I think it was because of the court case. Nobody remembers it now, but people were talking about it when Clay and I were growing up."

Hannah leaned forward, all ears. "What court case is that?"

"Ray was out with his girlfriend the night of the senior prom. They were driving past Lady Lake on their way back to town when Ray swerved to avoid a deer. The car went out of control and ended up in the lake."

"That's scary," Hannah said.

"It was a lot more than scary. Ray wound up with lacerations and bruises, but he managed to get out of the car and walk home. His girlfriend wasn't so lucky. They pulled her out of the car the next morning."

Hannah shuddered. She couldn't help but remember the car in Miller's Pond with Doctor Bev's body inside.

"There was a lot of speculation about it at the time," Ross went on with the story. "The town newspaper called it another Chappaquiddick."

"Ray's girlfriend drowned?"

"No one's sure. The autopsy report was inconclusive. Her family brought suit against Ray, claiming that he had been drinking, but the case was dismissed before it even got to trial for lack of evidence. There was no proof that he had done anything wrong."

"Did you keep in touch with the Worthington family?" Hannah asked him.

"Just with Clay. Why?"

"I'd really like to talk to Senator Worthington. Perhaps he could tell me something about Judge Colfax's background that might relate to his murder. Do you think you could presume on that old acquaintance and convince him to see me?"

"I'm almost sure I could. I'll call him tomorrow and see what I can do."

"Thanks, Ross. If they worked in the same law office, they've known each other for a long time. Sometimes old friends know things about each other that not even their families know."

"You're trying to find something in Judge Colfax's background that connects to his murder?"

"Exactly. I've struck out with everyone who was in Judge Colfax's current life. Maybe an old friend from the past like Senator Worthington can help."

It had been one of the happiest evenings of

Hannah's life and she didn't want it to end. "Will you come in for a while, Ross?" she asked, when he opened the car door for her.

"I thought you'd never ask."

They walked up the stairs arm in arm, and when they came to the landing, Hannah stopped. "Do you remember what Moishe does when I open the door?"

"I remember. Do you want to catch him or shall I?"

"You can. He'd like that. But brace yourself. He was twenty-four pounds the last time Doctor Bob weighed him."

Hannah unlocked the door and opened it to release the flying orange and white blur.

Ross grunted when he caught Moishe in midair, and then he chuckled. "You *are* a big boy, aren't you?"

"Just put him on the back of the couch," Hannah instructed. "It's his favorite perch."

Once Moshe was settled, she shut and locked the door. Then she went to check on Michelle and found that her youngest sister wasn't back from her dinner with Lonnie. "Would you like coffee?" she offered when she came back to the living room.

"Sure," Ross said. "Michelle's not home yet?"

"Not yet." Hannah turned to go to the kitchen, but strong arms caught her and

warm lips nuzzled her neck.
"I don't think I want that coffee after all," Ross said.

CHAPTER TWENTY-NINE

Hannah woke up to the smell of freshly brewed coffee and a purring cat nestled on her head. She dislodged the cat, thrust her arms into her robe and her feet into her slippers and went in search of the coffee. She found Michelle standing at the kitchen counter, similarly dressed and sipping a cup of the aromatic brew.

"Here you go," Michelle said, pouring another cup for Hannah. "Go sit. I'll bring it."

"Good thing. I'd probably drop it," Hannah mumbled, sinking down onto one of her favorite vinyl-covered antique kitchen chairs. It was a clone of the other three chairs arranged around the Formica-topped table, but it was exactly where she wanted to sit.

The other chairs had views that did not lend themselves to work mornings. Two faced the wall between the kitchen and the laundry room that was hung with an array of collectible plates Delores had placed there when Hannah had first moved in. Hannah had never bothered to change them to something she liked better. They were pretty and were probably expensive, but she didn't want to even pretend to assess their value before she'd consumed at least a whole carafe of coffee. As far as she was concerned the plates were a nice, innocuous wall decoration, nothing more.

The third chair faced the wall phone, hanging above her favorite chair. Hannah didn't want to look at the phone. If she faced the phone, it could possibly encourage it to ring. And the last thing she wanted to do when she got up at the crack of dawn was to deal with an early telephone call.

Her favorite chair faced the clock shaped like an apple, and that was perfect for morning viewing. It reminded her that she didn't have to go to work quite yet, but it wouldn't let her tarry too long. It ticked off the seconds in a predictable manner that only a dead battery could halt. It moved very slowly when she trained her eyes on it and it granted her time to sip, stare, and cogitate until the little hand neared the numeral five and the big hand halted at the numeral nine. Two more sweeps of the red minute hand and it was time to rise from the chair, walk down the hallway, and take her morning shower. Ten minutes later, she would finish her shower, dress, feed Moishe, and arrive at work on the dot of five-thirty.

"You got a text. I heard Big Ben," Michelle told her.

"Thanks," Hannah said. It was time. The little hand was nearing the five, the big hand was on the nine, and the red minute hand had finished its second sweep and was well on its way to the third.

It only took a moment to retrieve the text. Hannah read it, smiled, and put the phone in her purse. Ross loved her, he was going to work, and he'd meet her at The Cookie Jar before five-thirty tonight. When he called Senator Worthington, he'd text her again and tell her what time the senator could see them.

Twelve minutes later Hannah had finished her shower, toweled off and dressed, and was walking down the hall toward the kitchen for one last cup of coffee.

"Hurry up, Hannah!" Michelle called out. "He's got another one!"

Hannah covered the last five feet of the hallway in two steps and burst into the living room, only to see Michelle holding a pink, frilly baby bonnet in her hand.

"Moishe?" Hannah asked, staring at the baby bonnet.

"Yes. He had it in his mouth when I came out of the guest bedroom. Andrea never had anything like this for Bethie, did she?"

"No. Bethie was a winter baby. She wore knit hats. That's a summer bonnet. Look at the flowers on the side."

"Do you think it could have been Tracey's?"

"I doubt it. Tracey's birthday is in September and it was already getting cold when she was born. Andrea bought her hoodies made of sweatshirt material, and Tracey had one in almost every color."

"Then it's the cat burglar," Michelle said with a sigh. "Do we have time to look at the tape?"

"We'll make time," Hannah decided. "I don't know about you, but this is really bothering me. It's almost as frustrating as trying to solve Judge Colfax's murder."

Of course there had been nothing on the tape and by the time Hannah and Michelle got to work, they were an hour late.

"The cat burglar?" Lisa guessed when they came in the kitchen door.

"Yes. We repositioned the camera in the kitchen. It's the only room we haven't tried," Hannah sighed deeply, "but I really don't have much hope."

"You can't give up now," Aunt Nancy told them. "Grandma Knudson thinks you're close to the answer. She was listening yesterday and we got to talking later. Between the two of us, we came up with an idea about what you should do next."

"You did?" Hannah was delighted. Grandma Knudson was a wise woman and Aunt Nancy had a good head on her shoulders. "What do you think I should do?"

"We want you to hold a yard sale next Saturday, but not a yard sale for money. Just make a display, right here at The Cookie Jar of all the items Moishe has appropriated. Lisa says everybody comes in here on Saturdays and somebody is bound to recognize something. If they do, you'll know at least one place Moishe went when he got out."

"That's a wonderful idea! I wonder why I didn't think of it myself."

"Because you're too close to the problem. And you're too busy with other things. Will you do it?"

"Yes, I'll do it."

"Good. We'll start telling people about the yard sale that isn't a yard sale to display the cat burglar's loot."

■ ■ ■ ■

It was eleven o'clock when the text came in. Hannah heard her phone chime and hurried to take it out of her purse. Just as she expected, it was a text from Ross.

Senator Worthington will see you at the Winnetka County Courthouse at five-thirty this evening. Worthington Law has rented it for the evening to hold their annual reunion and he's the guest speaker. The reunion dinner begins at six. If we get there promptly at five-thirty, he'll give us thirty minutes of his time.

While Hannah was reading Ross's text, another text message came in. Again, it was from Ross.

Correction. It's just going to be you, Cupcake. I have to work until eight. I'll meet you at your condo later. Give the senator my regards. I'll text him to let him know I won't be with you. Love, Ross.

"What's the matter?" Michelle asked, coming into the kitchen just in time to see the disappointment on Hannah's face.

"Nothing, really. It's just that Ross was

480

going to go with me to see Senator Worthington, but he has to work late."

"Do you want me to go with you?"

"No, that's okay. If you really want to help, start something for dinner. Ross should be at the condo by eight-thirty."

Hannah was dressed and ready to go. She'd had another phone lesson from Tracey, baked several more batches of cookies, and rushed back to the condo to change into an outfit that was appropriate for meeting a state senator. As she dressed, she thought of something that Howie had mentioned months ago, some rumors about how Judge Colfax had done a favor for someone powerful and gained his judgeship in the process. She knew that Howie was in his office on Saturdays so she glanced at the clock, saw that it was not yet five, and dialed Howie's office number, hoping that he hadn't left early.

"Levine Law," Howie answered on the second ring.

"Hi, Howie. It's Hannah. Are you going to the dinner at the courthouse?"

"What dinner?"

"Worthington Law is having their annual reunion and they rented the courthouse for a catered dinner. Senator Worthington is the guest speaker."

"Hmmm! This is the first I've heard about it. Of course, I never worked for Worthington Law so I guess I wouldn't be invited."

"Well, I'm glad I caught you. I have a meeting out there with Senator Worthington and I remembered something you told me a couple of months ago. You said there were rumors about Judge Colfax getting his judgeship in return for doing a favor for a powerful person."

"That's the rumor I heard. It's just a rumor, though. Nobody seems to know what the favor was or who asked him to do it."

"Oh." Hannah was disappointed. She'd hoped that Howie would know more than that. "I did find out that Judge Colfax was the senator's mentor when he was a law clerk at Worthington Law. It's entirely possible that Senator Worthington might know something about that old favor."

"Tread carefully, Hannah."

"Why's that?"

"What if the favor was for the Worthington family?"

"Oh. Yes, I see what you mean. That would be putting my foot in it, wouldn't it?"

"I'll say. I've got to go, Hannah. Kitty's making sauerbraten tonight and that's one of my favorites. I don't want to be late."

"Tell her hi from me," Hannah said and hung up the phone. She glanced at the clock, picked up her purse, slung it over her shoulder, and headed down the outside staircase to the garage. There was no way she wanted to be late, not when Senator Worthington had so generously worked her into his busy schedule. She just hoped that their meeting would be productive and she'd discover something that would lead to the identity of the person who'd killed Judge Colfax.

CHAPTER THIRTY

Hannah found a parking spot right in front of the courthouse. There were no other cars on the street. She thought that was odd until she remembered that almost all of the guests coming to the Worthington Law reunion would be lawyers, and lawyers had preferred parking in the underground garage.

She glanced at her phone to check the time. It was five-twenty so she texted Ross.

I'm here at the courthouse ten minutes early. I'll see you later. Love, Hannah.

Something prickled at the back of her mind as she climbed the courthouse steps. She was inside, heading up the first set of stairs when she realized what it was. She hadn't seen any caterer trucks. They'd better get here in a hurry if dinner was at six.

Her footsteps echoed hollowly on the

marble staircase that led to the courtrooms on the second floor. The courthouse had a deserted feel and it made her a bit uneasy. Had she gotten the wrong day? Ross had said she should meet Senator Worthington tonight, hadn't he?

Hannah stopped and pulled out her phone to check Ross's earlier text message. Yes, her appointment with the senator was tonight. She was to meet him in Judge Colfax's chambers on the third floor at five-thirty. He would give her thirty minutes of his time before the six o'clock dinner. But how could there be a dinner at six o'clock if the caterers weren't here yet? They would need time to set up and she'd seen no one hurry past with trays of food or linens.

Something was wrong and she didn't like it. Hannah felt a sense of dread as she stared at the railing that ran all the way up the staircase to the second floor and then curved around in an arc to start the down staircase on the other side. She tried to tell herself that everything was all right, that she was simply nervous at the prospect of meeting such an influential person. That didn't work, not even for an instant. Every fiber of her being was vibrating with the sense of danger. Something was wrong. Terribly wrong. There had to be a reason why her mouth was dry and her heart was pounding like a caged bird in her chest. Silly or not, overactive imagination or not, she was getting out of the courthouse right now!

Hannah turned around on the step and that was when she saw a tall figure standing near the heavy oaken doors. He had dark hair, carefully styled and streaked at the sides with silver. He had the well-muscled body of an athlete who had stayed in shape, and he looked even more imposing than he had in the newspaper photos she'd seen. There was a smile on his face, a smile that was knowing and threatening, a smile that made her knees start to shake. Hannah was certain that the gloating expression on Senator Eric Worthington's face was one his constituents had never seen.

"So you finally figured it out," he said in an impassionate voice. "Unfortunately for you, it's a little too late."

"Figured what out?" Hannah asked, hoping her voice didn't reveal how terrified she was.

"That there is no reunion and that I lured you here. You may even have figured out that I killed Geoffrey."

"You . . . did?" Hannah asked, taking a step back up the stairs so that she could put more distance between them. "But how did you murder him without being seen?"

Senator Worthington laughed and it was not a pleasant laugh. "I didn't kill him personally. I'd never do that. Geoffrey was a friend. As a matter of fact, we were going to have lunch together. That's how my man got into the courthouse. Geoffrey sent me a one-time pass for the parking garage."

Hannah moved back until she felt the next step up behind her heels. "If he was your friend, why did your man kill him?"

"Geoffrey had become a very dangerous liability. He was losing his mind, you know. For periods of time, he was living in the past. And that was not a good thing for me."

"I . . . didn't know that his mind was going. I never noticed that."

"But I did. You wouldn't notice. You didn't know him when his colleagues claimed that he had a mind like a steel trap."

"He was a brilliant lawyer?" Hannah asked, hoping he wouldn't notice when she took another step upward.

"Oh, yes. He made junior partner at Worthington Law before he was thirty. That's a rarity. But years passed, and his mind weakened so much that I couldn't depend on him to keep my secret any longer."

"But wouldn't people have thought that anything he said was the product of his confused mind?" Hannah asked, moving back until her heel was against the next step up.

"Perhaps. But somebody would have looked into it. You know how the media operates. Ever since the evening news began to get ratings, they're on the lookout for good, juicy stories, the more scandalous, the better." The frozen smile on his face as he moved forward was chilling.

Keep him talking! her mind told her, and Hannah knew that it was good advice. If she were lucky, Ross or Howie or Michelle would check on the Worthington Law reunion and discover that it wasn't being held tonight. *Ask him a question,* her mind prodded. *Hurry!*

"You were afraid Judge Colfax would slip and tell the secret about your son?" she asked, rising another step.

"You've done your homework." He took a step forward. "Too bad it won't do you any good."

"What do you mean?" Hannah took another step up. She was almost halfway up to the second floor.

"It's a pity, but now that you know, I'll have to kill you. And I'll do it personally this time. You see, my dear, you know too much. Contrary to most teachings, too much knowledge is a very dangerous thing."

Hannah wondered if she could whirl and run. But he still had the body of an athlete and she had no doubt that he could take the marble staircase with a speed that would far exceed hers. She had to climb a bit higher to give herself an advantage. "I haven't told anyone," she said, moving up another step.

"I'm glad to hear that. And I'm very glad that Ross didn't come with you. I wouldn't have liked getting rid of that boy. He was a good friend to Clay."

"I won't say anything," Hannah said, gaining another step upward. "No one's found out about it and no one needs to."

"Oh, my dear," he said in mock sympathy. "It's very generous of you to offer to protect me, but I can't take that chance. I'm declaring my candidacy for governor next Monday. If the press finds out that I influenced the autopsy and toxicology reports, it could keep me from winning the election. You see how that could happen, don't you?"

"Yes, I do."

"The local papers compared it to Chappaquiddick at the time, but they backed down when the case was dismissed for lack of evidence."

"And now everyone's forgotten about it,"

Hannah said in a way she hoped would he would find reassuring.

"But *you* could change all that."

Hannah knew she had to keep him engrossed in telling her the story. "I don't understand. How could you have influenced the autopsy and toxicology reports when they're done by outside labs?"

"Everyone has a price. It was simple. My father was the governor. He could help their careers. He bribed them all with promises and they did whatever he asked. That's how politics works."

"Did your father keep those promises?" Hannah asked, taking another step toward the landing on the second floor.

"Of course he did. My father was an honorable man."

It would have been funny in any other context, but this situation had no humor in it. Hannah rose another step and asked another question. "I still don't understand why you had to kill Judge Colfax."

"Of course you do. I just told you."

"Tell me again. I guess I didn't understand."

"My father bought him for me, just like he bought the medical examiner and the head of the police lab. He bribed them with political favors because he had big plans for me. My father knew that if they learned that Raymond was drunk and he left that girl in the car to drown, it could be the death of his dream and my political career."

"But how about Judge Colfax? Did your father bribe him, too?"

"Of course he did. There was a judgeship available and he promised to give it to Geoffrey."

"And did he?" Hannah asked, even though she already knew the answer to her question.

"Of course he did. My father always kept his word. That's the reason I was forced to silence Geoffrey. It wasn't something I wanted to do, but it was necessary. He knew and his judgment was becoming impaired."

"I understand now," Hannah said, gaining another step up.

"I have to govern this state. My father knew that. It's why he made sure that there were no impediments to my rise in politics. The governorship is my legacy. I must fulfill it!" He took another step forward in tandem with her step upward and the dying rays of sunlight spilling from the high windows built into the rotunda illuminated his features. His eyes were glittering with a consuming zeal and Hannah realized that Senator Eric Worthington was completely mad.

He would kill her. There was no doubt in her mind. The time for talking was over. She had to escape *now*!

Without hesitation, Hannah hurled her heavy purse at the man who was advancing toward her. Then she whirled and took the last steps at a run. She dashed down the hallway and through a door at random. It was the courtroom where her bail hearing had been held. She had to hide before Senator Worthington saw her!

She headed for the raised judge's bench and that's when she saw it, the hidden door in the paneled wall behind the bench. She was in the courtroom with the handicapped elevator and she could use it to escape!

Where was the call button for the elevator? It stopped her for a brief moment, but she realized that it had to be within easy reach. She dashed behind the bench and found it almost immediately, under the center of the bench. Hannah pressed it and the hidden door in the wall slid silently and smoothly open.

The elevator it revealed was small and reminded Hannah of a cage. Even though she'd never liked tight, closed spaces, she forced herself to get inside. She had no other choice and there was no time to waste. She wanted to go down to the garage, but the outside gates would be locked and closed. She couldn't get out of the building that way and there would be nowhere to hide in the deserted concrete space. He would expect her to go down so she would go up to the third floor. As she pressed the third-floor button, she heard Senator Worthington running down the hallway in her direction. A door slammed in the adjacent courtroom and she held her breath as the door in the wall slid closed and the elevator began to rise.

Text someone! her frenzied mind gave her instructions. *Do it now, before it's too late. They have to know where you are!*

Thank goodness her phone was in her pocket! Hannah pulled it out and pressed the button that Tracey had shown her. It was something her niece had called *broadcast* and Tracey had explained that it sent a group text message to everyone on Hannah's contact list.

For one panicked moment, Hannah wondered if Tracey had gotten around to entering the cell phone numbers on the list she'd made. But there was no way to ask and all she could do was hope that Tracey had done it. With shaking fingers, Hannah typed in a terse message.

Help! Worthington killer. In courthouse elevator. Hurry!

She hit the send button and sent up a silent prayer that she'd done everything right.

The elevator opened on the third floor and Hannah gasped as she stepped out and realized it had taken her to Judge Colfax's chambers. Senator Worthington was responsible for one murder that had taken place in this very spot. Would he find her there and accomplish another murder with her as his victim? Would he guess that she used the handicapped elevator to come up here? Howie had told her that the elevator had been installed less than a year ago. Perhaps Senator Worthington didn't know that the elevator existed and she would be safe.

He's a state senator, Hannah's mind vetoed that possibility. *He's bound to know. He probably voted on the proposal.* But there wasn't time to consider that. She could hear him running up the stairs to the third floor. She had to find a safe hiding place!

There was nowhere to hide. He would find her and kill her! Hannah's frantic eyes searched the room and focused on the elevator door. That was it! She'd seen the emergency button that would stop it between floors. She'd be inside and he couldn't get to her. She'd be safe!

Hannah made a lunge for the elevator and threw herself inside. The hidden door slid closed and just as she pressed the button to go down, she heard the door to Judge Colfax's chambers bang open. He was there! But she was no longer within reach. She was traveling downward, away from Senator Worthington and danger.

The indicator dial showed the second floor, and she held her breath as the elevator continued to descend. She was almost down to the garage when the light for the second floor began to glow and the elevator slowed. He must have realized that she was in the elevator and he'd pressed the call button. Senator Worthington was attempting to bring his victim back up to him for the kill!

There was only one thing to do and Hannah did it. She hit the emergency stop button. It took a heart-stopping second or two, but the elevator halted just short of the garage. She sent a silent thank you to Mr. Otis and everyone else who'd developed the first elevator and breathed a big sigh of relief.

The emergency bell began to ring loudly, pushing all other thoughts from her mind. Had anyone received her cry for help? Was there anyone coming who would hear it?

There was another sound, a high-pitched wail that she heard over the noise of the clanging emergency bell. A police siren!

Hannah looked down at her phone and saw a text message appear on the screen.

Stay put. I'll text you when it's safe.

The return cell phone number was Mike's. She realized that her knees were trembling and would no longer hold her upright. She sank to the floor of the elevator and relieved tears filled her eyes. She was still there when the clanging bell ceased and Big Ben chimed with another text message from Mike.

Ross tackled him in parking garage. We got him. Come down now. It's over.

Somehow she managed to get to her feet and push in the emergency button. The elevator descended, the door opened, and she went straight into Ross's arms.

CHAPTER THIRTY-ONE

It was late Sunday morning and Hannah and Ross were standing in front of the security checkpoint at the Minneapolis airport. Their arms were around each other and Hannah couldn't decide if she was sad or happy. The employment director at KCOW had offered Ross the job and Ross had accepted. He would become the head of original programming at KCOW Television next Monday. That meant he had only a week to pack up his things in California and arrange for a moving company to bring them to Lake Eden.

Ross was holding her like he never wanted to let her go, but at last he released her. "I almost forgot to tell you that some of your detective skills must have rubbed off on me."

"What do you mean?"

"I solved the mystery of the cat burglar."

Hannah was shocked. "You discovered

how Moishe was getting out?"

"Not exactly. I discovered how Moishe was getting *in.* He's not going out anywhere, not really. I put it all together this morning when I was sitting at your kitchen table and you went back to your room to get your jacket. I saw Moishe jump down to the top of the refrigerator."

"Down? Don't you mean he jumped *up* to the top of the refrigerator?"

Ross shook his head. "No, he jumped *down.* There's a hole in your ceiling, and I think it goes into the attic."

"That's exactly where it goes! They had to cut a hole when they installed my refrigerator. It was too big for the space and there was no other way to vent it. But there's a grate over the hole."

"Not anymore. The cat burglar managed to claw it loose and it's laying there on the top of your refrigerator. I used your stepstool to look. Do you know that the attic covers the entire length and width of the building? The people with upstairs units in your building use it for storage."

"I know that, but I don't have that many things and I've never needed to use it. The access is through the master bedroom closet, but Moishe obviously found another way. I may have to rename him Houdini!

He escaped and none of us knew how he did it . . . except for you. Please don't tell anybody about it. It has to be our secret for now."

"Why?"

"Because Lisa, Aunt Nancy, and Grandma Knudson are so excited about holding the yard sale that isn't really a yard sale on Saturday at The Cookie Jar. There's no way I want to spoil their fun and if I let the cat burglar get into the attic for another week, we'll have even more stolen items to display."

Ross laughed and pulled her into his arms again for another hug. "That's one of the things I love about you, Hannah."

"I let my cat steal things?"

"No, you think of other people's feelings first. And speaking of others' feelings, please tell Doc and your mother that I'm sorry I can't come to their party tonight."

"I'll tell them," Hannah promised.

"And tell Mike thanks for letting me tackle that . . ."

Hannah didn't let him finish. She just pulled him down for a kiss. "I will," she promised.

"And tell Norman I'll invite him out to the station as soon as I get settled in. He was really interested in post-production."

"I'll tell him."

"And tell Hannah Swensen that I'll miss her very much."

"I think she already knows that."

"And does she also know how much I love her?"

"She knows."

Ross pulled her into his arms again and after a minute or two, Hannah was aware of someone clearing his throat. She looked over at the TSA agent who was manning the first podium, and saw him beckoning to Ross. "You'd better go," she told Ross. "It's almost time for your plane to board."

"Right."

Ross gave her one last hug and went up to the podium. He showed his identification and boarding pass and he was waved on. Hannah watched with tears in her eyes as he put his carry-on and shoes in a bin and placed them on the conveyor belt that led to the X-ray machine. Then he turned to wave as he went through the screening device.

He stopped to talk to an agent on the other side as he waited for his bins to come off the belt, and Hannah saw the agent grin and nod. Ross slipped on his shoes, not bothering to tie them, picked up his carry-on, and then he was gone.

Hannah turned away. She'd never felt so alone. She knew he was coming back in a week, but that didn't really help right now. Ross was gone and she felt desolate.

"Excuse me, miss." One of the TSA agents, the one Ross had talked to while he was waiting for his shoes and carry-on, approached her. "Please come with me."

"Come with you . . . where?"

"To the scanner."

"But . . . I'm not flying anywhere. I just came here to see someone . . ." Hannah paused as she spotted Ross on the other side of the scanner. "There he is, the man I brought to the airport. What's happening?"

"It'll be fine," the agent said, smiling at her. "Just follow me, please."

Ross was beckoning to her. If he wanted her to follow the TSA agent, she would.

The agent led her to the scanner and he motioned for Ross to come through. "You'd better ask her in a hurry," he said to Ross. "Your flight leaves in ten minutes."

Ross hurried through the scanner and folded his arms around Hannah. "I couldn't leave without asking you."

"Without asking me what?"

Ross took both of her hands in his and dropped to one knee. "Hannah Louise Swensen . . . will you marry me?"

"Oh!" Hannah gasped. Suddenly, her knees began to shake and then she was kneeling by him on the floor. His arms closed around her, his lips met hers, and she knew she'd never felt so happy in her whole life.

The kiss seemed to last for eons, but then they heard the sound of applause. They looked up to see a circle of TSA agents surrounding them and clapping.

"You'd better go, sir." One of the agents helped Ross to his feet and another extended a hand to Hannah. "We called, but we can't hold the plane for more than five more minutes."

"I'll call you after the party tonight," Ross said, turning quickly and heading back through the scanner. He ran toward the corridor that led to the gate, stopped to blow her a kiss, and then he was gone.

"Ma'am?" The TSA agent took Hannah's arm. "You'd better go now. I wasn't supposed to let you in this far without a boarding pass, but . . . well . . . my wife would have killed me if I hadn't. She still believes in love. And that's after thirty years of marriage to me."

"She's right to keep believing," Hannah said. "Please tell her thank you for me."

Hannah turned. And then she floated all

the way down the corridor, out of the airport, and into her cookie truck for the drive back to Lake Eden.

It's been a great party so far, Hannah thought.

Doc looked happy and proud, and her mother looked radiant as they accepted the congratulations of their friends. Dinner had been superb, everything was beautifully decorated, and Sally had outdone herself with the Butterscotch Champagne Cocktail she'd made for the toast to the newly-weds.

"Hi, Hannah." Norman came up to her with a smile on his face. "I didn't get a chance to ask you at the courthouse last night. How many responses did you get to your text?"

"Sixty-seven," Hannah said. "I had to send out another broadcast telling everyone that I was okay."

"You have sixty-seven people on your contact list?"

"I do now. Tracey went a little overboard. She put in the ten numbers I had on my list and then she transferred fifty-seven of her own. I really had no idea what I was doing when I sent out that emergency text. I even sent it to Tracey's classmate, Calvin Jan-owski!"

Norman laughed. "I saw the Janowskis at the courthouse. There were a whole lot of people who drove out there to help you."

"I know. I was really embarrassed, but it's great to know that I have that many friends."

"Especially Calvin Janowski?"

"Especially Calvin," Hannah said with a smile.

"This is a great party, Hannah. Doc and Delores are having a wonderful time and the band is really good. Let's get out there and cut a rug."

"What?"

"Cut a rug. You know . . . dance."

"Sure, Norman. I'd love to dance with you. Where did you get that phrase?"

"From my dance teacher. You remember that I took those dance lessons, don't you?"

"I *do* remember," Hannah said, wishing she could thank Norman's dance teacher in person. Before he had taken dance lessons, he'd stepped on everyone's toes.

"My teacher is in her late eighties and she was a professional dancer. She used to always tell me to ask the ladies if they wanted to *cut a rug.*"

"I see." Hannah managed not to laugh. As far as she knew, they hadn't even used that phrase in her mother's day. Of course Delores wasn't eighty. Delores wouldn't even admit to sixty-five.

Norman took Hannah's arm, led her onto the dance floor, and they began to dance. After a few moments of holding her close, he cleared his throat. "You know I love you, don't you, Hannah?"

Hannah's sensors went on high alert, but she quieted them quickly. "I know you do," she said.

"I just wanted you to know that my proposal still stands. I've always wanted to marry you and I still do."

There was only one thing to say and Hannah said it. "Thank you, Norman. That means a lot to me."

"I know that you love me," Norman continued. "I can feel it in my heart. You *do* love me, don't you?"

"Yes," Hannah said. "I *do* love you, Norman."

"And you *do* know that we could be happy together?"

Hannah drew a deep breath and answered quite honestly. "I know that, too."

"All right then. That's good enough for me. I just wanted to let you know that my feelings for you haven't changed."

Hannah smiled. She felt warm all over. Norman loved her and that was a wonderful thing. "I know," she said and went back into his arms.

She was sitting at a table with Michelle and Andrea when Mike walked up. "Want to dance, Hannah?" he asked her.

"Sure." Hannah got up from her chair and let Mike lead her to the dance floor. The band was playing their last number, "Good Night Ladies." It was a signal that the party was about to end and very soon it would be time to go home.

They danced for a minute or two before the band went into the final stanza and the song ended.

"Uh-oh," Mike said. "No more music. Do you know any songs, Hannah?"

"I know 'Love Me Tender.' They played it at Mother's wedding. Believe it or not, she asked for it."

" *'Love Me Tender'?* That's Elvis, isn't it?"

"Right."

"Okay, that'll do."

"Do you know it?"

"Good enough to get by. My mother was crazy about Elvis. And I don't want to stop dancing now."

Hannah laughed and started to sing the chorus of "Love Me Tender." It didn't really matter that she was off-key because when Mike joined in, he was off-key, too.

They danced their way into the hallway and out of the dining room, singing loudly all the way. Both of them were laughing and Hannah would have assumed she'd had one too many glasses of champagne if she'd had any at all, which she hadn't. Mike was fun. There was no doubt about that. Despite the fact that Ross was gone, she was having a wonderful time.

"Through here, Hannah," Mike said, opening the door and dancing her into the kitchen. They danced past the dishwashers, the cooks, and the sous-chefs, and into the back hallway.

". . . Love me tender, love me true," they sang as Mike danced Hannah through another door.

"We're in the janitor's closet!" Hannah exclaimed, almost tripping over a mop and pail.

"I know. We're here at last. I've been waiting for this all night."

"Waiting for what?"

"For this." Mike pulled her into his arms and kissed her.

"What was that for?" Hannah asked when he released her.

"For fun. And for I'm really glad you're all right. You had no idea how scared I was when I got your text."

"I was scared, too."

"I'll bet you were! But you're all right now and I just wanted you to know that I still want to marry you. I'll always want to marry you. Maybe I won't be a perfect husband, but I promise you that I'll try really hard. I love you, Hannah. Do you believe me?"

"I believe you, Mike," Hannah said.

Her mind was overloaded. That must be it, because she hadn't eaten a morsel or had anything at all to drink. Hannah stood in the hallway outside the janitor's closet and stared up at the sprinkler on the ceiling. Three proposals in one day. That had to be some sort of a record.

Her mind was spinning and all she really wanted to do was go home and fall into bed, but she couldn't seem to make her feet carry her to the outside door. Instead, she was stuck, thinking about the three men in her life and how much they meant to her.

"Is there something wrong with that sprinkler?"

A voice spoke behind her and Hannah whirled around. Sally was standing there, staring at her curiously. "No. I'm just fixated on it, letting my mind idle. I'm so tired, I don't know what I'm doing."

"Well, I do. You haven't eaten all evening

and you're exhausted. Your mind can't work if your body needs fuel. Come with me, Hannah. We're having a postmortem."

"A what?"

"A postmortem, at least that's what Doc calls it. I call it a post-party wind-down. All the guests are gone and I've got fresh appetizers, including the little meatballs you like so much, and champagne cocktails. It's all ready for you to enjoy in front of the fireplace in the lobby."

"Who's there?" Hannah asked.

"Delores and Doc, and Michelle and Andrea. That's all. It's just the newlyweds and your sisters. Everyone else has gone home."

Hannah began to smile as she followed Sally down the hallway. Family, a champagne cocktail, and several of Sally's delicious meatballs were exactly what she needed. Her family would give her love without asking anything in return, the champagne cocktail would relax her, and Sally's meatballs would nourish her. It was a perfect ending to a perfectly exhausting day.

"Oh, good! Sally found you!" Delores said, getting up to hug her eldest daughter. "I was worried that you'd already left."

Michelle reached in her pocket and brought out Hannah's keys. "I told you,

Mother. I had the keys to the cookie truck."
Then she turned to Hannah. "I'm driving
home. Have a couple glasses of champagne.
You deserve it after all the work you did
today."

"Thank you for a wonderful party, girls,"
Doc said. "It was great to come home to
something like this. The food was incredible, the music was great, the dining room
looked beautiful, and I couldn't be happier."

"The same goes for me," Delores said,
raising her glass in a toast. "I never dreamed
a wedding and honeymoon could be so
much fun."

"Honeymoon?" Doc asked, turning to her.
"You haven't had your honeymoon yet."

"But I thought the cruise to Alaska
was . . ."

"Our wedding cruise," Doc interrupted
her. "It was merely a taste of what's to
come. We're about to embark on our honeymoon."

"We are?" Delores smiled at him and all
three of her daughters saw the love in her
eyes. "Where are we going on our honeymoon, Doc?"

"To the Garden Estate."

"The Garden State?" Delores sounded
incredulous. "You mean we're going to New
Jersey?!"

"No, dear. We're spending our honeymoon at the Garden *Estate,* not the Garden State."

"Where is the Garden *Estate?*"

"It's local," Doc told her. "And Sally is going to cater a family dinner there tomorrow night." He turned to his stepdaughters. "Of course you're invited. Your invitations are in the mail and you'll receive them tomorrow, complete with the address of the Garden Estate. Don't forget to bring your bathing suits. There's a great pool."

"But where is the Garden Estate?" Michelle asked. "You said it was local, but I've never heard of it."

That was when it struck Hannah with the force of a blow. She knew the exact location of the Garden Estate. She turned to look at Andrea and saw the very same realization dawn on her face. No wonder Howie had told Andrea not to worry about her big real estate sale. They'd been duped and they should have known better!

"The Garden Estate is a wedding present for your mother," Doc told Michelle. "And Andrea? You may already have guessed where it is."

Hannah laughed out loud. She couldn't help it. Andrea looked positively stunned.

"I think I know," she said in a small voice.

"I should have checked the spelling on Nightlife! It starts with a K, right?"

"Right," Doc said with a smile, and then he turned to Delores. "Are you ready to go, Mrs. Knight?"

Delores smiled. "I'm ready. I just love your surprises, dear."

The three Swensen sisters watched their mother and stepfather leave, and then Michelle turned to Andrea. "Okay . . . give! Where's the Garden Estate?"

"It's the penthouse suite at the Albion Hotel!" Andrea said, all smiles. "If I'd only looked to see how the buyer's corporation was spelled, I would have realized that the Knightlife Corporation belonged to Doc Knight!"

"Wow!" Michelle exclaimed, clearly impressed. "What a great wedding present! I can hardly wait to jump in that pool. I wanted to swim there the first time I saw it and it wasn't even finished yet."

"Doc really fooled me," Andrea said, but she didn't sound that upset about it.

"Me, too," Hannah admitted. "He was smart. If we'd figured it out, we might not have been able to keep such a big secret."

"He could have told me," Michelle said. "I'm very good at keeping big secrets. I've been keeping one from Hannah for six days now."

"What secret?" Hannah asked.

"This secret." Michelle handed her an official-looking envelope.

Hannah looked at the envelope. The return address of the Food Channel in New York was printed on the upper left corner. "What's this?"

"Open it and see. I entered your name in their dessert chef contest and sent them a sample of your Double Fudge Brownies. This letter came for you on Monday."

Hannah opened the letter and read it quickly. "It says they accepted me as a contestant!"

"And that's not all," Michelle looked exceedingly proud of herself. "I called them and they're sending us two plane tickets and a voucher for a week in a New York hotel right across from their kitchen studio. I checked with my advisor and the school gave me the time off, so I'm going to go with you to New York!"

"Oh, my!" Hannah said, feeling a little faint with excitement. "I'm going to be baking on national television?"

"That's right," Michelle said. "And you're going to win, I just know it. The producer told me that the judges thought your brownies were the best they'd ever tasted."

Hannah's heart was racing so hard, she had trouble even speaking. She took another sip of champagne, drew in another deep, steadying breath, and then she said, "Thanks, Michelle. I've never been to New York and I can hardly wait! And now, I have a surprise for you two."

"What is it?" Andrea asked her.

"You probably saw me dancing with Norman earlier." Both Andrea and Michelle nodded, and Hannah continued. "He proposed to me again, tonight."

"Oh, boy!" Michelle breathed. "As if you didn't have enough on your mind!"

Hannah smiled. "That's true. And when Sally came to find me, I was staring up at the hallway ceiling, trying to decide what to do. That was right after I danced with Mike and he proposed again, too."

Both sisters just stared at her in shock and Hannah laughed. "Oh, that's not all! When I drove Ross to the airport, he proposed to me right before he boarded the plane."

Both of her younger sisters were obviously at a loss for words, and Hannah smiled at them. "I know you both thought that I could never choose between Mike and Norman. And now, with Ross in the picture too, it must have seemed even more impossible. I just wanted to tell you that I did it."

There was a moment of silence and then Andrea gave a little gasp. "You did what?" she asked.

"I reached an informed decision."

"And you're really sure about this?" Michelle asked, looking more than a little worried.

"Yes, I'm very sure. I just want you two to be the first to know that I'm going to marry Ross when he gets back to Lake Eden."

BUTTERSCOTCH CHAMPAGNE COCKTAIL

1/2 ounce butterscotch liqueur *(Sally used DeKuyper Buttershots Schnapps)*

Brut Champagne *(Sally used Korbel Brut)*

Pour a half-ounce of butterscotch liqueur into a champagne flute.

Fill the flute with Brut Champagne and enjoy!

Hannah's Note: Sally made Butterscotch Champagne Cocktails for Doc and Delores's wedding party because Doc's family is from Scotland.

DOUBLE FUDGE BROWNIE MURDER RECIPE INDEX

BAKING CONVERSION CHART

These conversions are approximate, but they'll work just fine for Hannah Swensen's recipes.

VOLUME

U.S.	Metric
1/2 teaspoon	2 milliliters
1 teaspoon	5 milliliters
1 tablespoon	15 milliliters
1/4 cup	50 milliliters
1/3 cup	75 milliliters
1/2 cup	125 milliliters
3/4 cup	175 mililiters
1 cup	1/4 liter

WEIGHT

U.S.	Metric
1 ounce	28 grams
1 pound	454 grams

OVEN TEMPERATURE

Degrees Fahrenheit	Degrees Centigrade	British (Regulo) Gas Mark
325 degrees F.	165 degrees C.	3
350 degrees F.	175 degrees C.	4
375 degrees F.	190 degrees C.	5

Note: Hannah's rectangular sheet cake pan, 9 inches by 13 inches, is approximately 23 centimeters by 32.5 centimeters.

ABOUT THE AUTHOR

Like Hannah Swensen, **Joanne Fluke** grew up in a small town in rural Minnesota where her neighbors were friendly, the winters were fierce, and the biggest scandal was the spotting of unidentified male undergarments on a young widow's clothesline. She insists that there really are 10,000 lakes and the mosquito is NOT the state bird.

While pursuing her writing career, Joanne has worked as: a public school teacher, a psychologist, a musician, a private detective's assistant, a corporate, legal, and pharmaceutical secretary, a short order cook, a florist's assistant, a caterer and party planner, a computer consultant on a now-defunct operating system, a production assistant on a TV quiz show, half of a screenwriting team with her husband, and a mother, wife, and homemaker.

She now lives in Southern California with her husband, her kids, his kids, their three dogs, one elderly tabby, and several noisy rats in the attic.

Email: gr8clues@joannefluke.com
Website: http://www.joannefluke.com